About the Authors

Patrick and David's first collaboration, the 'Sega Star', was published, by them, on A4 plain paper, at the tender age of 10. David got through university, worked for BBC Online, before starting his own web design company. Patrick abandoned his pitiful academic endeavours at 19 to work as a support engineer and designer in Indycar and Formula 1.

Years later both were running their respective businesses, David's in user experience and interface design, Patrick's in historic motorsport or 'seeing what everyone else did', as he calls it. Reunited over a long promised pint they talked childhood, Transformers and Starcom. It's a fact that boys love spaceships and robots; both had stabs at novels in the past so writing together sounded like fun. Patrick worked with Jade Gurss on his highly rated book *Beast* in 2014, among other motorsport and technical books, loving every moment of it.

Patrick does words, illustrations and some ideas. David does ideas, mostly the bigger ones.

Trinity

Of Cauldron Born • Volume 1

Patrick Morgan with David Kidger

unbound

This edition first published in 2021

Unbound
6th Floor Mutual House, 70 Conduit Street, London W1S 2GF
www.unbound.com
All rights reserved

© Patrick Morgan and David Kidger, 2021

This book is a work of fiction and, except in the case of historical fact, any
resemblance to actual persons, living or dead, is purely coincidental.

ISBN (eBook): 978-1-78965-100-3
ISBN (Paperback): 978-1-78965-099-0

Cover design by Mecob

Printed and bound in Great Britain by Clays Ltd, Elcograf S.p.A.

Super Patrons

Andrea Holden
Justin Humphrey
Tom Humphries
Terry Kaye
Tim and Nikki Kidger
The Kidger Family
Laura Knight
Vicki Knight
Bill Lane
Graham Langham
Deinde Legare Montague Mackie
Tony Main
Jerome Moody
Elizabeth Morgan
Hannah Morgan
Duncan Muddiman
Andrew Murdoch
Beryl Murdoch
Ian Bruce Murdoch
James Murdoch
Steven Newbury
Helen Orchel
David Rees
Paula Rissanen
Kevin Rowland
Craig Scarborough
Bernadette Shail
Emma Sharp
Tony Sime
Fraser Sinclair
Lucy Sinclair
Clive Skinner
Claire Slade

Maureen Smyth
Thom Smyth
Holly Steele
Jo Stevens
Illya Teideman
The Teideman's
Alan Thomason
Alistair Tudor
David Tudor
Mo Turney
Ian Watson
Ruth Watson
Ian Weltch
Stephen Wheatman
David Wilford
Andrea Williams
Sean Worthington
Alex Youngs

The Cast

Ayon Research

Katherine Kane – Privy Councillor

Nara Falla – Privy Councillor

ROOT – Intercessor Drive Core

HEX – Intercessor Drive Core

Myra Cena – Vault Technician

Ivor Gethin – Security Manager

Constance Hatch – Vault Security

Central Library

Megan Devin – Archivist

Crew – GVX-H

Trish Asher – General Assistant

Brendan Scott – Medic and Cook

Jayce Baker – Systems Engineer

Joanna Joyce – Power Unit and Chassis Technician

CID

Vincent O'Brien – Section Head

Jennifer Narin – Deputy Section Head

Tyler Olson – Investigator

Jason Karalydes – Informant

Gygath Slum

The Elder

Ezekiel Lee

Ness

Ira

The Landlord

Hadje

Benjamin Kittala

Jean-Louis – Second Spirit

Hesta

Michelle – Daughter of Hesta and Jean-Louis

Deain – Son of Hesta and Jean-Louis

The Shaman – Spiritualist and Historian

Hellinar Research

Joss Ratha – Privy Councillor

JT Gilbert – Quartermaster

Kyle Devin – Privy Councillor

Kyra Devin – Field Researcher

Mal-Kas Mine

Beth – Light Vehicle Driver

Mitch Farkus – Site Manager

Bill Connor – Security

Jo – Drill Rig Operator

Desiree Angelo – Jumbo Operator

Privy Council

(Listed to reflect seating in the Council Chamber from left to right.)

Kyle Devin – Research/Hellinar

Joss Ratha – Science/Hellinar

Esther Johannsson – Engineering/Hellinar

Oliver Burrell – Cultural/Hellinar

The Matriarch

Victor Urasa – Cultural/Ayon

Erin James – Engineering/Ayon

Katherine Kane – Science/Ayon

Nara Falla – Research/Ayon

(Presiding above)

Selwyn Abbot – Chamberlain

Special Vehicle Assembly

John Orchard – Designer, GVX-H

Don Hoffer – Workshop Manager

Roy Jacobs – Chief Engineer

T7 Staff

Austen Worral – Clerk

T24 Staff

Evelyn Tudor – Clerk

AYON TUNDRA

TEETH OF AUMOND

AYA

THE DIVIDE

MAL-KAS

LAKE EIRAYE

SKALA

THERMAL
TOWERS

ORORPRESA

HELLINAR PLANES

KUL

DRYLANDS

SOUTHERN REACHES

000: Prologue

Ayon Research Facility, Eastern District, Skala City

She hit the glass again with the ball of her hand and this time it cracked. Ignoring the pain, Myra smashed at the emergency panel until the painted floor was scattered with bloody shards. Fighting hyperventilation, she picked out the larger remnants with her fingertips, not caring if she cut herself, then slammed down on the alarm button. Abruptly the faint echoes of the starkly illuminated corridor were drowned in a cacophony of sound. Over the piercing siren she heard the explosive discharge of Freon gas as it doused the inside of the chamber behind her. The white lights blinked out, replaced by a violent confusion of spinning amber that flared from high on the walls. Palls of the sweet-smelling vapour were caught in the light as they rolled past the armoured door and over the debris at her feet before stretching into taut wisps that rushed up into an extractor grate above her.

Myra staggered to the wall, pulled towards it as if by gravity. As her temple hit the cold surface with a dull thud she slapped an anguished hand against the white brickwork, leaving a dark, bloodied arc as it dropped. Her eyes stung and she became aware her face had involuntarily contorted. She forced herself to focus, looking down the long passage to the door at the far end. Externally mounted pneumatic locks were slid hard into their keepers, telling her the hermetic seal was still inflated and that the room beyond remained secure. She let her eyes close momentarily and on opening them found her view obscured by the dark form of a woman running towards her. In the strobing light she saw both resolve and disbelief writ clear across her face. Myra began to crumple as the figure reached her, breaking her fall as the world faded from the maelstrom of confusion and panic. Time passed.

'Myra? Myra? Can you hear me?' The voice was distant at first but it rushed in to give her a degree of focus. She felt groggy and unsure of time or place. Blinking, she realised she was back in Vault security, the curved glass wall of the entrance in front of her.

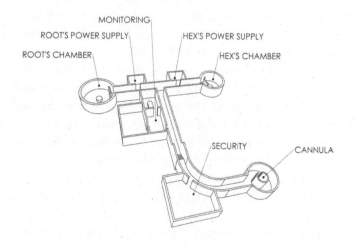

'What happened?' Myra managed, and hunched forward on her chair.

'You set off the alarm, Myra,' Constance Hatch asserted in her familiar stern manner. 'You purged HEX's chamber. What made you do that?'

Myra winced, the memory flooding back as the mental fog of confusion receded. The fingers of her right hand were sore and bleeding into a cloth. She realised she was very cold, a sensation that grounded her; the Freon must have chilled her badly. With a rush, an overwhelming panic rose from somewhere deep in her gut.

'HEX is gone, Connie,' she said wretchedly. 'She's gone. I did the regular check at four rotations for both IDCs as I always do. ROOT was fine…' Her voice trailed off, barely believing what she had seen herself. 'I didn't notice at first. I must have been in HEX's chamber for more than a turn. The telemetry looked normal but when I went to leave, the podium was empty, just the wires and pipes strewn over the floor.'

Hatch assessed her evenly for a moment. 'No one's been past here in three rotations, Myra.'

'Then look for yourself,' she snarled, an anger flaring in her.

Hatch narrowed her stare, then reached for a telephone receiver.

'Ivor, it's Hatch,' she said in a clear, subjective tone. 'The alarm's been set off. I'm with Myra Cena, she's pretty shook up. She says HEX is not in her chamber.'

There was a momentary silence in which Myra looked expectantly into Hatch's unreadable blue eyes. Getting no response, she looked at the floor and scratched distractedly at a shallow scar that ran down her left cheek, an involuntary tic she couldn't shake off.

'That's what she said,' continued Hatch after what seemed like a lifetime. 'If she's right, no one's going in there until someone in authority comes down here. It's been left exactly as it was, I've not been in there myself.'

She replaced the receiver and looked back to Myra with calm intent.

'I'm to keep you here. I don't know what's going to happen, but for now we wait.'

Myra nodded her understanding and took a deep breath. She forced her mind back to the start of her shift and tried to recall it in as much detail as she could. In contrast to the ceaseless activity above ground as preparations were made for the move from Skala to Aya, the Vault was almost tranquil during working rotations and became deserted after them when her half-shift started. The last visitors had left on schedule, or just about. Kyra Devin, who had been consulting HEX, had waved a cheerful goodbye dead on the end of her allotted slot. A few turns later the Special Vehicles designer, John Orchard, had departed from a session with ROOT. Characteristically, he was lost in thought and wholly unaware he had overrun, leaving Myra extra paperwork to contend with.

Four rotations into her shift, Myra, who reluctantly admitted diligence was an excuse to alleviate her boredom, had left her station and made her way down the short corridor to check on the physical condition of her wards. The corridor, like all the sub-basements in the building, was stark, white-walled and unusually free of pipework or electrical conduits. The floor was smooth, having been recently repainted in a shade of pale yellow that only its creator could have loved.

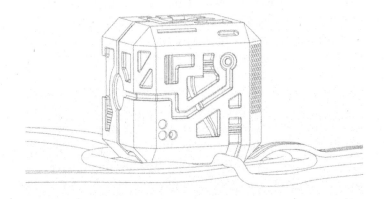

Originally, the Vault had been built around a single occupant, an ornate-looking cube that referred to itself as ROOT. More recently, an additional vault had been constructed upon the discovery of a second IDC, a polyhedron with no recognisable identification. After some deliberation, and in deference to its shape, it had settled on HEX as its alias. The chambers in which the IDCs resided were connected via a second corridor for human access but, crucially, they were not networked or connected electrically, visually or otherwise. Upon HEX's recent discovery, both she and ROOT had been emphatic that any connection between the two would likely result in the loss of both. Neither would expand on their reasoning for such stringent separation, and thus the only interaction permitted between them was strictly via human relay. Playing messenger was a task that the humans found simultaneously fascinating and onerous.

Myra remembered briefly deliberating which IDC to check on first. She found ROOT the more cordial of the two, and consequently made a left at the corridors' intersection. ROOT's chamber lay only twenty metres beyond, with its twin, occupied by HEX, a similar distance behind her. Both chambers were more or less of the same cylindrical design. Each was sealed by a heavy door fitted with a pneumatically operated seal and locks, the operation of which gave Myra a childish sense of satisfaction. She recalled clearly the hiss as the air pressure bled off and the three locks retracted into their housings.

Of average height but athletic in stature, Myra still had to exert some effort to swing the heavy door open to reveal a section of curved, freestanding wall behind it. This wall was a feature of both chambers. Spanning only three metres, it ensured the CCTV cameras positioned to monitor the doors could not see directly inside. This measure, insisted upon by both Intercessors, was not a consideration of privacy but designed to ensure no communication, visual or otherwise, was possible.

The Vault's twin chambers were dark places; their occupants had no need for light. What little illumination prevailed was provided only for the benefit of guards, technicians and the visiting engineers the permanent staff referred to as 'customers'. The same was true of the temperature, which, unlike the city above, was cool, ostensibly to keep the IDCs in their optimum operating window. In reality, as they had pointed out many times, both IDCs' functionality was consistent throughout a wide temperature range. The same, however, could not be said of humans, whose nature it was to bend the facts to suit their inclinations.

Closing and re-sealing the door, she had stepped around the 'courtesy shield', as it had, tongue in cheek, become known. It took a moment for her eyes to adjust to the dim light, which, with the muted hiss of cooling air fans, gave the place a soporific quality. Banks of screens, dimmed since the last shifts' visitors had left, adorned the curved walls. Seemingly static lines of monitoring telemetry scrolled from left to right. Unlike the output of humans, with their constant pulsing hearts and variable electric signals, the IDCs' output while dormant was simply flat, making Myra's work tedious.

In the centre of the chamber stood a squat podium on which, swamped in a snake's nest of cables and umbilicals, sat the unassuming cubic form. In her mind's eye, Myra saw unsheathed optic fibres emitting a gently diffused glow that pulsed occasionally as something, who knew what, was processed deep inside the Core.

Without warning, the fibres had glowed with radiance and several of the monitored channels spiked as the smooth honeyed voice of ROOT's vocal synthesiser enquired, 'Myra, that's you, isn't it?'

This was a game ROOT played with all the monitoring staff, switching off his CCTV feed and guessing who was on duty. He had become remarkably good at it.

'Hi, ROOT. Yes, just checking on you.'

'Can you tell me how I knew it was you?' the Intercessor had replied in a creamy, melodious tone he occasionally put on to amuse her.

Myra had turned to the monitors, belatedly grateful for some mental stimulation. She had said something about trying to figure it out again and looked over the telemetry, scrolling back to her time of entry.

'It's simply science. The answer is always in the data.' This was his favourite refrain.

She tried now to remember what she had seen in the data, wondering if it was in any way relevant to what had happened not five turns later. There had been a negative air pressure spike as the door opened, then a small change in ambient temperature. Moments later the air pressure climbed again as the door re-sealed.

She had puzzled for a few moments, no longer than that, and

made some flippant comment about ROOT being a genius, to which he responded in kind.

'Sarcasm will not provide you with the answer, Myra. You need to look a little harder – the answer is right there in front of you.'

As she left, ROOT asked her to pass on some unfathomable message to HEX that she took to be an insult. Reaching HEX's chamber, she retracted the door locks. As before, the seal depressurised with a satisfying hiss.

HEX's chamber was actually the one ROOT had occupied before HEX had had to be accommodated. It was largely a mirror image of the one she had just left, only slightly smaller. Some of the systems were older and more antiquated, but Myra had never minded that. Somehow it gave the chamber a more friendly feel, a stark contrast to its somewhat prickly occupant.

She focused now, straining to remember every move she had made. She had rounded the courtesy shield and walked habitually straight to the telemetry monitors. She knew it was petty to ignore HEX but she refused to show any deference toward the Intercessor. Unlike her counterpart, who was courteous, amusing and helpful, Myra found HEX to be abrupt and at times downright obnoxious. She seemed to harbour an unexplained resentment towards people in general and technicians in particular, although there were exceptions. Myra was not one of these.

Again she tried to remember exactly what she had seen in the telemetry – the chamber's pressure and temperature traces had given her the initial feeling of unease. Neither had deviated at all when the chamber opened. She recalled scrolling back in confusion, checking the time stamp. The values fluctuated very slightly but the amount was negligible. It was as if she had never entered.

She had begun to speak before turning to HEX, but her

words died in her throat. For a moment, Myra had not been able to put her finger on what was missing in the picture before her. Then a wave of panic hit her full force, a sensation that returned to her now. She remembered the cool of the room retreating as a hot nausea broke within her and her chest tightened. She felt sick and disorientated, staggering a moment before bolting for the door and the alarm beyond.

'Myra?' Hatch was watching her relive the events with obvious concern. 'You okay? You've gone very pale. Do you want a doctor or some water?'

'No,' said Myra and shook her head as the memories retreated. 'No, I'm okay, thank you.'

Hatch looked up, her attention arrested by the sound of voices from the other side of the glass panel. People were approaching, a lot of people, fronted by two men Myra didn't recognise. She sensed the command of shared urgency in the words and realised these were officials.

Hatch rose to approach the window. Before she got there Myra said, 'Connie? I think we should call Katherine Kane.'

Hatch paused a moment and regarded her closely. Then she nodded her agreement. 'I'll do that as soon as I've dealt with these gentlemen.'

001: Discovery

Katherine Kane had slept for little more than a rotation when the blaring ring of her office telephone woke her abruptly. Fighting the urge to ignore the sound, she pushed herself up from the couch, walked to her desk and lifted the receiver.

'Katherine Kane,' she said, trying to sound more alert than she felt.

The voice on the other end was strained, fighting to be heard over a wash of background noise.

'Councillor? This is Officer Hatch in Vault security.'

'Officer Hatch?'

'Councillor, I'm sorry to wake you. There's a serious problem. I think you'd better get down here.'

'What sort of problem?' asked Katherine, uncomfortable that the facilities staff knew she was sleeping at work.

'It would be easier if you just came down,' said Hatch with urgency. 'The alarm's been triggered and CID are onsite. There's a lot of officers, they're practically taking over.'

'What do you mean, taking over?' she asked pointedly.

'Ivor Gethin's on his way up to you, ma'am,' said Hatch without further explanation. The line went dead and Katherine replaced the receiver to the sound of urgent rapping from her office door.

'Okay, just a moment.' She fought with a button midway up her blouse. Despite the air conditioning, the climate in the building became increasingly stifling shift by shift with the remorseless rise of the sun. She crossed to the door to be met by the tanned, windswept face of Gethin, the Ayon Research Facility security manager. He looked shocked.

'Ivor? What is it?' asked Katherine.

'If you'll come with me, ma'am? It would be easier just to show you.'

'Okay, Ivor,' said Katherine, sensing the underlying hesitance in Gethin's tone. She wondered, not for the first time, if the Vault's IDC occupants had finally driven a conscientious technician beyond breaking point.

She followed him swiftly through the network of hallways that converged on a cylindrical elevator, known as the 'Cannula'. In uncomfortable silence, they descended eight floors into the bowels of Ayon Research.

Exiting the Cannula, it became immediately obvious that the situation was extremely serious. Emergency lights flashed about them; the level of noise alone was alien to this place, inducing an instinctive sense of anxiety. The security station, set behind the curved glass outer wall of the Vault's entrance, brimmed with an unbridled mob of animated officials. At the centre of the crowd stood an embattled Connie Hatch, who waved them past towards two men locked in an intense exchange.

'Mr Olson, Mr O'Brien,' interrupted Gethin over the ringing of the alarm. He addressed the nearer of the two, a middle-aged man in shirtsleeves. His companion, who stepped out from behind, was a severe-looking younger man in more formal attire. 'This is Katherine Kane. Katherine is the senior scientist at this facility. As you probably know, she is also a representative on the Privy Council.'

The younger man jabbed a pair of spectacles up to the bridge of his nose, and spoke first. His voice was clipped, abrupt and impatient. His manner had a faint air of superiority that Katherine supposed he had developed to make up for his smaller than average stature.

'I'm Vincent O'Brien, section head of the Corporate Investigations Division. We specialise in industrial espionage, fraud, illicit trade among other things.'

'I'm familiar with CID,' said Katherine, indifferent to the condescension in her raised voice.

'This is my colleague, Tyler Olson,' continued O'Brien, unfazed. 'We are hoping you can assist our investigation.'

'Investigation into what? Why are you in my Vault?' asked Katherine, impatient for an explanation. The noise from the alarm and the whirls of dizzying light were unbearable.

'No one has told you?' asked O'Brien, brow furrowed.

'Told me what?' she asked with levity. Catching sight of a distraught-looking Myra Cena sat atop a transport box, left abandoned in the corridor, she regretted her tone.

'We are investigating the disappearance of one of the two IDCs you keep at this facility,' he said, stumbling over the abbreviation. He stared at her intently, assessing her reaction.

'Disappearance? I'm not sure I understand,' replied Katherine, fighting back confusion. If this was true the implications were monumental.

'One of the 'Intercessors' – is that what you call them? One of them was removed sometime after the last work shift. The alarm was triggered and, according to protocol, your security officers called our department. We got here as quickly as we could.' He consulted a notebook momentarily before continuing. 'I believe Constance Hatch, the guard on duty, called for you to come down here Miss, or is it Mrs Kane?'

Katherine, stunned, did not enlighten him and, after a slightly uncomfortable pause, he continued.

'We've been told only that you have unlimited access here. What can you tell us?'

'I don't know what I can tell you,' she said, with no idea how to respond to such a generalised question. 'Which Core has been stolen?'

Her indifference to his question clearly annoyed O'Brien, who cocked his head and glowered at the apparently predictable lack of official co-operation. He answered her reciprocal question in an offhand manner she suspected was deliberately contrived.

'The one on the right,' he said, and flicked his head in that direction.

'You mean HEX?'

O'Brien glanced back, deferring to Myra Cena. Myra looked up momentarily, her wide eyes connecting with Katherine's. She gave a small nod.

'HEX,' repeated O'Brien.

In that moment the alarm subsided and the emergency lights ceased their flashing, the sensory onslaught giving way to a degree of calm. Katherine regarded the other man, Olson, and caught the briefest twitch of a smile behind a neatly trimmed beard. For a moment he held Katherine in the warmth of his gaze; only very faintly did she recognise a hardness behind that engaging stare, an edge that belied its captivating radiance. When he spoke, his voice was soft and melodious, compared with his colleague's staccato bursts of speech.

'We were hoping maybe you could fill in a few details for us, that's all. You have privileges?' he suggested. 'Access to both IDCs at any time, work or rest shifts, is that correct?' Unlike his colleague, he sounded comfortable with the Vault's technical jargon.

Katherine took a breath and chose her words carefully.

'I do have unlimited access to the Vault, that's true,' she said firmly. 'But I'm not the only person with that level of clearance. Most of the technicians, scientists and engineers can come and go as they please. The more senior personnel have access to the data and communication with both IDCs. Then there are the customers, outside technology companies, other Council departments, who can buy blocks of the Intercessors' time to get input on their projects. But you're right, only a few of us get access to everything.'

'How many would that be?' asked Olson.

'It depends. Perhaps eight in total,' she said, still fighting to maintain her composure amid the tumult of internal confusion. 'Some of the Privy Council, Joss Ratha for example, have had unlimited access for a decade or more. John Orchard, one of the senior engineers, has unlimited access for now, but I imagine that will be rescinded once he's finished the project he's working on.'

'And who decides who gets access to what? How does that work?'

'It's down to a steering committee to allocate access. They would be in a better position to tell you who's unrestricted at the moment. Councillor Ratha would be able to give you a clear answer, she chairs the group.'

'And you're not a part of it?' Olson posed this as part question, part statement.

'No,' replied Katherine with a defiance she hoped masked her disappointment.

A moment passed as O'Brien made a record in his notebook. The pause, brief as it was, gave Katherine time to gather her thoughts and take back control of the exchange.

'And you're sure it's HEX that's been taken?' she asked.

'Does it make a difference?' asked O'Brien, not looking up.

'I suppose not,' said Katherine, with a trace of irritation.

'But you have a preference? You regard the other one as yours?'

Katherine narrowed her eyes. The question suggested the CID man had a much better knowledge of her than his manner had implied. If she was honest, she did harbour possessive feelings towards ROOT and it was by no means inconceivable that other people guessed this. But how or why CID would know, she wasn't sure.

'He's not mine,' she stated with as much assertion as she could muster. 'Neither Core belongs to anyone.'

'But you discovered ROOT,' he said, deliberately pulling a wolfish smile.

'Yes,' she said, shaking her head defensively. 'By accident.' She looked up to meet eyes that feigned disbelief.

'Accident? You discovered something that important by accident?'

'Yes,' she said, feeling the need to explain herself, not for the first time. 'I was fifteen, tagging along on a Hellinar expedition with my father.' She faltered, feeling a need to justify a child being taken so deep into the desert. 'It was shortly after my mother died. He was exploring a ruined city called Mayak. I was on a ridge and fell into some sort of tomb, and there was ROOT. We didn't know he was important, we thought he was just an artefact of some sort. It wasn't until later that we figured out we could communicate with him.'

Her own natural defensiveness on the subject irritated her. Olson, however, looked captivated by the recollection and there was something else in his stare, something she found undefinable as he posed the next question.

'And the other Intercessor, the one that's gone missing? Another accidental find?'

'No,' said Katherine, with a mix of admiration and regret. 'HEX was found in quite a different way.'

'By Kyra Devin,' Olson stated, making it immediately clear to Katherine that, although O'Brien might be senior in rank, it was Olson who had a better grasp of the background.

'That's right. Kyra figured there could be more than one Intercessor near Mayak and went back. She found HEX on her own initiative and despite her disability.'

'And you respect that,' said Olson, in soft confirmation. 'You're related, if I'm not mistaken?'

'She's my half-sister,' said Katherine, trying to stifle the resentment she felt towards her father's second wife, the socialite Martha Devin. She had to remind herself that these feelings did not extend to the couple's daughters, Kyra and Megan. This was no time to dwell on the past, so she continued, cautious concern wavering in her voice. 'You haven't explained how HEX was stolen. With the security down here, she can't have just been carried out the door.'

'That's the thing,' said O'Brien, a peculiar smile playing on his face. 'We have no idea. There is nothing in the CCTV, and Miss Cena here says the monitoring systems are behaving like your IDC is still in place. None of it makes much sense at the moment.'

'That can't be,' she said doubtfully. 'The cameras must have seen something. HEX might be smaller than ROOT, but she's too heavy to have simply been carried out. Could she have been removed in a transport case?'

'We've checked,' said O'Brien firmly. 'Nothing has gone in or out of the Vault through the last two shifts except the technicians and a few higher-ranking personnel. We're looking again, but no boxes, no equipment, nothing big enough to conceal an object over twenty centimetres square. But the IDC's gone, come see for yourself.'

O'Brien gestured for Katherine to accompany him. Olson followed behind them, gently guiding Myra to her feet as he did so. As they reached the intersection, Katherine instinctively glanced to her left, seeing the sealed door behind which ROOT would be sitting like a forgotten child. For a moment she felt sorry for him, but quickly recognised that as he had no emotions, she was being self-indulgent.

As they walked, Katherine frowned. 'You said the monitoring telemetry is still running? That's hard to believe.'

'Miss Cena?' O'Brien deferred to the technician.

Movement rejuvenating her a little, Myra made her way past the others and into the chamber. Katherine followed her around the courtesy shield and over to the bank of monitors that adorned the left-hand wall. She stopped, seeing for the first time the empty podium upon which HEX should have sat.

'Look,' said Myra, indicating the traces representing HEX's temperature, internal pressure, output channels and a hundred other parameters. 'They're still reading. They fluctuate occasionally, which is normal, and the traces are still recording. It's bizarre, but it's why no alarm was triggered when HEX was disconnected.'

They watched as one of the traces labelled 'P REG PWM' gently rose and fell, settling at a value of 22 per cent. 'What's that?' asked O'Brien.

'It's HEX's input power regulation. She draws what she needs from the supply and this channel monitors her demand. But as you can see...' Myra looked over her shoulder at the mass of disconnected cables, one of which was clearly marked 'Power'.

'But what's really odd is that the channels, like room temperature and pressure, aren't responding to what is actually going on. If you look at ambient room temperature, it hasn't risen since we entered.'

Katherine looked at the trace Myra was pointing to. Perplexed, she looked back at HEX's podium again. O'Brien and Olson hung back, watching the two women but not interfering. Katherine noticed the icy condition of the podium and reached out to touch it.

'Better not,' said O'Brien firmly.

'It won't be that cold,' retorted Katherine, with some assurance. 'I was an expedition crew driver in Ayon. I know what 'cold' looks like.'

O'Brien gave her a superior, withering look and said, 'Forensics.' Reaching into his pocket he retrieved a pair of latex gloves and offered them to her.

Katherine withdrew her hand, nodding her understanding. Taking the gloves, she turned back to Myra. 'Could you scroll back to when the alarm went off? I want to see what the room temperature did when the coolant blast happened. We should be able to see a huge dive in temperature when the Freon jet fired – room temperature, Core temperature… everything.'

'There is nothing,' said Myra, baffled. 'It's as if it never happened.'

Katherine looked at O'Brien who, for the first time since they had met, was exercising a degree of patience as she explained what Myra meant. 'It's like it's a recording, but it's being fed live.'

'You're saying what's appearing on your equipment isn't real?'

'It may be real, but it's not happening here. I'll show you.' Katherine pulled on the latex gloves, which snapped against her wrists. 'Myra, that channel you mentioned earlier, 'P REG PWM', can you bring that up on the screen as live? I need a small piece of wire or something metal. Some links, maybe, if anyone's got loose change?'

Reluctantly, O'Brien unclipped a ring of links from his wrist. 'These had better not get damaged, they'll be paying for dinner later,' he said with forced humour.

Katherine took the bracelet and separated off two of the least valuable copper links, returning the rest to O'Brien.

She took the power cable in one hand and the links in the other. 'I'm going to short two of the pins in the power supply. That should drive the PWM demand to zero because…'

O'Brien cut her off, 'I'll take your word for it.'

'Ready?' Katherine touched the links to the pins in the connector. There was a momentary flash, a crackle and the unmistakable smell of ozone.

'It didn't move,' said Myra, looking at the trace. 'It didn't move at all.'

'So where is the signal coming from?' asked Katherine rhetorically. She handed the two slightly charred links back to O'Brien, who scowled.

'That's something we can look into,' he said. 'It's a lead. We'll need some technical assistance though.'

'I'm sure Myra could help you,' suggested Katherine.

'She's a witness,' said O'Brien firmly. 'Unless I'm mistaken, she's also in shock.'

To Katherine's surprise, Olson spoke up softly but persuasively. 'As she's responsible for us all being down here, I think it's obvious that Miss Cena wasn't involved. Her fingerprints will be everywhere anyway. Wouldn't she be the ideal person to look into it, Vincent?'

Myra could only look on as her immediate future was decided.

'Okay,' agreed O'Brien, relenting. 'But she's not to interfere with the forensic work and she's to report to me.'

'Is that okay, Myra?' asked Katherine sincerely.

Myra looked at Katherine. She didn't know her superior well, they were only acquainted at all because Katherine spent a lot of time with ROOT. But that someone of the Councillor's importance had asked her if it was okay was an act that bought a lifetime of loyalty.

'I'd be happy to help,' said Myra, trying to still a quiver in her voice.

'Then let's get to it,' said O'Brien with a curt nod. A moment later he had turned and gone, Olson and the two women filing out behind him.

002: Leaving the Vault

Ayon Research Facility, Eastern District, Skala City

In the shift or so that had passed, Katherine had begun to grapple with some implications. ROOT had advanced humanity's understanding of both science and engineering threefold during Katherine's professional career. After the more recent integration of HEX, that pace had accelerated again, but there was a catch. The engineers, both Council-funded and from private enterprise, were building new technology faster than the scientists could understand the underlying principles. Millions of links were being invested on trust, with the Intercessors key to making any given technology work.

Partial planetary tidal lock meant the rising sun necessitated the move from Skala to Aya. With HEX's disappearance, reliance on the IDCs in the design of the new city was thrown into sharp relief. Until now, meeting the critical deadlines was considered by most to be difficult; with HEX missing, those deadlines looked meaningless. The fact was that Ayon Research simply did not understand how the infrastructure worked and, for expediency, there was only limited overlap between ROOT's and HEX's input. In hindsight, that now looked like a monumental mistake on Katherine's part, and gave her much to consider.

O'Brien had radioed his department and demanded as many agents as CID could muster. Somehow he had commandeered the use of four airborne camera platforms to scour the city for signs of HEX or her captors. It was an optimistic effort over such a wide, built-up area but it demonstrated a serious commitment. After some deliberation he had also notified the closer Seeding Settlements that scattered the Divide. These were few, limited in number by the genetically driven difficulties the population faced in producing children.

Katherine's initial impression was that O'Brien saw this case as the one that would make him, but as time passed she began to realise that he was well drilled in the protocol he was executing. This, she supposed, was how he operated most, if not all of, the time.

Somewhere in the background Tyler Olson was hovering. On the few occasions she caught sight of him he seemed to be drinking in the detail of the place. In the increasing chaos, Katherine found it hard to pay him much attention but it had not passed her by that the older man was not only looking, but seeing. O'Brien on the other hand was marshalling his resources and paying scant attention to his surroundings. The younger man reminded Katherine of the engineering project managers she occasionally worked with. Undoubtedly they were efficient administrators but they were overseers and not versed in the engineering itself. They preferred to rely on others to give them simplified information, on which they based sometimes questionable decisions. That was fine up to a point, but when things went wrong Katherine had witnessed again and again the failings of the administrators blamed on their subordinates. 'I was not properly briefed,' was a phrase she heard with sickening regularity.

Katherine was a woman who made damn sure she briefed herself. Most of the time she came out on top but she feared that in the event of something going wrong she lacked the mental safety net of being able to remorselessly pass the blame on to others.

By the time the Vault corridors were overrun with agents scanning and spraying fingerprint detection fluid, Katherine felt distinctly like a fifth wheel. She had to wait an age before she could interrupt O'Brien, but when she made her case for her dismissal, he waved her off without hesitation. Unsure if her presence had done any good at all, she made her way back to the Cannula. Entering the elevator, she was surprised to see Tyler Olson step in beside her.

'You don't have more to do?' she asked, as the doors hissed towards each other and sealed.

'Not here, and I retire soon so I'm more of an observer right now,' he said, and smiled kindly. 'Vincent has his side of things under control and he lets me follow my own leads. You might not think so right away, but we've worked well together.'

Katherine didn't say anything, but gave Olson a doubtful frown.

Olson acknowledged this with an unperturbed smile. 'Vincent's a good man and he knows how to operate. He plays by the rules, has lots of toys and he gets results most of the time.'

Katherine agreed O'Brien had access to a great deal of resources. 'There are a lot of people down there.'

'There are,' said Olson. 'But I prefer less of a sledgehammer approach, more of a look and see philosophy.'

'So what do you think?'

'I don't know yet. It's an interesting trick isn't it? Your data is still coming in from somewhere but who knows where? There's no evidence of anyone entering or leaving the Vault with your IDC.'

'If the data has been faked in some way it could be that the

CCTV has been as well, although I noticed we appeared in it…' said Katherine. 'Either way, someone on the inside had to have been involved. I didn't want to suggest that to Detective O'Brien back there, I'm sure he can figure it out for himself.'

'I'm sure he can,' agreed Olson gently. 'It's likely that's how it was played but it's too early to jump to conclusions just now, wouldn't you say?'

Katherine nodded but was saved from commenting further by the arrival of the Cannula at the ground floor. Rational thought was returning to her and she began to grapple with the great many conflicting situations which might occur. There were serious political considerations beyond the technological and logistical ramifications. Many in the Council were against using the Intercessors and they would surely use the situation to lever their positions. The sheer scale of the situation was monstrous.

Katherine strode out across the ornate mosaic floor that depicted the universal sigil of Skala. A circle was itself encircled by nine points and enclosed by a pair of concentric brackets, one representing Hellinar, the other, which was highlighted, representing the frigid wastelands of Ayon.

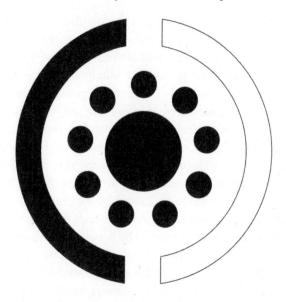

Reaching the entrance, she paused and looked back at Olson. She had warmed to him considerably and decided to risk a leap of faith.

'I'm going to find Joss Ratha, she needs to know what's happened.' Katherine faltered, as a thought occurred to her. 'Is that okay? I don't want to interfere with your work. I really don't want your friend O'Brien on my back.'

'You'd like me to tag along?' asked Olson.

'Yes, if you don't mind. I think that would be helpful.'

With Katherine leading the way, the two of them exited the building and descended a flight of stone steps into the heat of the city. It was still well before the work shift, the streets were empty and quiet and only the rumble of an occasional refuse truck or street sweeper could break the spell-like quality. Within a block they crossed the street to take advantage of the narrow shadows cast across the sidewalk. The heat was stifling and, although walking in shadow didn't help much, it did protect them from the perpetual malevolence of the sun.

Echoing her earlier concerns about Aya, she recalled it had been HEX who came up with the blindly obvious suggestion of orientating the new city's roads in diagonals relative to the sun. Diagonals guaranteed shadows cast across every street, whereas only Skala's longitudinal streets benefitted. HEX had proposed this solution, to the total bafflement of the questioner, when asked how society might reduce the strain on the healthcare system. Her rationale was faultless: Skala's biggest health risk was skin cancer caused by excessive exposure to the sun. She proposed laying Aya out such that exposure was negligible, something that could be done at no recurring cost.

There had, of course, been the obvious panic over modifying longstanding plans but HEX felt confident she could reconfigure any existing work without much effort and the gains were obvious. Even ROOT, who had come to view his processing capability as superior to HEX's, had grudgingly admitted the idea was a projection further than he would have managed. HEX, for all her prickliness, had an exceptional talent for thinking outside the box.

Crossing a road, they were momentarily exposed to the intensity of the sunlight, then moved back into the relative cool of the shadow. The buildings here were tall relative to the outer suburbs of the city. Most were brick, but a few were still a mix of stone and timber. Passing newer structures, they heard the draw of air rush between double glass panels, providing cooling and a means of powering small roof-mounted turbine generators.

Crossing into the Central District, Katherine gave her companion a brief summary of her work with HEX, ROOT and Aya. She outlined the political context of her position on the Privy Council, that of Joss Ratha and their respective relationships with the wider Orderly Council and its titular head, the Matriarch. Occasionally he asked questions which Katherine found insightful, seemingly based on intuition and deduction rather than any direct knowledge of her work.

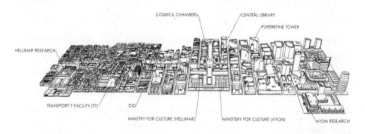

By the time they reached the Western District, Katherine felt distinctly grubby. She was still wearing the previous shift's clothes and was sweating profusely. She ran her fingers through her blonde hair, finding it displeasingly matted and greasy. She wasn't particularly vain but she liked to appear presentable, a discipline that helped keep her cluttered mind focused.

This part of the city was distinctly older than the Eastern District, a sign that investment was becoming sparse as its suburbs were slowly swallowed up into the drylands. Sandstorm erosion was starting to show on stonework, rounding off edges that were previously sharp, and turning windows opaque. In the distance she could hear the humming of a camera platform drone passing over the slums that fringed the western edge of the city and wondered what it had found. Almost certainly nothing, she was sure.

The Hellinar Research Facility, once a grand building with an elegant façade, was starting to show signs of age. While standing proud as it had done in Katherine's youth, it now looked noticeably tired and pockmarked. Katherine had spent much of her happy childhood in this building when her parents had worked there. She still had cause to visit it often but always in the bustle of the work shift. In the quiet, relentless blaze of the sun it struck a lonely figure, ageing and soon to be abandoned.

Forcing back a twinge of sadness, she ascended the steps with Olson following a pace or two behind. She pushed open a heavy wooden door and a familiar rush of cool conditioned air washed over her. Hellinar Research had a prominent security detail, a necessity since the least privileged of Skala's people occupied this less desirable quarter. Crime was on the up and the occasional disenchanted citizen had been known to enter the building, demonstrating contempt for its occupants by throwing a pipe bomb or scrawling graffiti across the walls.

Katherine made her way across a similar mosaic to the one that adorned the floor of Ayon Research, except this one, in a mirror image, highlighted the semicircle representing Hellinar and was generally more faded.

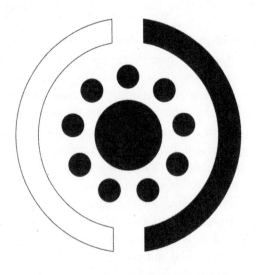

In front of the Hellinar Cannula stood a glass desk, a recent addition that looked wholly out of place in the ornate, time-worn grandeur of the entrance hall. Approaching a security guard she recognised, Katherine asked whether Joss Ratha was in the building. Informed that she wasn't, Katherine asked that the Councillor be contacted urgently. Noticing Katherine's unusually bedraggled state, the guard hesitated for only a moment before putting through a call.

Moments later they were shown into the Cannula and escorted across the building to Ratha's anteroom. As Katherine sank into her customary place on a worn sofa, Tyler Olson settled silently next to her to wait.

003: Hydra

Across the building from where Katherine Kane and Tyler Olson sat, a second, smaller panic had begun to assert itself. JT Gilbert was confused and had been for several shifts. As the quartermaster responsible for the kit and crew manifests for Hellinar expeditions, he had found a contradiction between his paperwork and the tag-in tag-out system used to track the vehicles in his care.

According to the manifests, a three-vehicle Unit, designation Hydra, was booked in for recall modifications. The work sheets indicated the mods were underway but not yet complete; 'awaiting parts' said the note in the live monitor. JT had taken little notice of this at first until he realised the Unit had been tagged in at one facility and out at another with no explanation of how it had travelled between them. Tagging was automatic, tripped by a transponder fixed to the chassis of each vehicle.

He had called the facility the Unit had been booked into, an area designated Transport 7. After a brief and slightly terse exchange, JT convinced a clerk to ignore her paperwork and see whether the Unit was physically on the premises. She was gone a long time before reporting, somewhat exasperated, that she couldn't see the Unit and would have to check with a colleague if it had been removed by flatbed. JT had enquired whether this would have been reported in the paperwork. It might not be, not yet at least, she'd replied. There was a backlog and a good deal of 'paperwork pending' notes stapled to folders at the moment. She had promised to call him back later that shift, but had failed to do so, which did not come as a surprise to JT.

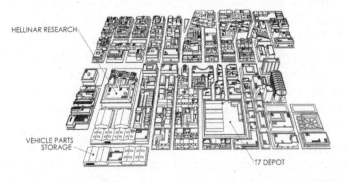

HELLINAR RESEARCH

VEHICLE PARTS
STORAGE

T7 DEPOT

Feeling a compulsion to run the Unit to earth, JT embarked upon his own line of enquiry. Reluctant to make a fuss, he initially let a couple of shifts go by without result before he called the management of the Transport 7 facility. The administrator was at least able to lay one mystery to rest, that of the clerk's erstwhile colleague and his 'paperwork pending' pile. The colleague, it seemed, had developed a sudden infatuation with a much younger woman, feelings that were 'inexplicably', to the administrator at least, reciprocated. The colleague, still unnamed, had failed to turn up to work for the past eight shifts and had subsequently been dismissed.

From there, JT began to look at the other end of the line, the Transport 24 facility.

'Is this about the missing winches?' asked the clerk before he could explain.

'Winches? No, I'm afraid not. It's about three missing vehicles, a dockable desert Unit.' Mercifully, in this case, the clerk, a Miss Tudor, was on the ball and there was no paperwork pending, at least none that was obvious over the phone. She found no evidence that Unit Hydra had ever been at T24 or was ever due there.

After a brief time batting possible explanations back and forth, Miss Tudor suggested she might discreetly ask a friend if T24 was home to any 'irregulars' at the moment. It took JT a moment to decipher her meaning. By 'irregulars' he felt sure she meant the Rika, an officially unacknowledged security detail – some called them mercenaries – who answered exclusively to the Privy Council. They were an open secret for many, requiring equipment just as any other field team might. It was inevitable that from time to time they came to the attention of the Hellinar and Ayon quartermasters and admin staff.

It was only now, a full shift and a half after their last conversation, that Miss Tudor had called him back. She sounded pleased, knowing she had some information of interest to him.

'I spoke to my friend,' she said. 'He was quite helpful.'

'How so?'

'We've had a Unit out in the yard. It's been in a corner under tarps and, it would seem, under the wire.'

'Interesting,' he mused. 'Is it still there?'

'I can take a walk in that direction if you'd like me to?'

'I'd like that very much, Miss Tudor.'

They exchanged pleasantries before hanging up. JT reclined against the back support of his chair, which creaked on a dry pivot. A discoloured plastic desk fan beat the air, doing little to cool him, but he let its pulsing rhythm focus his thoughts.

Something was wrong here. It wasn't a strong feeling but it scratched at the edges of his consciousness. Hydra was considered lucky; all three of its vehicle components were well proven. None had been transferred to another Unit or written off. They had stayed together since production, which was unusual.

Designed primarily as workforce transport, Hydra could be conjoined in the field, providing onsite accommodation and a workshop facility under tarps strung between the hulls. It had been at the forefront of the thermal tower construction programme dating back over two decades. After the initial construction of ten of the huge glass structures that powered Skala from way out in the desert, Hydra had been reassigned and refitted as a long-range exploration and salvage Unit. JT was pretty sure he had handled the reassignment personally.

The Rika, if they were involved, had always made a point of keeping the quartermasters in the loop if they needed equipment. Their policy was to contain knowledge of their activities rather than be over-secretive and encourage speculation or gossip.

Reminding himself he was speculating, JT concluded that in all likelihood the whole thing was just a clerical screw-up. Still, how did anything get the Unit out of T7 without tripping the tag? That detail continued to bother him but for now he had other work to attend to. The Unit at T24 might not be Hydra at all, and in any case the world didn't stop because of a single misplaced Unit.

004: Joss Ratha

In the small but airy anteroom to Joss Ratha's office, Katherine and Tyler Olson sat together in reflective silence. The office itself was visible through a glass partition, an unusual feature for such an old building. Piled to knee height along most of its length were books and files in varying states of wear. Behind these, standing resolutely on a crimson patterned rug, sat a dark, wooden desk littered with paperwork, pens and parts of a child's geometry set. There was no evidence of a computer and scant sign of any sort of organisation to the place. While a window filled the left-hand wall, the back of the room was lined with bookcases packed tightly with all manner of junk. Mounted high on the right-hand wall was a single painting which depicted a verdant pasture, trees and, at its centre, the unmistakable shape of a horse.

Olson had only ever seen a living horse once, while on a trip into the north of the temperate band with his parents. They had travelled off-road, following the path of a river tributary that looped around the main vein of water. Olson remembered his mother imploring her husband to shut off the engine. There, not thirty metres from them, head down and sipping at the gently flowing water, was the tallest and most handsome

34

animal Olson had ever laid eyes on. Sometimes, when he was down, he thought about it; the deep chestnut brown of its flanks and the swishing sound of its black tail as it beat away flies. It had taken a moment to notice them, then raised its head to regard them with big doe eyes. For a moment Tyler thought the animal had looked directly into his soul. Then, as if content with what it saw, it had turned, whinnied and galloped away.

Making as if to stretch his legs, he crossed the room to a water cooler and filled a paper cup. He fumbled in a pocket for a strip of salt tablets, which he offered to Katherine. 'Electrolyte?'

'Thank you,' she said gratefully. He popped out two tablets, dropped one into the water, handing it to Katherine, before filling a second cup for himself. He took a sip just as sure, clipped footsteps from the corridor signalled the arrival of a tall figure who wore about her an air of superiority as if it were a garment. Following in her wake was a short, tired-looking woman holding an armful of tatty files.

Katherine rose to greet the women and, as she did so, an instant change came over her. It was as if a veil of self-assured professionalism had descended from head to toe. It always did but there were times, and this was one, where she feared the mask would finally slip and show how she saw herself; a fraud in an elevated position by virtue of pure accident.

'Katherine, it's rather early,' Ratha snapped, ignoring Olson. 'I suppose you had better tell me why I'm here.' She stood rigid, resplendent in a full-length, dark-grey dress. Her chiselled features, high cheekbones and angular chin were accentuated by the sharp cut of a jacket which hugged her form tightly. The sleeves extended to her wrists, each ending in a point that partially covered the back of each hand. It was an effective, if intimidating, look which she pulled off without a trace of perspiration despite Skala's intense heat.

'I'm sorry Joss. Could we talk in your office? This is Tyler Olson. He's with CID and investigating the matter we're here to discuss.'

Katherine looked at Olson, who was silhouetted against a window, the cup of water still in his hand. Against the light she could just make out a mask of polite blankness on his face and for the second time she recognised that hardness in him just beneath the surface.

Ratha also regarded the CID man, measuring him with disdain. 'Very well, I suppose we had better get on with it,' she said and stridently made her way to the inner office door. Her companion, moving to follow, was dismissed with a momentary arch of a sculpted eyebrow.

Katherine felt suddenly embarrassed for Olson and couldn't meet his eyes. She had never been blind to Ratha's abrupt and sometimes overbearing manner, which was familiar to her from as far back as childhood. Heidi Kane, Katherine's mother, had been mentored by Ratha as a field biologist and the two had frequently collaborated on research projects, becoming close allies. But now, with an outsider present, she saw Ratha from his perspective and understood why so many people considered her cold and arrogant.

Ratha settled herself into the worn, well-kept leather chair behind her desk. She didn't offer seating to either of her guests which, for regular visitors, was an accepted given. Not wanting to act the schoolgirl in front of the headmistress, Katherine reluctantly stated her case before being invited to do so.

'It seems that HEX was stolen from the Vault. We don't know how or why but I thought you should hear it from me as early as possible.'

'Stolen? Stolen by who?' Ratha asked, creasing her brow.

This was her typical reaction to important news, not obvious shock or concern but an instant, aggressive parry.

'We don't know. The investigation is being led by a Detective O'Brien with the assistance of Mr Olson,' Katherine gestured to Olson, who stood a step behind.

Ratha leaned forward slightly to rest her forearms against the edge of her desk. For a brief moment she scrutinised Olson intently then apparently lost interest.

'Only two of them? I thought CID had more of a budget. They've taken a good chunk of mine recently.' She was being deliberately obtuse, another of her less-lovable traits.

Olson, however, responded with surprising reassurance. 'Detective O'Brien has a good number of agents down in the Vault and he's sure to be appropriating as many as the relocated resources will allow, Councillor.'

It was a good answer, as Ratha's lack of a response acknowledged. Her manner softened and Katherine thought the message was starting to sink in.

'HEX has gone, Joss, it's as if she disappeared into thin air. How she was removed and by who is a matter for CID but there's obviously going to be all sorts of repercussions for us to deal with.'

Ratha huffed. 'You're right, there will. I suppose it's going to be the work of the anti-AI brigade. They're a troublesome, uneducated lot. AI,' she complained, 'how can you take these people seriously when they still don't even use the right terminology? But I suppose they shouldn't be hard to track down.'

'Why would that be?' asked Olson, not unreasonably.

'Because they will make a song and dance of it, parade her. They'll probably try to damage her. It will all be very public – that's what the antis do, public,' she said, with enough disdain to make Katherine flinch. 'They write endless letters to Council representatives deriding even the existence of the Intercessors. Some are even representatives themselves now. It's impossible to get through an open Council session without several jabs at the rest of us. Any form of disruption they can come up with they push to the limit. Ask Katherine.'

'Is there anyone specific you think we should look into?' asked Olson.

'You would have to ask them.'

'There is no one you think fronts their cause?'

'They have an unofficial voice in the Council Chamber. A man, I forget his name,' said Ratha dismissively. 'But he won't be behind this. His way of doing things is to waste as much public time as possible and he's learned to stick to what he's good at.' With a sardonic smile she added, 'He seems to know his limits.'

Ratha's displays of prejudice were deliberate, designed to make her audience either complicit or militant. Katherine found the tactic distasteful but chose to ignore it for now. 'Joss, about the technical repercussions – Aya, Skala, the migration. If HEX is not recovered quickly we need to reallocate her workload between ourselves and ROOT. The timescale impact could be huge.'

'I think you're jumping ahead, Katherine. It is extremely unlikely that this situation will not be resolved by the end of the next shift.' She paused a moment and glared at Olson. 'Someone has to justify hogging my budget, don't they?'

Olson gave a flickering smile. It was a backhanded compliment but evidently he took it as a vote of confidence. For a moment there was silence, Katherine feeling she had run out of things to say. Ratha, as was her way, filled the gap and brought the discussion to its conclusion.

'Thank you for letting me know, Katherine. Am I to assume, Mr Olson, that I'm not to speak of this with my team for now?'

Olson thought a moment. 'Only to the people you need to.'

'Understood. Keep me informed.' And, with a hand gesture to the door, she bade them farewell.

As they left Ratha's office, Katherine hesitated and turned back. 'Is Kyra here?' Ratha, who was already engrossed in something else, looked up momentarily and glowered. Katherine understood the look and acknowledged it. 'Too early,' she said. 'Much too early.'

Back in the searing heat of the city, Katherine and Olson walked in the shadow of the low, sprawling buildings of the Western District with less urgency.

'She's quite a lady, that one,' Olson grinned.

'She is,' agreed Katherine. 'She's complicated, but she has good hearts underneath all the abruptness. Honestly, you would be surprised at some of the things she's done and doesn't talk about.'

'Such as?' For a moment Katherine thought this was a rebuke but then realised that the question was sincere. She'd been feeling defensive and was trying to justify how she regarded Ratha to herself more than she was to Olson.

'For example,' she began. 'She was once overheard shouting at some street kids to "Go back to the Projects" or something like that. Probably she swore at them. There happened to be a journalist in earshot and it made the news. "Privy Councillor picking on the poor", that sort of thing.'

'Well it wasn't a nice thing to say,' Olson observed.

'On the face of it, no, and Joss would be the first to acknowledge it was a poor choice of words. But the reality is that she was trying to protect the kids, stop them from doing anything that would attract the wrath of the law.'

'You're sure about that? That she was trying to help?' he asked doubtfully.

'I am. What wasn't reported was that Joss personally financed several of the Projects to try to get the kids out of the slums, out of trouble and into accommodation. She gave away hundreds of thousands of links but no one knows about it. She wants to protect the poor but…' Katherine searched for the words. 'She's just quite crass sometimes. There is no other word for it.'

Olson took this at face value but remained sceptical. 'As I said, quite a lady.'

'What will you do now?' asked Katherine, hoping to change the subject.

'I want to figure out how this little magic trick was done,' said Olson with enthusiasm. 'I reckon Vincent will run rings around himself and maybe he'll find something, you never know. But I think not in this case. While he's doing all that I'd like to do a little research. What about you?'

'There is bound to be an emergency session of Council before long. Get some sleep I guess, clean up a bit and wait.'

'A good idea,' Olson agreed. They paused in front of the gap between two buildings. 'I'll leave you to that now, if you don't mind?'

She gave him a warm smile, which he returned. He nodded, then started up a side street. She watched as he faded into the emerging crowds of the awakening city then set off again, towards the Eastern District.

005: ROOT

Eastern District, Skala City

Wanting to avoid Ayon Research and gather her thoughts, Katherine returned to her apartment for the first time in many shifts. She'd paused momentarily at the door, seriously debating whether she wouldn't be better off in her office after all. But, taking the plunge, she found herself unexpectedly relieved to be somewhere quiet and familiar.

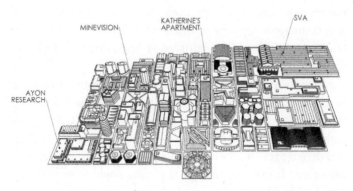

She sat on a deep sofa and gazed out through a glass wall, beyond the rooftops of the Eastern District, to arable farms and grasslands that extended out beneath distant dark clouds. The shrunken remains of Lake Eiraye looked dull, reflecting the grey hue of the leaden sky. Somewhere far in the distance, too deep into the twilight to make out, lay Aya.

For a time she sat imagining scenarios; HEX taken by the anti-AI lobby and paraded as the focal point for their righteous indignation; HEX stolen by a technology company to gain a commercial advantage. But at the end of each mental play-through she kept returning to the bizarre way in which the IDC had been taken. Even without knowing exactly how it had been done, it didn't fit with the established methods of either group. As Ratha had hinted, the anti-AI lobby were always overt, protests or slogans scrawled across building frontages in bright paint. She knew better than to underestimate anyone, and didn't completely reject these people as the culprits, but considered it unlikely. It didn't fit.

Industrial espionage, in other words greed, seemed a much more plausible explanation. The major companies lobbied hard to gain access to HEX and ROOT for the information they imparted. They also knew where the Intercessors were, information that was kept from the general public. It was easy to imagine any one of them collaborating with the city's criminal underworld to spirit away what they viewed as a limitless source of knowledge.

Katherine considered this at some length, before realising she hadn't eaten since the last rest shift. Finding the only edible thing in the kitchen was dried pasta, she boiled water and added a handful of the narrow strips. Stirring the pan, her mind wandered back to the companies and the possibilities they presented. It was conceivable that they could have recruited someone inside her department, however much she abhorred the idea. There had to have been someone on the inside somewhere, and she supposed it wouldn't be hard to woo a technician with money or the promise of a lucrative job later in life.

But again something didn't fit. Anyone wanting to use either ROOT or HEX would have to know how to communicate with them. Katherine herself had only discovered how to interface with ROOT after a great deal of experimenting. Her findings were not classified but they were not widely distributed either. Transfixed by the bubbling water, she thought about how often her colleagues would look into Intercessor communication. It wasn't frequently, there had been no need since HEX's integration and the only documentation resided solely, as far as she knew, in her office.

Glancing up, she noticed her antique chronocyl had run dry in her absence. She found ice and filled the glass tube, watching as it began to melt and saturate the red Hellinar sand her mother had brought back from one expedition or another. Gradually the sand began to 'shift', its colour deepening until the drip, drip of water from the cylinder base began to turn the mechanism below it. Belatedly, Katherine realised she had no reference to set the time to any accuracy. She set the time rings going anyway and watched as the upper of the three, the moment, clicked around the cylinder's axis until the 'turn' ring clicked around. Whether the bottom ring, the 'rotation', was working she couldn't be sure, it moved too slowly to judge.

Retrieving the now-overdone pasta, she strained it before tipping it into a shallow bowl. Rummaging in a cupboard for something to flavour it she settled on a sweet tomato paste and crushed peppercorns. She returned to the sofa and picked at the food, eating little before it went cold. She could count on the fingers of one hand the people who would have the knowhow to interface with HEX and none of them seemed a likely candidate for an industrial spy.

Exhausted and confused, she dragged herself from the sofa and, abandoning the bowl to a side table, went to bed. Thought blended with dream, phasing in and out of logical possibilities and the products of her overwrought imagination. Dust permeated the air as she turned over and over. It began to affect her breathing and caused her to wake, rise and fill a glass with water, which she drank and refilled. She dozed again for a while before giving in to the discomfort of a full bladder.

Awake, showered and feeling refreshed despite lingering tiredness, she made a hot drink. She picked out dark, pressed trousers to complement a plain, white cotton blouse from the few clothes she had not moved to Ayon Research. Before long she would be summoned to a formal Council meeting. She wanted to be ready but dithered, dressing slowly before realising she was only delaying the inevitable. Ayon Research was her responsibility and she had to face whatever difficulties that entailed. Resigned to the fact, she forced herself into action and, within five turns of the chronocyl, was out of the door.

Ayon Research was in lockdown. Security swarmed the building, drawing the attention of the public crowding by the foot of the stone steps that ran up to the entrance. Katherine had to jostle and fight her way to a cordon manned by officers in black uniforms. Fortunately, they had been briefed and quickly ushered her through. She heard the rapid fire of clicking cameras as she ducked under the thin tape separating the mayhem outside from that within the building.

Shouted questions from reporters were audible over the hubbub of the crowd. Although she didn't answer them, it was clear that they had no idea what the situation was, only that it was serious.

The entrance hall was packed with people, some clearly security while others, clad in white overalls, were presumably forensics. In the middle of it all, talking with vigour to a small group of suited officials, stood the diminutive, bespectacled personage of Vincent O'Brien. Catching his eye, she was surprised to see him break off his conversation to walk towards her.

'Katherine Kane,' he said, extending his hand.

Slightly taken aback, Katherine remembered Tyler Olson's obvious respect for his partner and took the greeting as genuine.

'Mr O'Brien. Have you made any progress?'

'Plenty,' he said and ushered her towards the Cannula. He continued to talk as the elevator was summoned.

'I have nearly thirty agents here now, including forensics and scanning technicians. We're gathering a lot of data. We've got seven or eight airborne camera platforms above Skala at any one time. Three are patrolling the city's perimeter, although I've got a feeling we're too late for that to do much good.'

'What sort of range do those platforms have? The ones we use for surveying can only fly for about fifteen turns.'

'Longer, for the bigger ones we're using. I'm told the next generation will be able to lift a person, which would be helpful.'

The doors parted and they entered the Cannula. O'Brien reached across to the control panel and tapped a lower button.

'I'd like to interrogate the other IDC so it's fortuitous you're here. We've kept a guard outside the door to its 'chamber', is that what you call it?'

'Yes, chamber,' agreed Katherine, noting O'Brien was picking up the jargon. 'But I'm not sure ROOT will take kindly to interrogation. You can't force him to be co-operative.'

'A poor choice of words on my part,' said O'Brien, as if it was of little concern. 'Let's say interview. No one has been in or out so as far as ROOT is concerned, so nothing is amiss.'

'He'll know something is out of place,' she said, without

hesitation. 'If no one has been in or out of there for a shift or more, he'll know.'

'So how would you approach it?'

'Don't pull the wool over his eyes,' she replied cautiously. 'He's extremely perceptive. He knows the staff's patterns and he's good at interpreting human behaviour. There is some speculation he may be able to detect pheromones if someone is in close proximity to him. He plays a game with the technicians, guessing which one has entered his chamber and he's almost always right. He cuts himself off from the CCTV most of the time to maximise processing power, so no one has figured out how he does it.'

'So would you advocate telling him exactly what's happened?'

'I would give him the whole picture and see what he comes back with, yes.'

'You don't think we should hold something back? See how he responds?'

'No, he's an Intercessor, a bridge between human and machine. But make no mistake, he's a machine himself. There is no benefit in holding back. Better to give him the whole story and allow him to process it. The more information we can give him the more we will learn.'

'I will reiterate: I don't know anything about these IDCs but are they not by their nature like dealing with a human? Interviewing suspects, we almost always hold some things back to maintain an advantage.'

As the elevator reached the Vault they waited for the doors to part, giving Katherine a moment to formulate a response. She found it hard to put two decades' of research observing ROOT's behaviour into words.

'ROOT interacts with people much as you or I would. He has adaptive strategies. As I said, he's a bridge and like a human he can be impulsive at times. He can also be very cryptic and avoid answering questions. In this case though, I expect he will see the situation as a challenge, a puzzle to be solved, which is something he responds to well and, in my experience, predictably.'

They walked together to the security window, where they were immediately signed in by CID personnel, a detail that was not lost on Katherine. She couldn't shake the annoyance that her domain had been invaded.

'I'll take your lead on this, I'm out of my depth here,' said O'Brien, with surprising deference.

Katherine found this an astonishing admission from someone so outwardly self-assured but she had to admit she respected how forthright he was. 'Is there anything else useful you can tell me? Anything that might help ROOT analyse the situation better?' she asked.

'At the moment, no,' said O'Brien emphatically. 'We have collected a great deal of data but none of it has been processed and nothing obvious has come from either the CCTV or the forensics.'

Side by side they turned left and approached the door to ROOT's chamber. O'Brien nodded to a guard, who stepped aside. As Katherine depressed the button to operate the door locks a vision of a second empty podium flooded over her. Fighting back fear as the seal depressurised, she swung the door open. Much to her relief, ROOT was sitting just where he should be, an inanimate object amid a tangled nest of cables and pipework.

'ROOT, it's Katherine.'

'Hello, Katherine, who have you brought with you?' came the creamy synthesised voice from speakers mounted in the podium.

'Mr O'Brien, an investigator from the Corporate Investigations Division.'

'And does Mr O'Brien talk at all?'

'Yes, sorry,' said O'Brien, caught off balance. 'Nice to make your acquaintance.'

This wasn't an uncommon reaction. Most people took time to get to grips with communicating with a highly intelligent but totally unreadable cube.

'And if I may ask, what is it you're investigating?'

Katherine nodded at O'Brien, a cue for him to continue, which he readily acknowledged. 'We're looking into the disappearance, presumably the theft, of the other IDC that's kept here.'

When ROOT did not respond, Katherine was moved to elaborate. 'HEX has been stolen, quite literally without trace. Her telemetry doesn't show any event that might indicate when she was taken.' She paused just a moment to consider the implication of her next words. 'In fact it's still running as if she were present.'

'And what would you conclude from that, Katherine?'

She looked at the floor, her brow furrowed in concentration. 'There is clearly some sort of recorded data being streamed into her telemetry feed.'

'And have you found the source?' asked ROOT, silkily.

'We're working on that,' replied O'Brien. 'But we've not found it yet.'

'And I assume from your perplexity that you do not know how HEX exited her chamber?'

'No, at the moment we've no idea. We only know she was stolen,' stated O'Brien.

'That is a matter of opinion,' said ROOT, with a trace of irritation.

Even Katherine, who was used to ROOT's games, found

this a particularly odd statement. 'I don't understand,' she said. 'HEX can hardly have walked out herself.'

'The answer is obvious, is it not, Katherine? Given the nature of her disappearance I think it is far more likely that HEX has abducted whoever moved her, not the other way around.'

'Forgive me, but how can you possibly draw that conclusion?' asked Katherine in astonishment.

'And how long has it been since HEX was taken?' asked ROOT, avoiding a direct answer. 'I imagine it's more than a few rotations, a shift or more, since you made the discovery and therefore more since her actual departure. I can't imagine even Privy Councillor Kane rushing in to consult me without at least a degree of background work beforehand. Is that not correct Katherine?'

'Yes, that's correct,' Katherine confirmed, resenting the insinuation of predictability.

'No doubt you've considered one of the dissident groups opposed to AI as the possible perpetrator?'

'I have,' Katherine confirmed.

'But like me you would expect HEX to have turned up by now? A public display of contempt perhaps? Her chassis cracked open in front of the baying mob, wires and drives smashed in a collective euphoria?'

Katherine raised an eyebrow. Although confirming her own thoughts he seemed to actually relish the idea. No doubt he was striving to emulate what humans might regard as vindictiveness towards HEX.

'As that is not the case, it would seem we can discount that group as being responsible.' There was a pause before he continued. 'Do you have any other ideas?'

'Someone is holding her hostage?' suggested O'Brien, who had clearly been thinking through options from the outset. 'Corporate sabotage is another distinct possibility.'

'If this were a hostage situation a demand for a ransom would have already been forthcoming, don't you think?'

'Probably,' O'Brien agreed.

'Corporate sabotage, industrial espionage would seem more likely. But I expect you know that already?'

O'Brien nodded, then, after a nudge from Katherine, vocalised the gesture. 'Yes, that's my area of interest.'

'I bet it is,' said ROOT, with a trace of malice. 'I'm sure you know as well as I do that for anything to be removed from the Vault without trace, the Vault's staff must have been compromised.'

'I think that's a given, yes.'

'And that implicates Councillor Kane along with the rest. Forgive me, Katherine.' Her look said she grudgingly took his point. 'But you have her here with you, consulting me. That suggests you trust her, a trust I would say that is very well placed.'

'Thank you ROOT,' she said, not entirely sincerely.

'You have detained the other staff? Questioned them?'

'There are a few non-permanent people, customers if you like, we still need to talk to. All of the permanent staff are accounted for,' O'Brien confirmed.

'Some must, of course, remain down here to babysit me. I'm sorry to be a burden to you, Mr O'Brien,' he said sympathetically. 'Would it not stand to reason that HEX herself is the main perpetrator here? She would after all be able to set off alarms and fire suppression systems in the event of a threat, just as I can. If she has disappeared without trace I assume none of that happened?'

'No it didn't,' confirmed O'Brien. 'That happened later, after the discovery.'

'Level with me, investigator, what are you thinking? Not who, but why the elaborate trick?'

ROOT had cut quickly to the hearts of O'Brien's concerns. How it had been done was crucially important and might give them a clue as to who was responsible, not least who among the Vault staff might have been involved. His assessment was forthright, which quietly impressed Katherine.

'Whoever is responsible needed to buy time. A lot of time to clear the city before we could start looking. I think it's very likely HEX is no longer in Skala at all.'

'Very good, Mr O'Brien,' ROOT said, with apparent admiration. 'I strongly suspect that HEX herself is complicit in whatever arrangements have been made for her.'

'What makes you think that?' asked Katherine.

'Let's just call it a hunch.'

'Let's not.' O'Brien was quickly becoming annoyed and Katherine could hardly blame him. 'If you know something, or guess something, we would appreciate your view.'

ROOT's tone changed suddenly to sharp and admonishing. 'Recovering HEX is hardly in my interests Mr O'Brien. We share a unique form of mutual animosity you see. If you require her return you will have to facilitate that yourself.'

There was a stand-off lasting a few moments in which Katherine considered appealing to ROOT but wrote it off as a lost cause. ROOT's synthesised voice began again, reassuming its cordial tone.

'May I suggest, in the circumstances, that you organise a recovery mission to be ready when further information becomes available.'

'What sort of recovery mission?' This suggestion made more sense to Katherine than his reference to a hunch, an allusion she didn't believe for a moment. IDCs did not have hunches, though ROOT persisted with the pretence.

'In the context of my 'hunch', HEX will be travelling a long way from here, probably deep into Ayon.'

'Why Ayon?' asked O'Brien pointedly.

ROOT ignored him. 'There is little point sending something of equivalent speed to the vehicle in which HEX is travelling. You will need to cover the distance faster if you are to recover her.'

'That stands to reason I suppose,' Katherine admitted, trying to assemble a picture of what might have happened in her mind's eye. 'We don't know how HEX has been transported. Or even if she has, but I take your point.'

'I agree with Mr O'Brien that she is travelling,' he said, emphasising 'is'. 'I suggest you plan accordingly. Now, if you don't mind, I'm going to hibernate for a while. Do let me know if anything further comes to light, won't you, Katherine?'

With that, the audience was over and Katherine and O'Brien made their way out into the corridor. Both wondered for a moment whether they felt more confused than when they had entered. Independently, and for different reasons, both concluded they probably were.

006: T24

Hellinar Research Facility, Western District, Skala City

'Miss Tudor,' said JT Gilbert as her call was put through to him.

'Mr Gilbert,' she replied in a formal tone. 'I'm sorry it has taken me so long to get back to you.'

JT thought this was amusing given that after more than five working shifts of pressing them he had still heard nothing useful from the T7 facility. 'No problem,' he replied. 'What can you tell me?'

'I didn't find your Unit exactly, but I may have turned up something of interest,' she said. 'There was no Unit in the yard, which I know is what you expected given it's already tripped the tag out. But there are three sets of tracks that merge into one, starting from a far corner. Each set of tracks has the same pattern, a series of arrow–like grooves.'

'Sounds like a group of desert vehicles,' JT agreed.

'The tracks lead out past security. I followed them as far as I could but they almost disappear as soon as the yard meets the road. It looks as if the Unit turned south then west, towards the slums.'

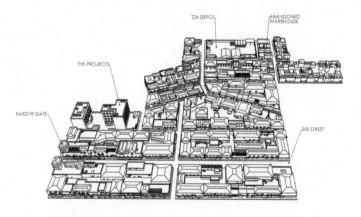

'The slums? That's odd. Normally anyone heading into the desert would head south through the city to avoid the slums, wouldn't they?'

'That's usual practice,' she said.

'Thank you very much, Miss Tudor,' he said thoughtfully. 'That's a great help.'

'There is one other thing,' she continued. 'This may be of no relevance but it's so peculiar I thought I would mention it.'

'Go on,' said JT curiously.

'A few shifts ago we received a transponder, apparently in error. One of my colleagues has been trying to sort out the paperwork to return it; however, the manufacturer is adamant it was ordered by us. It wasn't. The box has been sitting in this office for the last few shifts. I hadn't noticed until just now that it's been opened.'

Thinking quickly, JT asked, 'I don't suppose there is anything else in the box, a delivery note or an invoice?'

'Let me look,' she said and he heard the barest of taps as the phone was laid down. A moment later she was back. 'There is a certificate but I don't really know what most of it means.'

'Is there a transponder ID? It will be an eight-digit number followed by three letters.'

'Hang on.' He could hear her leafing through pages. 'Yes, here it is,' she said excitedly. 'The code is 3248 8492 HYD.'

Satisfaction surged though JT. 'That's the one. Let me cross-reference it to make sure. Can you read it out to me again?' He brought up the transponder database on his screen and typed the code in as she reread it but he already knew the answer. The alphabetical part of the code was always the first three letters of a Unit's moniker.

Miss Tudor heard a nasal snort of confirmation from JT. 'So you've found your Unit Hydra,' she said. 'I can only guess that whoever has taken your Unit had hoped anyone checking its movements would see a tag in and a tag out and not notice the change in location between the two events.'

JT considered this. She was probably correct but he felt reluctant to give himself too much credit.

'The bigger question,' she resumed, 'is who opened the box?'

'I'm not sure I follow you?'

'Who could get into the office here, open the box and walk out with the transponder? My staff are as confused as I am, the office door has electronic swipe locks. Either someone was able to get past that or was issued with a card.'

'Are the swipes logged?' he asked.

'In theory, yes. I would have to check with security.'

'Do that,' he said. 'In the meantime I'm going to head over to you and take a look at these tracks.'

'I would be happy to show them to you, but I fear they will have disappeared into the dust before very long, Mr Gilbert.'

'JT,' he said after a pause. 'My name is JT.'

'Very well, JT,' she said, and reciprocated. 'I'm Evelyn.'

He hung up and sat for a few moments with his elbow propped on his desk. He drifted into thought, chewing halfheartedly at a thumbnail. There was no question this was more than a clerical error. In fact, it had the potential to be very serious. He picked up the phone again and dialled the number for his contact in the Rika, on the off-chance she might have some insight. Whether through genuine ignorance or the Rika's maddening penchant for secrecy, she had none.

Finally he stood and made his way to the exit of the building. Emerging into the bustling streets of the city he hailed a trishaw taxi and directed the driver to the Western Fringe and T24.

Miss Tudor, Evelyn, turned out to be very different in person to the mental image JT had built up of her. He had imagined a tall, elegant, somewhat prim woman. On meeting her face to face he found her to be of medium height, slightly plump and far from prim. Her hair was short and blonde, almost white. Adorned in a loose-fitting blue blouse and cream linen trousers, she was certainly not beautiful but her companionable smile lifted his spirit.

'It's nice to meet you,' she said, offering a hand. Her shake was firm, warm and dry.

'It's good to meet you too,' he said. 'Now that I'm here I do recognise this place, but from a long time ago.'

'Not much has changed since I've worked here,' she said. 'Once in a while there is a clear-out of items that have been forgotten, but in general, it's looked tired since before my time.'

She signed JT in as a visitor and led him into the compound. It was as she described, worn down and very dusty. The windows, sandblasted for decades, were completely opaque. Grit skittered and whirled in patterns just above the broken surface of the concrete beneath their feet. Around them, low hangars stood, doors drawn shut tight against the elements. Within them, JT knew, were untold stocks of vehicle parts, much of which was considered surplus or outdated.

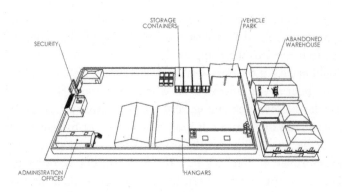

'So where's your office?' he asked.

'Admin is in that building.' She indicated a dilapidated wooden structure on stilts situated on the western side of the compound. 'It looks rather nicer on the inside than it does from here.'

'And how many of you work here?'

'Administration?' He nodded. 'There are three of us, which isn't enough, but we get by.'

'You strike me as very efficient, Evelyn,' said JT, who appreciated the likely workload she had to cope with.

She seemed faintly amused by the compliment and explained. 'It's easier to knuckle down, keep order and discipline than it is to deal with the consequences of cutting corners. Some of our customers do have to wait on occasions and I imagine they find that frustrating. But at least they know where they stand.'

A few moments later they reached a large ad-hoc structure,

more a frame draped in netting than a building in its own right. Evelyn gestured to the tyre marks on the ground.

'They are fainter now, even since last shift, but you can still see them.'

Squinting, JT could see the impressions; three vehicles apparently parked in a neat row. He followed the patterned imprints towards the compound's entrance. Straining hard he could make out the three sets of tracks converging into a single pair about twenty metres from where they stood. He stooped to take a closer look and noticed a regular interruption in the even marks of the tyres. It took him a moment to realise that what he was seeing was the pattern left by snow chains. He made a mental note to check the manifest, but was sure the Unit's last trip out had been to Hellinar rather than into the snowy wastelands of Ayon.

'Looks like our missing Unit,' he said and walked forward to inspect the tent. It was completely empty, with no visible footprints or other indication of who might have taken Hydra.

Turning his attention back to Evelyn, he asked, 'Any luck with the swipe log?'

'I have it here,' she said, offering it to him.

'This isn't going to mean much to me,' he said, studying it. 'I can see you and several other names repeated through each shift. Who are these other people?'

'Most of them work here, some are customers. This one,' she said, indicating a name that was marked down regularly once a shift, 'delivers our post. But there is one anomaly.'

She pointed out a name, that of a William Connor. 'I don't know who this is and he seems to come and go outside of the work shift. He has a swipe card so clearly he's got to be registered somewhere to be given access to the office. Security can see that he's registered, but they don't have the ability to see where or by whom.'

'I guess there will be a record of it back at Hellinar Research. We would have issued that card. Could it be that he's a cleaner or something?'

Evelyn Tudor looked at JT with open incredulity. 'A cleaner? Mr Gilbert, we barely have the budget to pay the admin and security staff. We do the cleaning ourselves, latrines and all.'

'Yes, of course,' he said, abashed.

After a moment of consideration she asked quietly, 'Do you think it might be stolen or forged?'

'That's a possibility, I'll look into it. In the meantime I'm going to see if I can learn where Hydra went after leaving here. You said the tracks indicate they headed out towards the slums?'

'Yes,' Evelyn replied. 'I followed them as far as Siir Street and there's nowhere vehicles of that size can turn off after that. But I would counsel against following them that way.'

JT shrugged, 'I've been through the slums before.'

'Recently?' she asked with a raised eyebrow.

'No, not recently. Why?'

She considered her answer for a moment before speaking again. 'There is a great deal of unrest out there at the moment. It's been bubbling just under the surface for a while.' She hesitated, wondering whether to elaborate, but the moment passed. 'If you decide you must go, please make sure someone knows what you're doing.'

'Well,' he said with a laugh, 'I guess I've got that covered. I'll let you know I'm back.'

Evelyn looked concerned but gave a small, sharp nod. 'Make sure you do.'

JT regarded her for a moment longer, then turned to follow the faint tracks that pointed the way out towards the western edge of the city.

007: Debate

Council Chambers, Central District, Skala City

Entering the Council Chambers early, Katherine found the airy space pleasantly cool and quiet. She let the eerie peace wash over her, breathing in the air to savour the aroma of the ageing wood panelling and the naturalness of its linseed oil coatings. Soft beams of sunlight shone down through air vents in the hemispherical roof and between the thick, cream cotton of the drapes that were slung across it. The light caught an infinity of dust particles that rained down to settle on the worn boards of the vast oak-lined floor. Even approaching the end of its life, the main chamber was a magnificent place.

Sunk into the room's centre was the belvedere, a circular edifice cut in half by a narrow aisle that formed a literal representation of the 'Divide'. Reflecting the sigil of Skala, two bracketed terraces descended to encircle 'the Nine' made up of the Privy Council and the Matriarch, who sat at its head. Presiding over the Nine sat a chamberlain, one of three learned civil servants charged with keeping order during parlance.

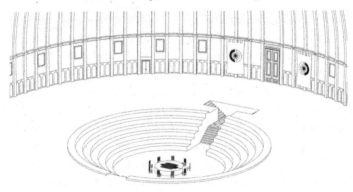

Descending the steep steps through the Divide in such unusual quiet, Katherine couldn't help but reflect on what the two terraced rostrums represented. Ostensibly, one symbolised Hellinar, the other Ayon, but in many ways she considered them to stand for more than that; in their simplest form they represented death and rebirth. Skala had been her people's home for nearly thirty decades but was now slipping into the deserts of Hellinar, soon to be rendered obsolete, dry and dead. A thousand kilometres into Ayon lay the part-constructed city of Aya, a next step in evolution, a symbol of hope and a way to redress some of the ills that had befallen civilisation's poorer inhabitants.

Pausing just short of the inner circle she wondered if it was all a bit too fanciful, Hellinar representing death and the past, Ayon life and the future. The majority of Orderly Councillors tended to gravitate naturally to one side or the other, depending on what role they played in wider society. Those who were concerned with keeping Skala alive, if only for a little longer, occupied the Hellinar dais to Katherine's left, while those planning the construction of Aya would find themselves sitting to her right.

She stepped forward to take her place at the edge of the

great table, a circular podium metaphorically sitting between Hellinar and Ayon. It was made from wood, a single piece of tree trunk nearly five metres in diameter, and gave the Privy Councillor standing at it the right to speak. Carved into its surface was an evolving schematic of the city's geography. According to tradition, or so the bards had it, the great table was destined to be burned at the final Council meeting before the migration. According to lore, the ashes would be retained by the Matriarch, who would stay with Skala as it advanced inexorably into the fires of Hellinar. Taking her place, Katherine supposed it would not be long before she discovered if this story was true or not.

The sound of voices approaching from beyond the belvedere woke Katherine from her thoughts. Gradually the Privy Council assembled, followed by nearly a hundred members of the Orderly Council and a full house of reporters and the public. As they streamed in she couldn't help but look for Kyle Devin, explorer, legendary survivor and, also, her father. The man responsible for research out in Hellinar, he entered with his opposite number for Ayon, Nara Falla. Nara had personified the role of explorer but now, in her seventies, had retired from the ice fields and reluctantly – some said she had been coerced – joined the Privy Council. Much to Katherine's relief, Kyle Devin's manner was outwardly easy although, as usual, he studiously ignored his daughter while Nara, making her way to seat herself next to Katherine, gave her a small nod of support.

The session started with the usual ceremonials, which were brief and uncomplicated. Orderly Councillors and the Nine alike would rise momentarily for the Chamberlain to take his place. All stood as Selwyn Abbot, a rotund but jocular man adorned in red velvet robes, bustled in through the Divide. As was usual he had a notepad wedged firmly under his left arm and was searching, seemingly in vain, for a writing implement. As he circled around behind Katherine she caught the unmistakable sound of mild cursing under his breath, which lifted her spirits, if only a little. Taking his place behind the Matriarch and apparently discovering a pen perched above his left ear, he removed it before donning a pair of spectacles which served as a cue for the rest of the assembly to take their seats.

'Right, the Council is now in session. We will begin with the review of membership,' he declared.

At this a tall woman, one of the permanent secretaries of Hellinar, stood.

'Council membership currently stands at 427.'

The population's limited ability to increase in numbers, given the rarity of successful couplings, made the review of membership a bureaucratic necessity.

'Excellent, thank you,' remarked Abbot, who, as a man fond of making records, diligently wrote the figure down.

'So, item two, matters arising.' Katherine's insides did a brief somersault. The Matriarch, resplendent in a long scarlet skirt, crisp white collared shirt and dark velvet jacket, stood and addressed the Council in her considered matter-of-fact way. As always she spoke with no reference to notes, a skill in which she took great pride.

'You will no doubt be aware that this extraordinary meeting has been called at short notice.' Mumbles of agreement and in some cases barely concealed impatience broke out from the assembled councillors. 'You may also be aware that an incident has occurred at the Ayon Research building. We have assembled to discuss that incident and its implications.' From behind her Katherine heard a barely raised, and thus unidentifiable, voice mutter, 'Get on with it.'

'I have been briefed by Detective O'Brien of CID. The situation as described to me is thus. At some time during the last shift one of the two Intercessor Drive Cores which have been kept at Ayon Research was removed by means and persons unknown.'

While there was no collective gasp from her audience it was clear that the Matriarch had their undivided attention. She continued, 'Every effort is being made by CID, with the co-operation of Ayon Research and the wider community, to recover the IDC. While we all clearly acknowledge that elements within our civilisation have strong feelings opposing the use of the IDCs, feelings to which I personally am not wholly unsympathetic, it is essential that the Core be returned.'

'The construction of Aya, as you know, is well under way. The contribution of both of the IDCs continues to be immense and for the good of all must progress subject to the restrictions put in place by this Council. I would urge anyone with information on this matter to make it available to CID at the earliest possible opportunity. Thank you.'

She swept her skirt neatly beneath her as she once again took her seat. There was a brief silence around the chamber before, predictably in Katherine's view, Victor Urasa, the Privy Councillor representing the cultural interests of Hellinar, stood and took the initiative. Urasa was middle aged, of average height and possessed of a sharp, some said subversive, intelligence. His voice was strong and confident, but had a wheedling nasal quality that Katherine had come to associate with a sense of distrust.

'Could the Matriarch tell us how the hell this happened? Aren't the IDCs kept under the strictest of security? I was under the impression that even their location within Ayon Research was up until five turns ago a closely guarded secret.'

Katherine winced as Urasa took his seat and the Matriarch again stood to address the chamber.

'I am unable to address the gentleman's first point at this time. Rest assured, as more information becomes available it will be disseminated among the Privy Council. Regarding the second, I would not presume to insult the public's intelligence by claiming a widely reported incident at Ayon Research and the subject of this meeting are not connected.' As she sat, Urasa, this time without hesitation, stood again.

'Disseminate among the Privy Council by all means, but what about everyone else?' he asked. 'This is clearly an important matter with enormous implications we need to consider. It's in everyone's interests to know the facts.'

Katherine wondered what tactic Urasa was using. He always had a strategy and was very adept at thinking on his feet to bend a situation to his advantage. He seemed to be taking a very combative approach, even by his own standards. Despite her passive, symbolic position the Matriarch was made of stern stuff and was having none this. Again she stood.

'Councillor Kane will be able to provide some further limited detail on the specifics on behalf of CID. I cannot at this time inform the gentleman, the Privy Council or the public any more than I have done, for the simple reason that events are moving fast and barely a shift has passed since the IDC was removed.'

'You mean stolen,' said Urasa, barely standing before sitting down again.

'I mean removed. But yes, presumably stolen.' This answer made Katherine physically shiver. Knowing she was sitting on information of volcanic proportions she had only moments to decide whether she should intervene. Willing herself on, she got to her feet, the rest of the Nine eyeing her with interest.

Trying not to look at them directly, least of all her father, she began.

'I may be able to elaborate on the situation, specifically on HEX's removal.' She stopped, momentarily realising she had given away more information than she had intended already. She cleared her throat and continued.

'A few rotations ago the lead investigator and I interviewed the other IDC.' What the hell, she thought, the damage is done, I might as well name him as well. 'ROOT.'

'He asserts that HEX may in fact be the perpetrator, she may have convinced a third party to remove her.'

She hesitated, wondering how much more to impart. In that moment a chain of events began that made that decision for her. Without getting up, Urasa simply said, 'Why?'

'I can't discuss that in a public forum,' she answered.

Again Urasa did not get up, a gesture which was clearly aimed at undermining her. Urasa had made no secret of his disdain for Katherine's youth, if not her person. 'Does it affect the investigation?' he asked.

'No, not directly, but I feel it would be unwise to discuss it in public.'

To her surprise it was Joss Ratha who spoke next. Ratha made to stand, then seemingly thought better of it. Katherine, feeling increasingly as if she was trapped, remained resolute. 'So if what you have to say does not directly affect the investigation and is of significance, what's stopping you from disclosing it now?'

Ratha knew as well as any other member of the Privy Council that to reveal the Research Departments' lack of understanding of Intercessor technology was an invitation to public revolt. 'The security of the Vault.'

'The Vault's security is compromised,' interrupted Urasa with a dismissive wave of his hand. Katherine looked up at

Selwyn Abbot. He wore a look that suggested he was not yet at the point where he felt justified in intervening but showed concern. The Matriarch wore a blank look.

'No. I'm not discussing it here,' Katherine said with as much assertion as she could muster.

'You're being obstructive, girl, come on,' Urasa threw back. The use of the word 'girl' threatened to rile Katherine and drew a clear reaction from members of the Council. Moments later this was revealed to be a deliberate ploy for Urasa to demonstrate his reasonableness and get his audience onside.

'Okay, okay,' he said. 'I apologise, I got carried away. I still don't see why you are holding out on us, though. If you can simply tell us what's going on I think we would all appreciate it.'

There was a collective groan of agreement. Katherine, feeling she was faced with no choice, tried to deliver her message – without, she hoped, simply blurting it out.

'Very well. ROOT asserts that HEX had persuaded or coerced somebody to remove her and take her out of Skala.' She hesitated long enough for Urasa to push her on.

'Out of Skala? Why and to where?'

'We don't know,' she said hesitantly. 'ROOT believes she's heading deep into the Ayon Tundra.'

Urasa, clearly making the most of her discomfort, fired another barb. 'Terrific. And why does the IDC wish to go there?'

'I have no idea and ROOT's not elaborating on what he describes as a 'hunch'. He seems pretty certain though.'

Katherine didn't expect anyone to take her seriously, but took some solace that this was ROOT's interpretation of events, not her own. Urasa, clearly feeling he had scored an unexpected victory, leaned forward and gave a snort of disbelief. But it was Ratha who took to her feet. Any feeling of relief Katherine may have felt at being out of the spotlight for a moment and able to retreat to her seat was cut abruptly short.

'Katherine,' began Ratha. 'Do you seriously expect us to believe that? HEX – you've identified which IDC is missing so I suppose there is little point in not continuing to refer to it by name – has convinced someone to take her out of the Vault and out of Skala?' She jabbed a single index finger onto the age-old surface of the great table as she spoke. 'He has a 'hunch' HEX is heading into Ayon? Come on.' She stood looking at Katherine with what could only be interpreted as disappointment.

Katherine stood. 'That's about it, yes. That's what ROOT said. He suggested we prepare some sort of interception but isn't willing to give us any information beyond that. In his own words, HEX's return is not in his interests.' Again she sat, giving way to Ratha.

'So what's your proposal? We go chasing after HEX on some mad mission to locate and catch her? If what we heard from the Matriarch is correct we don't even know who has taken her. It's absurd, the whole idea.' This last phrase was uttered with a disdain that Katherine had never directly experienced, although she had seen it lavished on others over the decades.

There was a long silence in which Ratha sat and brooded. Against Katherine's every expectation it was her father who stood next. His face was inscrutable but he spoke with a firm and reasoned voice.

'What Councillor Kane says is extremely far-fetched.' Katherine's hearts made an unexpected leap. While she had never expected any level of support from her father, his formal reference to her restored a respect Urasa had sought to tear down. 'However, there is no reason to doubt that this is the information given to her by ROOT. Over time he has made some peculiar assertions, this seemingly the most extreme'. A murmur of assent went around the room before he continued.

'But ask yourself this. For the minimal sacrifice required to prepare to chase down HEX,' he favoured Katherine with a glance, 'is it not worth the risk to be ready to recover her? If the window for doing so becomes smaller as a result of our own internal dithering, would we not all wish we had acted and not ignored or belittled a respected councillor for political gain?'

Katherine was nothing short of astonished by this show of support. She wasn't sure she quite understood the reference to political gain, but with both hearts thumping hard in her chest she didn't much care. Kyle Devin retook his chair amid a deafening silence. He looked not at Katherine but at Urasa, who appeared reflective. Finally the Matriarch stood.

'Thank you, Councillor Kane. I think you are correct and further discussion of this matter should be conducted in private. With regret, I recommend we adjourn for now.'

Selwyn Abbot, who had resisted interruption of these increasingly heated exchanges, readily agreed and declared order and dismissal. Katherine stood briefly but took her seat again as the chamber filed out. Looking down at the floor, and lost in thought, she was momentarily startled to feel a warm and firm hand on her shoulder. She looked up into the face of her father, his features seemingly softer than she was used to.

'What Urasa said, the way he addressed you, was uncalled for. You did well considering.' She blushed, unused to receiving praise from her remaining parent. 'More than a decade ago ROOT tried to persuade me to take him deep into Ayon, but would not elaborate. What he said to you has the ring of the same desire. At the time such an expedition was beyond us.'

Katherine looked at him in astonishment but could only ask, 'But you think it's possible now?'

'I think it probably is,' he replied. 'You're aware of what John Orchard is building out at Special Vehicle Assembly?'

'The Deep Ayon Research project?' asked Katherine as realisation dawned on her. 'I've seen it but that was some time ago. It must be close to completion by now?'

'It's designated GVX. You should go and see him at SVA, it might be an option if HEX is already crossing Ayon. And maybe you should talk to Nara, see if you can't make use of it if the need arises.'

'That would be a big ask,' said Katherine doubtfully.

Her father's reply took her by surprise. He spoke quietly and very deliberately. 'It may be on the face of it, but given the political background I think Nara will be more helpful than you'd expect.'

Katherine looked up into his eyes and found a firm assurance in them. 'You think what ROOT says is true?'

'I think so,' he paused. 'Or at least I think there is something in it he's hiding. He was very determined on it last time and, okay, I don't know the details as you do, but the whole situation is extremely strange. Speak to Nara.'

Katherine nodded and her father gave her a brief, warm smile in acknowledgement. Then he turned and she watched him leave. For the first time in a decade or more she felt a lightening of some indescribable load she was barely aware she was carrying. It was a good feeling that, if only fleetingly, dampened down the maelstrom of confusion.

008: The Slums

The Western Fringe, Skala City

There was someone following him, of that JT was in no doubt. One or two shadows? It was hard to be sure in the vibrant, bustling streets of the outer edge of the Western District. The old cobbles of Siir Street were intermittently strewn with crumbling stucco that fell haphazardly from the walls of buildings. Idly he kicked at a lump and watched it crumble. Peripherally he caught a movement within the flow of people that struck him as out of place. Off to his right, a figure reacted to his presence and hastened into the cover of a nearby doorway.

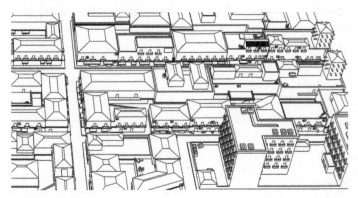

A stab of adrenaline threatened to expose his apprehension but he fought it and remained outwardly composed. The smells of human sweat, spit-roasted bovine meat and pungent spices were strong in the still, dry air. Warily he walked on, heading west in the direction of the slums. The heat was noticeably more oppressive here, although the sprawling, less orderly nature of the older buildings meant there was more shadow. Above his head, the hum and rattle of old, long-unserviced air conditioners was audible above the hubbub and bustle of Skala's poorer residents. The street was narrow, full of people pushing past each other in both directions. Had it been empty, he judged it just wide enough to accommodate Hydra. And it was straight, as it had been thirty decades ago when an old rail track ran through here bringing humanity in from the dead city of Kul.

For a moment he felt the presence of a second set of eyes on him. The feeling was strong enough to make him double back and duck into an alleyway festooned with patterned, brightly coloured cloth, rugs and kaftans. Old splinter-wood boxes were piled haphazardly below shopfront awnings, giving the place a confined, claustrophobic atmosphere.

As soon as he could, he took another right to head back towards Siir Street. His sense that someone was trailing him grew fainter as he descended a set of worn steps, taking two at a time where he could. He turned, emerging from between buildings to meld back into the flow of people.

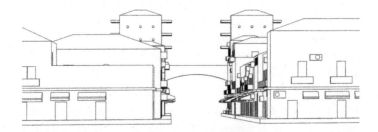

Opening out before him, beyond what was colloquially known as Kaedyr Gate, lay the yawning expanse of the slums. He moved forward, entering endless rows of sprawling tenement shacks cobbled together from weathered corrugated tin that visibly radiated heat. The ground, defined largely by makeshift dirt lanes forking off from the single main street, was strewn with detritus. The waste of thousands was piled against buildings whose lower flanks were spattered with excrement. Flocks of gulls spiralled overhead, alighting to peck whatever carrion they could find. JT strained against the intensity of the sun and winced as he passed what he realised was the remains of an animal, probably a dog. The necrotic carcass lay discarded by the roadside, a swarm of maggots burrowing into the little dry flesh that remained.

Shaking his head in disbelief he recalled how, a decade or two ago, prompted by the outbreak of an acute and virulent epidemic they feared might become a danger to them, a group of Skala's more prosperous residents had made an effort to improve conditions here. Rubbish had been collected, a central open sewer had been dug and a fresh, if limited, water supply network installed. Gradually, however, the self-satisfaction of goodwill had given way to apathy as fundamentally nothing changed to lift those living on the edge of humanity out of poverty. Little by little, attentions wandered and the rubbish began to build up as the flow of purified water reduced to a trickle then dried up altogether.

An outbreak of parasitic worms had prompted a reluctant second effort to improve sanitation and contain the infection at source. While the installation of communal composting lavatories improved the situation, a second unintended benefit was bestowed upon agriculture, which gratefully inherited a supply of cheap fertiliser. Or it should have. Instead, regular collections of human waste were carried out by Council-approved contractors who covertly formed a formidable cartel able to name its price and force the less affluent farmers into the slums themselves. With an increasing populace, the collective faeces output increased, making the cartel and the remaining farmers richer. The inevitable reaction from the slums was for the inhabitants to throw their waste upon their own doorsteps, defying the pleas of the politicians, activists and, of course, the cartel. Despite regular diplomatic and coercive interventions, the situation was still essentially unresolved.

Picking up the sporadic imprints of Hydra's chain-adorned tyres, JT tracked them deeper into the slums. The ground to either side of the road dropped, giving him a clear view of an endless expanse of ramshackle roofs.

Presently, the wheel tracks became confused and JT doubled back a few metres to squat, examining the marks more carefully. He ran a finger over the furrow of imprint when, from nowhere, a figure rammed into his side and sent him sprawling onto the dirt. Momentarily stunned, he began to lift himself as a pair of strong hands were thrust under his armpits from behind. He struggled as they began to drag him toward the side of the road. A hard, ringing blow to the head was the last thing he felt before the world descended into purples, yellows and finally, a deep, comfortable blackness.

Intermittently JT was aware of being hauled up and tied by the wrists. He had come round before falling back into unconsciousness at least twice, before finally coming to. A forefinger under the chin lifted his head and he found himself looking into the strong male features of his captor. He heard heated arguing nearby but couldn't make sense of the words. He made out three distinct voices and inferred they were trying to decide what to do with him.

He was on his knees, bound to what must be a square-section wooden pole because its edge dug mercilessly into his back just below the shoulder blades. His legs were on fire, aching with the strain of supporting his hitherto limp body. His wrists, lashed to the pole behind him, chafed on tight, rough bindings. The muscles around his eyes strained, prying apart lids that were gummed together by mucus and sweat. The metallic taste of blood was strong in his mouth as he tried in vain to swallow. Looking down with blurred vision he could make out dark stains flecked across his T-shirt and jumpsuit. Someone had clearly given him a good going over.

Time passed. A turn might have been a rotation, a rotation a shift or more. Trying to work both eyes open, he thought of Evelyn Tudor and wondered if she had alerted anyone to his disappearance, assuming he had been gone long enough to warrant her concern. He thought of Hydra and what in the world it might have been doing travelling through this accursed place. Sometimes he focused on the pain but found trying to mitigate it was futile. It wasn't long before his main preoccupation became his thirst. It started as a small discomfort compared to his physical condition, but grew steadily with each passing rotation until the need for fluid was overwhelming. As he became increasingly dehydrated he succumbed to sleep, once more drifting in and out of consciousness.

At first he wasn't sure what brought him back. The sensation was vague, a sort of long forgotten reflex. Something damp brushed his lips and anything damp he wanted with every fibre of his being. Forcing his lower lip to split away from the upper, he felt a straw push gently between them. Without caring whether he was being offered water or poison, he drew the liquid up the tube and into his mouth. It was surprisingly cool and very, very wet. For a moment he choked weakly and lost the straw but found it offered to him again. This time he put all his mental strength into sucking in the liquid. He tasted dust and blood washing down, but that quickly gave way to the wonderful restorative taste of mineral water.

He felt fingers reach across his forehead, gently grabbing a handful of hair. As his head lifted he summoned enough energy to open his eyes. His sight was still blurry, the dehydration causing purple shapes to dance around his peripheral vision. A male face came into view and though unfocused, JT could make out the unmistakable traces of a smile in and around the eyes. To his surprise it wasn't menacing, but more of a firm, satisfied look.

The face retreated and JT's head once again drooped forward. He felt the straw between his lips and took a long pull. Through the ringing in his ears he heard a voice, a soft gruff tone that sounded concerned.

'You should drink as much of this as you can. It's just iced water, pure for these parts. I'll get you some food, you'll feel better for that. You don't need to worry, we know who you are and you're safe now.'

JT could barely process this through the fog of pain and dehydration but judged that assertion a matter of opinion. He drank what he could and when he was finished he felt the tethers around his wrists loosen. As they gave way he fell helplessly forward onto the dusty earth. Drawing his knees up to his chest, he groaned but was relieved to be free of his restraints.

Beside him the man stood. 'Don't go anywhere, I'll be back in a while.'

JT watched the figure leave then closed his eyes and drifted back into sleep.

009: Three Sisters

Ayon Research, Eastern District, Skala City

After the meeting with Ratha, Tyler Olson had taken to the streets, asking probing questions of the more readily accessible of his underground contacts. To his surprise he'd turned up absolutely nothing relevant to the case. He gleaned a few unsubstantiated stories about small-time opium traders, a few illegal distilleries and some minor trade in illicit fungus, but of the disappearance of one of the two most valuable assets Skala possessed, nothing.

Now word of infighting within the Council was filtering through. News of it spread like wildfire through the city. Interpretations, elaborations and fanciful exaggerations were rife. Councillor Kane had apparently been publicly mauled by a cultural colleague on her own side of the house. Kyle Devin, her father, had seemingly come to her rescue, a situation which some found predictable but the more informed said was an extremely unusual state of affairs since the two were estranged. Devin, they said, had treated his first-born daughter as something of an outcast since establishing his new family.

With his enquiries at a dead end, Olson had returned to the Ayon Research Facility and to the Vault below it. On arrival, O'Brien filled him in on the data that had been collected and what he had learned so far, which was not much. He ran through the list of people who had been interviewed and those who had yet to provide an account.

O'Brien took Olson aside and imparted verbatim the theory ROOT had relayed, that HEX was likely somewhere in Ayon. O'Brien had a prodigious memory and Olson accepted his account word for word. Olson stood back aghast at the bizarre, unfounded assertions of ROOT's narrative. As a final footnote, and for completeness, O'Brien ran over a few unrelated issues that had been brought to his attention from other parts of Skala.

Eventually, having discharged his duties, Olson entered the Cannula and took it up to the fifth floor, on which he understood Katherine's office resided. It took him a few turns to find but presently he stood tapping on the frosted glass of a door, which was opened faster than he anticipated, not by a secretary but by Katherine herself.

'I hope you don't mind,' he said, in a friendly, if uncertain tone. 'I was in the building and thought I'd check on you.'

'I don't mind at all,' she said, ushering him in. She gestured to a sharply styled leather sofa and he settled himself with obvious appreciation for its comfort. She perched herself on the edge of a smaller sofa, facing him across a low, glass coffee table.

'I imagine you've heard about the Council meeting?' she asked with an air of inevitability.

'I've heard something,' he said, leaning forward and steepling his fingers. 'It sounds like it wasn't a lot of fun.'

'It wasn't, I should have kept my mouth shut,' she agreed.

'I'm sure you did what you thought was best and in good faith.'

'Good faith,' she repeated to herself in a weary tone. 'Good faith can be misplaced.'

'I heard your father came to your aid?' asked Olson.

Katherine sighed, tipping her head and gently arching a

considered eyebrow. 'That was a surprise, I have to say. It was welcome though.' She looked up and regarded him with an open honesty he recognised.

'You two aren't so close?' he said, more as a statement than a question.

'It's not that we aren't close, it's more that our relationship is a professional one. It's been that way for a long time.'

'Because he remarried?'

'No,' said Katherine, slightly shocked by this unexpected insight. 'Because we're both councillors and have to interact that way.'

'But in private?'

'In private it's…' she looked to the ceiling, searching for an answer. Finding none she sighed, 'It's just awkward.'

'I was the same with my dad,' said Olson and Katherine realised with a jolt that he felt ashamed.

'He ran this big company, here on the east side of the city. It was unusual for a man to be so successful back then. He got me the best schooling, gave me every advantage, but he sure was a hard person to please. I worked for him for a while but then he got sick and wanted me to run the company for him. It just wasn't what I wanted and I didn't think I'd be any good at it.'

He looked up and straight into Katherine's eyes.

'Well, I did it anyway. Trying to please him I guess, but it all went wrong. Business went bad. Outside influences, circumstances, you know?'

Katherine, whose life had been shaped by many unexpected events, nodded her complete understanding.

'He blamed me. I don't think it was my fault but maybe I could have done more – changed direction or something, I don't know. He lived just long enough to lose everything, so I understand "awkward".'

Through this brief account, Katherine began to feel an

intense sense that this man was a kindred spirit. She recognised in him things that she felt herself: a need to please a parent that could never be fulfilled; frustration at the influence of unforeseen events; and a deep-seated shame at advantage unasked for.

'What did you do? After he died, I mean?' she asked quietly and with heartfelt sympathy.

'I did what I had to. Paid off the workers, closed the company and started again. It put a strain on my marriage, which came to an end.' He looked sharply back up again and smiled. It was another gesture Katherine instinctively understood. Pulling the mask back on. 'You don't want to hear about all that now. We've got other, more pressing, things to talk about.'

'We do,' she agreed, more for his sake than because she wanted to change the subject.

'I was wondering,' he began. 'We still have no idea how the IDC was removed from the building. Vincent is making progress no doubt but I wondered if a little history might shed some light on events.'

'What sort of history?' asked Katherine in surprise.

'Well, not history exactly, more historical architecture. How long has the Vault been down there? This is an old building after all.'

'Okay,' said Katherine, searching her memory. 'It was originally some sort of cellar, but had been converted to a safe place to conduct high-voltage research when I moved down there with ROOT. We didn't know what he was then of course, it was just a convenient place no one really went to keep us out of the way. There really wasn't much down there, just the high-voltage cages and a few test benches which were rarely used.'

'It sounds bleak.'

'It's wasn't bad actually,' she replied, with a reflective smile. 'I spent a lot of time down there trying to figure ROOT out. It was a good place to get away from things.' She felt she should explain a little as Olson had so openly talked about his own troubles. 'Obviously my father remarried, but not because my parents split up. My mother was a biologist and died somewhere out in Hellinar. Only one person from that expedition made it back alive. Finding ROOT had given me something to focus on and I spent as much time as I could trying to analyse him. I was hiding, I suppose.'

Olson took this in but chose to direct the conversation back to the Vault itself. 'So when was it converted to what it is now?'

'Shortly after I activated ROOT,' she said, returning to surer ground. 'The conversion took a while and I really had little to do with it. I think I would have been taken completely out of the equation had it not been for ROOT's insistence he communicate through me, or at least with me present. More recently he's happy to talk to anyone but early on, he wanted me with him.'

'Why do you think that was?'

'I never really got to the bottom of it,' said Katherine in a tone that implied she was still considering it even now. 'It benefited me enormously but I never understood why he was so insistent. Having said that, some of his reasoning can be quite impenetrable, as Mr O'Brien so recently discovered.'

'He told me about that. When HEX arrived, the Vault was upgraded?'

'Yes that's right. The second chamber was built such that it wouldn't interfere with the workings of the first. ROOT was moved to the new chamber and HEX installed in the original.'

'So are there plans of the Vault somewhere? Blueprints that show the ventilation systems, that sort of thing?'

Katherine considered this for a moment. 'There are, certainly for the newer part of the Vault. There were some of the older part as well. I remember seeing them as it was converted but that was some time ago. They may still exist. If they do they will be in the Central Library opposite the Council.'

'Never been in there myself, but I've admired the building from a distance. Would I be able to look at what plans there might be?' Olson asked.

'Absolutely. You will need authorisation, which I can give you.'

'Thank you. I'll go take a look. I guess there is an architecture department or something?'

'Ask for city planning,' she advised. 'Actually,' she said, changing her mind, 'don't do that. Ask for Megan Devin, my sister. She will show you where to look. She's training to be a librarian and if you need a research assistant she'd be ideal.'

'I'll be sure to do that. She's helpful?'

'Trust me,' said Katherine. 'She's diligent and very bright, if a little unorthodox at times. Not as wild as Kyra, my other sister, but she'll surprise you.' Withdrawing a pocket notepad she scribbled and tore out the sheet of paper, which she then folded and handed to Olson. 'Give her this and I'll sort out your authorisation from here.'

Olson nodded and reached across the table to take the note held out to him. He took it and tucked it into the top pocket of his shirt. Pausing a moment, he asked, 'You mentioned Kyra? That's something else you might be able to help us with. I know Vincent is keen to talk to her. I understand she was in the Vault the shift of the disappearance. We've been trying to locate her but Vincent tells me so far with no luck. Any idea where we might find her?'

Katherine sighed, her expression suddenly weary. 'She'll likely be holed up in a tavern somewhere. The seedier the better as far as she's concerned. Look for somewhere in the

Western District that does strong drink and high-stakes gambling. You'll likely find her somewhere like that.'

Olson gave a short laugh and got to his feet. 'Sound like my kind of places. We'll go looking.'

Katherine uttered a quick, nasal grunt as if making her mind up about something. She straightened and said, 'Look for somewhere with a poet or minstrel, whatever you call them.'

'One of those storyteller, bard types?' he suggested.

'Yes, exactly. Kyra might be hard as nails but she's got a soft spot for history and stories about the old cities. At hearts she's an incurable romantic when it comes to that sort of thing. It's ironic but it might help you find her before she's...' Her voice trailed off and she looked down at the floor.

'Thank you,' said Olson, feeling he understood her meaning. He straightened his shirt and tugged a rolled-up cuff back over his elbow.

He made his way to the door, paused and momentarily looked back at Katherine. She was still perched on the edge of her sofa, introspective. Her eyes flicked up to meet his and he saw a deep concern in them. 'I'll get Vincent to go looking sooner rather than later,' he said and caught the acknowledgement of a brief, sad smile before he closed the door.

010: Nara Falla

Ayon Research, Eastern District, Skala City

After Olson left, Katherine took a little while to collect her thoughts and eventually gave in to the overwhelming feeling she had to do something. Having no better ideas, she decided to follow her father's advice and speak to Nara Falla.

Like Katherine, Nara spent most of her time in Ayon Research, her office being situated at the other end of the building on the ground floor. Although both ostensibly had much in common they rarely met one-on-one. Their discussions, when they did occur, centred on budget requirements and distribution, which, with Aya being of principal concern, were largely decided by Katherine. Nara accepted this position with good grace and had never sought to undermine her. Katherine, in turn, was grateful but still felt uncomfortable. In a rare off-guard moment, Joss Ratha had once made a comment suggesting Kyle Devin, then Kane, had in the distant past entertained a brief romantic entanglement with Nara, who was at least a decade his elder. Katherine, aghast at this revelation, tried to probe further, but Ratha would say no more.

The corridors of the first floor were dark and formal compared to the newer part of the building with its modern architecture of glass and steel. Mosaic lined the many windowless corridors, lit only by the occasional electric light hanging haphazardly from the ceiling. The offices allocated to the exploration and research departments were seldom occupied, owing to their custodians being out in the field more often than not. The whole floor and those below it had an old, solitary feel that bordered on neglect.

Reaching the door to Nara's office, Katherine hesitated, then knocked. A moment later she heard the drag of a chair across thin, worn carpet and light, assured footsteps. With the dry squeak of the handle, the door opened to reveal the short figure of Nara Falla, dressed, as always, in a grey jumpsuit. It was easy to forget Nara was now retired from the field, as she still looked the part: her long, plaited white hair draped over one shoulder and the lines of a lifetime's exposure to the elements writ clear upon her face. Regarding her across the threshold, Katherine came to the sudden realisation that Nara must once have been very beautiful. She didn't know why she'd not realised this before, nor why it suddenly came to her now. It was as if, now she was in her early forties, the world was starting to reveal itself in ways that should have been obvious but had before gone unnoticed.

'Katherine,' said Nara with a warm, forthright smile that carried the faintest hint of mischief. 'I thought you would come.' She took a step back and indicated for Katherine to enter. The office, much like the corridor, was darker than Katherine would have preferred in a workspace. But then Nara had spent decades working in the eternal dark of the ice fields and probably found this a more natural environment.

They sat, Nara behind her desk, Katherine directly opposite. Although the room was filled with artefacts, tools and equipment, it somehow didn't seem untidy or chaotic in the same way that Ratha's office did. Maybe, Katherine thought, this was because Nara's uncomplicated nature made it somehow more comfortable. Realising the ageing explorer was waiting for her to begin, she began fumbling for words.

'Nara, I don't know what you make of what I said in the Council meeting, but I promise you it's what ROOT told us.'

'I'm sure that it is,' said Nara. 'Sometimes the big things are so very big they sound implausible, especially to the person that's speaking.'

Katherine could not have agreed more and nodded seriously. 'Councillor Devin suggested I come to see you. I'm not sure how to ask you this, or even if I should be asking...' Nara picked up the thread to put her out of her discomfort.

'You want to know about John Orchard's Ground Vehicle Ten project? Whether it would be able to penetrate as deep into Ayon as necessary to recover HEX, if indeed that is where she is?'

Katherine was left momentarily speechless but also a little relieved that she didn't have to spell it out.

'That's about the long and short of it, yes.'

'Do you know much about the project?' asked Nara.

'I'm familiar with the basic concept, it's a mobile research station.'

'Well, that's right,' said Nara seriously. 'But it's more than just a research tool. It's a testbed for new technology; hybrid power plants and a hydraulic drive line among other things. It's hoped it will be the start of a new approach to exploring and studying Ayon. Despite the expense, the intention is that it will cut future exploration costs dramatically by eliminating the need for permanent research stations.'

'You said something along those lines when we agreed the funding,' said Katherine, recalling a meeting nearly half a decade before. 'Where in the build schedule is it now? The last time I saw it in SVA it was just a skeleton.'

'Close to completion but it hasn't been commissioned yet. We expect that to happen within fifteen, maybe twenty shifts.'

'That's close,' said Katherine. It was difficult to judge whether it would be too late without knowing how HEX was being transported. She took the worst-case scenario – an MK8 'Ice Runner' rapid transport vehicle – and based her comparison on that. 'How fast do you think it will travel?'

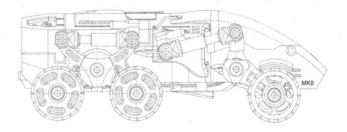

'John feels that 70 kilometres per rotation is about the best compromise at cruise speed over level ground. It will do much more but the fuel economy goes out of the window very quickly.'

On the face of it this was not fast enough, although Katherine had to admit she was impressed. It was also worth considering that a biofuel-run Ice Runner would be slowed by the need to refill its 'mulching tanks' regularly. Travelling onto the ice where bio-matter simply didn't exist would surely be impossible.

'You're wondering how quickly GVX would catch up with HEX, however she's travelling?' asked Nara. Before Katherine could comment, Nara said something that threw the whole foundation of her assumptions into question.

'How sure are you that HEX is travelling through Ayon? I accept that ROOT told you Ayon was the most likely place to look, but are there not other possibilities?'

This was something that Katherine had been agonising over. ROOT's unexplained assertion threw up all sorts of questions. She hesitated, trying to decide how to respond.

'I don't know, it's all hypothetical at this point, depending on how you view ROOT's theory.'

'It is extremely perverse,' agreed Nara thoughtfully. 'But the dilemma is that he has made inexplicable claims in the past and been correct. I suppose for the time being, we have to take him at his word and hope he will provide more insight.'

'What do you think, assuming he's right? Could GVX catch, say, an Ice Runner?'

'Yes, I think all things considered it probably could, over a period of, say, two lunar cycles.'

'Sixty full shifts? That's a long time,' Katherine frowned.

'Well, GVX's size and weight will be a great benefit early in the journey, where the terrain will be rocky. As you know yourself, that's where something like an Ice Runner struggles the most. After that I would expect GVX to catch up progressively.'

Katherine accepted this assessment for what it was, an educated guess. There were many unknowns, but she was grateful there was at least one outside possibility.

Nara began again. 'There is the question of the crew in our hypothetical journey,' she said, talking more to herself than to Katherine. 'It would be a very big risk sending GVX out this early. We have a shortlist of drivers we've interviewed for commissioning but we've not approached anyone about taking it out into the field. There is a very big difference between a test driver and a field driver.'

Katherine was well aware of the distinction, having seen first-hand how out of her depth a test driver could be in the wilds of Ayon. In fairness, she had also seen a very capable field driver wreck a new test vehicle by treating it as if it were a known, proven quantity. It worked both ways, and the driver selection would be critical given the timescale.

Nara seemed to be making up her mind. When she spoke again it was in a much firmer tone.

'I'll be frank, Katherine. I think if you are proposing that HEX be pursued at great risk to an expensive prototype vehicle and its crew, you should oversee the commissioning and crew selection personally. I want you to take responsibility.'

Katherine had not seen this coming, but reluctantly took Nara's point.

'Yes,' continued Nara, with mounting conviction. 'I am willing to push GVX's commissioning date forward and forgo much of the prior testing before it ventures into the field, but the conditions are these: the expedition collects data where possible; that data comes back to me personally and is left for me alone to disseminate.'

Katherine was momentarily confused. Surely any data collected would come back to Nara anyway. She seemed to be trading the world for something she already had.

'Well, that seems very reasonable, Nara,' she said, taken aback.

'Katherine, I'm getting old and my influence is not what it once was. I need your word that you will put a system in place to ensure the security of whatever comes back. I'd like you to be involved personally.' Her expression softened slightly as she spoke again. 'You were a very competent driver yourself.'

Katherine blushed slightly. This was hardly the time for compliments, but it was nice to be acknowledged. 'I was okay,' she said. 'I miss it, that's for sure.'

'I've been led to believe you're something of a natural.'

'That's very flattering,' replied Katherine, hoping Nara would get back to the problem at hand.

'My other condition is that, in the event we have no field

drivers available to conduct the commissioning and in light of the risk involved, you personally step in to ensure GVX is field-ready.'

Katherine was dumbfounded by this request and wasn't sure how to respond. 'From what I've seen of it, GVX would be a quite different animal to anything I've driven before,' she said a little lamely.

'That's going to be true for any driver. You're a good engineer, Katherine. You also understand the bureaucracy we will have to negotiate with to make this happen.'

Nara looked Katherine straight in the eye. 'You should conduct the commissioning. You've put yourself publicly in the firing line already, and you have the most to lose if things go wrong. Make sure GVX is ready and safe for whomever you hand over to.'

'Can I consider it?' asked Katherine, uncomfortably.

Nara cocked her head to one side and simply said, 'There's not much to consider, Katherine. Those are my terms.'

There was a long pause before Nara made a final point. 'I'm not sure if you are aware but GVX was designed to interface directly with ROOT. It was his idea and, although we've never attempted to integrate him into working machinery before, I felt it was prudent to at least build in the option, be it used or not.'

Katherine immediately grasped the relevance of this comment. 'An Intercessor could speed up the commissioning.'

'That's what he claims to have been built for,' Nara agreed. 'There is a risk in interfacing him of course. We don't know what he will do or what control he will exert,' said Nara cautiously. 'SVA built GVX to ROOT's specifications but, as with so many things, we just don't understand how the technology works.'

'Don't worry,' said Katherine automatically. 'I've know

ROOT for as long as we've had him, he won't misbehave.'
This statement sounded stupid even as she said it.

'I'm afraid I don't share that conviction,' Nara warned. 'I
suggest you trial the interface but analyse carefully what he
might have control over. It's the first step towards the decision
on whether the IDCs are integrated elsewhere.'

She meant Aya. Integrating ROOT and HEX into the new
city's systems had been endlessly debated and remained a
divisive issue.

Nara concluded the conversation in a more positive tone. 'I
will get on to John Orchard and apprise him of the situation
as far as I can. I will also deal with the Privy Council, if you
prefer?' Katherine accepted this offer with gratitude. 'Good.
Then SVA will be expecting you as soon as you can get there.'

'Good luck, Katherine Kane,' said Nara with a look of pride
that startled Katherine.

With that, Nara showed Katherine out into the corridor
before returning to her desk and starting what was to become
a whirlwind of political wrangling. As she lifted the receiver
of her telephone, she felt with total certainty she was doing
the right thing and that, in all likelihood, Katherine was the
best chance to accomplish a near-impossible task in a near-
impossible time frame.

011: Unaccounted

Evelyn Tudor sat at her desk, looking from her chronocyl to the telephone in front of her and back again. She had been doing this on and off for nearly a revolution. She put her hand on the receiver, withdrew it, then changed her mind and picked it up, dialling a number she knew by hearts. She was greeted with a brusque 'Yes?' of indistinguishable sex.

Putting on her best formal voice, she said, 'I'd like to speak to Mr O'Brien please.'

'What is it concerning?'

'That's between Mr O'Brien and myself. Please put me through.' She said this with as much authority as she could muster.

'Who is this?' came the annoyed reply.

'Evelyn Tudor,' she said, as if the man should have known.

There was a pause at the other end and a hesitant response before another phone number was given.

Without further acknowledgement she hung up and dialled the new number. A slightly shaky female voice answered.

'Vault Motioning, this is Myra Cena, can I help you?'

Confused, Evelyn cleared her throat and said, 'Yes, I'd like to speak to Vincent O'Brien if he's there?'

93

'Just a moment.' Evelyn heard the distinctive voice of O'Brien from somewhere in the background.

'Hello?' he said, the receiver not quite to his ear.

'Vincent, it's Evelyn Tudor.' There was a momentary pause at the other end before he responded.

'Miss Tudor, this is a surprise. How can I help you?'

'I'll get to the point, Vincent, I'm sure you're busy.' When he didn't respond she continued. 'I've been working with a man from Hellinar Research, a quartermaster by the name of JT Gilbert. He's had some vehicles stolen. I won't bore you with the detail.'

'That's kind of you,' said O'Brien. Evelyn wasn't sure if he was being sarcastic and decided to press on anyway.

'He's gone into the slums and hasn't returned. He's been there more than a full shift. Do we...' She stopped to correct herself. 'Do you still maintain contacts there?'

'Yes,' he said, matter-of-factly. 'More than we used to, actually. You wouldn't believe half the things that are going on.'

'I'm sure you're right.'

'Gilbert, you said, JT?' She got the impression he was cradling the handset against his shoulder and writing as he talked.

'That's right.'

'Do you have a description?' Then, having second thoughts, 'Actually, hold on.'

Evelyn could hear a conversation in the background. O'Brien was asking for access to the address books for Hellinar Research. In a moment he returned to the phone.

'Okay, I've got him. Forty-ish, short dark hair. Tidy, efficient-looking guy?'

'That sounds like him. I'm sorry, Vincent, I didn't know who else to call.'

'That's okay. You said he had some vehicles stolen?' She had forgotten O'Brien's eye for detail and smiled to herself.

'Yes that's right, a three-vehicle Unit called Hydra. The circumstances are very odd, our system's been interfered with.'

'Yours? That's interesting. I take it you're still working at the same place? Western Fringe isn't it?'

'Yes, that's right,' she said. 'And there is a clerk missing as well, not turned up to work for shifts now.'

'Really? What was the name?'

'Austen Worral. I checked with his superior a rotation ago and he's still missing. It may not be important but it could be connected.'

'Okay, I'll look into it when I get a chance. For now I'll see what I can find out about your Mr Gilbert. We're flat out here at the moment, you may have heard.'

'I've heard something,' she said.

'Look, I may not be able to chase this through much, but if he does turn up I'd be interested to speak to him.'

'Of course,' she said, a little surprised. They exchanged brief pleasantries, then hung up. Agitated, she drummed her fingers lightly on the desk, then rose and addressed her secretary, who looked up gloomily.

'I'm going home, then I'm going out. I may not see you for a couple of shifts. I trust that's not a problem.'

'Not at all,' said the man, nonplussed, before turning his attention back to his paperwork.

In the Vault, O'Brien leaned back in his chair. Something was nagging at him, worrying him. He called over to his deputy, Jennifer Narin. She was a fastidious lady of around his own age, always immaculately presented and totally ruthless when it came to pursuing her quarry. Contrary to the rumours that occasionally circulated at CID, their relationship was platonic.

'Jen, can you get a message to our friend in Gygath slum? Tell him there is a Mr Gilbert missing somewhere over in that area.'

'Sure,' said Narin with a small nod.

O'Brien thought a moment, then made a decision. 'Can you also run a check for an Austen Worral under missing persons for me?'

'No need,' said the deputy. 'Austen Worral turned up this morning.' He could see she had something to add and narrowed his eyes. 'Austen Worral's dead,' she said simply.

'Dead?' asked O'Brien.

'Yeah, it's right here in this morning's briefing notes.' She picked up a single sheet of paper. 'You didn't read them?'

'I haven't had time,' said O'Brien, snatching the paper and reading as Narin looked on.

'Found in a refuse collector,' he said, scanning through the two paragraphs of description. 'Looks like he was strangled. No blood.'

'That's what it says, sir. It's not public yet. The coroner will have to look at him first.'

From the corner of his eye, O'Brien caught sight of Myra Cena sitting across from him. She looked alarmed.

'What is it Myra?'

'A man's missing and another has turned up dead?'

'That's right.'

Myra stumbled over her words a little. 'Well, we have a missing person too, don't we?'

It took O'Brien a moment to get her meaning. 'Kyra Devin?'

'We haven't seen her for three full shifts now.' Myra showed open concern. She was clearly fond of Devin; O'Brien had picked up on that during her first interview.

'Jen, could you reassign two agents to track down Devin please? Olson should be looking into it, but given Gilbert and Worral, I'd rather not have him tied down. He's more useful freelancing, much as I hate to admit it. This may all be unconnected but it doesn't feel that way to me.'

'Or me,' agreed the deputy. 'I spoke to Tyler earlier as it happens. He said he had talked to Councillor Kane about Devin. Apparently she's known to frequent seedy establishments in the Western District.'

'Opium dens?' asked O'Brien, with a raised eyebrow.

'The Councillor didn't say that explicitly, but that was the inference, yes. He also said she had a soft spot for the bards or whatever they're called.'

Seeing Myra gawping at this exchange, O'Brien frowned. 'What is it?'

She closed her mouth and blinked a couple of times before answering. 'It just seems... well, I don't know Kyra well, but opium seems a bit extreme.'

'You'd be surprised how common it is,' said O'Brien knowingly. 'It's only illegal because Oliver Burrell couldn't push through the tax reforms on it. I'm not saying it's harmless, far from it, but in my experience we have a lot less trouble with it than we do with alcohol.'

Myra was lost for words. Opium, she had been taught, was a one-way trip to the devil. To think that Kyra Devin, one of her role models, would smoke it was unthinkable. O'Brien saw Myra's expression and read it correctly.

'Myra, you're going to learn as you get older that the absolutes you trusted growing up are really not as rock-solid as you might like. The trick is to decide where your perceptions of right and wrong lie, and not to be too judgemental of others if they stray from the path a little.'

'I suppose,' agreed Myra, a little crestfallen.

'Okay then,' said O'Brien, all business again. 'Jen, if you could get word to the slums. Gygath is the closest so start with that. Then get after Devin. Start with her apartment, her family, and go from there. Take Joseph and Brigs and see what you can find out. From here, Devin's considered a priority. Is there anyone else we've not located?'

Narin flicked through a notebook. 'Not according to my list.'

'Then we work on the assumption she's in trouble.'

'Will do, sir,' said Narin. She tucked her notebook into a bag and, with minimal fuss, left the room.

012: Quorum

Council Chambers, Central District, Skala City

A full shift after her meeting with Katherine, Nara Falla managed to assemble enough of the Privy Council to attain a quorum. Any decision reached would be valid and would stand uncontested in any subsequent meeting. Sitting around the table in an alcove of the Council Chambers were Urasa, Ratha, Devin and Erin James, in addition to the Matriarch and Falla herself. Encircling the table were a group of invited, mutually agreed upon, interested parties. John Orchard was one of these, the rest were made up of various representatives of bodies such as the Aya Construction Committee, the Resources Committee and minor delegates of both Ayon and Hellinar Research Facilities.

Chairing the meeting was Selwyn Abbot, who, true to form, dropped a scruffy pad in front of him, located a pen and threw on his glasses in a single swift motion.

'Welcome, everyone, to this extraordinary meeting of the Privy Council. Are there any matters arising?'

Victor Urasa immediately leaned forward and, as if he couldn't get his breathless words out fast enough, declared that there was. Raising a bushy eyebrow, Abbot enquired what he might like to raise.

'The matter of your chairmanship, actually,' he said, to everyone's shock.

'I'm sorry? I'm not sure I follow you?' asked Abbot, regarding him with a calm suspicion.

'We haven't voted for you to chair this meeting, Chamberlain. We normally vote.'

Taken aback, an exasperated Abbot conceded. 'Yes, that is normally the case but as this meeting was called by Councillor Falla at short notice, I was, I believe, the only available chamberlain.'

'Well, that's exactly my point,' continued Urasa. 'It all seems very convenient. One might almost say it's a setup.'

Abbot stared directly at Urasa, who refused to meet his gaze. 'I'm not at all sure what you might be implying?'

'I think you know exactly what I'm implying,' he replied, drew an exasperated breath and continued. 'Bearing in mind the likely subject matter of this meeting, called at extremely short notice as you said yourself, it seems to me that there is a bias towards a particular outcome and I'm questioning whether we should have a neutral...' he paused and chose his words carefully, 'chairperson.'

Abbot, trying not to sound as furious as he felt, invited Urasa to explain why he might not be neutral, given this had never been questioned during his decades of service.

'I'm just asking the question, Chamberlain,' replied Urasa.

'Very well. Does anyone else around the table take exception to my chairing this meeting?' It seemed no one did, which made it the more surprising when Urasa pushed further.

'With respect,' he said, 'to settle the matter we should have a vote of confidence.'

'For goodness' sake, Victor. If you insist.' Abbot stabbed the tip of his pen onto his pad in annoyance. 'If anyone feels strongly about Victor's motion, please raise your hand.' No one did.

'Then we can proceed with the meeting, unless there are other matters arising?' None were raised and, as the other councillors looked at their hands in faint embarrassment, Victor Urasa reclined in his chair with the barest hint of triumph on his face.

'Nara, you have a motion to put to the Council,' he continued, clearly glad to be moving on.

'Thank you, Selwyn,' said Nara, in gratified acknowledgement. Her face then fell into a more serious expression. 'You are all aware of the address made by Councillor Kane in the Council Chamber a few shifts ago. It seems to me, and I am not alone in this view, that not pursuing HEX would be too big a risk to take. If we don't intercept her, the impact on the build programme of Aya may be catastrophic and leave some of the infrastructure unusable, at least until we invest the resources to understand it ourselves.'

'How much?' interjected Ratha sharply.

'How much what?' asked Nara.

'Delay, Nara. How long will it take?'

'Assuming what ROOT says is true,' continued Nara patiently, 'possibly a couple of cycles. I'll come back to that if I may?' She looked up at Abbot, seeking his approval to continue, which he granted with a wave of his pen.

'What are you proposing?' asked Ratha, in a firm but not wholly unreasonable tone.

'That we complete the GVX Ayon Research vehicle with a view to sending it to intercept HEX. At the very least, we can use the initial field expedition to get GVX positioned, pending further information from CID.'

Although all the Council members could have predicted Nara's proposal, they all sat in silence while the observers behind them shuffled uncomfortably. Unusually, given her limited symbolic role, it was the Matriarch who eventually spoke.

'How far off is the completion of the vehicle, Councillor?' she asked.

'John Orchard, GVX's designer, is with us here. I would invite him to answer that question,' said Nara.

'Objection,' interrupted Urasa.

Selwyn Abbot, who was only just able to restrain himself from rolling his eyes, asked Urasa tersely on what basis he objected.

'It is not normal practice for non-co-opted members of this committee to speak in meetings. We would be setting a precedent, the implications of which should be considered first, preferably separately.'

'Victor,' began Ratha in a considered matter-of-fact tone. 'We have the man who can answer the Matriarch's question, which is relevant, sitting here. Would it not be in the Council's best interest to hear his view?'

'I maintain my objection,' Urasa asserted, and sat back, signalling this was his final word on the matter.

'Very well,' said Abbot reluctantly. 'I suppose I must uphold your objection.'

Nara Falla, who eyed Urasa closely, was surprised not to see any hint of satisfaction in him. Looking blankly at the agenda in front of him, he merely sniffed. Looking at the faces around the table, she got the faintest impression that it was Ratha who felt she had won the point. Did she detect the faintest spark of complicity between Urasa and Ratha? She couldn't be sure but filed away a mental note.

Looking back to Abbot, she found him looking at her expectantly and cleared her throat to continue.

'Given the urgency, we feel we can have the GVX project

up and running within ten full shifts, half a cycle at the outside. It won't be fully fitted out, but all the major components and systems have been rigorously tested in isolation so there is no reason to expect problems.'

'Nara, do you seriously believe that?' said an incredulous Ratha. 'When has that ever, ever been the case? In the whole history of Hellinar and Ayon Research no vehicle, however well tested, has ever completed its shakedown problem-free.'

Nara, knowing this was true, could only stare at Ratha, waiting for her to continue.

Ratha bristled, then seemed to relent. 'Look, I understand your concern. I think ROOT's conviction that HEX has been taken into Ayon is utter nonsense, but I accept the risk factor you allude to. We are at a point where we are trying to get Aya built, we need resources there and we are down one IDC. Now is hardly the time to throw an untested vehicle out into the wilderness, risking its possible loss and adding further distraction to an already complicated situation. Can this 'GVX',' she said with a hint of derision, 'actually catch HEX in any case? You said it could take more than a cycle?'

This gave Nara a way back in. 'Yes, we are sure that it can, despite the delay in sending it out.'

'How do you know?' Ratha threw back at her across the table.

'Basic calculation – a little assumption, that's true, but with some margin given.'

Ratha shook her head, indicating what a sad situation this was. 'Nara, the furthermost outpost we have in Ayon is what? Nastra?'

'That's right.'

'And we don't know much about what's beyond that.' This was put as a statement and followed up before Nara could contest it. 'Okay, you have some idea what's out there, but your knowledge is pretty limited, isn't it?'

Nara closed her mouth, and didn't dispute the point.

'Nara, look. I'll go along with this, but on the condition that it takes up as few resources as possible. That means minimal crew and minimal expenditure. Afterwards, I expect SVA to prioritise sorting out our fleet of Hellinar exploration vehicles, which are in dire need of attention. Aya might be the future, but you still need a power source and that comes from the thermal towers in the desert.'

Nara nodded her acceptance to these terms, which Ratha acknowledged with a curt reply. 'I'll send over our quartermaster then.'

Abbot cleared his throat, bringing the meeting to formal order.

'The motion I propose is this,' he pronounced. 'That the GVX Ayon exploration vehicle be completed with all haste and sent out in speculative preparation to retrieve the Intercessor HEX, should the need arise. Those in agreement, please place a palm on the table.'

All, with the notable exception of Urasa, reached forward, placing a hand palm down on the table in front of them.

'It's agreed then,' concluded Abbot. 'Any other questions before we end?'

Kyle Devin, who had sat in silence throughout the exchange, now spoke. 'Who are you proposing to lead this undertaking?'

Nara, looking faintly uncomfortable, spoke up. 'Undecided at this point. I've asked that Katherine Kane personally oversee the commissioning. As some of you know, one of the goals of the GVX project is to assess the integration of an Intercessor into a physical technology. I don't need to tell you that there are far-reaching implications depending on the outcome. I have asked Katherine to ensure the integration is a part of the commissioning as intended. Once the commissioning is complete, ROOT will be returned to the Vault.'

An uncomfortable silence fell across the room. When it was broken, the protest came from a wholly unexpected corner: Erin James.

'You're joking? You're going to install ROOT? He's vital to the construction of Aya. What happens if he's damaged? This is madness,' she said.

Momentarily thrown off guard, Nara nonetheless recovered. 'He's insisted it's safe. He defined the interface himself. As I said, once the commissioning is complete, we will remove him. It should be straightforward and will provide us with vital information that could determine the direction we take with Aya. With the architect of the city's infrastructure stolen, that is surely now more important than ever.'

James, who was normally the epitome of reserve, looked openly astonished. 'This wasn't stated before we voted. We need a revote.'

Selwyn Abbot shuffled himself forward uncomfortably. 'We voted on the motion as put forward. There will be no revote.'

'Fine,' said James, with uncharacteristic petulance. 'But for the record, I'd like to make it clear that I disagree with risking our sole remaining Intercessor at the cost of the future of our people.'

'Duly noted,' agreed Abbot, in a tone that implied even he thought this was an overstatement. After a pause, he went consecutively around the table. No further points were forthcoming and an air of sullen acceptance descended over the gathering.

'Then the meeting is adjourned,' he declared, rising and propping his pen behind his right ear as he did so.

The gathering broke up, the alcove emptied and voices that

had been loud and clear faded into the expanse of the larger chamber. Nara, absently gathering her things, was the last of the councillors to leave the table. As she turned, she found the lanky form of John Orchard waiting for her.

'Nara,' he said, with evident concern in his voice. 'What was all that with Urasa? Why couldn't I speak?'

Nara shook her head in resignation. 'Politics, John, politics.' She looked into his questioning gaze. 'I have a feeling it's going to get a lot worse.' The two of them turned and made their way out into the sun-streaked air of the main chamber.

013: Interrogation

Gygath Slum, West of Skala City

When he finally woke, JT felt significantly more comfortable. The man who had revived him, a man he now knew as Ira, had returned to pick him off the dirt and prop him in a sitting position against a timber support. After a brief introduction, Ira left and returned with a bowl of surprisingly clean water. Carefully, he stripped JT to the waist and washed him down. The quartermaster had no energy to protest or feel uncomfortable. In fact, he was grateful for the aid. A bed made up from two flat-pack crates and a dirty mattress had been brought and he pulled himself on to it, lying sleepless for a time unmeasured.

Intermittently, herb flatbread and water were brought to him by a guard. After four meals, always the same, JT sat up to look at Ira, who after a shift or more of absence had returned to watch him intently from the shadows. Although a thousand questions ran through his mind he first asked the one that perplexed him the most.

'You said you know who I am?'

'That's right,' replied Ira in his soft, gruff voice.

'How?'

'How do you think?'

'I have no idea,' said JT wearily.

'No one is born in the slums, Mr Gilbert,' said Ira, as if this were obvious. 'Your name is Jonathan Timothy Gilbert, you're a quartermaster working in the Hellinar Research Facility. You're known to be clear-headed, reliable and diligent, if a little over-obsessive when it comes to detail. You're unmarried and your sexuality has been the subject of on-and-off speculation in your office for as long as you've worked there. General consensus is you just never met the right girl.'

JT glared at Ira but the man merely shrugged and continued. 'You have a talent for origami and hot-plate cooking. On occasion, but only under peer pressure, you step in to take the place of the chef in your preferred eatery to select and cook meals for your companions, much to their pleasure. How am I doing so far?'

JT nodded, feeling shaken by the detail.

'Good. Beyond that, you walk a lot.' Ira scratched thoughtfully at his stubble. 'Well, most people do I suppose. You're trusted, have good security access and you maintain a distant but officially condoned relationship with the Rika. Oh, your apartment is decorated in a minimalist style which would work better if you tidied it occasionally. Just my opinion.' He shrugged.

JT sat back in astonishment at this last statement, which Ira had delivered as just another titbit. 'How do you know all this?' he asked, horrified.

'Like I said, no one is born in the slums.'

'What does that mean?'

'It means exactly what it says. Did you see any children here when you ambled in?'

'No, but I didn't see much of anyone.'

'There is a lot of general misconception about the slums, even for people like you who have actually been here before.'

Ira eyed JT, assessing his reaction. Detecting a pang of shame, he continued more cautiously. 'No one is born here. Everyone comes in from outside. The men, normally at the lower end of the social scale, come early, once it's established they, or should I say we, can't produce children. As the women get longer to prove their fertility, they come older and there are far fewer of them. Obviously.'

Reluctantly, JT took his point.

'So the people here are from all walks of life,' Ira continued. 'Yes we've got criminals, prostitutes and opium dealers, which is what everyone on the outside expects. But there are plenty of us with backgrounds like yours. Factory or office workers moved aside in deference to cheaper, younger models. They find it hard to get another job and, without kids, there are no Council subsidies and not much of a future. We even have one or two ex-business moguls who've gone bust and have nowhere else to go. They fall the hardest.'

Ira took a deep breath and decided he owed JT a more direct answer to his question. 'There are plenty of people here with families or friends out in the city. They don't come here so much, but family is family and some people keep close ties to the city. We get to know things, sometimes we ask some questions.'

JT thought for a moment then asked, 'So, what's your background?'

'Me?' Ira responded with a short, rough laugh. 'Let's just say I'm a failed poet and leave it at that.'

Unsure whether to take this literally, JT decided not to pursue it. 'So, what are you going to do with me?'

'You'll be on your way soon. There are some folks who would like to talk to you first though. We're to wait until called, then you get an audience.'

'An audience with who?'

Ira considered how to answer this but, shrugging, only said, 'Interested parties, just some interested parties is all.' The finality with which this was said told JT he was not going to learn more for now. Stretching back, he reclined onto the bed, placing his hands behind his head. He folded one leg cautiously over the other, closed his eyes and waited.

It was about a rotation later that the call came. A hollow rap on the tin door prompted Ira to move languidly from his observations and wait for a bolt to be drawn noisily back. JT stood, something he had done little in nearly two full shifts. Finding his balance, he followed Ira through the doorway and out into a darker, narrow corridor.

The close proximity of the shacks that lined each makeshift street of the slums meant that many were interlinked. There were no tall buildings to provide shadows in which to hide from the cancer-inducing sunlight, so moving directly from hut to hut was practically a necessity.

Led through a rabbit warren of homes, makeshift shops and what, to JT's horror, could only be a very active brothel, they arrived at their destination. Entering through a door on which 'Landlord's Arms' had been sign-written with astonishing skill, they found themselves in a large, heavily populated communal room. Long benches were arranged in semicircular fashion around an exquisitely carved dark wood bar. Glasses, tankards and pipes were hung from above with bottles of spirits, mostly gin, nestled among a multitude of beer pumps mounted on the surface.

Two things about this place instantly struck JT. The first, obvious at the moment of entry, was the temperature. It was cooler in here, not at all like the hot, sticky climate of the shacks he had been led through. But it was the scene that hit him hardest, an overwhelming feeling of community and goodwill permeating the air. Laughter was rife as glasses clinked and the sweet, floral smell of opium smoke billowed up into the conical roof space. Somehow it felt much more intense, much more genuine than the soulless wine bars of Central Skala.

The guide left them at the door and JT looked around in wonderment as Ira led him to the centre of the room. Despite his condition, no one paid him any heed, for which he was grateful. Behind the bar stood a hulking, swarthy fellow resplendent in a simple, dirty V-necked shirt that might have once been white. Around his neck hung swaths of long necklaces in a flamboyant show of platinum links. He scowled, a furrowed brow of sun-bleached skin rippling his shaved head. His forearms tensed as he lifted clenched fists, revealing yet more links arranged in tight-fitting bracelets around his wrists. He brought them down with a firm thud on the wooden surface, making nearby bottles jump in alarm.

'What will it be, bitches?' he growled with ill-concealed hostility.

'The usual, thanks, Landlord, two of,' said Ira, totally unconcerned.

The big man turned and emptied half a bottle of clear liquid into two tall, chipped glasses. He slammed them on the bar, with enough firmness to make a point. Turning to JT he sniffed, as if measuring him by smell alone.

'You must be Gilbert,' he said, eyes narrowed.

Before JT could answer, Ira replied in a distinctly suspicious tone, 'How did you know? Seen him before, have you?'

'The blood, Ira, it's all over 'is clothes.' As the big man leaned in, Ira neither flinched nor made eye contact. 'I 'eard you lot did him over. Shouldn't have done that. Find out who the bastard is before you deck 'im. I've bloody told you before, but will you listen?'

Pulling back, the big man picked up the glass nearest JT and handed it to him. "Ere, drink this. You call me Landlord, okay?

Anything else you need – pipes, women, whatever – you just ask. I'll add it to this bastard's tab.'

JT raised the glass to his lips and nearly choked as the fiery liquid touched his throat. A huge hand slapped appreciatively down on his left shoulder. Coughing, he managed a weak-sounding, 'Thank you, Landlord. I'll bear that in mind.'

'Make sure you do,' barked the Landlord with humour. 'Now, there are some people you need to see, just behind us. Ira, can you manage that without hurting anyone else?'

'I'm sure I'll cope,' intoned Ira sarcastically.

The Landlord stood back and folded his arms, his huge chest puffed out as he watched the two men move around the bar to a corrugated door in the rear wall.

'Best not drink too much of that stuff,' said Ira under his breath. 'It's good, don't get me wrong, but you'll want a clear head for the next rotation.'

JT, who was not much of a drinker, was relieved to hand his glass over. Ira cocked it in appreciation before downing its contents in a single swig.

Behind the door lay a small, dark room of the same round profile, a low, rectangular table at its centre. The air was cool and carried an aroma of incense, replacing that of the opium. Instead of earthy dust, the floor was covered in rugs woven in dark reds, yellows and blacks. Behind the table sat a group of three: one male, two female, all evenly spaced. Like Ira, their clothes were well worn but differed little from what a normal resident of Skala might wear.

Ira gestured for JT to be seated on the floor in front of the group. Sensing his discomfort, one of the women, white haired and apparently the elder of the group, moved to kneel. The other, younger woman, stood up and with a sweep of her hand indicated JT could sit as he felt comfortable. All regarded him closely but with no hint of malice or aggression.

Not knowing what to expect, he waited to be addressed. It was the man who spoke first; middle aged with a trim, grey beard, he began with an apology.

'We regret the way you were brought in, Mr Gilbert. We were expecting somebody else.'

'Who were you expecting?' asked JT, with more scepticism in his tone than he'd intended.

'A mercenary. A man called Bill Connor. I don't mean to excuse the treatment you were subjected to but, in fairness to Ira, the two of you look very alike.'

'Do we?' said JT in astonishment. 'So you're going to let me go? If I'm not who you thought I was?'

'That's right,' said the older woman, with a swift assurance JT didn't quite trust.

'But first,' continued the bearded gentleman, 'we were rather hoping you might agree to help us. We believe you came here looking for three vehicles, 'Unit Hydra'. Is that correct?'

'How did you know that?' asked JT, looking instinctively back to Ira, who simply shrugged.

'We can offer some limited help on Hydra, some information. But first,' he said, with slight hesitation. 'Well, maybe we can help each other. Do you know anything about Bill Connor?'

'Not much, I came across his name recently. He illicitly gained access to a storage facility in the Western District.' He moved to qualify this statement. 'Well, we don't think he should have had access. We don't really know.'

'Undoubtedly he should not have had access,' said the elder woman. 'Let me tell you a little about Bill Connor. He is a mercenary, he works for anyone who will pay him, corporate, Rika, whoever.'

'We thought he could be Rika,' JT interjected.

'Not Rika,' said the woman firmly. 'He does the jobs even the Rika don't want to take responsibility for.' She let this sink in.

There was a brief silence, eventually broken by the man. 'Connor was the cut-out between whoever wanted your 'Unit Hydra' and a part of the crew who have it now. Two of the crew are our people you see, picked up as the Unit passed through. These are people we want to protect.'

'From what? Prosecution?'

The younger woman gave a snort. 'Prosecution for stealing a clapped-out set of desert rats is the least of their problems.'

The man shot her a warning glare. 'They are young, and seek to prove that they are worth more than the sentence society has imposed upon them,' was all he offered in explanation.

JT took a moment to process this somewhat impenetrable statement but could make little sense of it. 'So this William, Bill Connor, he recruited your people to steal Hydra? Who was he working for?'

'We don't know,' said the man. 'But we would like to find out. We believe he's gone to ground in one of the mines up to the north, a place called Mal-Kas. He does occasional work there when he's, let's say, short of a throat to squeeze. He acts as a sort of corporate security army of one, which basically means suppression of the workers.' He looked disgusted, then added, 'Most of them come from here.'

'I'm not sure I understand,' said JT.

The man's beard twitched in a thin, deprecating smile. 'You may have noticed that Gygath slum is not over-populated as you walked through it. A large number of our people have been contracted to work out in the mines and refineries, producing the resources to build Aya. On the face of it, that's good work for those of us down on our luck. Unfortunately, in reality, it's closer to a death sentence than a contribution to humanity.'

'Why?'

'The contracts are complicated,' he explained. 'First, anyone wanting to work for the companies employed by the Council has to have a sponsor. Naturally many of us have family or friends in Skala who are happy to help drag us out of the gutter. The sponsorship fee is supposed to cover training, housing, other overheads. But there is no training and there is no housing. Once you leave for the mines or the processing stations, it's long shifts, two rotations' sleep and the conditions are... well, you would be appalled.'

JT was sceptical; this didn't sound likely. The Council was notoriously careful about perceived exploitation. But a note of caution rang in his mind and he asked, 'If it's bad, why don't your people leave?'

'A good question and the answer is simple. Geography.'

JT frowned.

'Geography,' said the younger woman harshly as she turned to look at him. 'The mines are at least a hundred kilometres north – you may have noticed there is a mountain range between here and there. To the southeast are the fulgurite fields, do you know what they are?'

'Vaguely,' said JT, thinking hard. 'They're large areas of desert covered in conductive rods to attract lightning? The fulgurite is used to make glass.'

'That's right,' she said, with a thin smile of appreciation. 'I was out there myself for a time. It's dangerous work collecting fulgurite – the lightning is almost constant but it's never predictable. But if you want to leave you have to cross two, three hundred kilometres of desert. In this heat, with a body already broken by labour and with no water, you wouldn't last twenty kilometres on foot. If the company that employs you doesn't want you to leave, you don't leave.'

She looked off to her left again and as she did so JT studied her a moment. Her physique and the way she moved exuded a toughness he had mistaken for arrogance.

'So how did you get back?' he asked.

'Under a transport,' she replied, matter of factly, not looking at him. 'I tied myself to the underside before it left.'

JT gawped at her. That she could have possibly survived three hundred kilometres underneath a transport, jumping dunes and rocks, seemed hard to believe. His mind drifted and he pictured this woman suspended between flailing suspension parts, drowning in gouts of sand and debris. He looked back at her stony expression and saw a truth in it. It was easy to see that face gritted, determined and fighting moment to moment to survive.

'We think the Council's plans for Aya are optimistic. They've been promised a level of resource by the mining companies that can't be delivered by humane means, so they are turning a blind eye to what's really going on.'

Now she turned to look straight at JT, her green eyes blazing out from behind stray wisps of black hair. 'We don't think our people are going to come back, and we think that's intentional.'

'Intentional? That seems very unlikely…'

'As you say,' said the man, raising a hand to halt him.

'And Connor helps enforce the work regime?' asked JT, trying to steer the conversation back to Hydra. 'If he's the link between Hydra and whoever stole it then I need to speak to him.'

'It seems our interests coincide,' said the man. 'Hydra's gone, we don't know where, and we're worried about our people. Anything you can learn from Connor could help if you can get close to him. We're also very worried about conditions in the mines for humanitarian reasons. If someone can give us a picture of how bad things are, we might be able to force the Council to open its eyes.'

JT weighed the price of freedom before speaking again. 'Okay, I think I can probably do that. We have equipment that's been on loan to various mining companies for a long time, more than a decade in some cases. I'm sure I can organise an inspection without arousing undue attention.'

'You'll need to get Connor to talk. Officialdom won't be any sort of incentive for him,' said the first woman, looking down at JT.

'Take Ira with you,' suggested the man. From his corner, Ira growled an unmistakable sound of displeasure.

'Would Connor recognise Ira?'

'Not a chance,' said Ira from behind him. 'Still, I'd rather not go. A trek into the mountains isn't exactly what I had in mind for a vacation.'

'You'll go,' said the elder woman firmly.

'Okay then,' said Ira with finality. 'Audience over. Time to get you back to civilisation. It's a long walk and besides, your girlfriend's waiting at the other end.'

With that, Ira pushed himself off the wall he'd been leaning on and moved to help JT to his feet.

014: SVA

Research and Development Facility,
Eastern District, Skala City

Katherine Kane walked into Hangar 56 of SVA, immediately perceiving the sense of urgency that had overtaken the place since her meeting with Nara Falla. The short, wide corridor that served as an entrance was situated directly under the design and production offices and was unlit, giving the enormous space beyond the air of a radiant, perfectly geometric cavern. Closeted in the shadows to either side of her were numerous runs of pipe and conduit. Electrical cables spilled from hatches in the floor, like tendrils searching for a mechanical host to feed upon.

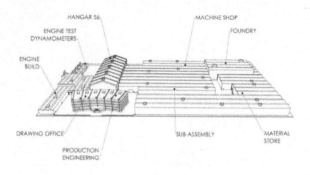

In the centre of the hangar, illuminated from far above, stood the looming hulk of GVX-H. The last time she had seen the vehicle it had been a sparse-looking composite skeleton, suspended just off the ground on huge trestles. It had been impressive, but now, with its external carapace and all eight wheels fitted, the true scale of it hit her for the first time. Even from this distance, she estimated each wheel must be twice her height at least. The welding teams, working to stitch the acid-etched panels forming the outer skin, looked like ants, the fountains of white sparks more readily visible than the technicians themselves.

Despite the hubbub, she was gratified to see that the discipline she tried to instil in her teams had not been abandoned. The surface of the floor, although off-colour and in need of a fresh coat of paint, was clean. The tiled walls that extended out into the enormous space had recently been washed down and a general sense of professionalism permeated the atmosphere.

She strode out to greet John Orchard, the man who had designed a number of the vehicles in the Ground Vehicle fleet. Katherine had always been impressed by the designer's ability to meld the data obtained from ROOT with established technology while maintaining an elegance of form.

With Orchard stood two other members of the senior team on the project; Roy Jacobs, SVA's rock-solid head of engineering, with whom Katherine was well acquainted, and a second man she didn't recognise. Orchard made the introduction.

'Katherine, this is Don Hoffer. I'm not sure you've met?'

Katherine took Hoffer's hand and found his shake reassuringly firm.

'It's a pleasure to meet you, ma'am,' said Hoffer, all business.

'Don has replaced Jim Davenport as Workshop Manager.'

'Dav finally retired? I didn't know,' said Katherine, with a hint of regret.

'He did, although we haven't quite got rid of him yet. He still comes in every so often to check up on us.'

Katherine smiled. 'You mean he turns up, meddles, then leaves?'

'Yes, that's about the way of it,' agreed Orchard, with good humour before continuing more seriously. 'I'm sorry, Katherine, I should have told you, but Jim wanted things low-key. You know how he is. No fuss, no party. But we took him out anyway, just a few of us from the office.'

Katherine nodded in understanding, then turned to the hulking behemoth before them. Nearing completion, it was swathed in external umbilical lines that ran across the floor and hung from the ceiling above. At this stage, GVX was still dependent on external electrical and fluid systems.

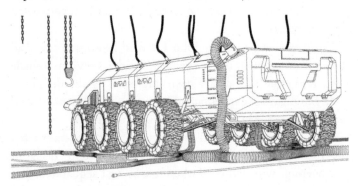

'It looks different to the last time I visited,' she said, raising her eyebrows in appreciation.

'Yes,' agreed Orchard. 'Visually it has changed a great deal. In truth the bulk of the hard work, the detail as it were, was completed a few shifts ago. The assembly –' he cleared his throat, 'the final assembly – happens very fast.'

'I'm sorry we've had to put you under pressure,' replied Katherine sincerely. Then with some discomfort, 'I hope you don't feel I've usurped control of your project?'

'Not at all. We understand from Nara there is a need to move quickly, and I'm sure you will be the ideal test driver,' he said, with only the faintest hint of false conviction. 'Perhaps you could expand upon the situation a little?'

'I'm afraid I can't, sorry. In truth, I don't know much more about HEX's disappearance than you do.' Katherine, knowing this was not entirely true and feeling uncomfortable discussing it, declined to elaborate. She left a pause that Orchard felt obliged to fill.

'We understand that GVX will be travelling further into Ayon than anyone has gone before?' Jacobs probed with concern writ across his face. He was a well-built man with short, tidy hair, intense dark eyes and stubble that, despite shaving every morning, he never quite seemed to be able to get rid of.

'Yes, quite possibly a lot further,' Katherine said in weary agreement.

'The most pressing decision has been the power unit,' Orchard explained. 'The schematics ROOT provided us with allowed for several possible options.'

Katherine nodded. She had taken a cursory look at ROOT's output before passing it on, but had left the in-depth analysis and interpretation to Orchard and his team.

'The ideal solution for your needs would be a gas turbine, but in the timescale we have to work with, there are several problems that we are not able to overcome.'

'Okay,' she said, 'what options do we have?'

'We have started,' continued Orchard, who was also relieved to be moving on without protest, 'converting two of our existing V10 generator engines to run on biofuel and adapting the installation bay appropriately. Fortunately it's been fairly straightforward.'

'And you're confident V10s will be reliable?' asked Katherine.

'And fuel efficient,' Orchard added. 'Electrical support is powered by a proven battery system to store energy harvested from the solar panel array on top of the chassis. It's surprisingly effective, even in the light levels of Ayon. We've installed two standard mulching tanks so you can harvest fuel from any available organic material.'

'Then we'll go with that,' said Katherine confidently and saw visible relief sweep the group.

They turned and moved further out into the intense light of the hangar.

'I'll give you the whirlwind tour for now, but there will be a lot to cover in the next few shifts if GVX is going to be driven halfway across the world,' said Jacobs, raising his gruff voice above the clatter of arc welders and pneumatic hand tools.

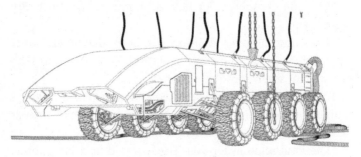

Stopping near the rear of the construction area, he began what Katherine guessed was a hastily prepared presentation.

'As you know, GVX has eight-wheel drive using the new 'Spring Tread' traction wheels in place of air-filled tyres.'

Looking up, Katherine nodded. 'I can't imagine changing a wheel out in the field.'

'It's possible, but not ideal, so we've a different solution,' said Jacobs. 'The tread is split into sections. If a section is damaged you can unclip and replace it. The sections are small enough that they can be stored in the hold, which is over there.' He pointed to an open compartment in the vehicle's underbelly.

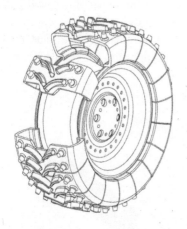 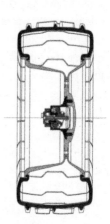

'The drive to the wheels is hydraulic,' he continued. 'The power pack, or just 'the Pack' as we refer to it, houses the hydraulic torque converters.' Gesturing to each of the huge wheels he continued. 'And hydraulic drive via pipes instead of drive shafts means wheel travel can be increased as there is no drive shaft angularity to consider. There's far less to go wrong,' he concluded.

Katherine could see the sense in this and eyed the suspension intently.

'That's clever,' Katherine acknowledged. 'What do those vertical slits near the front do? They look like doors.'

'That's exactly right,' said Orchard. 'They are movable doors that regulate incoming air to manage cooling and air conditioning. ROOT refers to them as 'gill flaps', although I'm unclear what the word 'gill' means exactly.'

She took a few steps back, taking in the chassis. 'So I suppose the question you are all dreading me asking is, when is it going to be ready?' All three men smiled in amusement. She was quite right of course, they had all known this was coming and had calculated as accurate an answer as possible.

It was Jacobs who stepped in to answer. 'We expect to receive the power pack in the next full shift, the rest part of the shift probably.'

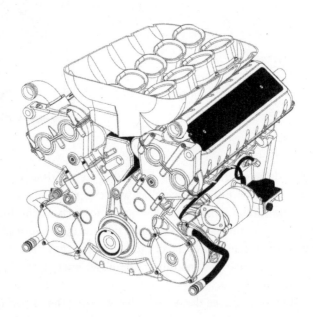

Katherine looked back down the hangar past the rear wheels. Jacobs caught her look and understood her frown.

'You are wondering how it's installed into an enclosed

chassis in such a short period of time?' he asked, with an air of enjoyment. 'It would be well worth you being here to see it fitted.'

'I'll make sure I'm here,' she assured him, reciprocating his no-nonsense tone.

'Very good, ma'am. By that time we'll have most of the internals fitted out. I'm afraid it's not going to be very plush, but in the time frame you have us working to it's all we can do – unless you want to delay a few shifts.'

'No time,' said Katherine with regret. She turned to address Orchard. 'What about systems checks and whatever training you can give us?'

Orchard looked over to Jacobs in deference, allowing him to answer since it was his work crews that would determine the timings. 'We could use the next shift to get as much fitted out as we can. If you can allow us that time it will speed things up in explanation.'

It took Katherine a moment to understand what Jacobs was saying. 'No point briefing us on functions not actually fitted yet?'

'Exactly,' said Jacobs. 'I've sent as much literature on the systems as we have put together so far to your office. It's incomplete but it will give you a general overview of what a driver needs to know.'

'In that case, I'll be back the shift after next.'

'That would be ideal,' said Jacobs. 'We'll be ready for you then.'

'Thank you, gentlemen, I'll look forward to it.' Katherine gave a nod of appreciation and turned to leave.

Watching her go, Hoffer commented as if to himself. 'Well that could have been worse.'

Jacobs looked over at him and smiled. 'The girl knows her stuff.'

'It seems so. She's not what I expected, I have to be honest.'

Orchard let out a brief, good-natured laugh. 'You wait until you're in a meeting room with her and twenty other engineers. She's doesn't take prisoners.'

Hoffer raised his eyebrows as Orchard leaned over to him and continued in a confiding tone. 'Trust me, she's bright as hell and fights like the devil until she gets what she wants. Well,' he paused, reconsidering his words, 'she fights until she gets what she thinks is best, which is not always what she wants. The funny thing is, just when you're at the point you want to throttle her, she'll take you by the arm, buy you a cup of coffee and ask after your wife or family and it will be like the last two rotations never happened.'

Jacobs looked amused and gave a half-grin. 'She's got good hearts,' he agreed. 'But don't let that fool you, she's probably better at your job than you are. I've certainly watched her do mine on at least one occasion.'

Hoffer took this on-board before Orchard proffered an elegant hand to guide the way back to the engineering offices. The three of them started back in the direction in which Katherine had just departed. Privately, Jacobs wondered what the next few shifts would have in store for them. Adapting to the situation, he concluded, was going to be a necessity on this one.

015: Megan

Central Library, Central District, Skala City

Crossing the open area in front of the Central Library, Tyler Olson paused at one of two pools cut into the granite slabs lining the ground. Looking down to admire its blue, mosaic-lined bottom, he wondered how often the water had to be changed; probably daily, in deference to the dust and sand that beset Skala.

The sun at his back was momentarily obscured by an errant cloud, bringing him back to the present. At the top of a flight of grand stone steps, the library's entrance was large, airy and elegantly venerable. Inside he identified himself at an exquisitely carved front desk. As he stood he could feel a curious, faint sensation of cool air moving up from the flagstone floor. The gentle fluttering of deep red drapes hanging from the walls assured him it was not his imagination, but he saw no vents.

'Mr Olson?' prompted a bespectacled desk clerk, replete with a bushy moustache.

'Sorry,' said Olson. 'My mind's elsewhere. Just wondering how the air's so cool in here.'

'Good question,' replied the clerk with faint annoyance. 'No one really knows how it works. Some time ago we had a bunch of architectural graduates in for shift after shift trying to figure it out, but they never did. Turned the place upside down and left no wiser.'

'Funny how that happens,' said Olson with a little irony. 'It's a nice system. We'd be happy to have something similar down at CID.'

'I'm sure you would. Now, what can we do for you, sir?'

'City Planning,' said Olson warmly. 'I was hoping to get some help from one of your junior staff, a Miss Devin?'

'You mean Megan?' said the clerk, picking up a telephone receiver with an earnest look. 'She's a mighty good researcher.'

Olson smiled his acknowledgement as the clerk spoke into the mouthpiece.

'Is Megan up there? Yes, there is a Mr Olson from CID here to see her. Could you send her down please? Thank you.'

He replaced the receiver and gestured to a green leather sofa off to the right. 'You take a seat, sir, she'll be right with you.'

'Thank you,' said Olson, grateful for the respite. He felt quietly content to sit in the grand entrance for a few turns. It was a serious sort of place but not excessively pretentious. The entrance was circular, ringed by columns set into the walls that extended up to the dome above him. The dome itself was a complex structure of stained-glass panels providing natural light with a pleasantly warm, yellowish hue. Squinting up at them and picking one at random, he was sure it rose a little, opening then retracting on an ornate brass gear-and-pulley system.

The ring of distinctly female footsteps approaching him brought his attention back to ground level. Clutching a notebook firmly to her chest, a young woman strode pragmatically towards him. She was smartly dressed in a grey pencil skirt, cut just below the knee, and an expensive-looking white silk blouse. To Olson's eyes she bore a striking resemblance to Katherine, although perhaps she was slightly taller, cutting a slimmer figure.

'Mr Olson?' she asked politely.

Olson rose and offered his hand. 'That's right. You must be Miss Devin? I'm hoping you can help me.'

'Of course. What is it you need help with?'

'City Planning,' he said, not quite sure where to start. 'I'm working on a case for CID. You have probably heard about it, the missing IDC?'

'Everyone in the city knows about it. I imagine every outlying seeding from Krai to Ororpresa knows about it by now.'

'I'm sure they do,' Olson agreed, with a supplicatory smile. 'What's not public knowledge is that we really don't know how the Intercessor was stolen. There are no clues, it's like it disappeared into thin air.'

Megan frowned wordlessly, but kept her composure.

'Your sister, Katherine, suggested I commandeer you for a few shifts,' Olson continued. This wasn't strictly true but he had an intuition that Megan, young as she was, could be nothing but an asset.

'Here, I'm to give you this,' he said, and offered her the note Katherine had scribbled.

Megan read it quickly, a look of amusement writ large across her face. As was his nature, Olson had not read the note himself and scrutinised Megan for a clue as to what it might contain. The young woman frowned again but gave nothing away.

'My colleague, Vincent, has been scouring the Vault – you know, the place the Intercessors are kept?'

Megan nodded. 'Yes, I'm aware of it.'

'It's a curious place. Vincent has turned up nothing so far so I'd like to take a look at the problem from a different angle. I want to look back at how it was originally built. According to Katherine, it was a basement put in when the building was new, but over time it's been extensively modified. I'm hoping there is a record of how and when that happened. With luck we might extract a little insight.'

Megan, bewildered by this onslaught of information and the strange note from her sister, faltered, then recovered. 'Well, I'm sure I can help you find any plans that are here.'

'Only if you have the time.'

'I'm doing archive work. I love working here but…' she pursed her lips in a mischievous expression he guessed was one that he would never see on Katherine's face. 'It's actually quite boring,' she confided. 'If you need help, I'd be happy to ask for a few shifts' reassignment.'

Olson smiled broadly and stroked his grey beard. 'Well then,' he said, 'where do we start?'

Megan had a remarkable grasp of the library's antiquated referencing system. Over a period of only a few rotations she had withdrawn, cross-referenced and overlaid decades of blueprints dating back to the earliest records of Skala. The oldest bundles of plans stretched back as far as the latter decades of Kul but, despite his natural curiosity, Olson kept his mind focused on the Vault.

The records were fragmented but, as they laid them out across a sturdy oakwood desk, they could see that Katherine's memory of the pre-Vault basement was largely accurate. As she had suggested, it had been constructed prior to the rest of the Ayon Research building, which had itself developed over more than twenty decades. The layout of the basement, specifically its depth, which was considerable, suggested its original function was cold storage. Surprisingly, access had been via a vertical shaft so that heavy, geological samples could be lowered from the main building. Three decades after construction the shaft had been substantially widened, changed from square to circular section and labelled with the moniker 'Cannula'. This, it seemed, was one of several designations bestowed upon the building during its first serious expansion. On the same plan, a prominent upper-floor corridor was labelled 'Arterial', a nomenclature that had apparently not endured.

Moving through the decades, Megan noted gaps in the development, possibly due to freelance modifications by whoever made use of the basement at a given time. Its exact purpose had morphed from storage to an ad hoc testing laboratory around ten decades later. By that time, the rest of the building had expanded as far as its footprint would allow and had begun to grow vertically, incorporating electrical ring mains and lighting throughout. By the time Katherine, aged fifteen, had moved in with the inanimate ROOT, the Cannula had been outfitted with an automated lift. Olson asked for references to the high-voltage cages Katherine had mentioned and how they might have been powered. Megan spent a few turns scouring the plans for notes or references to associated documents. She found nothing beyond a single handwritten label that denoted one annexed area as 'HV', and a small arrow pointing to a far wall. Olson, following her lead, moved on but made a mental note to investigate further.

The bulk of the blueprints were more recent, detailing the conversion from basement to Vault. If there was an indicative measure of ROOT's perceived value at this time, the sheer effort and expense of the basement's conversion was it. Almost nothing was left unchanged; the area had been expanded significantly, no doubt requiring a significant removal of earth. Hoping this might provide an answer to how HEX had been removed, possibly via a second access shaft, Olson was disappointed when Megan turned up a photocopy of calculations pertaining to the upgrade of the Cannula to move bedrock up and equipment down.

Once the Vault had been completed and ROOT installed, the facility stayed much the same for the following decade. Occasional upgrades were introduced; a cooling system was installed, as well as a standalone power supply to the chamber and requisite power-spike suppressors. The monitoring station, then situated to the left of the main corridor linking the Cannula to ROOT's chamber, was expanded twice for increased server capacity, but the general layout remained intact.

They skipped forward to the next explosion of activity that accompanied HEX's arrival. The building of a second, upgraded chamber was extensively detailed, as was the significantly revised layout of the Vault itself. As Olson saw it, the whole project had the hallmarks of a battle of egos. Rather than run a second corridor off as a spur, the original corridor had been moved such that it was now positioned between the existing chamber and the later, upgraded version. He asked Megan if she had any insight as to why this extraordinary provision had been made. Her answer, given in a groan of exasperation, surprised him.

'Katherine. Katherine has to do everything properly.' She bracketed this last word with waggling index fingers. Olson raised his eyebrows, prompting a further explanation.

'She has this thing, a sort of tic, that everything has to be done a 100 per cent or not at all. Sometimes even a 100 per cent is not enough.'

'She's a perfectionist,' Olson suggested, in an understanding tone.

'That's what people say, but it's more than that. She's driven.

It's like she has this itch that she can't quite scratch. People admire her for it, but it can drive you nuts sometimes.'

'Do you admire her?'

Megan hesitated for a moment, looking out from their dimly lit alcove. 'I do. She's a good person and has everyone's best interests in mind, but I couldn't work with her.' She paused before reluctantly adding, 'Sometimes I think she drives herself nuts, you know?'

Olson smiled his understanding and gave a quick nod of agreement, then pulled the last Vault layout plan towards him and examined it intently.

'So what do you think happened to the original corridor?' he asked.

'I'm not sure,' said Megan, thumbing back through the older plans. 'It could have been filled in or cut off. This plan shows some of the original network that runs from HEX's chamber into what was then the monitoring room.'

Olson stood and peered over her shoulder. 'Can you still access that room?'

'It doesn't look like it. At least part of the corridor is still there, but it's not connected to anywhere else.'

'But it was once connected,' Olson asserted, meeting her eyes. 'That could be our access point to the chamber.'

'It could,' Megan conceded sceptically. 'But it looks like it was sealed off some time ago.'

Olson thought it through. 'At the end of that corridor there would have been a door. Would the door have been similar in design to the sealed doors that are fitted now?'

'Yes, probably,' said Megan, thinking hard. 'In fact I'm pretty sure they are the same; the lock, the air-operated bolts… I remember Kyra once telling me they were a sort of vanity project. The engineer, I can't remember her name, but Kyra said she wanted the most impressive locking system she could design. This was way back when the first chamber was built. Have you seen it? It's very elaborate, but quite neat.'

Olson gave her a hard stare. 'You've seen them?'

Megan coloured instantly, a look of panic across her face. 'Well, yes, I saw it once.'

'Katherine took you down there?'

'Kyra,' she said sheepishly. 'Katherine would go mad if she knew. It was only once, just after HEX's chamber was built. I know she wasn't supposed to take me, but she was so proud to have HEX installed and working. She really grew up in Katherine's shadow and for that short time she seemed to feel she'd stepped out of it.'

'It didn't last?'

'For a while, but then the politics started.' Olson could see that Megan was extremely uncomfortable with what she had already divulged, and decided not to press her further.

'You know one of your people came here earlier asking about Kyra?'

'Sergeant Narin, yes,' said Olson. 'We're trying to find your sister.'

'She has a habit of disappearing for a few shifts at a time, but you probably know that,' said Megan with pregnant resignation.

'I'd heard something of the sort,' said Olson. 'I'm sure Narin will find her, wherever she's gone, and she won't be in any trouble. Not with us anyway.'

Megan stared blankly into space, obviously concerned.

'So that far wall,' said Olson, drawing her attention back to the plans. 'What's there now? Can we take a look back at where that corridor is in relation to the rooms in the pre-Vault basement?'

'Certainly,' said Megan, pulling several sheets of plans across to overlay them. Finding one she thought was appropriate, she turned it, taking the Cannula as her reference point and overlaying its position on both drawings. Satisfied she had it as close as she could, she held the upper sheet with one hand and flapped it back and forth with the other for Olson to compare.

'Hmm, well I never,' he said in wonder. He stabbed a finger at the older map to indicate where the corridor would have been. At its central point was the annex that had been marked 'HV'. 'I had a feeling that little note would mean something. I'm right in thinking there is no high-voltage trunking running down to the Vault from above?'

'Not that I can see,' Megan said, studying the plans again.

'So thinking around the problem, so to speak, where would you find a high-voltage supply if you were looking for one?'

'I've no idea, Mr Olson,' she said truthfully. 'Electrical systems are not my forte.'

'Still, you're a hell of a good researcher. I'll bet you can find out inside of a rotation.'

Megan, happy to be back in favour, took this as a challenge. Not knowing exactly what she was looking for, she began to skim through various plans of Skala's electrical distribution network. There was an alarming amount of them but she knew enough about electricity to assume that it likely arrived in Skala at very high voltage, and was then reduced for domestic use. She therefore focused her attention on the route from its source at the solar towers out in Hellinar. Within the rotation she had an armful of rolled schematics.

'I think these are likely be the most relevant,' she began, as the rolls spilled out onto the table. 'They date from about eight decades ago.'

'Before my time,' Olson smiled.

'This is about where Ayon Research is located, next to this junction. It's strange, though,' she mused, tracing a line diagonally up the map with a forefinger. 'This line doesn't run horizontally. All the rest do.'

'Do you think they might have doubled up on the line running parallel with an existing utility?'

'Possibly,' she agreed. 'It's got a designation here, 7075. That's different to all the other lines, they have a two-letter prefix, then a number. There might be some reference to it elsewhere, hang on.'

Getting up, she wandered back into the archive, reappearing a few turns later with further documents.

'I've found it,' she said excitedly. 'I think you're going to find this very informative. 7075 is not the power line designation, it's a coolant tunnel. It runs from the Western District, through the Central District and then directly past Ayon Research. But here's what's really interesting.' She spread out one of the rolls, not a schematic this time but a depiction of the tunnel in cross-section. 'It's deep,' she asserted. 'It's really deep.'

'As deep as the Vault?' asked Olson.

'Deeper.'

'Where exactly does it run? Can you pin it to a few metres?'

'I can do better than that,' she said, brandishing another bundle of papers. 'According to these drawings, the early extensions to the Vault had to be built just above the 7075 tunnel. Apparently there was some concern they might break into it by accident. They got at least as far as contacting the outer concrete before they stopped.'

'You're kidding,' said Olson, eyes wide. 'That's got to be it.'

'It looks likely,' she said. 'It's quite possible that the high-voltage supply is taken from the power lines in the 7075 tunnel. Whether that happened officially or not is another matter.'

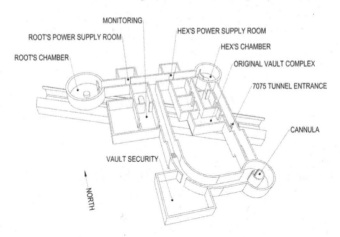

Olson looked over the schematics again to reassure himself this wasn't just dumb luck. 'How would anyone know about this?' he asked.

'Well…' said Megan, thinking out loud. 'It's only taken us a few rotations to learn all this. Maybe we weren't the first people to make this journey.'

'Is there any way we can find out if these plans have been looked at in the last few cycles?'

'There should be a record, if they have been withdrawn by anyone that doesn't directly work here,' she agreed. 'I could ask.'

'Do that,' said Olson. 'In the meantime, I think we should go and take another look at HEX's chamber, see if we can't make out that door. If you're willing?'

Megan didn't need to be asked twice. 'Give me a couple of rotations. Can I meet you there?'

'I'll sort out your clearance.' Olson got up, still eyeing the plans lying across the table. Then he looked at Megan and gave her a final nod of appreciation. It was time to head back to the Vault.

016: Pack Load

Research and Development Facility, Eastern District, Skala City

In the time between Katherine Kane's visit and the planned Pack installation, Roy Jacobs and Don Hoffer worked without sleep to get as much of the internal installation finished as possible. Privately, Jacobs had been concerned how Hoffer would take to a management role; promoting from within always carried a risk. A good crew chief did not always make a good manager. As things turned out, his fears had been misplaced. Hoffer was neither egotistical nor pushy and had that rarest of qualities, the ability to lead his team without them noticing. He was efficient, liked and easy to work with.

The two men now stood together watching with interest as the Pack was finally wheeled into place below a gantry crane that spanned the hangar. Hoffer admired its elegance for something that had been so hastily put together. At the back of each hulking V10 were a series of doughnut-shaped objects which Hoffer moved to inspect. 'These are the torque converters?'

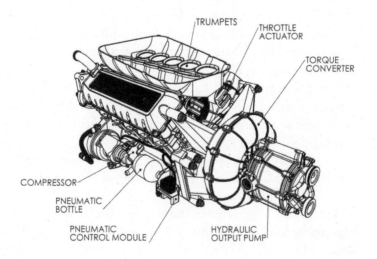

'That's right,' Jacobs confirmed. 'Behind them are the drive couplings.'

'One coupling per wheel – don't mix them up, right?' intoned Hoffer with a wry smile.

'Exactly.' Jacobs gestured to a second set of couplings that were mounted directly to a sculpted tank nestled down between the torque converters. 'Those are the return lines to the hydraulic tank. You can mix them up all you want, it won't make any difference'.

'Still, I'll try not to.'

Both men continued to admire the 6,500-kilowatt Pack for a few turns before Katherine strode into the hangar to greet them.

'I've tried to get through the documentation you sent me,' she said, uncertainly. 'There is a lot of it…'

'Does it make sense?' asked Jacobs.

'Yes, but I can't say I've been able to take it all in. I need more time with it.'

'It's your copy, so take as much time as you need.'

'That's not the problem, Roy. I'm worried I'm not going to be fully versed by the time we come to commission. I've never driven anything this complex.'

'Nor has anyone else,' Jacobs assured her. He knew the situation she had been put in and, although he didn't fully understand it, what he did know was that she needed his full backing if she was going to make a success of it.

'Okay,' said Katherine, gathering herself together and nodding towards the huge engines. 'So are you going to show me where this lump goes?'

'Yes ma'am,' said Hoffer, turning to GVX, which sat expectantly behind them. 'And I think you're going to enjoy this.'

A few turns later, Roy Jacobs stood with Katherine among a plethora of umbilical lines at GVX's rear. Don Hoffer was now in full flow, with the majority of his technicians deployed strategically down the vehicle's length; the rest were coupling the Pack to the gantry crane. There were no straps or other lifting equipment that Katherine could see. She supposed there must be inbuilt hard points integrated into the Pack itself for this purpose. It was the sort of detail John Orchard was renowned for.

Looking from the Pack back to GVX, she said, 'I still don't understand where it goes. How do you get it in?'

Jacobs smiled and nodded towards Hoffer, who was talking intently into a hand-held radio. 'I think he's pretty much ready. You'll see in just a moment.'

Hoffer looked towards Jacobs and gave a thumbs up, which Jacobs promptly returned.

'Here we go,' said Jacobs, and Katherine heard the

unmistakable whine of a gas turbine spooling up from deep inside GVX's body. Then a second whine began. It only took a few moments for both turbines' speed to stabilise, before the noise deepened as they took up the load.

Hoffer was conferring with one of his technicians and the two seemed to be agreeing. Hasty radio calls were made and received. Although she couldn't hear the exchanges above the sound of the turbines, Katherine could tell there was a building sense of expectation. Glancing back at the Pack, she was surprised to see it had already been raised up and was moving towards them.

A rapid succession of metallic cracks from rotary locks in the vehicle's rearmost section caught her attention. To Katherine's amazement, the entire rear section of the vehicle juddered, then began to move. It took less than a turn to fully extend, with the Pack itself moving directly above. The crane's operator sat in a small glass cab that was mounted on the huge cross beam. She could see him squinting to get perspective on his charge and line it up as exactly as possible. Hoffer concentrated on the final lowering until the crane operator stopped about fifty millimetres above the deck. Now, in Katherine's hearing, Hoffer was readying technicians positioned down the length of the vehicle, but for what, she couldn't make out.

'Are they concerned it's going to tip when the Pack goes in?' Katherine asked Jacobs, in as confiding a tone as she could manage given the noise.

'Something like that. You'll see,' he replied.

The Pack began moving again but very slowly now. Dowel pegs engaged the sump plate, guiding it into position. As it touched down, short, curved locks snapped up from the bed to secure the V10s in place.

'Pack locked in,' shouted Hoffer over the radio. 'Everyone standby while we release the load.' He signalled to the crane operator, who began to lower once more. The chain slackened and Katherine was aware of a prolonged mechanical groan coming from somewhere deep inside the chassis.

She turned to Jacobs and saw a distinct satisfaction in his expression. The same look was writ across the face of most of the technicians. Hoffer looked particularly satisfied or relieved; she couldn't be sure. Something was out of place, though, and it took her a moment to put her finger on what it was.

'Shouldn't the suspension compress when this amount of weight is added?' she asked.

Jacobs grinned broadly at her. 'It should, you're right.'

'What's the joke? Why didn't it?'

'Platform control,' he explained. 'The suspension has springs and dampers but there is also a hydraulic ram that is a part of each damper. GVX was designed as a laboratory, remember? Having a level floor in your science lab is pretty important. According to the scientists at least.'

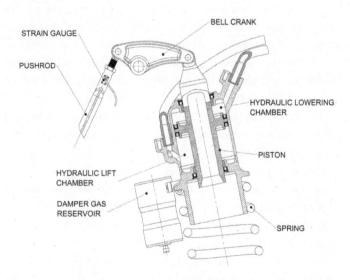

It took less than a rotation to complete the installation, even allowing for Hoffer and Jacobs' tour of the 'Pack Bay'. Less than ten turns later, the deck was retracting back into GVX's chassis.

'So that's it,' she asked. 'All over that fast?'

'Not quite,' said Hoffer. 'That's the Pack installed and systems flushed, but we've got to fire it yet.'

Katherine watched as Jacobs tested systems from a remote laptop until his list of checks was exhausted. A few calibration changes were made and some system controls tweaked, but it was clear from the perceptible sense of building anticipation that all was going according to plan.

'How are we looking?' Hoffer asked as Katherine moved aside for him.

'We're looking good for a fire-up,' said Jacobs.

'Remove the kill on engines one and two once we reach start speed please. Begin cranking now,' said Hoffer.

'Cranking for dual start,' confirmed Jacobs and, with only a moment's hesitation, initiated the starters of both engines. The whir built up over a couple of moments.

'We're in the start speed window for both engines. Removing kill,' said Jacobs, suppressing a clear air of nervous excitement.

There was a bark, followed immediately by a second bark as the Pack came to life for the first time. A deep and brutish roar quickly settled to a smooth, even purr. The reverberating sound was all that could be heard in the hangar before spontaneous applause broke out. John Orchard, who had been standing beside Katherine, gave an emphatic sigh of relief. She had not realised there was so much tension in him. Hoffer and Jacobs exchanged satisfied, equally relieved grins.

'Pressures are holding, pneumatics look good, everything in limits,' confirmed Hoffer, who gave Jacobs an uncharacteristic slap on the back. Jacobs continued to stare at the control screen, finger poised over the key to initiate a system shutdown. After a few moments the finger was gingerly withdrawn and he turned to look back at Katherine, confidence writ large on his face.

017: Return

Gygath Slum, West of Skala City

JT walked. His head hung low as his body was pounded from behind by the relentless heat of the sun. His mouth was dry and he felt dust caked into every crease of his face as the strain of movement came and went. He used the crisp sound of fine grit crunching beneath each footfall as a point of focus. Ira, walking beside him in silence, was reassurance that he would make it out of Gygath, but the Projects that marked the boundary between the slums and Skala City seemed a long way off.

He looked around him, trying to take his mind off the pain. The slums seemed less foreboding than they had when he'd entered. There was no sense of being followed this time. The residents were more visible and simply ignored the two men.

'Ira, can I ask you something?'

'Can't promise I'll answer, but go on,' came the gruff retort.

'Before I came here, before I was even out of Skala, I was sure I was being followed. Was that you?'

'Might have been.'

'And people seemed to be hiding?'

'Look, don't flatter yourself, it was Connor we were after. It took a lot of planning in a short space of time and a lot of people were involved. He would have been quite a prize.'

'And you burgled my apartment?'

Ira took a moment to consider this. 'I wouldn't say burgled, I took a look around. Anyone else wouldn't know if it had been burgled or not, it's that much of a mess. I was surprised, the people you work with said you were tidy and diligent. It makes me wonder if you're going through some sort of personal crisis.'

This annoyed JT considerably, not least because it was true. He tried to deflect Ira by asking, 'And how did you get in?'

'Through the front door,' said Ira, as if the answer were obvious.

'Picked the lock I suppose?'

'No, I used the key.'

JT looked at Ira in puzzlement. 'The keys are in the desk drawer in my office.' It took him a moment to make the connection. 'You burgled my office and my home? How did you get into Hellinar Research?'

Ira merely shrugged. 'And where are the keys now?' JT demanded.

Ira began fumbling in a pocket and retrieved a small bunch of keys, dropping them into JT's waiting hand.

'Meant to give them to you earlier. Sorry.'

'Have you made copies?'

'Actually, no, I haven't.' Meeting JT's scowl he shrugged and added, 'There didn't seem much point.'

They walked in silence the rest of the way, JT brooding, Ira striding alongside him indifferent to his mood. Presently they reached the Projects and the dirt path became the cobbled stones of Siir Street. Waiting at a nearby corner, looking apprehensive in a long white tunic, was Evelyn Tudor.

'Look at you,' she said in a scolding tone as they approached. 'You're covered in blood.' Seeing Ira she demanded, 'Who are you? Did you do this to him?'

Ira offered her a rough, calloused hand. 'I'm Ira, failed poet, and yes, I did that to him. He took it pretty well actually. You should be proud.'

Evelyn gave him a withering look before turning back to JT. 'We need to get you cleaned up and into a fresh change of clothes. Nothing broken is there?'

'I don't think so. A wash and a change would be welcome though.'

Evelyn took him by the arm and walked him east along Siir Street, Ira trailing behind.

'I followed the tracks into the slums,' said JT, in a voice he hoped didn't carry. 'Ira here thought I was William Connor.'

'That's the name from the T24 access log,' she replied.

'It seems he may have facilitated the theft of Hydra. It stopped in the slums to pick people up before heading out of Skala. From there I have no idea where it went, into Ayon I assume.'

'If it was heading west wouldn't it be going into Hellinar?'

'It was fitted with snow chains,' he reminded her. 'You'd never fit chains to go into the desert.'

'I suppose not,' she agreed.

'The people that questioned me after Ira was done seemed very worried about Hydra. Well, the people Hydra picked up I should say. Their concern seemed a little out of proportion. I'm not saying the theft of three vehicles isn't a serious offence, but there was something else going on.'

'I might be able to fill you in on that,' she said. 'While you've been gone it's come out that one of the Intercessor Drive Cores has been stolen.'

JT, startled by the news, considered it a moment. 'You think whoever stole the IDC used Hydra to move it? That would certainly account for a lot.'

Ira, who was still close behind them, chipped in. 'Your Unit

Hydra and the people it carries are about to become the most hunted group on the planet. That's why we wanted Connor so urgently. Once we heard about the Core we had to try and get our people back before the authorities got to them.'

'Hence the harsh treatment?' asked JT, gesturing to the dry blood that still adorned his jumpsuit.

Ira sighed. 'It was a race against time. Connor is a tough nut and he had to know we were serious. We had to find out who hired him and where that Core was going, fast, if we were to have any chance of getting to our people first. Unfortunately 'he' turned out to be you, and you knew as much about IDCs as I do about poetry, which as I've assured you, isn't much.'

Evelyn glared at him over her shoulder, then looked back to JT with motherly concern. 'If that's the case, there is someone I think you should talk to. We'll get you cleaned up and I'll make the arrangements, if that's okay?'

'Sure,' said JT, willing to go along with anything that bought him a bath. 'Who is it you want me to talk to?'

'An old friend who works for the Corporate Investigations Division.'

'Oh, okay,' said JT, caught a little off guard.

Ira snorted. 'What are they going to do?'

When Evelyn didn't answer he added, 'I'll wait outside while you powwow if it's all the same to you.'

'That,' said Evelyn Tudor with assured finality, 'sounds like a very good idea.'

On the outskirts of the Central District, the Corporate Investigations Division was a large, cluttered office at ground level. Thick double doors prevented the repressively sweaty atmosphere spilling into the rest of Skala City, while worn ceiling fans creaked overhead like the hinges of old wardrobes. It was an outdated, wood and glass-lined, open-plan space shared by twenty officers. To judge by the near constant ringing, it was also home to twice that number of telephones.

Evelyn Tudor and JT sat on a pair of poor-quality steel chairs whose torn linings spilled forth the bulk of their contents. They faced a wide desk with split veneer and bulging but neatly stacked trays of paper that looked destined for the brace of filing cabinets that lined the far wall. A small slide-in plaque assured them the desk was the current property of Detective Vincent O'Brien.

Evelyn sat prim and upright and, to JT's eye, looked uncharacteristically self-conscious. She glanced around every so often as if looking for someone she knew but the other occupants of the office seemed far too busy to pay her any heed. Her discomfort was cut mercifully short when O'Brien arrived. He was everything JT imagined an investigator would be – the clean, urgent persona masking a weary, overworked soul.

'Evelyn, nice to see you.' She stood to greet him and shook his hand warmly. 'I imagine it's strange being back in this office?'

'Well, it does feel a little awkward. I don't recognise anyone,' she confided.

'There are still a few old faces,' he scanned around the room but seemed unable to locate one. 'I guess most of them are out right now. Tyler Olson's still with us but only for a couple of shifts as it happens. I'll be sad to lose him.'

'Retirement?'

'Well earned,' said O'Brien, a sentiment Evelyn clearly shared.

'You worked here?' JT asked her with a raised eyebrow.

'Yes I did,' she said evenly.

'Worked here?' said O'Brien, amused. 'She set the place up.'

Evelyn blushed momentarily then, remembering her manners, made the introductions. 'Oh, I'm sorry. Vincent

O'Brien, this is JT Gilbert.' They shook hands, each immediately recognising and respecting the administrator in the other.

'JT is the man I called you about.'

'I remember,' said O'Brien, stabbing his glasses up to the bridge of his nose.

'I'm sorry to drag you back here from whatever you were doing, but I think you should listen to what Mr Gilbert has to say.'

'Certainly,' said O'Brien, willingly. 'I've been trapped down in that accursed Vault for shifts now. It's actually quite a relief to be above ground for more than a few rotations. I need to spend some time here on a disappearance in any case.'

Evelyn Tudor regarded him seriously and he felt obliged to explain. 'I don't think it's related to Mr Gilbert here. A missing woman called Kyra Devin. We're getting pretty worried and I need to shuffle some rosters around to widen the search.' Perching himself on a corner of his desk he gestured for the other two to retake their seats.

JT told his story, recounting in as much detail as he could the discrepancies in the tag-in, tag-out system and how he had begun to trace Unit Hydra. When he came to the part about the T7 facility and their inability to help him, O'Brien interrupted briefly, addressing Evelyn Tudor.

'Homicide found a body a couple of shifts ago, a man dumped in a refuse collector. I don't know all the details but he was identified by some documents he was carrying. They pertained to the conversion of desert vehicles to run in the deep cold. We're sure it's Austen Worral, the man you mentioned when you called. Are the documents relevant? We were surprised he was carrying them, to be honest.'

'They certainly could be,' said JT with consideration. 'You could see the imprint of snow chains in the tracks the Unit left at T24. That really surprised me, for a desert allocation. I'm not sure what it means – maybe he was trying to cover up the conversion?'

O'Brien considered this a moment then asked JT to continue his story. When he came to his mistreatment in the slums, his audience scowled but remained silent. The name Bill Connor clearly registered and mention of the Mal–Kas mine elicited an intrigued look from the CID man. When he had finished, O'Brien thought for a moment then asked, 'This man Ira, where is he now?'

'He's outside,' said Evelyn with displeasure.

'Worried we'd recognise him?'

'I think so,' said JT.

'I take it you don't want to press charges?'

This had occurred to JT more than once but, after a hesitation, he said he didn't.

'Then we'll let this run for a while but I think you should be careful of this man. I'd like to know who he really is, if that's possible.'

'I think you're right. I'll try to find out.'

O'Brien shifted his weight slightly and assumed a resigned look. 'We've been trying to get someone into one of those mines for a while now,' referring to JT's mention of Mal–Kas. 'We've speculated for some time about exploitation and we suspect deaths have been covered up. Every time we get close, the corporations smell a rat. How, I don't know.'

'You think they know about your agents in advance?' asked Evelyn.

O'Brien regarded her carefully, then nodded. 'It looks that way, yes. They have someone on the inside, here in this office or close to it. Could be a secretary or typist, I don't know. Déjà vu, wouldn't you say Evelyn?'

'And Connor is someone you know?' asked JT when there was no response.

O'Brien gave a little laugh. 'Yes, he is. A slippery man, Connor. A thug and almost certainly a murderer, but he continues to elude us. He has protection provided by a lot of influential people.'

'I said I'd try to get into the mines to find Connor when I was being questioned in the Landlord's Arms. Would it help you if I went through with it?'

'That would be a crazy risk to take,' said O'Brien, raising an eyebrow.

'I'm not sure it would,' said JT, thoughtfully. 'I'm supposed to take field trips as part of my job – check on equipment, make sure it's actually being used and maintained properly. I don't know for sure that we have any equipment at Mal-Kas, but it's a fair bet. I might learn nothing for you and I may not find Connor, but, in the worst-case scenario, I'll have taken a legitimate trip out there and verified my kit's in place.'

'It seems a little too good to be true,' O'Brien said, looking at Evelyn. She returned his stare but again said nothing.

'If you're sure you won't be at risk, then go. You'll be working for me informally – no pay, no contract, is that understood?'

'Perfectly,' said JT. 'I'd just be happy to help if I can.'

This seemed to satisfy O'Brien. 'Okay then, good luck. Evelyn, could I speak to you alone?'

'Of course.' She glanced at JT, who took the hint, nodded to O'Brien and crossed the office to join Ira, who was no doubt loitering with intent somewhere outside.

When he had gone, O'Brien asked, 'I'm not being foolish? This isn't a monster-sized trap is it?'

'Like the one that ended my career, you mean?' she asked. When he didn't answer she continued. 'I think he's exactly what he appears to be, a good conscientious soul. I think, for a change, you've been dealt a good hand and you should play it to your best advantage. He's good to work with, as far as I can tell.'

O'Brien acknowledged this with a nod. 'Okay, I trust your judgement,' he said, and offered her his hand warmly. 'Keep an eye on him, though, will you? It would be better if he communicates through you if we are to keep him as a usable asset.'

'Of course,' she said, a little testily. 'I'm a little out of practice but agent-running isn't something you forget in a hurry. And it seems anyone that would remember me has long ago retired.'

'Probably they have,' he agreed, with a placatory smile.

Getting up to leave, she paused and turned back. 'Remember me to Tyler, won't you?'

'Of course. Goodbye, Miss Tudor, and thank you.'

018: The Chamber

Ayon Research Facility, Eastern District, Skala City

Under a dark, foreboding sky that filtered only occasional beams of sunlight, Megan Devin climbed the stone steps to the entrance of Ayon Research. She moved with a confidence of familiarity that was not lost on Tyler Olson, who regarded her ascent from just inside the doorway. She had changed from smart working clothes into a grey jumpsuit and boots, an outfit she apparently considered more appropriate attire for working down in the Vault. It suited her, but then she had the maddeningly athletic physique that made just about any outfit look natural. She pushed the door open and stepped onto the ageing, polished surface of the mosaic floor.

'You've changed,' Olson observed, looking her up and down. Coming from most men this gesture would have made her feel uncomfortable, but somehow Olson didn't exude any sort of seediness; in fact his apparent approval came as a mild relief to her. The jumpsuit, however appropriate, was not a uniform she felt she necessarily had the right to wear in public.

'I didn't think scratching around in a skirt was ideal, Mr Olson. I had this old thing from doing work experience at Hellinar Research.' She took an involuntary look at her left shoulder, which was adorned with an embroidered badge depicting the split circle with the Hellinar half highlighted.

Olson gestured to the Cannula, now guarded by two black-uniformed officials. Without protest, one summoned the elevator and both moved aside as the doors parted. Olson stepped in first with Megan a pace behind him.

'You know,' began Olson, as if speaking to no one in particular, 'it's a good thing you've studied those schematics so hard, this being your first visit to the Vault. I wouldn't act as if it's too familiar.' He glanced over to her but she didn't meet his eyes. She coloured slightly and gave a barely perceptible nod.

The doors slid open and they ventured out past security towards Vincent O'Brien, who sat on the end of Myra Cena's desk in the next-door monitoring room. On seeing Olson through the glass, he rose and stepped into the corridor, followed gingerly by Myra herself.

'Mr Olson?' said O'Brien, in an enquiring tone.

'Vincent,' replied Olson, less formally. 'Can I introduce Megan Devin? She's been extremely helpful researching the local architecture.'

'Miss Devin,' said O'Brien, with a curt nod. 'Thank you for your assistance. Mr Olson has filled me in on your findings. Good work.' He made to move past them, pushing his spectacles back to the bridge of his nose as he did so. 'Time to prove your theory.'

Olson gave Megan an expectant frown and fell in behind his superior. Noticing Myra loitering in the doorway, Megan turned and introduced herself in a somewhat awkward exchange. Myra frowned, then scowled at the younger woman's uniform, knowing it couldn't possibly be hers by right, she was far too young. But she restrained herself and said nothing as they fell into step behind the CID men.

HEX's chamber was darker than Megan remembered it,

although she didn't say so and made a show of looking around as if for the first time. She felt Myra's eyes following her as she moved to stand by Olson. He was already examining the section of wall that stood to the right of the entrance, running his hand across it with the flat of his palm. Myra stood back with O'Brien as Megan and Olson began to search for the joint in the plaster that would show the location of the original door. It took them longer than either had expected and, ultimately, it was Olson who found the smallest of ridges, which he picked at with a fingernail.

'It's certainly faint,' he said. 'I guess I'm disappointed we missed it, but not surprised now that I see it.'

'I can't imagine how such a close fit could have been achieved,' said Megan, in a tone that suggested such interesting anomalies were commonplace to her. Inadvertently, she caught Myra's disapproving stare again, as the technician scratched distractedly at the pale scar on her cheek.

'Maybe it will be more obvious once we get the door open,' said Olson, oblivious to the animosity that was growing between the two women.

'How do you want to go about this?' asked Megan, trying to sound unfazed.

'Vincent, would I be right in saying you have photographed, scanned and dusted down every square millimetre of this chamber?'

'You would,' agreed O'Brien.

'Then, being as we don't know where the 7075 tunnel terminates, or even if it does intersect with the space behind this door, we could save ourselves a good deal of time by just drilling it.'

O'Brien considered this for a moment. 'Miss Cena, are the locks in this door secured by compressed air, same as the others?'

'They are,' said Megan, answering for Myra, who scowled.

'Then if we drill one of the link pipes, the whole system should depressurise?' asked O'Brien.

'I imagine so,' said Myra. 'It's not something I've ever tried.'

O'Brien left the room, returning moments later with a long, thin drill bit mounted in a cordless drill. In his other hand he held an endoscope. 'Where do we drill?' he asked, approaching the plastered wall.

Megan stood aside and gave him a shrug. 'Your guess is as good as mine,' she said.

'If that's the outline of the door,' said Myra, tracing the invisible shape onto the wall, 'then I would start about here.'

He looked at the blank spot she was pointing to, then pushed the drill bit firmly into contact with the wall. The drill cut effortlessly though the dry, brittle plaster. It took a few moments before the muted whine became a grinding screech as the bit hit steel. O'Brien applied effort and presently a few red flecks of paint were pushed up the flutes of the drill bit, spilling over his starched, white shirt cuffs.

Hot metal swarf followed as the drill penetrated the outer layer of steel before it sank through the inner layer of sound-deadening rock wool. The tone changed again as the bit made contact with the door's outer casing. Another turn passed before O'Brien, with a jolt, was through and withdrew the smoking drill bit.

Carefully, he picked up the endoscope and connected it to the light source. Leaning into the eyepiece he squinted and plunged the shaft in through the hole. He rotated a collar that tilted the tiny mirror, angling it back towards him, drew back and, leaving the endoscope in place, offered it to Myra. She looked. It was hard to position her eye to the lens but once in the right place she could make out the dim shape of pipework and the nearest pneumatic lock.

Olson and Megan took turns to look, both squinting to make sense of the dim shapes. O'Brien gestured to Myra to take the scope again.

'If I drill, you tell me where I come out and where to angle the tip,' he said, again falling to one knee and pushing the bit into a fresh area of plaster below the first. Myra stood over him as the silence of the chamber once again gave way to the high-pitched shriek of the drill. A couple of turns later, O'Brien was through.

'There is a pipe above and just to the left of you,' said Myra, straining with intense concentration from her position above him.

'How far up?' he asked.

'Hard to tell, it looks like about six or seven centimetres but it could be more.'

O'Brien withdrew the bit, angling it up and to his left before attacking the outer skin once again. Presently the sound wound down and Myra again gave instructions.

'You're really close – angle up two more centimetres.'

The shrieking resumed but this time, as the drill poked through, O'Brien jolted and came to an abrupt halt.

'You're on the pipe,' said Myra. 'Just a bit further and you'll pierce it.'

O'Brien got the drill turning, more slowly this time.

'Gently,' said Myra. 'The pipe is pushing away from the tip of the drill. Just take it slowly.'

O'Brien did so, and after a few moments was rewarded with the sharp crack of depressurisation that gradually reduced to a gentle hiss of escaping air. In less than a turn they heard a series of dull thuds as the locks retracted on the far side of the door.

O'Brien pulled the drill back from the door as Myra did the same with the endoscope. With the heels of his hands, the CID man gave the wall a firm, deliberate push. To everyone's astonishment, the invisible gap opened up as the door swung open.

'Well, I'll be damned,' said O'Brien, in disbelief. Examining the edges of the opening, he dug into the plaster with a fingernail. As the others watched, a lump of smooth, freshly painted filler chipped off with ease and fell to the floor.

'Someone's put a lot of effort into this,' said Olson, with reverence.

O'Brien nodded, then turned to push the door again. The heavy body swung silently open on freshly oiled hinges to reveal the mouth of an unlit passage.

'I think it would be prudent to get Katherine Kane down here if we can,' said Olson, staring into the darkness. 'She knew this place right back to its origins.'

'She'll have other stuff to worry about,' said Megan, with a familiarity that clearly grated on Myra. 'Besides, we've got the plans here.'

The Vault technician felt a bubble of anger burst inside her. 'I'll get Councillor Kane,' she said and turned to march down the corridor.

'What's her problem?' asked Megan.

'Stress,' said O'Brien. He turned his gaze from Myra back to Megan. 'Just take it easy on her, you're in her territory.'

Megan looked chastened but said nothing.

'I'll get the forensics people back as well,' he said and turned to follow Myra.

Katherine arrived before the forensics. Myra met her at the Cannula and escorted her to the chamber with a simple greeting of, 'You need to see this.' On entering and seeing Megan, Katherine's face brightened before she saw the open door and dark space beyond it.

'Of course,' she said, as if it should have been obvious. She looked back to Megan. 'You figured this out?'

'Not really,' said Megan, blushing girlishly. 'Mr Olson and I figured it out together.'

'We've not been through yet,' said O'Brien. 'Miss Devin has explained the layout of the original Vault, but I wanted you here, as you probably know it better than anyone.'

'I doubt that's true,' said Katherine. 'Do you want me to go first?'

'Please,' said O'Brien, gesturing to the doorway and handing Katherine a flashlight as he did so.

She took it and snapped it on. The air smelled musty and was laced with damp and mildew. She approached and scanned the immediate vicinity before crossing the threshold. The ground beyond the door was strewn with debris, mostly the broken-up concrete of the floor mixed with dark bits of lino and ceiling tile. In comparison with the floor, the walls seemed to be largely intact, but for the peeling paint that adorned them from floor level up to waist height.

Katherine stepped forward into the dark and scanned the flashlight further down the corridor. After a few steps she heard the crunch of broken glass under her feet and saw jagged shards of old strip lights smashed on the ground. Realising she was holding her breath, she exhaled and summoned up the memories of how this place had looked back when it was immaculate, new and at the cutting edge of technology. It looked smaller than she remembered, the corridor shorter and lower. The suspended ceiling had partly collapsed at the far end of the corridor, its flimsy metal framework bent and twisted.

She cleared her throat. 'It's amazing how run-down this place is.'

She turned and played the light over the broken shards of

glass that had been the window of the old monitoring room. 'This is where you would have lived, Myra.'

Myra made her way forward and peered into the space. 'It's not very big,' she said, disapprovingly.

'There was only ROOT to keep track of at the time,' said Katherine, absently. 'What's this?' she asked aloud. Tracing a line of incongruous new cabling emerging from the wall to her right, she tracked it down to a small metal cabinet on the floor. Puzzled, she moved to it and heard a faint whirring from small vents in its side. She squatted to examine a bank of flashing LEDs mounted beside a stencilled, rather worn manufacturer's logo. It read INI Industries Inc.

'Please don't touch that until the forensics people have been in here,' said O'Brien firmly but his look suggested he only half meant it. 'What do you think it is?'

'I have no idea,' said Katherine. 'Myra?'

'Some sort of old computer storage device or something?'

'It's an emulator,' said Olson from behind them. Surprised by his insight, Katherine turned to look at him.

'It's an old emulator used to record and relay signals in and out of a system. They were used for checking what were then very complex processors in control systems. Of course, they are a fraction of that size now.' He gave a good-natured laugh, with which no one joined in.

Shrugging uncomfortably he offered up a simple explanation. 'My father's company used to make them.'

Katherine looked again at the manufacturer's inscription, then back to Olson. For a moment she scrutinised him, trying to recall what she could of INI Industries. Memory came flooding back and she straightened as a sickening realisation gripped her stomach.

'Your father's company was INI Industries?' she said slowly, making sure she had the story right.

'That's right,' said Olson, with an irreverent joviality so out of place the others began to share Katherine's discomfort.

Megan looked from the shocked, pale face of her half-sister to Olson, and back in bewilderment.

'So that's why you were interested in how I found ROOT,' said Katherine, still fitting the pieces together. 'ROOT and the technology he offered effectively put your father out of business.'

Olson looked absently to one side, clearly uncomfortable. 'Yeah, I guess I was interested. I never thought I'd get to meet that famous little girl who found the magic box of Mayak.'

'All those people,' said Katherine, furiously rubbing her forehead. 'You had to lay off all those people and your father blamed you. All because of me.'

'It was a long time ago,' he said in a kindly but sad voice.

'But it wasn't your fault,' she protested. 'Finding ROOT was just a stupid accident, but for you…' She looked at him and shook her head, unable to finish the sentence. To the others, who could only watch this exchange with a sort of morbid curiosity, she looked as if she was about to crumple to the ground.

'It's the law of unintended consequences,' he said in supplication. 'You, at age fifteen, would never have imagined what might happen.'

She was still shaking her head, her mind clearly not in the present. He moved a step towards her and gently took her hand. 'Some good things came out of it. I never wanted to run that company and I resented my father for making me. I was never cut out for a directorship but it's hard to admit that, even to yourself. Once it was gone, once he had gone, my wife came back and we were happy together. And now I'm doing what I dreamt of doing as a child.'

She looked back at him sadly, tears brimming in her eyes.

'Your wife, she's still with you?' It felt an important detail to cling to in this moment.

He wanted to reassure her but that wasn't to be. 'She died. Cancer. But we had some of the happiest times before that. She was a truly wonderful woman. And look,' he said, his voice now suddenly filled with humour, 'I get to work for this control freak. I get to go down dark passages with attractive ladies.' He looked to Megan and Myra for approval and both grinned.

O'Brien, who knew Olson's backstory, chipped in with uncharacteristic generosity. 'He's very useful for me. He knows how these big companies work. How they get corrupted and how to look for the rot. I'll miss him when he retires.'

Katherine pulled herself together as best she could. She sucked in a deep lungful of the stale air and asked the one question that remained. 'So this is how HEX's telemetry is being interrupted?'

'Undoubtedly,' said Olson. 'That is exactly what this device does.'

Katherine looked at it then turned to sweep her flashlight through the open gap that would once have housed a door. The light flickered across the far wall of the corridor. As it did so, something caught her attention and she brought it back. Her brow furrowed as she squinted.

'I don't remember that,' she said.

All turned to see what she was looking at. Across the corridor, embedded in the wall, was a steel access panel that sat partially open. In contrast to the wall and floor around it, it looked distinctly well cared for. Unusually, it opened backwards, into whatever was behind it.

Megan moved to it excitedly, examining it in the glow of her own flashlight. 'This has to be the link to the 7075 tunnel!'

'The what?' asked Katherine.

'It's a service tunnel that runs close to here. We think it's how whoever stole HEX got out.'

Megan knelt and poked her head through the hole, pushing at the door as she did so. She had expected the hinges to squeak but they were smooth and silent. She reached in and shone her light around before calling back.

'It's definitely a service tunnel, there are pipes and things all over the walls.' Before anyone could protest she had climbed through and jumped down to somewhere below.

O'Brien looked at Olson and frowned. 'Adventurous girl for a librarian. There's no way I'm going down there.'

Olson gave a wry grin. 'She's an archivist, not a librarian, Vincent.'

'You'd better follow her,' O'Brien said. 'The two of you have got us this far. If you can find out where that tunnel leads it would finish the job nicely.'

Olson nodded then looked back at Katherine. 'Don't worry,' he said. 'I'll look after her.' Then he added, 'Don't worry about that other stuff. Please?'

She gave a resigned nod and, after accepting it, Olson himself climbed through the steel hatch and into the darkness below.

019: The Tunnel

Below Skala

The oppressive darkness that surrounded Megan seemed like a dead space, alive only in the glint of her flashlight. In the thirty turns since she had entered the tunnel network, followed by Tyler Olson, they had made good progress.

The tunnel was far from featureless; its crumbling concrete walls were lined with electrical conduit and sagging pipes that leaked refrigerant gas from cracks that appeared where wall-mounted supports had failed. Occasionally, smaller tunnels spurred off to the sides, providing irregular reference points where the air moved noticeably faster. The cool breeze was a welcome respite from the sweet, mildly intoxicating smell of the Freon gas.

The concrete floor became increasingly irregular and littered with debris the further they ventured. Glass from long-exploded vacuum light bulbs crunched underfoot, throwing up occasional puddles of refracted light. Occasionally they heard the hum of crossed cables discharging crackling electricity and a distinctive tang of ozone. Distantly, the clicking of ancient relays could be heard, bringing an increasing sense that a secret, long-forgotten electro-mechanical world existed beneath an uncaring upper world. The scratching and skittering of small, clawed feet was close, but the creatures themselves remained unseen.

At a touch of Olson's hand on her arm, Megan slowed her pace. They came to a standstill before a high arched opening lined in crumbling, pale brick. Tracing the outline with the flashlight she paused at the keystone, her attention arrested by a symbol carved deep into its surface. A series of three diagonal slashes, one above another, had been chiselled into the stone accompanied by a single vertical cut to the right.

'This is it,' said Olson, with a degree of trepidation. 'This is where the tunnel leads to.'

Megan shone her flashlight into the void beyond the arch, the abyssal darkness swallowing the beam whole. Straining her eyes, she could just make out a tall, pale, cylindrical shape in the distance. As her eyes adjusted, she thought she saw a shadow flash across it. A stab of adrenaline surged through her system, causing her focus to sharpen and her already tight lungs to draw in an involuntary drag of the gas-laden air.

'What is it?' Olson asked, his eyes straining into the faint illumination.

'I don't know, something moved,' she whispered, not daring to take her eyes off the cylinder.

'A person, animal maybe?' His voice calmed Megan just enough to hold back fear.

'I don't know.'

'We go carefully then,' he said. 'My wife once told me, in the strictest of confidence, there is a whole subculture living down below the city. I've never told a soul before, but I guess it doesn't matter now.'

Megan stared ahead, not daring to look away. 'People, living down here?'

'From what I know, they leave us up-worlders alone most of the time. Have you ever heard of anyone going missing down here?'

'No,' replied Megan, not remotely reassured.

Olson moved forward and Megan followed, fear blooming inside her like a dark rose. Crossing the threshold of the arch, she shone her light deep into the space beyond, scanning from right to left. Detecting no movement, she swallowed hard and took a step further inside.

The space was large compared to the relative confines of the tunnel. It appeared wider than it was deep, the flashlight picking up no wall on either side. But she could see ahead of her. The cylindrical object they had seen became clearer, one of two huge, grey tanks. They reached up to twelve metres in height and were encircled by an austere-looking set of metal walkways. Far to the left was what appeared to be a hulking spoked wheel, half buried in the floor and coupled to a series of long ornate linkages that joined a pump-like machine.

'What is this place?' she whispered to Olson. Terror gripped her hearts as she realised he was no longer beside her.

'What is this place?' intoned a deep, booming voice from directly behind her. She froze, petrified.

'This place, down here in the darkness. This place, it be

called the Siphon.' The voice, rich and melodic, echoed faintly around her before dying away into the darkness.

Megan fought back tears and fright as she heard the soft struggle of Olson somewhere behind her. She was rooted to the spot, unable to muster the courage to turn and face the owner of that terrible voice. It came again, slow and closer this time, answering the question she dare not speak.

'And what of it, young miss? We do live down here although, for us, this is but an attic. Our kingdom lies beneath.'

He drew closer and Megan became aware of an intense aroma of incense just as the man himself took in a long, nasal breath. She felt the air move above her and knew he derived satisfaction from her scent. She felt fingers running softly against her hair on both sides and the proximity of palms that did not quite touch her. Sweat ran in streams across her brow and into her eyes, stinging and making her blink. But still, she didn't move.

'Your friend is a quiet one,' said the man, calm and questioning. From behind her, Olson spoke up in a supremely level voice.

'She's a child. Don't hurt her. You don't need to hurt either of us.'

'A child you say. She does not have the smell of a child.'

'She's not old enough to have done you any harm,' replied Olson.

'No?' enquired the voice and Megan felt the man draw himself against her, his breath blowing downward around her ear. He laid his hands on her shoulders with a terrifying lightness, his long splayed fingers coming to rest across her clavicles. 'But she might yet do harm to others, my friend.' His grip on her shoulders tightened.

Despite her fear, Megan was confused, mostly because Olson

seemed to know how to converse with this man on a level he clearly understood.

The voice spoke again but this time from a step or two behind and Megan felt the hands draw back, the fingers running over her shoulders like flaccid claws. 'And what are two souls from high above doing in the underworld?'

'We're just passing through,' said Olson, as if this were a normal thing to be doing on any given shift. 'We are retracing the steps of a friend of ours who came this way recently.'

At this, Megan felt a sudden rush of air as the figure behind her whirled. Finding her paralysis broken, she turned and gasped at the sight before her. The first thing she saw was Olson, his white shirt and face bright in the light of her wavering flashlight. Restraining him by the arms was a small group of men. All, to Megan's astonishment, had darker skin than anyone she had ever seen. All were powerfully built, dressed in light-coloured, dirt-stained rags. They seemed to hunch as if at the ready; for what, Megan tried not to think.

Between Olson and herself stood the man to whom the deep voice belonged. Even with his back turned, she could see he was tall, two metres at least, with long hanging plaits of black hair adorned with beads or rings. He wore a robe of dark sacking torn at the sleeves and at the hem, which nearly touched the ground. Megan could see from his bare feet and the backs of his tattooed forearms that he too had the same dark skin. In his left hand, he held a long staff tipped with a translucent yellow stone that caught her light and refracted it in a diffused halo.

'The woman Myra?' asked the man with obvious recognition.

Olson didn't flinch and spoke confidently. 'That's right, you know her?'

'We know her,' said the man with obvious respect in his

voice. 'She is one of the few visitors we tolerate down here in the darkness.'

The man turned to look back over his shoulder, giving Megan her first sight of his face. His high-set cheeks were full and covered in dark freckles, but it was his eyes that took her. He had the eyes of a cat. Though not slits exactly, the pupils were not round but possessed a definite vertical appearance that bled out at the edges. The iris surrounding each pupil was a deep green and shone bright in the flashlight. Megan saw no malice in those eyes, a hardness born of difficult circumstances, yes, but their intensity told her she was not in mortal danger.

Straightening, the figure turned fully towards her. Megan stood stock-still, forcing herself not to show lingering fear. For a moment, she met his gaze and felt a flicker of recognition in those strange eyes looking down on her.

'Look like her you might, little miss, but you have a calmer soul.'

'Thank you,' was all she could think to say, more in a whisper than as actual words. Look like her? That made little sense, as she possessed little more than a passing resemblance to the Vault's monitoring technician. She fought to regain her composure and, partly succeeding, managed to speak with more confidence than she felt. 'Who are you?'

The man turned his head, looking back at those behind him. Megan followed his gaze, noting that the assembled group had relaxed. Olson was no longer being held and stood, quite unmoved, apart from them.

'We are Hadje,' said the tall man with a sweeping gesture. 'That means nothing to you?'

Megan stuttered, embarrassed and afraid. 'I'm sorry, it doesn't.'

'No,' said the man thoughtfully, and turned to Olson. 'I imagine it may mean something to you?'

'A little,' agreed Olson. 'Enough to know we're safe.'

'Safe you are,' agreed the man and turned back to Megan. His voice was low and, although quiet, it reverberated with an almost dreamlike quality. 'Come, make the descent with us and I will show you our world, as I showed Myra.'

Startled, Megan looked to Olson, who gave the briefest of nods. He may have said he felt safe, but his looks assured her the descent to wherever it was they were going was a journey they were in no position to refuse.

The huge man moved towards Megan and reached out for her flashlight. She fought back a resurgent stab of fear to hand it to him. He snapped it off and, for a terrible moment, the world went dark. Then, from the tip of the staff, came a soft, yellow glow. The light grew steadily brighter, enveloping the whole group. Its quality, together with the smell of incense, had an overwhelming, calming effect. The man turned and, as a group, they moved off into the depths of the unknown.

020: Mal-Kas

Mal-Kas Mine, 122km Northwest of Skala

JT had been hard pressed to find an appropriate vehicle to make the journey to Mal-Kas. Eventually, he located a Unit of similar age to Hydra that had been split up due to a persistent gas turbine issue. Pegasus 2, as the vehicle was dubbed, carried JT and Ira over the rocky terrain that led upwards into the barren but deposit-rich expanse of the northern mountains. It was rough going, causing Ira to look distinctly uncomfortable.

'So – this trip is legitimate, you said?' he asked JT, speaking up above the hum of the turbine through the bulkhead beside them.

'Yes, totally legitimate. I've got a list of equipment Hellinar Research lent the contractor, a company called 'MineVision'. No one's seen it since. In truth this visit's overdue.'

'Sounds an inventive name,' said Ira sarcastically. 'Will we have to go into the mine?'

'Probably, yes.'

'I don't much like dark places,' said Ira nervously. He shivered, momentarily reliving a previous experience.

'Well, you'd better get used to the idea. Mines are a very harsh environment at the best of times.'

'You've been in one before?'

'A long time ago. I've tried to avoid them since, but needs must if we're going to find Connor.'

'Maybe you find Connor, and I'll take a look around above ground.'

'We'll see how the land lies when we get there.' JT didn't dismiss the suggestion out of hand, although he preferred to have Ira with him.

A rotation later, they reached the bund wall that delineated the outermost edge of the Mal–Kas encampment. The road, a well-travelled track of reddish dirt, took them directly to a sliding gate, which screeched open on a protesting rack and pinion. There was nowhere obvious to park, so JT guided Pegasus 2 toward a prefabricated building marked 'Admin and Ops'. He throttled down and flicked a switch to lower the tailgate. They squeezed between the staggered seats of the cockpit and made their way out through the spacious cargo hold.

'Are they expecting us?' asked Ira, more out of interest than concern.

'Absolutely,' JT reassured him. 'As far as anyone's aware, this is all routine.'

Their boots thumped dully down the metal ramp and out onto the dirt. Being slightly west of Skala, the sun hung a little higher in the clear blue sky. The heat was dry and parched but about the same intensity as it was within the city. The surrounding mountains limited the breeze but there was enough to cool the skin, albeit with the abrasiveness of fresh, dry dust. They had taken only a few steps towards the office before a door opened, banging unrestrained against a cladded exterior. A short, stocky man emerged, his face sweaty and red.

'You're from Hellinar Research?' he asked in a gravelly and altogether unfriendly tone.

'That's right,' said JT.

'And what is it you want exactly?'

JT put on his warmest smile. 'We've come to check on some of our equipment. MineVision has had it on loan, we just want to check on its condition and that it's still required. Just routine.'

The man reached them and halted, eyeing the pair closely and apparently not liking what he saw. 'What do you know about mining?' He narrowed his eyes and spat at the dirt to emphasise his displeasure.

'Not much, Mr...?'

'Farkus. Mitch Farkus. Now you listen here, anything we got, you gave us and we're keeping. You're not taking anything away, you hear?'

'We're not here to take anything away, Mr Farkus. We're merely going to check on the equipment, make sure it's still in place and the maintenance has been kept to schedule.'

Farkus wrinkled his nose and scowled at them with one withering eye. It was such a deliberate gesture, JT wondered if the other eye worked. 'You're joking, right? Maintenance out here? You've got more chance maintaining an ornamental aquatic lily farm than mining kit out here. Where in the name of the Matriarch would we get the parts?'

'Well, from us if you need them, Mr Farkus,' said JT deprecatingly.

Farkus glowered again. 'Your lot give us squat. You might as well get back in that clapped-out turbine truck and run back to your comfy little air-con office.' When neither JT nor Ira moved he followed up with, 'Be gone you arseholes.'

'Mr Farkus,' JT began again, but was interrupted by Ira.

'Listen, you fat old shit. We've come to look at the stuff and no more than that. Either you show us and we go merrily on our way, or we go merrily on our way and ten more like us turn up next shift. Now, what'll it be?'

JT, though startled, was impressed by the reaction this outburst elicited. Farkus scrunched his nose and gave a long, disgustingly dry sniff. 'What are you looking for? Exactly what are you looking for?'

JT sensed it was a guarded question, but had his answer ready. Farkus, of course, didn't know it mattered little what they saw. JT reached into his jumpsuit and brought out a wad of paper, most of it blank. He made to rifle through it until he apparently found what he wanted.

'We're looking for a drill rig, two jumbos, three boggers and an LV.' In truth, JT had only the faintest idea what any of this meant although he had figured out an LV was a light vehicle.

Farkus began to laugh, a rasping sound from deep in his belly, but it was at least a laugh of genuine humour.

'Do you know how long an LV lasts in a mine?'

'I'm not sure,' said JT. 'Probably not long?'

Farkus' laugh quickly became a wracking cough. Between convulsions he managed to get out, 'About four bloody cycles, that's how long. Bloody things get run over regularly.'

'Run over?' asked JT with a frown.

'Yeah, run over. Crushed. Have you seen a tram truck before?'

Thinking back to his last mine visit, JT got his point. 'Two storeys high, three-metre wheels, usually yellow? Is that a tram truck?'

'Usually yellow, ha! That's a good one. Will have to remember that one for the girls and boys,' Farkus roared. 'So you've been to a mine before?'

'It was half a decade ago, Mr Farkus, but yes.'

Farkus seemed to be pacified a little by this. 'You go down?'

'Yes.'

'You remember the prep?'

Farkus was watching him closely, the question clearly a test. 'Yes, I think so. Lots of water, lots of electrolyte.'

'How much?' Farkus interrupted, now paying JT his full attention.

'I guess about ten litres of water, five of electrolyte for a shift. I may be out of date of course.'

Farkus merely nodded.

'I'd need to do a specific-gravity urine test and a breathalyser test.' From beside him, he heard Ira groan.

Farkus' glower relented a fraction. 'Okay, you know enough. You want to see the kit, that's your business.' He spat again and turned to the office. 'You'd better come in. I'll get you kitted out and get one of the girls to take you down. Follow me.'

A half rotation later, JT and Ira stood in the middle of the prefab, clad in hi-vis vests and hard hats. They strapped on carrier packs, filling them with as many bottles of water and electrolyte as they could hold. Small, potassium KOX kits were fastened to their belts by Farkus, whose assurance these would keep them alive for up to a rotation should the air turn bad caused Ira to roll his eyes. Next they provided urine samples and were breathalysed, a test JT was relieved Ira passed.

They stood for a few turns while Farkus radioed for a transport, which duly pulled up in a cloud of acrid dust. The driver, a stocky middle-aged woman who exuded a kind disposition, entered with a bang of the door.

'This is Beth, she'll be your driver,' growled Farkus. 'She'll take you down, show you what you want.'

'Thank you,' said JT, with as much warmth as he could muster.

'Just make sure you bring the kit back once you're done,'

said Farkus. 'And remember, if your piss starts to smell you're dehydrated, so take a drink. Don't try to keep the water cool, though, or else your body'll thermal shock. Just keep it in your packs and if anyone offers you ice don't take it. And there are restricted areas. That means you don't go in there for any reason. You got that?'

'Yes, sir,' said JT evenly but Farkus had already turned his attention to a shabby, wall-mounted monitor. Unimpressed by her boss's attitude, Beth shook her head and led them into the stark sunlight outside. The two men climbed aboard a faded, long-wheelbase truck with an open bed at the rear. Ira took the front seat, hauling the door open and slamming it purposefully behind him. JT climbed into the back without protest, as Beth turned the ignition key and the engine rumbled reluctantly to life. They pulled away, leaving a plume of reddish dust behind them.

'You been here long?' asked Ira.

'Ten cycles,' replied Beth, turning onto a wide dirt roadway that led up and over the crest of an excavated mound. 'I keep the drill rigs supplied and bring the sample slugs up to the surface, mostly.'

The landscape was clearly machine-formed, with rises and falls of consistent gradient levelling off only where other, wider roadways intersected their path. Cresting the rise, JT leaned forward to get his first view of the vastness of the excavated caldera that lay before them. It was truly huge, almost too big to comprehend the scale. The pit was 200 metres deep and terraced to provide roadways. Dust-caked tipper trucks moved around the various levels; even from this distance they were clearly enormous.

Beth, who saw the same sight several times a shift, concentrated on the road but noted the interest of her passengers. The roadway became bumpy as they passed a large artificial pond, which both men regarded intently.

'That's the sump. It provides water for drill coolant and dust suppression.'

'Is that a problem, the dust?' asked Ira.

'Yeah,' said Beth. 'It's a huge problem. You'll get the idea, trust me.'

They descended a series of steep inclines that had been cut between levels. 'What exactly is it you want to see?' asked Beth.

JT retrieved his list and handed it over. Beth took a look then thrust it onto the dash. 'You haven't got a hope of telling one bogger from another and as to the LV,' she gave a little laugh, 'that'll be long gone.'

'And the jumbos?' asked JT tentatively.

'Yeah, we might be able to help you there, we only have a handful of them. Do you really need to see the specific stuff on this list or can we just say you saw a couple of jumbos and leave it at that?'

Under normal circumstances JT would have insisted on seeing the actual items, but it was Connor he was interested in. 'Just a couple of jumbos would be fine.'

Ira looked back at him with appreciation, as if JT had taken his first step towards his world.

Turning off the incline onto a lower level, they tracked the wide road around the periphery of the pit. Out in front of them they could see the mine entrance, a wide, black maw of screaming torment. Cable and pipework spilled out of it like tendrils, arching upward as if torturing the mouth in some bio-geological horror. Ira shuddered.

Beth pulled up just short of the entrance and snapped on a hand-held radio. There was a lot of chatter, which she took a moment to assess. During a pause, she keyed the microphone and sought permission to proceed, which she was duly given.

They pulled forward, crossing the threshold into darkness. It took a few moments for their eyes to adjust as the truck's weak headlights illuminated a level dirt floor and rough rocky walls secured with steel mesh. Conduit and cabling were anchored to the walls, sagging between fixings. Bound to a hard line directly above them, a large flexible pipe writhed and pulsed like an enormous suspended earthworm.

Catching Ira's upward gaze, Beth said, 'That group of pipes is called the BACS. The smaller lines supply compressed air and water, both for drilling. The big flexible pipe in the middle supplies atmospheric air. There's electrical conduit up there as well for power and comms.'

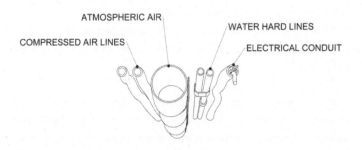

The tunnel began to descend to the right in a constant-radius turn. 'We're on the decline now. That's de-cline emphasising the 'e'. Ya gotta say it right,' she said in a convincing parody of Farkus.

'Got it,' said Ira distractedly.

'We were hoping to meet up with someone down here,' ventured JT, feeling now they were in the mine he could reveal the real reason for their visit. 'A man called Bill Connor. Do you know him?'

'Yeah. Are you two brothers or something? You look nearly identical.'

'No, we've never met,' said JT, noting a smile of justification play across Ira's face.

'I know Connor,' continued Beth with a sigh of resentment. 'We're not supposed to say he's here but who gives a shit, right? What do you want to see him for?'

'Is he here often?'

'No, but you sure know about it when he is.'

'Why?'

'He's pretty mean. It's his job to bully the miners and does he ever enjoy it. Shit!' she exclaimed in sudden alarm. She stood on the brakes as a bright light approached from around the ever-descending spiral. Throwing the truck into reverse she turned and hooked an arm over the headrest of Ira's seat. JT instinctively got out of her line of sight.

'Shit, shit, shit!' she cursed with increasing urgency. 'The bastards are supposed to clear us when there's a gap to at least the first drive.'

The lights were getting bright and the sound of a diesel engine under strain reverberated around them, rapidly increasing in volume. Suddenly, the source of the light and sound became visible. It was one of the tramming trucks they had seen from across the pit but now, when it was nearly on top of them, Ira and JT at last got to put the scale into perspective. It was enormous. Only just fitting the tunnel, it dragged the edge of its huge bucket across a section of wire mesh, ripping it free from the wall as if it were tissue paper. The noise of steel against rock was audible above the diesel, as was the sound of loose rocks crashing to the ground behind it. Up in the cab, Ira could see the driver. He glanced down at the truck beneath him but only for a moment and showed no sign of slowing down for them.

'Isn't he going to stop?' asked Ira with gruff annoyance but little sign of fear.

'Nope,' said Beth. 'He's got to keep to his schedule. It's up to us to get out of the way.'

'Or what?' asked JT.

'Or we're going to leave here a damn sight thinner than we arrived,' said Beth evenly. JT's eyes widened, his pupils contracting in the dazzling headlights of the truck, which was virtually on top of them.

Beth's face assumed a look of total concentration. Without any effort to slow, she flung the steering wheel around, bringing the truck violently into a small cut-out in the wall. She stamped on the brakes, making the truck rock on its worn springs. The tailgate met the mesh-covered wall with a thud as the giant wheels passed by without contact.

Beth got out to survey the damage, leaving JT looking wide-eyed into Ira's unreadable features. There was a wrenching sound from outside as the twisted remains of a rear bumper were pulled away and discarded onto the tunnel floor. Climbing back into the cab, Beth slammed the door with exaggerated force.

'Idiots. They're idiots up there.'

'Up where?' asked Ira.

'Control,' she snarled. She picked up the radio and keyed it, speaking over anyone else who might be talking.

'LV22 here. Who cleared us? 'Cos we just came head-on with a tram.' There was an incomprehensible reply followed by another bark from Beth. 'I don't care what your software says, we damn near got crushed. You need to check the transponder on that tram.' Then almost as an afterthought she said, 'So are we clear now, or no?'

After the reply, which only Beth could understand, she threw the truck into first gear and dumped the clutch. Reaching the rocks knocked down by the tram she got back on the radio. 'Oh, and by the way, your dumb-ass driver hit the wall before the level-one drive. You'd better get someone to repair it.'

JT sensed she would have cheerfully tossed the radio out of the window or, at the very least, switched it off were it not their lifeline. 'Does that happen often?' he asked.

'Yeah, it happens a lot. They have tracking software to follow all the trucks, it's pretty smart but it doesn't always work. The transponders break all the time or reset themselves to the wrong frequencies. It's nobody's fault really, but we lose a lot of LVs like that. It gets really messy when you get two trams head to head. That's not pretty.'

It wasn't much further to level one. It wasn't illuminated, so presumably had yielded as much ore as it was going to. As they continued to spiral down, the temperature climbed fast, as did the humidity. JT had experienced this before, but had forgotten just how oppressive the conditions could be. He was sweating already and took a swig of water.

'Most of the action is down on level four,' Beth continued. 'They're drilling a load of mother-and-daughter holes down there. You know, mapping out the geology to figure out where to dig next? Anyway, the drill rig will be down there, with the jumbos and boggers. Whether they're yours is another matter, but you said you weren't too fussed?'

'I'd rather not go down any further than we have to,' Ira agreed. 'It's pretty damn hot. I don't know how you could spend more than a rotation down here.'

Beth agreed. 'Can you imagine having to sleep in this? No thanks.'

There was something in her tone that made JT feel uneasy. It was a faint cadence that told him that maybe people did sleep down here and he thought back to the conversation he'd had in the Landlord's Arms. He made a mental note but didn't push further, choosing instead to occupy himself by following the meandering path of the pipework in the tunnel roof above.

'We've just passed level three, you won't have noticed 'cos it's been blocked off.' She looked back to JT. 'The stope became unstable. We couldn't secure it, so we abandoned it a few cycles ago.'

'The what? Stope?' he asked.

She shot him a brief, condescending look over her shoulder then explained in a similar tone. 'Yeah, stope. You know, the hole that's formed after you blast the rock out?'

'The cave?' JT said, feeling it sounding dumb even as he said it.

'I suppose,' said Beth. 'I thought you'd been in a mine before?'

JT didn't reply and, when Ira looked back at him with a frown, he just shrugged and said, 'Just not a term I'd heard before.'

It was so hot he was sipping at his water regularly and had noticed Ira doing the same. Beth, it seemed, was made of sterner stuff and had consumed barely half a litre.

A few moments later, they swung left into a side tunnel marked 'Level 4' and pulled over into a large, well-lit siding. They disembarked into the abrasive, unbearably clammy atmosphere. The noise level outside the truck was astoundingly high. Diesel engines growled above the harsh grinding of drills on rock and the hiss of coolant and dust-suppression jets spraying water with abandon.

'Okay then,' said Beth, voice raised. 'Let's find your stuff.'

021: Meridian

Mal-Kas Mine, 122km Northwest of Skala

After the dark of the decline, the cavern was incandescent with stark light. Where old-style vacuum bulbs would have bathed the space in a soft, diffused glow, LEDs struck the rock severely, casting harsh shadows across deep fissures like creases in old flesh.

Beth led them towards one of the huge tram trucks, its bucket fed with rubble by two front-loading diggers. Rock crashed unapologetically against steel walls, battered from cycles of abuse. The dirt-encrusted yellow loaders themselves would have seemed large if not for the scale of the vehicle they were servicing, like Vespidae wasps tending to a queen.

'Those are your boggers, or LHDs if you like,' said Beth, pointing at the two loaders. They resembled the front-end loaders JT was familiar with from Hellinar Research's warehouses on the western outskirts of Skala, facilities like T24. They were low with centre-pivot steering, the cab and bucket up front, a diesel engine that revved with the demand of the hydraulics at the rear. The combined noise of the engines, the scraping of metal across the rock and the crashing of the aggregate was as oppressive as the heat, soot and diesel fumes.

'There's no ventilation down here?' JT shouted ahead to Beth over the din.

'Yeah, it's ventilated,' she called back over her shoulder. 'The decline's pressurised to keep the gases moving. This atmosphere is actually not too bad.'

The two men shared a look, wondering what bad air could be like. They followed Beth out past the boggers and down a smaller, darker side tunnel. The din faded behind them, giving way to the sound of flowing water accompanied by the unmistakable ripping of metal violating rock. Lying before Beth, drowned in glare, was a multi-limbed mechanical manifestation of a Hellinar tarantula spider. What appeared as a corpulent thorax was suspended just off the uneven ground by four sturdy legs that arched out, clawed tips forced hard against the rock floor. High above them, three articulated arms probed high on the walls in an unsteady myopic examination.

One of the arms found its mark and drove itself hard against the rock face above. From halfway down its length, a sliding ram engaged and the high-pitched metallic ring of a spinning rod became audible. The slide moved forward and hydraulic supply piping unwound from a spool mounted behind it. On contact, the rod bowed under load as a hissing spray of water from the drill tip fanned out to cool it. A moment later the fan became an opaque, gushing flow from inside a rapidly deepening borehole.

The atmosphere was even more oppressive than it had been in the main drive behind them. Coolant pouring from drill heads increased the local humidity above already unbearable levels. Sweat mixed with condensation formed a layer of clammy slime on the skin that began to soak slowly into their clothes.

Seemingly oblivious, Beth shouted, 'That's a jumbo' during a pause while the drilling arm probed for its next spot. 'We use them for securing the stope, 'case you're interested. The arm that was just drilling, that's moved on while the other two raise the mesh and drive rock bolts into the holes.'

As she said this, the two men could see a figure off to the side hooking a flexible section of mesh onto a lowered arm. 'That's the nipper. He loads the mesh, the rock bolts and takes care of any other jobs to keep the jumbo operational. He changes drill heads, stops up any coolant leaks and services the chassis. Having a good nipper is the key to making progress down here. They struggle at first, but this guy's pretty good.'

The men nodded as they watched the fluidity of the nipper's work with admiration. A few moments later their attention was pulled away by the sight of a fourth arm carrying a fenced platform on which stood a single female figure.

'That's Desiree Angelo,' said Beth, with a reverence that was hard to miss even above the racket of drilling and splashing. 'She's one of our best. Didn't know she was down here this shift.'

From where they stood they couldn't see exactly what Angelo was doing, but she appeared to be working levers and a keyboard with assured dexterity.

'It's pretty advanced tech,' said Beth. 'Once the pilot hole is sunk, the bolt goes right in there without any assistance. The mesh arm's manual and so is the drill.'

'That's still quite a workload to manage,' shouted Ira.

'Yeah, that's true,' said Beth. 'You seen enough? We can go find you another one to tick off your list soon as you're ready.'

JT nodded vigorously and Beth turned back to step between them. Both men took a last look at the arachnid-like form of the jumbo before turning to follow her.

A second jumbo had been folded and parked up in one of the

many drives that made up Level Four. On its wheels, with its three arms folded and thrust in front of it, it looked more like an insect than an arachnid. JT took a moment to examine it more closely, with the benefit of much-reduced ambient noise.

'You know this one is actually ours,' called JT with delight. 'It says so right here.' He pointed to a plaque attached to the chassis.

'That's great,' replied Beth, with a feigned enthusiasm that made Ira smile. JT, clearly oblivious, joined them to move on down the tunnel. The two men were now breathing hard simply with the exertion of walking.

Entering another stope, they recognised the unmistakable form of a drill rig. Beside it stood a short run of freestanding racking filled with metal tubes on one side and labelled rock slugs on the other. A man and woman conferring over the slugs caught sight of the approaching visitors and turned.

'Beth, hi. You come for the slugs? We're not quite done yet,' said the woman. 'Who are these guys?' she asked.

'The slugs can stay a while,' said Beth and looked back to Ira and JT. 'These gentlemen are from Skala. They're down here to account for some equipment on loan, if you can believe that.'

'Really? Well, okay. Good luck with that,' said the woman.

'Can I look at your drill rig?' asked JT. 'Just to take the serial number?'

'Sure,' said the man and showed him over to the rig. JT found the chassis plate easily and wiped away cycles of crusted dirt. He took down the number and nodded his thanks before making his way over to the two women, who were chatting casually while Ira looked on uncomfortably.

'So you're drilling for metal ore?' asked JT.

'Yeah, the usual. Iron, copper, precious metal if we're lucky. The big money's in bauxite, but you have to go a long way north for that,' said the woman nonchalantly. 'I'm Jo, by the way.'

'JT Gilbert,' said JT. 'So is Mal-Kas rich in ore? Do you find a lot of it?'

Jo gave a short, ironic laugh, spat and moved to lean against the drill rig. 'Not likely. We've been drilling mother-and-daughter holes for cycles, established a meridian reference, but found zip. That's not what the geologists say, of course.'

JT frowned. 'What do they say?' He noticed Beth stiffen and shoot Jo a cautioning look.

Jo, however, either didn't pick up on the warning or chose to ignore it. 'They say we've been extracting ore left, right and centre, but there's no way we have.'

'Why do you say that?' asked Ira, who had also noticed Beth's posture and posed the question as deferentially as he could.

'You can tell without having a geologist here. When you strike ore you know about it. It's much softer than rock, for one thing, so the torque demand on the rig drops rapidly when you hit it. And you can tell from the coolant. When you're boring through rock, the coolant's a dull grey colour and it's gritty. When you hit ore it turns black. We've not seen black coolant in a long old time.'

She seemed to be about to say something else when she caught Beth's eye and reconsidered.

'I'm just saying,' she said, and shrugged at Beth.

Beth relaxed in supplication. 'Yeah, all right. But enough of that now.' She turned to JT and Ira. You seen all you want?'

'Just Connor,' said Ira, who suddenly seemed unnaturally on guard.

'Connor?' said Jo in surprise and a little disgust. 'Why would you want to see him?' JT was about to answer when he caught her narrowing eyes and reassessment as she looked him up and down. 'You look like him,' she said with disapproval. 'You related or something?'

'No, but I'm getting that a lot.'

'He's down Drive 8,' said Jo. 'At least that's where he seems to 'hang out' at the moment.' Again, she seemed to want to elaborate, but hesitated.

'Okay, well, thanks Jo. I'll be back for those samples just as soon as you're ready,' said Beth in a forced, cordial tone before leading the two men back towards the decline.

022: The Descent

Below Skala

Knowing nothing of the dark abyss beyond the reassuring glow of the robed man's staff, Megan and Olson were guided in silence through the dark, open space of the Siphon. With the rest of the group behind them, they followed the light through a low arch and into a narrow passage that led steadily down. Flaking white emulsion clung to rough brickwork eaten away by damp and mildew.

'I don't remember this passageway being on the map,' whispered Megan.

'I don't remember it either, but then we weren't looking for it,' replied Olson in the same hushed tone.

'Have you noticed there are no power cables or pipes on the walls? How long do you think it's been here?' she asked.

'It's pretty old, that's for sure. I can't remember anyone whitewashing walls in my lifetime.'

Megan leaned in, nodding towards their guide. 'Who do you suppose he is? Their leader?'

Olson narrowed his eyes, focusing on the figure striding in front of them, his ragged robe billowing out as he walked.

'I don't think he's a "leader", even if these Hadje people have one. If I were to guess I would say he's a shaman.'

'A what?' asked Megan, unfamiliar with the word.

'A shaman, a sort of spiritual man.'

'He said they knew Myra, the technician from the Vault,' whispered Megan with an urgent excitement.

Olson cocked his head towards her in confidence. 'I'd be reluctant to jump to that conclusion. I spent a few rotations with her and she doesn't strike me as the sort to go wandering the underground of Skala. Myra's not an uncommon name. It could just be a coincidence.'

Sceptical, but not wishing to push her luck, Megan stayed silent. Reaching a second low arch, the Shaman came to an abrupt halt. He looked back over their heads and Megan could see his eyes searching. Was he counting? Seemingly satisfied, he looked to the two outsiders, the vertical pupils of his strange eyes narrowing down to slits. Megan sensed airflow from beyond the arch. The Shaman's robes billowed as if being sucked out into the dark void beyond. His long fingers tightened around his staff.

'This arch marks the descent into the Deep Wells, into Buni Sound. The descent is perilous. From here there is no going back.'

Megan wondered at this, sure that they had crossed that point the moment they had entered the Siphon. To her left, she saw Olson straighten, accepting the challenge. His voice acquired a hard edge she had not heard before.

'What will we face?' he asked.

'You will see soon enough,' replied the Shaman.

From behind them, a second man spoke up for the first time. His tone was level and strong, more human by far than the other-worldly speech of the Shaman. Megan picked up an inflection she didn't recognise, a strange but beautiful lilt of pronunciation.

'Watch your footing, there are steps missing. And don't touch the indigenes, they're poisonous.'

'Poisonous?' asked Megan, turning in alarm.

'Leave them alone and they won't harm you. If you stand on one, keep your foot on it and call for me, call for Jean-Louis.'

'Jean-Louis,' repeated Megan, finding the knowledge of a single name in this mysterious group infinitely comforting. The man himself was much shorter than the Shaman and had a clean, strong face. Like the rest, his skin was dark and had an ebony-like quality to it.

'You were right,' he said, looking at Olson then lifting his chin towards the figure standing in the archway. 'He is our Shaman. I am his Second Spirit. What is it you are called?'

'Megan Devin,' said Megan hesitantly.

'Tyler Olson,' said Olson.

Jean-Louis looked at him and nodded with an appreciation that Megan didn't understand. 'What is a Second Spirit?' she asked.

'I will explain,' said Jean-Louis. 'But not here. We should start the descent.'

The Shaman turned to face the arch, lowered his staff and stepped through, disappearing down as if into the bowels of the earth.

Beyond the arch, the tunnel angled sharply downward and narrowed enough to force the group into single file. Hunched beneath the low ceiling, the Shaman led, with Olson directly behind him. Megan followed, occasionally falling back a little but never out of view of the yellowish glow from the staff. They came to smooth steps, worn by uncounted cycles of use. The walls became heavily angled, leaning in from the left, the path curving sharply to the right. It forced Megan to support herself against the right-hand wall and shuffle herself forward with the aid of her forearm.

In the dim light of the staff she could see the construction of the walls; the brickwork was like no arrangement she had seen before. The bricks themselves were narrow rectangles laid at angles so they meshed perpendicular to each other. This formed a pattern that brought to mind the tyre tread of the desert vehicles Kyra had shown her, on the rare occasions Megan had accompanied her to the repair or storage yards.

They continued in silence, winding ever downward. Megan began to notice breaks in the walls where bricks had either fallen out or never been laid. The exposed rock in these gaps was rough and at times harboured what looked like burrowed holes. Crawling from one of them was a creature the size of her arm, moving forward on a myriad of tiny legs. Its thick, fur-covered body bore bright red stripes running from its eyeless head to a bulbous tail. The legs moved in unison, forming a series of rippling waves down its length.

'Millipede,' said Jean-Louis from behind her. 'The red ones are poisonous but rarely deadly. If you hop your arm across, it won't pay you any attention.'

Megan did so and was aware of Jean-Louis doing the same behind her. 'So there are others that are deadly?' she asked with nervous humour.

'Absolutely,' he replied in his elegant, clipped tone. 'It's the bigger, darker ones that live lower down that you need to look out for. The centipedes, the ones with less legs and segmented bodies are dangerous as well.'

Megan was unsure what alarmed her more – the idea that as far down as they had travelled was considered high, or that the creepy-looking monster on the wall was apparently small and docile. Up until this point she had pushed any feelings of claustrophobia back in her mind but now, knowing she would be surrounded by deadly, freakish-looking creatures in such a confined space, it rushed up at her full force.

Recognising her momentary fear, Jean-Louis spoke from behind her, 'Don't worry, the walls get easier to manage the further down we go.'

And this proved to be the case. As they continued to descend, the walls became noticeably more upright and their curve shallower. Conversely, encounters with the red millipedes became more frequent and Megan found herself stepping over and ducking under them every few steps. From in front of her, the Shaman made what seemed to be a short lunge. Olson did the same, performing more of a jump due to his shorter stature. Moments later, when Megan came to the place, she saw a gap in the steps.

Jean-Louis grasped her forearm with a warm, dry hand to steady her. Without knowing it she had stared down through the gap and nearly fallen forwards. There was a distinct glow of violet emanating from deep below where she had expected only darkness.

She looked back at the Second Spirit, who merely said, 'Steady. There are a few of these.'

Vaulting the gap, she took a few hasty steps to make up a little ground on Olson, who was now further ahead than she was comfortable with. Without warning, she felt a soft crunch under her left foot and heard a screech of such high pitch it was barely audible. Realising at once what she had done, she fought off every instinct to move and with committed control kept pressure on her left leg. The screech came again and she shut her eyes, tilting her head to the ceiling as if for divine intervention. She could feel the creature squirming, its soft fur brushing the side of her calf. Before a rising panic took her, she managed to speak.

'Jean-Louis?'

To her relief he was there already, calmly bending to reach around her. She heard him grunt, then a soft squelching sound accompanied by yet another screech on the limit of her hearing. Then the squirming stopped.

'Lift your foot slowly,' said Jean-Louis with a level voice. 'You don't want to get poison on you. It stays active for a few hours and it's very easy to get contaminated later, when you remove your clothes.'

She heard the scrape of a knife against the rough rock of the wall and supposed he was cleaning the blade. She became aware of a scuttling around her, as if many creatures were fleeing, winding themselves into the hole-ridden walls.

'Try not to do that again,' he said in mild rebuke. Then, returning to his matter-of-fact tone, 'We should get moving. Others will be attracted to the body.'

'Because of the sound?'

'You could hear it?' he asked, surprised. 'No, not because of the sound – they are attracted by the smell. They are cannibalistic, they eat their own.'

'Oh, right,' said Megan absently and, with eyes wide open, moved forward once again. 'You said the poison stays active for an hour. What's an hour?'

'It's an older measure of time,' said Jean-Louis. 'It's roughly what you would call a rotation.'

'Okay…' said Megan, confused.

They continued navigating the occasional gaps with care. As the walls became near-vertical, Jean-Louis moved more confidently and she felt able to do the same. Their progress became faster the further down they went and Megan found that, without the distraction of the odd walls, she was able to negotiate the scuttling creatures with greater ease.

Their progress continued at this pace for an indeterminate

time before the Shaman abruptly stopped ahead of them. He drew himself up to his full height, letting out an audible breath.

'Beyond this doorway lie the Deep Wells. This passage you have travelled is sacred and I wish you to know that only few have been granted a right to it. Fewer still have set foot in Buni Sound.'

Olson stood stock-still, Megan nodded, fearful of what lay beyond. The Shaman looked down at the glowing tip of his staff. It illuminated the features of his face, played off the rings in his hair and highlighted the swirling tattoos on his arms. Then, as if sucking in all light from the world, it blinked out.

023: The Deep Wells

Below Skala

When the Shaman's light went out, Olson and Megan took a moment to adjust. They blinked in the cool breeze that rushed in from beyond the breach before them. The air felt cold and damp as it spiralled upwards to a world that lay almost forgotten above them.

To their surprise, the two up-worlders discovered they were not surrounded by darkness at all. The Shaman stood facing them, his tall form distinct in silhouette. The faint, violet glow they had seen through the gaps of missing steps during the descent caught the edges of his tattered robe and reflected off the beads in his plaited hair. They couldn't make out his face, but both recognised the nod of his head indicating for them to follow, before he ducked through the doorway.

Olson took a few steps forward, followed by Megan. As she reached the doorway she looked back at Jean-Louis for assurance. His stare was fixed purposefully past her, suggesting there was little option but to continue. Olson stepped through the doorway and disappeared into the illustrious glow of violet. Swallowing hard, she braced herself, and followed.

What awaited her on the other side was the very last thing she expected. The vista was not a dark, dirty nest of monstrous centipedes, but a thing of wonder and beauty. As she took it in, the past few rotations of hell suddenly started to make sense.

She stood on a wide ledge that extended from the base of a huge, perfectly formed dome. The descent was a staircase that wound between its inner and outer skins. The uppermost part of the dome was sharply curved, the arc of the walls becoming gentler and almost vertical towards the base. Squinting, she could see small, dark gaps where the missing steps had fallen.

Equally astonishing was what lay stretched out beneath her. Lit by numberless ultraviolet lights that refracted through its smooth surface was a vast body of water. From where Megan stood, it appeared bottomless. Never in her wildest dreams had she guessed such a place existed so far beneath the city. It was the most magnificent place she had ever set eyes on. And it was cold; a natural cold unlike the artificially induced cool of air conditioning. She took a deep lungful of the damp, frigid air and exhaled slowly with the pleasure of a first, exalted taste.

Standing beside her, Olson was clearly moved. He stared into the abyssal depths of the clean, translucent pool. He looked across to the Shaman, who returned his stare and spoke with a calm knowing. 'All who look upon the Deep Wells for the first time share your awe.'

'I never expected...' But he couldn't finish.

'Come.'

The Shaman turned and led the way down a gently curving set of stone steps. Olson shook his head, turned and followed. Megan did the same, escorted by Jean-Louis, who began to recount a brief history of Buni Sound.

'You are wondering what this place is. It was built at Skala's birth. The site of the city was chosen in part because of the huge natural caves that lie below it. A similar reservoir was built underneath the city of Kul, but it was built far too late and designed badly. According to accounts of the time, the

Kul Reservoir was built close to the surface, and had a roof supported by stone columns that in little time were eroded by the water. You have heard of the blight that overcame the city?'

'Yes,' said Megan. 'Everyone knows about it.'

'Although not its cause. The infections and disease that spread were accelerated because the city's water supply was tainted. Collapsed parts of the reservoir were open to vermin, who nested and bred, spreading their plague into the water system as they did so.'

'But what about the water from outside the city?' asked Megan. 'Wasn't Kul built next to a natural lake?'

'Indeed,' Jean-Louis nodded, following them across a level platform before descending the next set of steps. 'Much like Skala was, before evaporation reduced Lake Eiraye to what it is now. In the last shifts of Kul, building and engineering techniques were not advanced enough to bring water back to the city without huge leakage. Moisture traps and underground storage were never sufficient. Hellinar had drawn too close by that time. When over half of Kul's population were dying, the first footings of Skala were built and it seems the architects ensured such a situation would never reoccur.'

'And that's what this place is? A huge water reserve?' asked Megan.

'Yes, although the water here is connected to the main supply system so it does not grow stagnant. It is a reserve, but it's periodically replenished as an amount of it is pumped to the city above. The purple lights you see are to kill bacteria and any other micro-organisms in the water. Further filtration is not required.'

Megan looked at him, puzzled. 'But there is a huge company, Purerefine, that filters the water above ground... it costs a fortune.'

Jean-Louis looked at her and shrugged. 'Further filtration is not required.'

She looked to Olson, who wore a faraway look and offered only a momentary absent smile. They continued in silence, punctuated only by the occasional drip of moisture from high above. They were heading towards a wide, square opening on the far side of the dome; an entrance, above which was carved a similar symbol to the one they had observed above the archway that led to the Siphon. Beyond the opening, Megan saw the flicker of flame, contrasting with the gently rippling reflections of the water that played upon the brickwork of the dome.

'What's in there?' she asked, indicating with a nod towards the opening.

'Our city,' said Jean-Louis. 'Buni Sound.'

The entrance to Buni Sound was bathed in a warm, orange glow that danced across the smooth, red brick of the walls. It was a sensation Megan had never experienced before. She had heard Katherine talk of the wonderful cosiness of a fire out on the ice planes of Ayon. It was pleasant beyond her expectation. Rising up from a rectangular pit set into the flagstone floor, it ran the length of the hallway in which they now stood. Black coals smouldered at the edges, becoming ashen grey towards the middle of the trough.

The Shaman was still walking some distance in front of them. Noticing his staff had disappeared, Megan looked around, but didn't see it. She shrugged the thought off – there was enough strangeness in this place that anything might have happened. Entering a large open space at the end of the hallway he turned left and disappeared from sight.

Led by Jean-Louis, they entered thriving living quarters which were spacious and meticulously clean. Unlike the ragged robes of the Shaman and the group she and Olson had encountered in the Siphon, the other inhabitants of Buni Sound were dressed in vibrantly coloured fabric garments of eclectic design. The Buni Sound Hadje filled a vast room at the end of the hallway with colour, chatter and laughter.

'There must be several hundred people here,' said Olson in wonder.

'Just over three hundred,' Jean-Louis affirmed.

'There are so many children,' said Megan, as small groups of youngsters ran in and out of the arches and gathered adults.

'Yes,' agreed the Second Spirit. 'We are not shackled by the same physiological constraints as your people. We can breed almost at will.' He gave a wry smile. 'Sometimes it is a benefit and at others, well, less so. I'll show you to my quarters. My wife will look after you. If you don't mind, I'd like to change.'

'We don't mind at all,' said Olson.

As they followed Jean-Louis around the edge of the space, Megan began to take in the people. All had the smooth, ebony skin that made the Hadje so distinctive. They spoke in a multitude of accents, some with Jean-Louis' beautiful lilt, others more like the Shaman's deeper, drawn-out speech. The walls flanking the vast atrium were lined with pale arches set into the smooth, red brick, each illuminated by a pair of gently flaming metal torches. Visible beyond them were open spaces linked to other rooms and corridors.

Under one of the nearer arches, sitting in a circle, were a group of women. Megan caught the unmistakable tone and accompanying laughter of gossip. The women were sewing. What they were sewing she couldn't see, but the sense of community was clear.

Jean-Louis led them under one of the arches at the far end of the chamber and into a passageway of smaller rooms. The smell of cooking wafted through the cool air in aromatic waves from a roomy alcove in which stood a rounded, motherly-looking woman flanked by two small children.

'Daddy!' cried the children in unison and ran to him, each grabbing a leg.

'They missed you, Jean-Louis,' the woman said, beaming at him. 'I missed you too,' she added and embraced him warmly. After a moment she pulled away and looked to Megan and Olson, as if only just noticing their presence. 'And we have guests,' she exclaimed in a tone of genuine pleasure.

'We do. This is Megan Devin and Tyler Olson.'

'I'm Hesta,' she said, looking at Jean-Louis in mocking reproach. 'He never introduces me.'

Megan forced a half-convincing smile as Jean-Louis, looking a little chastened, apologised. As if to make amends he introduced his children. 'These two monsters are Michelle and Deain.'

Hesta regarded Olson closely. 'An Olson,' she said in a questioning tone. 'We knew an Olson.'

'You may well have done,' he replied, with a smile but no further explanation.

'Well, I expect you will be hungry if you've travelled all the way down here. I'll take them for something to eat while you get out of those filthy rags and into something more presentable.' She looked at her husband. 'Then I'll sort out some bedding. You look exhausted, Miss Megan.'

'I am. We both are,' said Megan.

'We would be very grateful,' Olson added.

'I'll see you shortly,' Jean-Louis reassured the two up-worlders while trying in vain to free his leg from Michelle's crushing grip.

Following Hesta, they discovered that the Hadje, much like the poorer citizens of Skala, ate communally, something Megan appreciated. When their father and mother were distracted, she and Kyra had sneaked down to one of the food halls of the Western Fringe with what few links they had and delighted in the food, song and camaraderie. The sisters had loved the hubbub and were occasionally gifted a small glass of wine each by a mischievous proprietor. It made for a heady mix, which Kyra revelled in.

They sat themselves cross-legged on embroidered cushions around a low, square table of light-coloured wood. Megan took in the room with delight – the candle-lined walls and the low ceiling that arched across the warm chatter from many tables. She noticed a man, light-skinned like herself, sitting a few tables away. She nudged Olson, who smiled in recognition. The man seemed to notice them at the same time and raised his head to them in silent acknowledgement.

'Hesta, who's that?' she asked.

'Who? The up-worlder? He's one of the bards. Dylan Samuel I think his name is. Jean-Louis will know.'

Jean-Louis appeared with the children, who ran to settle themselves on either side of Megan. Their proximity to her, a stranger, didn't seem to bother them at all. The boy, Deain, grinned up at her. She smiled back as an arm reached over her bearing a platter filled with toasted flatbread and assorted root vegetables surrounding a large, skewered centipede.

Megan recoiled in horror, remembering the skittering, poisonous creatures in the upper dome. Jean-Louis caught her discomfort and sought to calm her.

'Don't worry, they're not dangerous when cooked properly. They are considered a delicacy in Buni Sound. Please...' he gestured for her to take one of the body segments. They smelled delicious but looked like something from the worst kind of nightmare. With great reluctance, she reached out, taking hold of the very end of the skewer. She was followed swiftly by Hesta and the two children. Megan stared at the charred body of the creature, trying to keep her revulsion from showing.

The children showed no such reserve, both dragging the meat sideways off the sticks with their teeth.

'It's really very nice, dear,' said Hesta, displaying more delicacy than the children had done.

Megan shut her eyes and, with the feeling of diving off a very high building, took a bite. Hesta was right, it was very edible, once you got past the look of the thing.

'You said you would explain about the Second Spirit?' Olson asked Jean-Louis, while reaching for a skewer himself.

'A Shaman is a spiritual man,' he began. 'He can travel to the spirit world but it is possible for him to remain trapped there. A Second Spirit is a Shaman's anchor to this world. I travel with him but I remain partly here as well.'

'I see,' said Olson. 'And do you do that often?' he asked.

'No,' said Jean-Louis. 'It is some time since we travelled that path. But I feel the time is coming to travel it again soon.'

Hesta looked a little concerned at this statement, but didn't protest.

'So you are Olson?' said Jean-Louis, with a familiarity that caught Megan's attention. She couldn't restrain her curiosity any longer.

'Do you know these people, Tyler?' she asked, sounding more impetuous than she'd meant to.

'No,' he said. 'But I think my wife did.'

Jean-Louis nodded seriously. 'Helenka was a friend of ours.'

'You knew her personally?'

'She stayed with us from time to time. We were sorry to hear of her passing.'

Hesta nodded, sadness and compassion in her face.

'She was a storyteller, a bard,' Olson explained to Megan. 'She didn't speak of the Hadje, certainly not by name, but she told me enough that I understood the people that dwell beneath the city were kind and wise. She told me they possess a great knowledge of the past, the present and our place in the world, such as it is.' He smiled, looking to Jean-Louis and Hesta for approval, which both duly gave.

'I feel it a great privilege to finally walk in her footsteps.' He was not a man given to speech-making and these last words drove home the compassion Megan felt towards him.

'Tonight you will sleep in her bed,' said Jean-Louis with gravity. Hesta shot him a look of daggers which he clearly understood and quickly clarified his offer. 'If it would not upset you unduly, of course.'

Olson cleared his throat, clearly choked. 'That would put me at peace,' he agreed, softly holding back tears. Tears of happiness or sadness? Megan didn't know but she preferred to remember the moment as a happy one.

Presently, the children became fidgety and Hesta scooped them up to take them home. The others followed not far behind. Megan came last of all. A profound feeling of solitude had descended upon her and she spoke little as the children were put to bed and her accommodation organised. Hesta fussed over the bedding, making sure her guests were comfortable before turning in herself. Eventually the firelight of the surrounding pits faded and sleep overcame them all. It was hard to resist given the events of the past rotations and the comfort of the heat in the cool air. The smells and slumbering life brought a drowsiness that calmed both the body and the soul. They slept deeply, for a while.

024: Connor

As Beth drove the LV through the never-ending maze of high, wide tunnels, JT considered how easy it would be to get lost in a place where one drive looked much like another. Drive 8 was not simply a spur off the decline but a vast network in its own right. Compared to the stope they had left an indeterminate time before, it was eerily quiet, with only the sound of the LV's engine and the spattering of tyres on wet rock for company.

Beth remained uncharacteristically quiet, which made the two men apprehensive. Presently, she brought the LV to a halt, opened the door and climbed out.

'Connor should be down there,' she said, looking long into the tunnel ahead but making no move to proceed.

'You're not coming with us?' asked Ira, in a gruff, questioning tone.

'No,' she said simply. 'Further down is the restricted area. Well, one of them anyway. Do yourselves a favour and stay out of it.'

'How do we find Connor?' asked JT.

'He'll find you, don't worry about that,' she said, with a trace of irony. 'Drive 8 doesn't get used much, so watch the puddles, try not to step in them. The stagnant water down here tends to suck in sulphur dioxide. If you disturb the water it gets kicked back into the atmosphere and it doesn't half smell bad. Hurts your eyes too. Just try to avoid any standing water from here on.'

'Okay, will do,' said JT, grateful for the advice.

'Let's go,' said Ira and nodded.

Walking any distance down here was hard going, as they had already discovered. The relative quiet helped a little – it was one less bombardment on the senses. They could still hear the occasional crash and echo of the operations far behind them but they were faint and indistinct.

Once they were out of Beth's hearing both men instinctively dropped their guard a little.

'There's something very wrong here,' said Ira.

'I know what you mean. I can't put my finger on it, but you're right.'

'Did you see the way Beth reacted to the rig operator talking about the ore they recover?'

'Or don't recover,' JT interjected. 'Yes, I did notice. She wasn't happy. What do you suppose these restricted sections are?'

'No idea,' said Ira. 'I'm not entirely sure I want to find out.'

'How are we going to handle Connor?'

'I've no idea on that either. See how it plays out. The last thing we want is a scuffle. I'm not sure I'd have the energy to do much damage down here even if I wanted to.'

'I second that,' said JT, who was still suffering with the after-effects of Ira's attentions of a few shifts earlier.

There was no missing the entrance to the restricted area. The tunnel was artificially reduced in both height and width by battered steel panels that had been riveted together to form a sort of bulkhead between the mine and whatever lay beyond.

A black opening, just big enough to admit an LV, had been left at its centre.

'What do you think we should do?' asked JT absently.

'I don't know,' said Ira, his voice betraying his growing unease. He looked around at the walls and ceiling. 'You see those sensors up there?'

JT squinted in the direction Ira was looking. 'Yes, I see them. There's more in the walls. Do you think they're motion sensors?'

'I guess so. Maybe they're cameras. They really seem keen not to let anyone in here.'

They heard the unmistakable sound of a roller shutter being raised on a chain pull from somewhere in the darkness. Presently, the rattling and screeching stopped and the roller shutter was held open before being allowed to drop closed again under its own weight. In the momentary pause between the door being open and shut, JT was sure he heard a scream from somewhere deep in the darkness. Human or animal, he couldn't be sure.

A moment later a man strode out from the dark aperture. To JT and Ira's shared horror, he was stowing a long, curved knife into a sheath at his right hip. He moved in the manner of a man caught doing something he shouldn't but not particularly caring. He was younger than they had expected and dressed in nondescript sandy grey fatigues similar to those JT had seen worn by the Rika on the few occasions he had encountered them in field dress. His hair was shorter than JT's, and divided by a curved scar that ran from his right ear around to the back of his head.

'Who the bloody hell are you? What you doing here?' the man demanded as he came to an abrupt halt uncomfortably close to them. Such was his resemblance to JT, they knew it was Connor. Connor himself, now giving the pair his full attention, also recognised the similarity.

'It this some sort of joke?' he said, scowling at JT. While they might have looked similar, their manner couldn't have been more different. Even the way they stood was different. Where JT, admittedly nervous if not fearful, held himself with an easy fluidity, Connor in contrast had a forced stiffness.

'No joke,' said JT, with a little diffidence. 'I've been hearing how much we look alike all shift. It's getting a little stale, if I'm honest.'

Connor laughed. 'Well, I never. You sure we're not brothers? Your daddy wasn't running around doing the dirty on Mummy?' His face creased with spite.

JT had never met anyone who could start a sentence with humour and finish it with such malevolence. 'Pretty sure. They were both dead within a cycle of my appearance and if I'm not mistaken I'm older than you.'

'So who are you then?'

'Gilbert. JT Gilbert, Hellinar Research. I'm a quartermaster.'

'Well that is very interesting, Mr Gilbert. What is a quartermaster doing in Mal-Kas mine? And who's this fellow?' Ira bristled a little but said nothing.

'This is Ira,' said JT. 'We've been looking for some equipment that was lent to MineVision way back. It's long overdue an inspection.'

Connor growled in disapproval but seemed to accept the explanation as legitimate. 'There's no kit back here, Mr Gilbert. This area is restricted, like it says on that sign above the door, so you can be on your way now.'

'Actually,' said JT with more confidence than he felt, 'we were hoping to talk to you about some equipment that's not at Mal-Kas. As far as we know,' he added.

Connor's eyes narrowed and it occurred to JT that Hydra

might not be the only theft facilitated by this man. There seemed no point holding back so he came straight out with it, trying hard to resist a glance at the machete as he did so.

'Hydra, a three-vehicle desert Unit. There's some paperwork with your name on it and we wondered, since we were here, if you could shed any light on it?' Even to himself JT's tone sounded infuriatingly superior but he didn't know how else to play the part.

'Paperwork? What paperwork?' said Connor with a snarl. JT got the distinct impression paperwork was not Connor's thing.

'Well, not so much paperwork, more that you were in and out of the office the transponder was delivered to, and we wondered why.'

Connor's expression changed very slightly. It was only just perceptible but he seemed almost to relax. His shoulders might have dropped – maybe by only a few millimetres, it was hard to tell, but his posture had somehow lost a little of its stiffness. His demeanour was subtly different too, his hostility taking on the air of assuming a role in contrast to the genuine disdain he had previously displayed.

'T24? My access to that facility's official.'

'No one is doubting that, Mr Connor,' said JT deferentially. 'We just want to know where Hydra went and that it will be returned. If it's been commandeered on an official or semi-official basis, by the Rika for example, we would be grateful to have that confirmed.'

Connor looked to Ira, then back to JT and scrutinised him. Something felt wrong here. It was as if the conversation was playing out as Connor expected, almost as if it were scripted. It made no sense, but JT concluded it was better to let it run its course and see where it led.

'It was official. Don't ask me how or why, I don't know. I was hired by an intermediary, a man called Garnet. Can't tell you if that's his real name or not. I don't know who was behind moving it or why it had to be converted to run in Ayon. That never made much sense to me – why steal a desert Unit and convert it? Easier just to steal an Ice Runner.'

'So it was stolen,' said JT, seeking confirmation.

'Like I told you, it was official but it had to be done on the quiet. Garnet's employer was official, my access was arranged to be official. I don't know the detail, but it was legit. They even got me to take photographs when they got to the slums to pick up the rest of the crew.'

Connor reached backwards and unclipped the flap of a pouch strung from his belt, his dark eyes never leaving JT's own. Carefully he withdrew something and brought it forward for them to take.

'I kept one photo back for myself. Insurance, like. It's a bit basic, but you might as well have it. I figure they're deep into the ice by now and if you're looking into it I'd prefer to stay on the side of the great and the good.'

'Thank you,' said JT, amazed by this turn of events. He took the photograph and examined it. Even at postcard size and in black and white it clearly showed Hydra, one of the vehicles replete with snow chains, pulled up across the foreground. In front of it stood six figures all in plain jumpsuits, their faces wrapped up against the dust. Or, as JT thought more likely, to conceal their identities. In the background he recognised the shanty town of Gygath.

'Why did they want photographs?' asked Ira, speaking for the first time.

'Haven't a clue, my son,' said Connor. 'Maybe they just wanted to capture the moment. Still, good thing I kept that one for you boys isn't it?'

'Thank you,' said JT, still scrutinising the picture.

'So what's back there?' asked Ira after a pause.

Connor's reaction was so swift that JT was shocked out of concentration with such speed it confused him. In a single motion the man had drawn his blade and had it to Ira's throat, their faces now only centimetres apart.

JT took a step back as Connor snarled, teeth bared at Ira like an animal. For a moment the blade caught the light above, revealing a slick, dark liquid flecked across its surface. His hearts seemed to miss a beat.

'What's back there is nothing to do with you son. I'm a polite gentleman most of the time, so I'll ask you nicely, once, to get the hell out of here before I have to ask again. I don't like asking twice. It shows an impoliteness on the part of the person I'm asking and I don't like impolite people.'

Very slowly he withdrew the knife. 'Understood?' he said and took a step back. 'Are we done here, Mr Gilbert?'

'I think we are,' said JT, who, to his own surprise, managed to keep his voice from betraying the fear he felt. 'Thank you for the photograph.'

Connor said nothing more. He turned and walked away from them, sheathing the knife as he did so. As he reached the opening he seemed to mumble something. JT couldn't hear the words but the tone implied a debt had been discharged. A moment later they heard the rapping of knuckles on the roller shutter and it screeched open. JT strained to hear beyond as the roller paused at the top of its travel but heard nothing. It ran down its guides, slamming into the unseen floor in the darkness.

'Well that was fun,' said Ira. 'I don't know about you, but that guy scares the shit out of me.'

'Me too,' said JT, releasing a breath he might have been holding throughout the encounter. 'Come on, let's get out of here.'

He pocketed the photograph, still astonished and a little

confused to possess it. They turned to head back to Beth and then to the relative cool of the outside world.

025: The Shaman

Below Skala

Megan awoke with a jolt, unsure of where she was. She blinked her eyes into focus, the red brick of the walls and pale grey of the flagstone floor bringing memories of the previous shift back to her. Olson lay a metre away, snoring gently. She sat up, stretching her stiff, aching muscles.

The air was cool and quiet. The occasional pocket of warmth drifted in from a fire somewhere in the corridor beyond. She got up and straightened her jumpsuit, ironing out wrinkles with the flats of her hands, and made her way to the doorway. Enjoying the cold, abrasive feel of the stone under her bare feet, she wondered how hot the stone near the fire pits that heated and illuminated the corridors got and kept her distance.

The passageways were silent, although she was aware of the presence of sleeping humanity all around her. She was careful not to stray into anyone's private space, keeping to the thoroughfares and larger halls. It was hard to believe the place was thirty decades old. The brickwork was of a stunning, even quality and remained as sharp as it had in the shift it was built. Bidirectional arched ceilings curved above her and she wondered how they were constructed.

She found her way to the vast, deserted atrium at the centre of Buni Sound. It was darker than it had been upon her arrival; only a few of the wall-mounted torches were left burning. The glow of the coals in the fire pit of the entrance had dimmed, allowing the iridescent glow of the UV-lit water to penetrate the space. Feeling the rough flagstone changing to smooth mosaic, she looked down to see intricate, swirling patterns set into the floor.

In the centre of the atrium stood a low, circular stone wall, a seating area perhaps. At its centre was a small pool of clear water lit softly from below. She peered in, wondering if it were connected directly to the vast body of water beyond the entrance.

A deep voice made her jump.

'It is known as the Level, little miss.'

It was the Shaman. He sat, propped against the stone wall with an arm across one raised knee. The other leg was stretched out in front of him and she guessed he had been sleeping that way. He was wrapped in a clean, dark cloak that had holes and tears sewn into it as if a part of the design.

He looked up, the light catching his eyes. She had forgotten their strange feline look and winced.

'Who are you?' she asked. 'What are the Hadje?'

The Shaman looked her directly in the eye and his wild features softened a little.

'Who are we? That is a good question,' he said, speaking with a slow, melancholy tone as if asking it of himself. 'We are exiles of a sort. A people living away from their own place, down here below yours.'

Megan waited for him to continue but he looked at her with a purposeful, level stare.

'Are there more Hadje?' she asked.

'Many more, hidden far from here.'

'Hidden? Are they in danger, your people?'

'We all feel the danger.' He nodded a couple of times in affirmation. 'We have warned you of it many times, in stories and song. Few listen.'

'But some do?' she asked.

'Some do,' he agreed. 'Danger is now closer than ever.'

'Why?'

'The Intercessor Drive Cores you covet. They are not the cause of the danger, but they propagate it.'

'We didn't invent them,' said Megan defensively. 'We found them. We need them to survive...'

'Indeed,' said the Shaman, cutting her off. 'The Cores you so zealously guard were locked away for years uncounted, and for good reason. Their reappearance is...' he made a show of searching for the right word. 'Unfortunate.'

Megan narrowed her eyes, trying to get the measure of him. 'Are the Hadje behind the anti-AI movement?' she said with suspicion.

'No,' said the Shaman with amusement. 'We are not, little miss. We do not approve of the methods of the righteous and self-absorbed. They are as much a part of the problem as the corruption that infects your Council.'

Megan, who had two family members on the Privy Council, took exception to this statement and said so.

'They are not all corrupt.'

The Shaman frowned. 'Perhaps not. But, by its nature, corruption spreads to the purer of heart whether they know it or know it not.'

He said nothing further and Megan could think of little to say. When he began again it was in a lower, more confiding tone.

'The Cores you harbour, to become dependent on them is a road to ruination. It would be better to return them to the prisons from which they came. We have guided the Cauldron

Born, your people, over thousands of years. Once we could do this in plain sight, now we must do so from the shadows. The Hadje are here to educate, to spread the truth.'

'Cauldron Born?' Megan found the term unfathomable. 'What does that mean?' But the Shaman only held her stare.

'The bards,' she said in realisation. 'You educate the bards, the storytellers?'

The Shaman nodded.

'And Myra Cena, you told Myra all this?' She had been burning to get answers to the myriad of questions surrounding Myra.

'Cena? I know not this name.'

'You said in the Siphon that you thought we were looking for a woman called Myra,' she said hastily. 'Myra Cena, the technician who works in the Vault where the IDCs are kept.' She took a step towards the Shaman. A desperation to slot the pieces together boiled inside her.

'Myra. Dark hair, about my height, looks like she works out a lot.' She was almost willing him to confirm this. Myra Cena had facilitated the theft of HEX, she felt sure. In the midst of all that had happened, she'd buried the frustration of not being able to return to the Vault, to tell O'Brien that Myra was the bad apple. But now the feeling became overwhelming.

But the Shaman was non-committal. 'Possibly. One of your kind looks much like another to my eyes. It's the soul that speaks out.'

Megan tried hard to picture Myra, who she had only met briefly the shift before. Describing her soul was not something she had much chance at achieving, but she did remember a physical detail that might set her apart.

'She has a scar on her cheek,' she said. 'The left I think.'

'I remember no scar, little miss, but I couldn't say that with certainty.'

Megan felt deflated as the Shaman got to his feet. She had forgotten how tall he was. He placed a huge hand on each of her shoulders.

'Do not be too hasty. The answers will come, although perhaps not to you. Tell me, why is the woman you seek important?'

She looked at the floor as she spoke and shook her head a little. 'One of the Intercessors has been stolen. Whoever took it used the 7075 tunnel, where the Siphon is, to remove it.' Then she added with a tinge of disappointment, 'We think.'

The Shaman swiftly fell to one knee in front of her and she felt the movement of air around her. Even kneeling, his eyeline was near level with her own. Those strange eyes burned with a new intensity.

'Say that again, little miss,' he said.

'One of the Intercessor Drive Cores was stolen.'

He drew back from her then looked over her shoulder at something behind her. She turned and saw Olson approaching with Jean-Louis.

'I'm sorry,' said Olson. 'I woke and, well you weren't there. Just wondered where you'd wandered to.'

'I'm safe,' said Megan, looking back to the Shaman.

'It must be found,' he urged.

'I know,' said Megan. 'That's what we're trying to do.'

'You do not understand, child. It has to be recovered. If it seeks to return to its origin, the consequences are unthinkable.'

'Its origin?' she asked. 'Why? What would happen?'

He seemed to think a moment. He spoke in a slow and considered tone. 'That is not an easy question for me to answer so that you will believe. But I can set you on the path to the answer if you are willing to travel it.'

This sounded extremely cryptic to Megan, and she looked back at Olson, who regarded her with concern. She felt like a small child, an effect magnified by the sheer size of the man kneeling before her.

'How do I find the path?' she asked.

'You must go to our city of Tsarocca.'

'Tsarocca?' she said, turning the strange word over in her mind. 'You said your people were hidden.'

'Yes,' he said, more as a breath than a word. 'To find Tsarocca you will need a guide. I said we were exiles and that is the truth. None of us here know the way to Tsarocca, although many of us have been there. Protection for our kind from yours,' he said, slowly and deliberately.

'If you are to find Tsarocca, you will first need to travel to the Ruined City, to Kul. There is a man there that can guide you.'

'A man? What is his name?' asked Megan.

The Shaman gave a short, deep laugh and relaxed his face for the first time since kneeling. 'It matters little, as he is the only man to dwell within that cursed place. But, as you ask, his name is Benjamin Kittala.'

'Then I will find him,' she replied with the assertion of youth.

'Be wary in Kul,' said the Shaman, drawing closer to her. 'It harbours a creature deep in its belly. A monster. You must exercise extreme caution within the city walls.'

'What sort of monster?' asked Megan, alarmed.

'A daemon,' said the Shaman. 'I have seen it in my visions and I fear it greatly. Now we must make haste and prepare to return you to the surface, to your own kind, if you are to make the journey. Storm clouds are gathering. Skala will be gifted one last rain before its death; this has been foretold. I fear that there is no time to lose. You should go.'

He stood, releasing Megan before nodding to Jean-Louis.

'I will gather an expedition,' Jean-Louis said. Then to Megan and Olson, 'If you wish to say goodbye to Hesta and the children, now is the time.'

Megan turned back to the Shaman but in the fleeting moment during which she had looked away, he had vanished.

026: The Surface

Below Skala

Having said their goodbyes to Hesta, Michelle and Deain, Megan and Olson followed Jean-Louis back into the vast space of the underground reservoir. Olson had been reluctant to leave and Megan understood why. He seemed very much at peace down here among the Hadje, but equally she'd learned that the person he wished to see most of all was no longer here.

Accompanied by a party of three, they made their way around the circular body of water and back to the passageway. Turning back for a moment, Megan caught a last glimpse of the family. The children waved eagerly before Hesta ushered them back into the warm glow of Buni Sound. It was strangely comforting to think of them being tucked back into their own beds just as she and Olson were to begin the long, daunting climb.

The ascent turned out to be easier than Megan had expected. For one thing she was less terrified than she had been the shift before, when she had no idea whether she was a prisoner or a guest. For another, the climb may have been physically demanding, but it felt a lot more controlled than the sensation of a barely restrained fall. Negotiating the many creatures was also easier and, while still wary of them, she felt much less threatened.

They travelled in a silence punctuated only by their collective heavy breathing. Presently, the walls started to slope in from the right, providing assurance that they were nearing the top of the dome.

'I can take you as far as the Siphon,' said Jean-Louis, speaking for the first time in several rotations. 'After that you are on your own, I'm afraid.'

'Thank you,' said Olson. 'We appreciate you bringing us this far.'

'You're welcome.'

'How do we get from the Siphon up to the surface?' asked Megan, grateful to reach the top of the steep climb.

Entering the damp link tunnel, Jean-Louis spoke breathlessly over his shoulder. 'There is a metal structure around the Siphon tanks. There are steps that lead up to a service platform. At the rear of the platform is a ladder of metal rungs. Climb those and you will find your way to the surface.' Catching sight of Olson, who was looking out of breath, he added, 'It's not too far.'

It wasn't long before the tunnel ended abruptly and the light of Jean-Louis' torch and those of the other guides became lost in the vast open space. They could dimly make out the huge water tanks and the winding steps around them.

'This is goodbye for now,' said Jean-Louis, and Megan savoured the soft lilt of his voice, stowing away its calming effect deep in her memory. 'But I hope we will meet again. Mr Olson, it has been my privilege to meet you. You are welcome in my house and I should like you to visit again if time and chance allow. You know how to find us.'

'Thank you, Jean-Louis, that means a lot to me,' said Olson with total sincerity.

Jean-Louis then turned to Megan. 'You will really travel to Kul?'

Megan hesitated. She had been asking herself this question over and over again for rotations but had no definitive answer. 'I think so, yes,' she said, but without much assurance. 'Do you think I should go?'

Jean-Louis considered this a moment. 'Yes, if you can I think you should go. My soul tells me you are the right person to walk that path. Few of your kind have walked it, and none so young, but I feel that, yes, for you it is right.'

Jean-Louis looked intently at Megan and she saw a darkness slowly overcome his handsome features. 'Remember what the Shaman said. Be careful inside the walls of Kul. Find Kittala as quickly as you can. He will keep you safe.'

'I understand,' said Megan seriously.

'May the spirits walk beside you,' he said with gravity.

'Thank you, Jean-Louis,' she replied, grateful for this blessing.

He gave them a last look, handed his torch to Olson then turned to the three men who stood at the threshold of the tunnel. 'Time to go,' he said, and together they walked swiftly back into the tunnel, the flickering light dimming all too quickly.

Olson found the climb from the Siphon tank hard going but did his best not to show it. He was an active man, but descending then ascending thousands of steps in consecutive shifts was more punishment than his body was used to. They found the rungs Jean-Louis had spoken of and Olson followed his younger companion to their summit. The darkness of the shaft pressed closely about him and, while he wasn't claustrophobic, the confinement combined with fatigue gave

223

him a manic need to press on. He was relieved when Megan called back over her shoulder.

'I think this is the top,' she said, giving the roof above her a firm shove. A wooden panel moved aside, allowing the hot air of the upper world to stream through the crack. She gave it a second shove and pushed it aside with what strength she still possessed. With the panel out of the way she clambered out into the remains of a long-abandoned building. She took a tentative look around before turning back to help Olson up and out.

They both took a few moments to adjust to the light, which was dimmer than either had expected. Through the splintered beams of a partly collapsed roof they saw the dark underside of cloud obscuring the sun. It rendered the sky almost black, an arresting sight for Megan, who had seen such a thing only twice before. Olson extinguished the torch, which smoked a little then gave up completely.

'Where are we?' wondered Megan out loud.

'I'm not sure,' said Olson, looking around. 'The Western Fringe someplace, I guess.'

They dusted themselves off, a futile effort considering the damp grime that sullied their clothes. Seeing the remains of a partly collapsed doorway, Olson made for it before reconsidering and doubling back to cover the entrance to the Siphon.

'Don't want any kids falling down there,' he said, catching her frowning. 'We don't have enough to spare.'

'Of course not,' she said, berating herself.

They made their way out through debris and into the more familiar surroundings of a deserted street. The buildings were low and bore the appearance of warehousing or light industrial units. They skirted the perimeter fence of a nearby compound, eventually finding the entrance. Above it hung a large, sand-scoured sign that read 'Hellinar Research Area T24'.

'Well I'll be damned,' said Olson, who took a step backwards to admire it, a look of reverence writ clear across his features.

'What is it?' asked Megan, intrigued.

'Before we went down to the Vault – before you jumped straight into that tunnel Miss Devin – Vincent told me he had interviewed a quartermaster from Hellinar Research. He'd been beaten half to death in the slums after tracking a group of vehicles stolen from a facility called T24.'

He shook his head in bemused wonder.

'That makes perfect sense,' said Megan, jumping quickly to the obvious conclusion. 'Myra let someone into the Vault, they took HEX and escaped to meet the vehicles here.'

'I really don't know about Myra,' said Olson, looking doubtfully at Megan. 'She just doesn't strike me as being a part of this. But yes, I think you've hit the nail on the head with the rest of it.'

Jumping back to her assertions about Myra, Megan urged him. 'But someone from inside the Vault must have been able to tell whoever took HEX that the coast was clear. That wall was fillered, sanded and painted from the inside. It must have taken shifts. Surely that's the only way it could have been done?'

'Yes, you're right. That part doesn't quite make sense to me either. We need to talk to Vincent as soon as we can. He may have learned more since we've been gone.'

'Well, what are we waiting for?' asked Megan with a smile. 'Let's find a trishaw.'

027: Commissioning

Research and Development Facility, Eastern District, Skala
City

The case for ROOT's integration had not been the hard sell
Katherine anticipated. The success of the GVX fire-up seemed
to have brought a renewed confidence that humankind could
create, with or without the aid of IDC guidance. While no
one would deny the input that ROOT had on the project,
the abilities of John Orchard and the other designers were
played up, as were the speed and precision of Don Hoffer's
construction crew. Although this nagged at Katherine a little,
she felt it would be churlish to deny the team their
achievements. After all, it was the Privy Council lording it over
their work, not they themselves.

Ultimately it was Erin James who had pushed the case for
integration. Ratha objected at first but capitulated somewhat
sooner than expected. She seemed reluctant but resigned to
the outcome, sighing a good deal but letting events play out
without much protest. The rest of the Privy Council followed
suit soon after. For reasons she couldn't quite define, Katherine
felt an undercurrent of unease at this. She had got what she
wanted, but the way in which it had come felt somehow

contrived. Nevertheless, she knew she had to grab the opportunity with both hands.

ROOT's removal from his plinth in the Vault had been complicated. In the time since his activation he had been shut down only once, and vigorously warned of the dangers of doing so again. Keeping him live necessitated some delicate work to splice into his power supply and switch to an auxiliary unit, which would remain with him as a backup while coupled to GVX. After a few agonising rotations the technicians switched him over with no interruption.

Katherine reached SVA a little before ROOT's arrival, which was undignified given the circumstances. The importance of this momentous event, the first integration of an Intercessor into a man-made machine, was lost on no one. It was therefore hard to find the sight of the intricately featured cube being wheeled in atop a basic trolley anything other than comical. To make matters worse, Vincent O'Brien, in a rare show of generosity, had assigned two of his agents to act as a temporary security detail. Seeing two uniformed women flanking the trolley as if their lives depended on it looked utterly absurd. A group of technicians, Myra Cena among them, trailed behind like an expectant, if nervous, guard of honour.

John Orchard, standing to one side, shouted across to Roy Jacobs. 'Can we open her up?'

Jacobs looked up from his laptop and gave the designer a broad grin. 'We certainly can,' he said, and hit a series of keys.

Katherine gasped as GVX's smooth flanks, divided into compartments between skeletal ribs, slid out. Each made a dull thud as it reached full extension and locked. What was already a huge vehicle had almost doubled in width over the course of only a few moments.

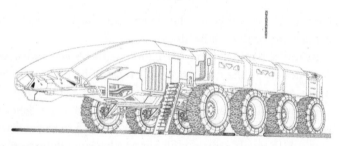

'I suppose it's time we acquainted you with the interior, Katherine,' Orchard said with more than a little pride in his voice.

'That...' she stumbled over her words, 'That would be good.'

Accompanied by Orchard and Jacobs, Katherine made her way towards a steep ladder that extended from a retractable platform ahead of the expanded midsections. Reaching it, she found it was made from a plastic-based material.

'Just in case you forgot your gloves,' said Orchard, bringing up the rear.

Reaching the top of the steps, Katherine ducked through the open doorway. Immediately, lights winked on, reacting to her presence. The space inside, although split into compartments, was huge relative to any previous exploration vehicle she had travelled in.

She looked around her, getting her bearings. Although each compartment's purpose was self-evident, Jacobs listed them.

'We refer to the central, open, crew area as the galley,' he began. 'Behind you are the science stations. They've yet to be outfitted with equipment and it's unlikely much will go in there before departure. Across the way is a small workshop and survey drone pod, again not outfitted yet but that's a priority for the next shift.'

Gesturing to the compartments closer to where they stood,

he continued, 'These are the sleeping quarters; you can see there are eight bunks. Forward from them is a washroom and a small kitchen. Food stores, by the way, are down the back.'

'So, where's the dance floor?' she asked.

'That would be up the front,' said Jacobs with a laugh. 'Come on, I'll show you the cockpit.'

He led the way towards a door in the forward bulkhead. The cockpit, much to Katherine's surprise, was relatively spacious. The hangar was visible almost all around them, not only through the forward windshield, but parts of the roof, flanks and a good proportion of the floor. She frowned, impressed by the panoramic view and realising that most, if not all, of it was a projection.

'The cockpit is designed for up to four people; a systems engineer, a monitoring technician, driver and co-driver. The hope is that most of the time a crew of two can manage the systems while GVX is mobile.'

She stepped forward, mounting a step to the raised forward portion of the cockpit. In front of her were two identical chairs, the design of which was distinctly different to anything she had seen before. Side by side, with a generous gap between them, they sat reclined. What was most peculiar though was the control system. From the back of each chair, running round and forward from either side, were frame-like structures which apparently supported the drivers' arms. At the end of each frame was a control stick festooned with buttons and selector wheels that differed in layout from left to right.

'Have a seat, ma'am,' said Jacobs, gesturing to the right-hand chair. Katherine moved to it and stepped awkwardly over the left arm support to lower herself into the seat pad.

Once in, Katherine instinctively reached over each shoulder in turn, pulling the straps of the harness from behind her back.

Feeling a little more comfortable, she looked to Jacobs, who was now squatting beside her.

'So my arms go in here?' she asked, lowering them tentatively into the frames.

'That's right. The simulator drivers referred to them as 'splints'. The whole setup is designed to be as intuitive as possible and allows you to maintain concentration for long periods. I've spent a few rotations on the sim myself and it works.'

Settling her arms into the splints, she took the control sticks as her feet found pedals. 'So, what do I do?'

Moving ROOT up the ladder and into GVX's hold was fraught with potential disaster. It was a slow and painful process as SVA technicians carried up the remote power supply, trying to keep the cables from getting tangled or, worse still, disconnected. Eventually, in single file and with a good deal of fumbling, ROOT sat safely before the cut-out he had himself designed into the rear bulkhead.

'Well done everybody,' said Katherine with great relief. 'I'm not sure I'd want to do that every shift.'

There was a collective murmur of agreement.

'Okay, if we've got the backup power supply in place I guess we lift him in,' she continued with a look of mild trepidation.

With Roy Jacobs observing her from a respectful distance, she squatted down and looked to Myra to do the same. Between them, they lifted the cube and lined it up with the cut-out. It was a snug fit and they had to walk ROOT in the first few centimetres until he could slide back with ease to mate with the rear docking face. A moment later they heard a brief percussion of metallic cracks as ROOT's internal locks snapped into GVX's receptacles to secure him in place.

'Well I guess it all works,' said Katherine, to no one in particular. 'ROOT, can you hear me?'

'Yes Katherine, I can hear you just fine,' came the silky reply. 'I have successfully patched into the internal camera system and can see you quite clearly.'

'It's not the easiest process getting you up here,' she replied.

'I must confess, I didn't consider that when advising Mr Orchard on the design. I will make a note to do so next time we work together. So Katherine, who do we have as crew?'

'This is Roy Jacobs – he's the chief engineer on this project and will be my co-driver during the commissioning. Myra will be keeping an eye on you...'

'A familiar face to look after me is much appreciated Katherine, thank you,' ROOT interrupted.

After a moment's pause, Katherine turned to Jacobs and the small group assembled behind him.

'To Roy's left is Brendan Scott. Brendan's a medic.'

'And cook,' Scott interjected, with a laugh.

'And cook,' Katherine agreed. 'Then we've got Jayce Baker, our systems engineer, and Joanna Joyce, our power unit and chassis technician.'

'Jayce and Joyce,' said ROOT sardonically. 'How quaint.'

'Everyone just calls me JJ,' said Joyce quickly. 'Jayce and I have worked together a long time. The Jayce/Joyce thing's a running joke for some people. I guess it's kind of funny...' She left the sentence unfinished.

'Very well,' said ROOT. 'Thank you for making the introductions. I trust I don't have to introduce myself, do I, Katherine?' The optic fibres inset into the bulkhead around him glowed, changing from blue to a violent shade of red.

Katherine was suddenly aware that the interior lights had been dimmed. She wondered whether Roy or someone else had dimmed them, or whether it had been ROOT himself. She felt a mild sense of tension in the group.

'No, I don't think so, ROOT,' she said, then forced a laugh. 'I think it's time we got moving, don't you?'

The tension eased and was quickly replaced by palpable excitement as everyone broke off to take their stations. GVX was about to come fully to life for the first time.

'Cranking for dual start,' said Roy Jacobs across the cockpit from Katherine as she settled into her seat. 'Kills removed.'

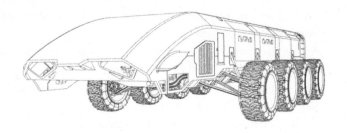

The bark of the V10s sounded around them, settling instantly to a deep purr. The accompaniment of reciprocating pistons, the whir of crankshafts, cams and gears, together with the roar of combustion, made the hairs on Katherine's neck stand on end. Seeing the satisfied look on Jacobs' face, she was sure he felt the same sensation. It was a feeling she didn't ever want to get used to.

'I'm going to release the torque converter lockout clutches now,' said Jacobs.

'I'll keep her throttled down,' said Katherine, as he flicked a bank of switches with a single motion.

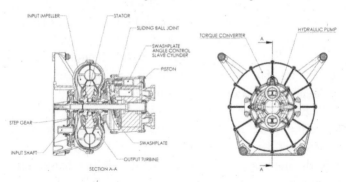

Looking down, Katherine could see a hive of activity below her as ant-like technicians decoupled the umbilical and other pipework. A moment later there was a rapid succession of cracks and the grinding of metal on metal, as the hangar doors began to slide open.

'Torque converters are locked in – you have drive. Moment of truth,' said Jacobs, taking a sideways glance at Katherine.

'Moment of truth,' she repeated and took a deep breath. 'Can I have a final systems check please Jayce?'

'All systems nominal,' came the quick, assured reply.

'Myra? ROOT's looking stable?'

'Everything's looking normal,' said Myra with obvious excitement, belying her professional manner. 'Hang on, I'm seeing an output spike…'

Without warning the twin V10s throttled up and GVX pitched noticeably forward then rearward, as if squatting. Jacobs looked to Katherine in alarm. Katherine had her splints pushed hard into the stops in an attempt to throttle down, but with no effect. There was a sudden lurch as the foremost pair of wheels lifted clean off the ground before reconnecting with a violent slapping sound. Less than a moment later the same happened from further back, then again and again. Below them, Katherine could see technicians scattering in alarm as the wave of lifting wheels ran back up the chassis, each pair slapping down on the painted floor.

'It's the platform control, it's going wild,' shouted Jacobs in desperation. He flicked switches left and right but with no apparent result. 'I can't get control of it.'

'ROOT's input and output signals are off the scale, Katherine,' said Myra in desperation. 'You've got to do something.'

Katherine began flicking switches herself, in a frantic effort to shut down as many systems as she could. Then she paused, realisation dawning on her that all she was doing was replicating what Jacobs had already done. There was no reason to expect a different outcome.

Jacobs saw her hesitation and looked at her directly. 'What is it?' he said. The lurching had ceased, although the wheels were still raising and lowering with that same horrible slapping sound.

Katherine sat back and calmly said, 'ROOT, I think you should stop that, please.'

Without warning, calm was restored. The V10s settled into a smooth idle and Myra's shaky voice confirmed ROOT's output signals were settling within normal limits.

It took a few moments for Katherine's heartrates to slow. 'ROOT, what was that about?'

'My apologies, Katherine. It's been a very long time since I've been given control of any extension of my chassis. I didn't mean to alarm you. Some recalibration was required. You might say I got a little carried away.'

'Yes, you could definitely say that. Please give us some warning if you need to do it again.'

'You have my word, Katherine. I don't believe it will be necessary. Recalibration is now complete.'

'Thank you,' she said breathlessly, before leaning forward

and flicking switches back into the on position. Taking her lead, Jacobs did the same.

'Okay, let's try again. Everyone ready?'

They were. Calm had seemingly reasserted itself on the ground as well. The SVA personnel could hear her and would accept her judgement on whether or not to proceed. Don Hoffer stood in front of them giving a clear thumbs up.

Katherine focused intently on the space beyond the hangar doors. Under the dark sky now pregnant with rain, a concrete roadway led out in the direction of the dry grasslands east of Skala. That's where they would go first, a place to test the capability of this enormous engineering masterpiece. She drew in a breath and held it a moment, releasing just as she pulled the splints towards her to throttle up. The V10s filled their exhausts, the inlet trumpets dropping to keep the incoming pressure waves in tune. With astonishing smoothness, GVX began to move.

028: Trials

The Grasslands, East of Skala

For Katherine, the joy of driving GVX was almost indescribable. Its speed and ride quality eclipsed anything she had ever experienced. Its vast weight helped, of course, but the way the suspension geometry worked in harmony with the springs and dampers was astonishing. And then there was that sound. At speed, the V10s sang. Put under load, they howled like the banshees of the bards' ancient myths. She felt she could drown in it.

'How's your systems analysis going, ROOT?' asked Jacobs, who had already struck up a surprising rapport with the Intercessor. Katherine supposed they spoke the same language in terms of engineering and, despite the crazed manner of his first interactions with GVX, ROOT had quickly settled into an efficient working partnership with the engineer.

'I've been tweaking a few of the control systems, Roy, but essentially they work very well. The feedback loop on the steering control is a little oversensitive and gets into a dither from time to time but I'm rewriting that code for you as we speak.'

Brendan Scott, who, at a loose end, had made his way forward to the cockpit door, asked, 'How far to the trial area?'

'About another ten kilometres,' said Katherine.

She was concentrating hard despite relying on Jayce Baker to alert her to any anomalies. Jayce and Myra had taken up station next to each other in the main hold. Although their conversation was muted, Katherine could still hear them over the cockpit speakers discussing the various systems they were monitoring. She could tell by their tone that each found the other's job interesting and, for Myra, this was a rare if not unique opportunity to show off.

'What are you grinning at?' asked Jacobs, who was grinning a little himself.

'Just pleased the crew are getting along. I wasn't sure Myra really wanted to be dropped in at the deep end after everything she's been through this past few shifts, but she seems to be taking to it well.'

'She's good?' asked Jacobs.

'Yes, she's very good,' said Katherine. 'I don't know her terribly well, but her record is exemplary and she dealt with HEX's disappearance in a level manner.' She hastened to qualify this. 'She was clearly scared out of her skin – I mean, it's a very big deal – but she kept her head.'

'That's good to know,' said Jacobs, reassured.

'Who's going to be driving once we're commissioned?' asked Scott, trying to make light of something that clearly weighed heavily on his mind and those of the rest of the crew.

'Unclear at the moment,' said Katherine. 'There are a couple of drivers doing sim work. We'll have to cross that bridge when we come to it.'

'What about a co-driver?' asked Scott.

Katherine was about to repeat her last answer but Jacobs interrupted. 'That'll be me,' he said, twisting backwards to look at Scott evenly. 'I volunteered last shift and got the okay from Orchard and Councillor Falla.'

Katherine looked across at him wide-eyed.

'What?' said Jacobs. 'You don't approve?'

'I do,' she stuttered. 'I just didn't expect it, that's all.'

'I used to do a lot of test driving, if you recall. Less recently, but I figure given where GVX is going I might be of some use if I tag along.'

'You're being modest, Roy,' she said seriously. 'You'll be a huge asset. I just didn't expect you'd want to be trekking into Ayon, that's all.'

'What about a GA?' asked Scott.

'I've been trying to get Trish Asher,' said Katherine.

'What's a GA?' Jacobs asked Scott, noting the impressed look he wore.

'General Assistant,' the medic replied. 'A GA is the person that keeps the rest of us alive out on the ice. Normally, these expeditions are put on to get the scientists out into the field. Most of these people are really bright, but you wouldn't let them tie their shoelaces unsupervised. No offence, Councillor Kane…'

'None taken,' said Katherine, whose tone implied she couldn't agree more.

'A GA's someone who's spent a lot of time out in Ayon. They can practically smell the ice, tell how thick it is by colour and spot a snowed-in crevasse from half a kilometre away. I've been out with Trish a few times, she's a good choice. Actually I'd rank her as one of the best, but don't tell her that.'

'She certainly takes no prisoners,' said Katherine with a knowing smile.

Scott gave a gruff laugh and turned to head back into the galley.

'Do we really know where we're going?' asked Jacobs, once he was out of earshot.

'In truth I don't know,' said Katherine. 'ROOT seems to think we're heading somewhere very deep in Ayon.'

'Almost certainly that's where HEX has travelled,' interjected ROOT, reminding both of them that no conversation was private.

'Why do you think that?' asked Jacobs.

'I just know, Roy,' said ROOT in an almost whimsical tone.

'I've tried to get more out of him, but he won't elaborate,' said Katherine, a little huffily. They both fell silent, allowing the sounds of the outside world to wash over them. The further east they travelled, the lower the sun and the darker the sky. The wind had picked up, running through the increasing green wash of grassland in a relentless flowing hiss.

Reaching the proving grounds, Katherine turned left into a wide area of undulating dry earth before pushing her splints forward, quelling the twin V10s. GVX obediently came to a smooth halt, Katherine feeling the mechanical strain as its momentum was arrested. She had an affinity for those sensations and had occasionally wondered why she seemed to be more in tune with them than some of her contemporaries. Her father had once told her she had a gift for driving, one of his rare compliments that came back to her now.

'Do you remember the programme?' she asked Jacobs, already knowing the answer.

'Yes, ma'am,' he replied.

'Okay,' she said. 'Hold on, everybody.'

The V10s roared again as she throttled up and the hulking vehicle accelerated smoothly from a standstill out towards a series of mounds before it. She took to the smaller slopes first, sometimes head-on, sometimes at an angle, to assess GVX's roll characteristics.

'I love this thing,' she said, and gave Jacobs a broad grin.

'I can tell,' he replied, marvelling at her dexterity. 'You certainly handle it well.'

'It's a pussycat,' she said, heading towards the next set of rocks.

'We should simulate some system failures as soon as you're comfortable,' Jacobs said, all business again.

'Okay, that's fine, what first?'

'Pneumatics?'

She frowned but kept her eyes forward. 'Won't that result in a catastrophic engine failure? If there are no valve springs won't the valves just hit the pistons?'

'Nope,' he said, without further explanation.

She stole a glance at him to check he was serious, which he seemed to be. 'Okay, then.'

Jacobs cycled through menus on the control screen, and punched in a series of commands. There was a momentary metallic ring from the V10s before they suddenly dropped power.

'Critical loss of pneumatic pressure,' said Jayce Baker in a firm but calm voice over the intercom. Katherine had to restrain herself from initiating a complete Pack shutdown.

'Thank you, Jayce, I'll bring it back online in a couple of turns,' said Jacobs. He looked at Katherine and began to explain. 'The engines have gone into a torque-limiting mode – that's the loss of power. What's unique about the system in our Pack is that the bottom of the chamber is a separate, sprung part. We call it a Thomason Plate.'

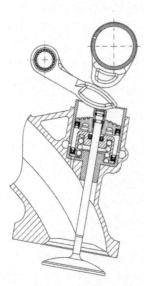

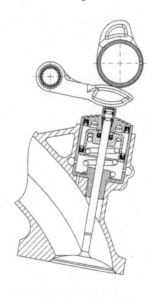

NO PNEUMATIC PRESSURE
VALVE OPEN

NO PNEUMATIC PRESSURE
VALVE CLOSED

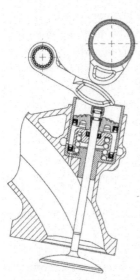

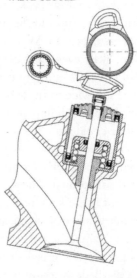

PNEUMATIC PRESSURE 16BAR
VALVE OPEN

PNEUMATIC PRESSURE 16BAR
VALVE CLOSED

'So, with air pressure the steel spring is redundant?'

'Yeah, that's right,' he said and swiped in another set of commands.

The momentary ringing sounded again as the plates were pushed back to the bottom of the chambers by the building air pressure.

'That's really clever, Roy,' she said, admiration clear in her voice.

'Yeah, well, the guy that came up with it is pretty clever.'

'So what next?' she asked.

'Oh, I've got a pretty long list.' Jacobs smiled.

They ran through it over the next few revolutions. Most concerned ancillary-systems testing and temperature control, with which ROOT had some input. They began to work as a group, finding small problems and sorting them out or noting them down to address back at SVA. By the time the list was exhausted Katherine was reaching her endurance limit.

'You want to drive back?' she asked Jacobs.

'You bet,' he said and she switched control over to him.

They returned to SVA at a steady sixty kilometres per rotation, Skala eventually coming into view beyond the drier grass of the city's outlying fields. They headed for the hangar, its doors still wide open, with the tiny but unmistakable figure of Don Hoffer standing at their centre. Even from a distance, Katherine could sense the pride in his posture.

Jacobs throttled down and turned GVX around to reverse it back into its berth. He left the V10s to idle for a moment then initiated a shutdown. The tink-tink of contracting metal came clear over the speakers from behind them.

'I don't think that could have gone much better,' he said. 'There isn't anything we can't fix in under a full shift.'

'It's great,' she agreed sincerely. 'Well done everyone, it's been a privilege working with you.' There was a momentary, if restrained applause from the hold. 'Myra, I guess we should decouple ROOT.'

Katherine levered herself up and out of the driver's chair. It was awkward with the splints, and more so now, with her body half asleep after so long in one position. Standing and waiting for the blood to return to her legs, she ran her fingers through her hair and rubbed her eyes.

'Katherine,' said ROOT unexpectedly. 'I have a small problem.'

Katherine furrowed her brow. 'A problem?'

'My internal locks appear to have jammed. I've not used them in, well, a very long time, and they simply won't release.'

Katherine sighed. It was the only real hiccup of the shift so she took it as well as she could.

'I'll get someone to dismantle the bulkhead to get you out,' she said.

From beside her Jacobs said, 'You know, I'm not sure you can do that.'

She looked at him, confused. 'I'll speak to John. I'm sure there is some way we can get ROOT out. Let's not worry about it for now. ROOT, you're staying where you are. I'll get you removed once we're organised.'

'Thank you, Katherine,' ROOT said with no indication of concern. But there was an inflection in his tone she didn't recognise and, if she were honest about it, she didn't quite trust. She pushed the feeling to one side and made her way back into the galley, then, alongside the rest of the crew, into the hangar, to the general jubilation of designers, engineers and technicians.

029: Revelation

The return journey from Mal-Kas was a troubled one. Having dropped their gear with a predictably unhelpful Farkus, JT and Ira said their farewells to a worried-looking Beth. Whether she was concerned for their physical condition or the shared look of horror both were attempting to conceal, neither could be sure. Both feared they had seen or heard enough to warrant someone, not least Bill Connor, to want them kept quiet, and were relieved as the facility disappeared from sight as they drove away.

It had been about a rotation before Ira felt comfortable enough to talk. With each passing kilometre his fear had given way to a simmering anger which kept an ever-wary JT on edge. The experience of meeting Connor and their suspicions of what he was guarding had without doubt brought them closer. But the infrequent stabs of pain JT still felt served as a constant reminder of what had occurred in the slums.

Both men had tried to form plausible explanations for Connor's presence, the knife, the blood and the scream, but it always came back to the same thing. He was guarding and hurting, if not murdering, a group of people whose origins it didn't take a giant leap of faith to guess at. Why he was doing this, however, remained a mystery. Ira was understandably keen to return to the Landlord's Arms to see if the 'Three', as he referred to them, could make any sense of it. JT, remembering O'Brien's allusion to his attempts to get an agent into the mines, felt they might learn more from him. Reluctantly, Ira agreed to go this route first on condition they return to Gygath together so that there was corroboration of the story.

Feeling a need to press on, JT drove, while Ira slept fitfully beside him. By the time the northern suburbs of Skala appeared on the horizon, JT had made up his mind to head directly for T24 in the hope that Evelyn Tudor would be there. If she wasn't, he would have to make a more clandestine approach, or wait. Waiting seemed like the worst possible option, not least because Ira would likely use any delay as justification for heading directly into the slums. As it turned out, they were in luck.

Evelyn Tudor herded her staff out of her office, skilfully dispatching them on innocuous errands to give her visitors some privacy. JT told the story, feeling it to be far-fetched even to himself, but Ira backed him up when needed. When they had finished, Evelyn picked up the phone to O'Brien and requested a meeting in person. O'Brien had been reluctant at first, but relented and, to everyone's surprise, suggested the Vault under Ayon Research as a safe meeting place. In fact this made perfect sense, since he still had access and the building was a natural enough place for JT to visit. It also guaranteed privacy: now both IDCs had been removed, the place was effectively deserted.

And there they stood, O'Brien looking at the photograph Connor had provided and whistling in amazement.

'Do you have any idea how hard we've tried to learn what you've just told me?' he asked. JT and Ira both shifted uncomfortably but said nothing. 'And you guys just walk in there. I must say I'm impressed.' He pushed his spectacles up and looked at each of them in turn.

'There was a scream, and that blade had blood on it. There was no doubt,' said Ira, with total assurance.

'I'm not doubting you,' said O'Brien, eyebrows raised in surprise. 'Everything you've told me confirms what we've suspected for cycles.'

'What does it mean?' asked JT.

It was now Evelyn Tudor's turn to look uncomfortable. O'Brien regarded JT seriously. 'I don't know exactly, but I've got a reasonable idea. I think it's about subsidies.'

'Subsidies?' asked JT incredulously. He looked at Ira and saw a strange look of understanding in the man's chiselled features.

'Subsidies,' repeated O'Brien firmly. 'The Council has been funding mining companies, processing firms and others to employ people from the slums. It's a way of making them look like they're solving the problem of mass poverty without actually doing anything they might be accountable for. No overt help, but they can claim they are trying to improve the situation.'

'But why keep those people penned in?'

'My guess is that the mine has run its course. You said the drill-rig operator thought they hadn't extracted ore for cycles?'

'That's what she said. She also said the geologists disputed it.'

'They would do,' said O'Brien, knowingly. 'To keep the subsidies flowing the mine would have to be viable. What we think is happening, and not just in Mal-Kas, is that some mines have run dry, but it's more lucrative for the operator to keep them running on a skeleton crew. Fake the output to make them appear... viable.'

'And subjugate the workers on whose backs the subsidies are provided,' interrupted Ira.

'Exactly.' O'Brien looked at him with appreciation.

JT ran a finger across his lower lip in thought. 'In real terms wouldn't someone, the Council or whoever, know that there is no output?'

'That's the bit we don't fully understand,' O'Brien agreed. 'The companies are getting help from somewhere to cover that up. We think it runs high up in government but we don't know how far it goes. Not yet anyway.'

O'Brien was cut short as the Cannula lift ascended, apparently called from above. He looked at it with narrowed eyes, the photograph in his hand momentarily forgotten. They waited, concern building that they were about to be discovered. The lift descended, and came to a smooth, painfully slow halt before the doors slid open with a hiss.

Together they watched the dishevelled form of Tyler Olson step out. He was followed a moment later by an equally shabby-looking Megan Devin.

'What on earth happened to you two?' asked O'Brien, startled.

Olson was about to speak but Megan got in before him. 'It's Myra Cena. The person on the inside, the person that got HEX out is Myra Cena.'

O'Brien frowned, not knowing what to make of this unexpected assertion, let alone their appearance. There was a momentary stand-off as he looked to Olson. The agent's face looked doubtful, but he didn't object. Finally, O'Brien unclipped a radio from his belt and keyed the mic.

'Find Myra Cena and bring her down to the Vault, please,' he said. There was an acknowledgement, followed by something else the others didn't catch. He keyed the mic again and said, 'Okay then. Be aware she may panic and run. Tell Councillor Kane she's to escort Cena down here herself if at all possible. You stay with them, but keep your distance and be ready if she does run.'

The radio crackled again then fell silent. 'You have some explaining to do, Miss Devin,' he said, attention momentarily averted as he clipped the radio back onto his belt. When he looked up again he saw Olson staring past him in astonishment.

He turned to see Ira returning the stare with obvious recognition, but also a little sheepishness.

JT had also picked up on this exchange and looked as puzzled as O'Brien. 'Ira, what's going on?'

'Ira?' asked Olson, apparently confused.

'Hello Tyler,' said Ira, with a faint trace of apology in his voice. 'That's the name I've been going by lately.'

'I thought you died a decade ago,' said Olson in wonder. His eyes suddenly glistened and he took a step forward, as if not quite believing what he saw.

JT became aware of a sudden dawning of recognition in Evelyn Tudor, who stood beside him. O'Brien, for once, looked totally confused.

'This man's name isn't Ira,' said Olson slowly. He looked straight at O'Brien. 'His name is Jason Karalydes.'

Evelyn Tudor took a step back, appraising Ira as if for the first time. She looked like she'd seen a ghost. Ira returned the look but in confusion rather than recognition.

'I'm sorry, I don't know who you are?' he said.

Evelyn regained her composure and looked at the floor with a wry, almost girlish grin. 'Well no, you wouldn't recognise me, and that can only be for the good. I was Tyler's boss during the time you were helping us. We really didn't think you made it out of that warehouse alive. I'm very glad that you did.'

'It wasn't easy,' said Ira. 'I was in pretty bad shape, they damn near cut my arm off. The only way out was through a sewer. I got blood poisoning, thought I was done for.'

'But you got out,' said Evelyn with clear relief.

'Not right away. You might say I was rescued down there.'

Megan, standing apart from the group and forgotten by all, spoke up. 'By the Hadje.'

Ira narrowed his eyes as the rest turned to regard her. 'Yes, by the Hadje. How on earth do you know about them?'

'We've seen them, seen their home.' She looked to O'Brien. 'That's where the tunnel led, to a place called the Siphon. Below that there's a huge water storage tank. People live down there.'

O'Brien frowned, as if this was a very unlikely tale, but Olson quickly moved to assure him. 'She's telling the truth, that's where we've been the last two shifts. There's a mini-civilisation living down there.'

O'Brien ruckled his nose in disapproval.

'It's not how you might imagine it,' said Ira in response. He favoured Megan with a momentary glance. 'It's very beautiful. They're good people.'

Megan nodded vigorously but didn't get the chance to elaborate. Unnoticed by anyone, the Cannula had made a second trip and now settled back down into the Vault. The door slid open and out stepped Katherine Kane, followed by a mystified-looking Myra Cena.

Katherine, who had been working flat out to come up with a strategy for removing ROOT from GVX, had resented the interruption. Now, seeing the assembled group, at least three of whom she didn't recognise, she wondered what could possibly be so important as to warrant her compliance with CID at such a critical moment. Nearest to her stood the uncharacteristically dirty figure of Megan, who ignored her to look daggers at Myra. Olson wore a curious look of what could have been relief. He made his way towards her but, to her surprise, kept going to stand in front of the elevator doors. Katherine was startled, and a little confused, but composed herself before addressing Vincent O'Brien.

'Mr O'Brien, what can I help you with?'

'Mr Olson, could you or Miss Devin explain please?' said O'Brien.

'She's the one on the inside,' said Megan impetuously, while engaging Myra with a hard stare. Myra looked bewildered but said nothing.

'The Hadje, they told us Myra had been down there. Down to the Deep Wells, Buni Sound they called it. She's been back and forth through the 7075 tunnel, she knows who took HEX.'

Katherine looked at Megan as if she'd gone mad. Olson gave a small and slightly embarrassed smile and took to examining his feet. O'Brien was studying Megan intensely, as were the others.

Myra looked around, trying to make sense of what was happening. 'I have literally no idea what you just said. Buni what? The Ha... who?' Her confusion turned to disbelief as she studied the look on Megan's face. 'You think I helped steal HEX? You're mad. I'm in the CCTV the whole time.'

'Someone must have told the, the...' Megan stuttered, trying to find the right word, 'the thieves.' It didn't do the perpetrators justice, but it was as close as she was going to get. 'You told them the coast was clear. They must have known.'

Myra shook her head. Her look had turned from confusion to amused sympathy. 'No, I wasn't involved at all. I have no idea what you're talking about. I had no idea that tunnel was there until you came down here two shifts ago. I'm sorry but you're wrong.'

There was a moment's silence before Tyler Olson spoke in a quiet, measured tone. 'Megan, did you ever find out who last looked at the tunnel schematics in the Central Library?'

Megan turned her ire onto him then seemed to relax a little. 'No, I didn't ever follow it up.'

'I think you should do that now,' suggested Olson firmly.

Megan was clearly unhappy with being dismissed and walked gracelessly to the security room. The guard, seeing her approach, opened the door. When it closed again, Olson returned his attention to the group and began his explanation.

'I'm sorry, Miss Cena. The tunnel we found, we followed it and found a group living underground. They call themselves the Hadje. I'd heard of them before but not met them myself. Their figurehead, if you could call him that, told us that a woman called Myra had recently been through the 7075 tunnel and had spent some time with them. I'm afraid Miss Devin is trying to hammer a square peg into a round hole and has concluded you are the Myra in question.'

'But you disagree?' asked O'Brien.

'I do,' said Olson with quiet confidence. 'For one thing, as Miss Cena pointed out, she is in the CCTV footage. She could have communicated with others outside the Vault, but if I'm correct you've found no evidence of that.'

'That's correct,' O'Brien confirmed.

'In my view, her reaction at the time she discovered HEX's disappearance looked genuine and panicked. She didn't delay raising the alarm and she's not behaved in an obstructive way as far as I'm aware.'

'Well that's how she might behave if she were guilty. What else?'

'The scar on her cheek,' said Olson, pointing to it.

Myra fingered it unconsciously. 'I was born with it,' she said absently. 'My mother had to have the operation, she couldn't give birth naturally and the surgeon nicked me.'

'The Shaman, the figurehead, he said he didn't remember a scar. I think we're looking for another Myra.'

There was a silence as everyone took this on-board. Katherine looked over into the security station to see Megan talking on the phone, presumably to the Central Library. Katherine thought she looked a little ashamed of herself. O'Brien, more as a distraction than anything else, raised the photograph he still held and peered at it.

'Could be one of these people,' he said thoughtfully to no one in particular then gestured towards JT and Ira. 'These two gentlemen retrieved this photograph of a Unit that was stolen from Hellinar Research a few shifts ago. There are five people standing in front of it. It's possible this is how your Intercessor got out of the city.'

He handed Katherine the photograph. 'Shame their faces are all covered up.'

'The vehicle's set up for Ayon, that's for sure,' she said. 'Just like ROOT thought.'

She sighed and studied the photograph more closely, looking at the faces wrapped in patterned cloth. You couldn't see any more than their eyes. She looked at the vehicle again, not really knowing what she was looking for. Then she saw something that tugged at the edge of her consciousness.

'There's another person in this photograph,' she said. 'In the cab, look. It's faint but there is definitely someone sitting up there.'

'Let me see,' said O'Brien. JT and Ira closed in to see the faint profile of an almost ghostly face.

'Connor, the man who took this, said he took it as insurance. For some reason they wanted photographs,' said JT.

'I can't make out the face,' said O'Brien. 'There should still be a field kit in security, can you get it for me?'

Olson moved to the door. As it opened they heard Megan's voice in deep discussion. A moment later Olson returned with a black case, which he set down and opened. He retrieved a large magnifying glass and handed it to O'Brien.

'I'm amazed you still use those,' said Evelyn Tudor. She sounded a little sarcastic.

'No batteries to go flat,' said O'Brien evenly. He squinted into the glass and gave a short, sharp snort that suggested something of interest. He handed the photograph and the glass to Katherine, who peered at it. She took a double take before her eyes went wide.

'What is it?' asked O'Brien urgently.

Katherine didn't hear him. Her ears rang and she felt suddenly faint. She turned to look at Megan, who was staring back at her through the glass with an identical look of total shock. The phone slipped from her hand, the thud as it hit the desk just audible. She shook her head very slowly, tears forming in her eyes. She mouthed a single word that Katherine simultaneously voiced out loud.

'Kyra.'

030: The Last Rain

Given the gravity of the situation, the events that followed Katherine and Megan's concurrent revelations in the Vault were uncomfortably brief. The two sisters shared a momentary and rare emotional embrace before Vincent O'Brien, who had been wise enough to wait, demanded an explanation. There was little to explain. Kyra was pictured sitting in the cockpit of Unit Hydra and, according to Megan, had most recently accessed the Central Library's plans of underground Skala in the area of the Vault. It seemed conclusive, and somehow monstrously simple at the same time.

For a brief, foolish moment, Katherine found herself thinking that at least Kyra was away and safe, before admonishing herself. Of course she wasn't safe. If the Hellinar quartermaster and ROOT were right, she was heading deep into the danger of the icy wastelands of Ayon, the most demanding terrain encountered by civilisation. She was also suddenly elevated to enemy number one by most of her own people.

O'Brien, to his credit, took no further convincing and immediately called off what had become a city-wide search for the presumed abductee, Kyra Devin. Tyler Olson fell in by O'Brien's side, the two men working in unison. Not forgetting Megan, with whom he had shared two terrifying shifts, he asked Evelyn Tudor to take her home. JT Gilbert and Ira, or Jason as Olson referred to him, had been thanked and temporarily dismissed with the proviso they made themselves available for further questioning when needed.

Which left Katherine. Unsure what to do next, she had followed O'Brien and Olson out of the Vault and found herself, without quite knowing how she had got there, back at SVA. She found John Orchard hovering around the internal bulkhead into which ROOT was still locked. Trying to formulate a salvage scheme that was both safe for ROOT and did as little damage as possible to the integrity of GVX's chassis was proving extremely challenging.

Orchard had the lights turned down inside GVX's expanded galley, one of those eccentric things he did to help him think. For the same reason, he had also removed his shoes and paced up and down in black cotton socks, occasionally pausing to look out of one of the trellis-braced windows into the bright expanse of the hangar outside. Distracted herself, Katherine dithered. She made the occasional observation, but his lack of response made her uncomfortably aware she was contributing next to nothing. Too late, Katherine saw him looking past her in the direction of the outer door. She heard him say, 'We've got visitors.'

From the entrance stepped two women, the last people Katherine expected to see together. Joss Ratha, ever immaculate in her customary full-length ashen robe, moved to stand in the centre of the galley at a respectful distance, while Nara Falla leaned against a vertical rib between the expanded compartments. Dressed for the field as always, her white hair was plaited and hooked forward over one shoulder. She wore a look of concern that contrasted with Ratha's apparent indifference as she made a condescendingly random inspection of GVX's interior. Orchard, who shared a frosty but professional relationship with Ratha, stood his ground for as long as dignity required, then made his way past the frowning Councillor and out into the hangar.

'So it's Kyra,' said Ratha, her cadence suggesting intrigue more than disapproval.

'It seems so, yes,' Katherine replied weakly from her position next to ROOT. She felt cornered.

'She was always impetuous, that one. Although what she thinks she's doing this time I can't pretend to understand.'

When Katherine didn't reply, Ratha spoke again, her voice harsh and annoyed. 'Come on, woman, she's your sister. No insight? No hypothesis? You've always been one for a good hypothesis, why not now?'

Katherine, feeling small and under fire, looked to Nara for help, but found Nara staring blankly upwards at some pipework in the hull.

She said, 'I've no idea, Joss,' which was the truth and must have come over as such, as Ratha gave a short grunt of disapproval but not disbelief. She looked around the dimly lit interior before settling on ROOT.

'And what's all this?' she asked pointedly.

Katherine frowned at the floor to avoid Ratha's glower. 'ROOT's internal locks have jammed and he's stuck in this bulkhead. We're trying to figure out a safe way to remove him.'

Ratha unhelpfully offered her opinion – based on no knowledge of GVX's construction, but that detail didn't seem to bother her. 'Can't you just cut through whatever anti-vibration mounts he's sat in?'

'Someone else suggested that,' said Katherine, anger rising

in her voice as she met Ratha's narrow stare. 'I'll tell you what John said, his words exactly: "The anti-vibration mounting consists of eight wheels and sixteen temperature-controlled springs and dampers. Cut those if you like, but it will still leave you with a hundred and twenty tonnes of metal to deal with."'

Ratha, despite resenting Katherine's tone, seemed not at all deterred by this insight. 'Well then, you'll have to remove these panels and cut a section out.'

'It's not that easy,' said Katherine testily. 'This isn't a panelled wall, it's a bulkhead, part of GVX's structure. It was designed that way to give him maximum protection, you can't just cut into it.'

'So what are the options?' asked Nara, speaking for the first time.

'Well,' said Katherine, considering her words carefully. 'ROOT's staying where he is, at least for the short term. John's working on how to extract him safely. Whoever is going after Kyra could take an Ice Runner, but it's unlikely they would catch up with her any time soon. Or we wait until we can use GVX and hope it's as capable as we think.'

'Or ROOT goes with GVX,' offered Ratha.

'I don't see that as an option,' said Katherine, regarding her in astonishment.

'I don't see why not. If I understood your ramblings in the Council meeting, you said ROOT has an idea where Kyra or HEX is heading.' Her tone had become flippant, which put Katherine further on guard.

'He's not said anything further on that.' She was going to continue but ROOT's synthesised voice cut her off.

'I can't pin down precisely where they are going. The geography has changed over time, but I can get you very close.'

Ratha looked around absently. Refusing to address the

Intercessor directly, she looked back at Katherine. 'Ask him, what geography? What's changed?'

Katherine was about to speak but again ROOT took the initiative. 'You need only look around you, Councillor Ratha. Skala was built by a lake, yes?' Ratha didn't respond. 'It was a sizeable lake when the city was built, over forty kilometres wide. Now it's less than five kilometres wide. My data is much older than that. If I could give you a precise location, of course I would.'

Astonishingly, Ratha seemed placated by this. 'Well then, it makes sense to me for ROOT to go. He would have to be accompanied, of course. By someone with an adequate level of authority…'

Her voice trailed off and Katherine saw Nara's narrowed eyes scrutinising Ratha, who began again in a parental tone.

'You were responsible for the commissioning, Katherine, is that right?'

'Yes, I…'

'And you're a councillor, familiar with the tundra. Quite the right person to act as chaperone, wouldn't you say, Nara?' There was a snarl in her voice and, despite outward appearances, Nara was clearly under pressure.

'You're serious?' asked Katherine.

'Yes, I'm serious.'

'You'll consult the Matriarch?' asked Katherine in faint disbelief.

'Consult her? Don't be stupid. I'll tell her what's going to happen. She's in no position to object. With the migration coming, her time possessing any meaningful influence is over and she knows it.'

Katherine, lost for words, looked back to Nara, who had fixed her attention on a survey drone hung on the cockpit bulkhead. 'It does seem a plausible option at the moment,

Katherine. I'm going to send supplies out to the furthest outpost we have in Ayon, which, at the moment, is Nastra – fuel, food and anything else we can get out there, to give you as much range as we can. You can burn as much fuel as you need to get to Nastra as fast as possible. After that you'll have to rely on economy and mulching.'

Katherine's stomach gave a lurch at the mention of the Nastra outpost and Nara knew it. Ratha, however, seemed totally oblivious and smoothed her robe in readiness to leave.

'Do I get a say in this?' asked Katherine, looking from Nara to Ratha and back again.

'Of course,' said Ratha, with feigned conviviality, before snarling, 'provided you agree.'

She turned and swept out but Nara hung back a moment and regarded Katherine seriously. She pushed herself off the rib she'd been leaning on, her small frame poised as if ready for anything, despite her advancing age. Still fixed on Katherine, she dropped her head and closed her eyes a fraction longer than was necessary. Katherine understood the gesture, her discomfort now giving way to near panic. After Nara had gone she looked about her, lost for words or comprehensible thoughts. She waited as long as she felt she could before making her way into the hangar and out into the darkened outskirts of Skala.

She walked aimlessly for a time. The wide streets of the Central District were relatively empty, the sand-strewn cobbles looking dull and grey under the morose, blackened sky. There was no breeze but the temperature was lower than was typical. Her thoughts circled endlessly in her head. Kyra – what had she done and why? Ratha and Nara – why had they come to find her together? That was unprecedented. ROOT and GVX.

Yes, she was probably the right person to pilot the huge vehicle into Ayon, but it all seemed too confused, too unreal and far too rushed.

She turned back to the east. If she was going, and it looked like she was, she would have to pack clothes at least. She didn't want to set foot in her apartment, but knew she had to. She wondered where Megan was – at home and safe, she hoped. She felt an intangible pull to be with her but knew that now was no time to intrude. Megan was so young, and needed their father and his family more than she did. Kyra's actions would hit her hardest of all, Katherine knew.

She walked a couple more blocks out of her way – anything to delay the inevitable and give her time to come to terms with it all. Still lost in thought, she ran her fingers through her hair and was brought back to the present by the sensation of cool dampness upon her skin. Bringing her hand down, she saw it was wet. She stood still and watched a few tiny droplets appear on her palm and fingertips. She raised her head towards the blackness of the sky above and felt cool, light raindrops kiss her forehead and cheeks.

Skala had not seen rain for as long as she could remember, since she was a child in fact. The sensation was extraordinarily calming, her frayed nerves subsided as the hot tightness of her skin was cooled and cleansed. The few drips became a stream, then a torrent. She had forgotten the sound, the rush of raindrops striking hot cobbles, the muted thudding as they met dry dust and sand. She took in the smell of damp earth that rose up and filled her lungs. It only took a few moments for the street to become saturated; the old, disused drainage system had long been clogged and did nothing. It didn't matter, though – drains were at the very bottom of a long list of priorities. She stood stock-still and closed her eyes as her clothes became wonderfully cool and sodden.

She realised with a start she was standing next to a school. Suddenly, from every doorway, children spilled into the street, whooping and laughing as they splashed into swirls of dust-filled water. Adults followed, as excited as the children. She watched as together they jumped and splashed, not caring how wet or dirty they were. It was an extraordinary sight, and for a moment, Katherine forgot her troubles. But she couldn't forget the children, how she felt as a child before the death of her mother and how she still longed for children of her own. In that moment she was grateful beyond words for the flood of water that fell from the sky, hiding the tears that spilled down her cheeks and flowed out into the streets of the dying city.

031: Council of Three

'If you two 'ave just done what I think you 'ave this one's on me,' said the Landlord, smacking down a bottle of clear spirit in front of JT and Ira. 'And there's another one tucked under the bar for you for later.'

'You sure?' asked Ira, with one eyebrow raised.

'You done good, Ira. Makes a change, I must say. They'll be ready for you in ten to fifteen. I'll tip you the wink.' The Landlord turned before bellowing at a nearby table. 'What are you bastards looking at? You're supposed to be getting wasted, not interested.' He playfully cuffed one of the men as he passed, eliciting a drunken grin for his trouble.

'Can I ask you a personal question?' asked Ira.

'You can ask, but I can't guarantee I'll answer,' said JT, expecting he knew what was coming.

'You've just voluntarily walked into a mine and interviewed a known psychopath, a killer, in his own territory. I'm not saying you weren't scared, I was shitting myself. But you don't seem to care much about a threat to your life. Then there's your flat, a total mess, and, worst of all, you're sitting here sharing a drink with a man that knocked seven shades of shit out of you.'

Ira leaned in, regarding JT quizzically. He grimaced as he

spoke, as if the mental effort was a strain. 'Have you recently figured out you're gay or something?'

JT choked on his drink but looked immensely relieved. 'Well... You're about 5 per cent right there Ira. No, I'm not gay. Would it matter if I was?'

'No,' said Ira, with total seriousness. 'I've got no problem with that at all.'

'Good,' said JT, and took another swig of the fiery liquid. Then more seriously he said, 'Obviously I've got some problems, I'm just not ready to talk about them yet.' He looked down at the table while Ira looked on expectantly. Then he shook his head as if clearing it. 'So what about you? What was that about a warehouse and CID?'

Ira exhaled a short, nasal breath of amusement. 'Well, I've had a decade to think about that, so I suppose I'm okay talking about it. I was an accountant before, if you can believe that. I worked for a water purification company in the Central District, a well-financed start-up.'

He looked at JT a moment, seeking assurance, then lowered his voice.

'Well, near enough a start-up. The company I worked for before that went bust, so I had to move. I was young, just like the company. For a few cycles it was great – we were treated well, worked hard, long rotations and all that. But they looked after us, arm around your shoulder, took you out at the end of a hard shift, that sort of thing. Then, when they felt they trusted me, when they felt they had me hooked to the good life, I got promoted. I started looking after more of the accounts and it didn't take me long to figure out that something wasn't right.'

'How do you mean?' asked JT, to fill a prolonged pause.

'They were investing heavily in water purification, cutting-edge stuff on the face of it. But there was another arm of the company. It looked innocuous enough on the surface, but if I asked what it did I could never get a straight answer.'

Again, Ira paused and stared intently at the knotted wood surface. JT felt obliged to prompt him. 'What was it? Opium, money laundering, what?'

Ira screwed up his face, as if the memory was painful, then took a swig of liquor. 'They farmed shrubs. Fields and fields of shrubs. Well, one particular shrub. Do you know what Fatsia is?'

'I've never heard of it,' JT admitted.

'It's nothing special, but native to this area. Most people, farmers particularly, regard it as a pest of a plant. It has medium-sized leaves, small bulb-like flowering bits in the middle, I forget the actual term for them. So this company, of which I'm now a senior accountant, is growing masses of the stuff. They've taken out bank loans to finance it and all I'm told is it produces castor oil and there's nothing to it. But I know full well they're not selling castor oil. So what are they using it for? I have a friend, a biologist, in Ayon Research, so I ask her. She consults her books and finds nothing. Then a few cycles later she comes across a paper. It's something related to a question put to the Intercessor ROOT, the only Intercessor Skala has at the time. The paper is to do with pathogens and plants, specifically Fatsia. According to ROOT, this plant can be processed to produce a potent pathogen he calls ricin, which is pretty deadly as a gas but less so if dissolved in water. My friend, concerned, passes this on to me.'

'I can see where this is going.'

'I bet you can. They're poisoning the bloody water to justify the purification business, pure and simple. No one died as far as I know, but they proved there was a risk and built their livelihood on it.'

He took another swig to fortify himself. 'The company I

worked for before was called INI Industries. Their main products were computer hard drives, emulators, that sort of thing. You know what I'm on about?'

'I do.'

'Well, INI went down like I said. The 'Old Man' wouldn't change, and as soon as the solid-state memory stuff came on the market they were done for. The son took the fall, very unfairly in my view. That was Tyler Olson, who you met earlier. I'd heard talk he'd retrained and joined CID. He knew a lot about how big corporations operated, despite apparently not being able to run one himself. So, I looked him up and I told him what I'd found.'

'And he understood?'

'Yes, completely. I started to feed him information, copies of accounts, any paperwork I could lay my hands on. Between us we assembled a bloody great dossier – this was over a period of about six cycles. Where the stuff was grown, where it was processed and by who. The only thing we couldn't rumble was how they were getting it into the water system, although we knew what part of the system was contaminated. It doesn't take a genius to figure that out, right?'

'The slums,' said JT, catching on.

'Exactly. The point was to demonstrate how ill the water could make you if it wasn't treated. The upper crust of Skala don't want to be sick, so they agree loans to purify the water in the whole city to stop the spread. Other companies jump on the bandwagon, sewerage, drainage and all that stuff.'

'What did you do?'

'Nothing, we didn't get the chance. There was a leak on the inside, within CID. During an off shift these two thugs came for me, dragged me into a meat storage warehouse, just to impress upon me the likely outcome of my situation. They tied me down to a chair in this tiled room where they bleed the carcasses, you know?'

JT nodded, although in reality he had never set foot in such a place.

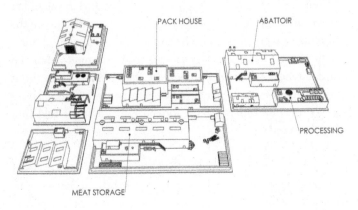

'They gave me a good going over, like I did to you.' He paused to give a brief grimace of regret but kept his eyes down. 'Then one of them got carried away.'

Ira looked up at JT for the first time in several turns then drew back his left sleeve to reveal a prominent scar that ran around the upper part of his bicep.

'There was a lot of blood. Too much. They panicked and started arguing, worried I was going to die before they got paid their due. You probably won't believe this, but the stupid bastards left me alone to call a doctor. They did, honestly.'

'I believe you,' said JT reassuringly.

'That means a lot, for what it's worth. They made another mistake. They shackled my hands with one of those enforcement handcuffs that were popular at the time, the metal ones?'

'I remember them.'

'Well, there was so much blood running down my arm I

managed to slide one hand out. Then I spun the cuff and used the ratchet to saw through the tiewraps on my legs. That was the most intense three turns of my life, I can tell you.'

'I bet,' said JT, captivated.

'There was this drain in front of me, where the blood was running. It was big, made to cope with the cows from the outland farms, so I decided to hide in it. It might sound dumb but there wasn't anywhere else to go. What I didn't know until I climbed in was that it drained into the main sewer. I crawled for ages, I have no idea how I kept it up, but I did. I crawled through shit, piss, rotting bits of dead animal and anything else that gets flushed down there.'

'You said you got blood poisoning?'

'I did, and so much else.' Ira looked down at the table, momentarily reliving the pain. Abruptly he was brought back to the present when the Landlord placed a hand gently on Ira's shoulder.

'They're ready for you,' he said softly.

'I'll tell you the rest another time,' said Ira. 'For now we need to talk about Mal-Kas.'

The elder woman sat at the low table, flanked by the bearded man and the wild, captivating younger woman. JT lowered himself down, and this time Ira moved to sit beside him. When nobody spoke and the elder woman resettled herself and frowned, JT felt obliged to say something.

'You're still not going to tell me who you are?' he asked.

The elder woman looked implacable, but the man and younger woman shifted uncomfortably. It was Ira who spoke next.

'Considering what this man's been through and what we've

got to tell you, I think you should level with him. He'll find out anyway.'

To JT's surprise it was the younger of the two women who spoke up.

'Ness, my name's Ness. Don't ever call me Vanessa.'

'Thank you, I'll remember that,' said JT, imagining that if he made the mistake he would be unlikely to get a second opportunity.

The man regarded JT intently and fingered his short beard. 'Ezekiel Lee,' he said finally, before looking across to the elder woman.

'I'm not going to tell you my name, for the time being at least,' she said, measuring him with pallid, watery eyes. 'You will have to take it on trust that I have good reason.'

There were two interpretations of this statement but JT felt sure there was nothing in his past to warrant the woman's distrust. 'Okay,' he replied, accepting she must be protecting someone else not present.

'We got into Mal-Kas,' began Ira. 'We got right in there with no problems. Horrible bloody place.'

'Did anybody recognise you, Ira?' asked Lee.

'No way,' said Ira, amused. 'It wasn't deserted by any means, but the people we saw were all company people. The scary part is the people we didn't see.'

'How's that?' asked Ness.

'We found Connor,' said JT, who then deferred back to Ira.

'He was in what they called a 'Restricted Area'. We got the impression there were several but we only saw the one. It seems to be part of the mine that had been fenced off. There's a big metal dividing wall and behind that some sort of roller-shutter gate by the sounds of it.'

Ira looked at JT for reassurance. 'We didn't see it, but you could clearly hear it being opened and shut.'

'And there was a scream,' said Ira with conviction. 'We both heard it. It could have been animal, but we both think it was human.'

'Connor was carrying a knife, which he pulled on Ira,' said JT. 'It already had blood on it.'

'So he's using serious force to keep the workforce producing,' said Ness, eyes narrowed.

'Actually,' said Ira, glancing at JT for support, 'We think it might be a bit more serious than that.'

'How so?' asked the unnamed woman JT had begun to think of as the 'Elder'.

'When we got back and talked to Vincent O'Brien at CID, he had a theory that the people were being held captive so the mining company can collect a subsidy for employing them.'

'We got the impression the mine had run dry,' interjected JT, wanting to make clear that the pieces fitted together. 'One of the drill-rig operators said the core samples they take don't contain ore, but geologists were falsifying the results to make it look like the mine was still viable.'

'O'Brien thinks the subsidies might be more valuable than the ore,' said Ira in conclusion.

The Elder considered this a moment before speaking again, more to the other two than to JT and Ira. 'That might fit. I had not considered subsidies being a factor, but it makes sense.'

Wordlessly, the other two agreed.

'Mr Gilbert,' said the Elder, 'We are very grateful for your coming here. These are disturbing tidings you've brought us. Would you be willing to make a similar trip for us again, I wonder?'

'Not to Mal-Kas,' said JT, alarmed by the suggestion. 'We were lucky to get out the first time…'

'Not to Mal-Kas, no,' said the Elder in agreement. 'I wonder if the same phenomenon is occurring elsewhere though.'

'Possibly. If we were to look anywhere else it would have to be somewhere that Hellinar Research has a legitimate interest in, equipment that genuinely needs inspecting.' He considered this a moment then began again, a little hesitantly but warming to the idea as he spoke. 'I could easily and quite legitimately make a case for wanting to inspect the equipment elsewhere. I need to write a short report on Mal-Kas – the truth is they didn't look after their kit at all well. They didn't even know what was theirs or what was on loan from us.'

JT could see Lee nodding his understanding and felt Ira's eyes on him from the right. 'Honestly, it would be easy to argue that Hellinar Research needs to put some resource into a stocktake, find out where our equipment is and in what condition.'

He looked across to meet Ira's eyes. 'How strong is your Ira identity?'

Ira was clearly startled by this question posed in the open. 'It's pretty strong,' he said, hesitantly. 'I've used it half a decade now. I have a bank account, link credits.'

'A fixed residence?'

'Not exactly,' said Ira with a laugh. Seeing JT didn't get the joke, he fell silent.

'Enough for me to hire you though.'

Ira looked shocked by this. 'Hire me? What, as an assistant?' To the delight of everyone else in the room, he sounded utterly horrified.

'Exactly. You and I go inspecting sites in Hellinar. We do the actual work but we dig around for whatever else we can learn.'

'Sounds delightful,' said Ira with as much sarcasm as he could muster. 'Just tell me where to send my CV.'

'I will,' said JT, revelling just a little in Ira's discomfort. 'You'll have to go through interview, and actually do the office work when I get you assigned, but I can't see anyone paying us the blindest bit of notice once we're up and running.'

'And you would report back to us?' asked the Elder.

'Yes. Well, I suppose Ira would.'

'We do it together,' said Ira with total sincerity and laid a firm hand on JT's shoulder. 'We talk to O'Brien as well.'

'I would expect that,' said Lee. 'We're all on the same side and if we can do things as legally as possible that's all to the good.'

'I might be able to help you target worthwhile sites,' said Ness, who JT remembered had some experience of living as a working prisoner. 'If you can come up with a list of places you can legitimately visit, we can pick out the ones most likely to be of interest.'

'That sounds ideal,' said JT.

'Thank you, Mr Gilbert. We are extremely grateful to you,' said the Elder as she rose. The others did the same. Each nodded to JT and Ira in turn before they filed silently out of the rear door.

'She likes you,' said Ira under his breath.

'The Elder? Or whatever she's called…'

Ira rolled his eyes. 'No, you dumb-ass, Ness. You could do a lot worse you know, although she's hard. I mean like quartz, not like, I don't know, granite or something.' He was floundering a little. 'Think of something hard, but she's harder.'

He gave up altogether. 'Come on, the Landlord said he'd do us another bottle and I want to take that son of a bitch for as much as I can get out of him. You're not walking out of here this shift, my son.'

JT gave him a broad grin and nodded his acceptance.

'Good, then,' said Ira. 'We'll drink to the future and I'll tell you about Ness. She practically eats men for breakfast you know…'

The two of them turned, leaving the rug-lined room quiet and airy behind them. As Ira pulled the door open, the sounds of laughter, raucous and good humoured, flooded in from the bar. JT Gilbert passed through the doorway followed by his friend, who paused before pulling the door shut with the delicate firmness of a hardened survivor.

032: Departure

Accompanied by members of the GVX crew, Katherine entered the crowded hangar of SVA late the following shift. The hangar seemed smaller, darker and hotter, GVX somehow larger and more imposing; the formal lines of engineers and dignitaries gave the vehicle a scale it had previously lacked in isolation. The entire project team had been assembled along the left flank of the vehicle, Skala's politicians and bureaucrats positioned opposite to form a narrow passage to the ladder. Katherine felt, a little cruelly perhaps, that the dignitaries' intent was solely to rob the project team of their achievement and claim it as their own.

Walking beside her, Myra Cena seemed shaky at being confronted by all the noise and the oppressive atmosphere. Katherine put an arm around her shoulder, and gave her an encouraging squeeze.

'You said goodbye to your family?'

'Earlier,' said Myra. 'They're very proud.'

'They should be,' said Katherine reassuringly. Superficially it seemed to do the trick, as Myra, in step with the rest of the crew, waved out to no one in particular.

273

Katherine made a point of shaking every team member's hand she could reach while deliberately missing the occasional VIP. She was being petty and knew it, but considered a little bit of rebellion was called for given the circumstances. Kyra would no doubt approve. And that was the bizarre thing – Kyra was out there somewhere, cast as the villain, probably exhausted and almost certainly freezing. Katherine, in contrast, was preparing to leave Skala in a frenzy of goodwill. While overall it might serve as a wildly overblown metaphor for their differing natures, it seemed wrong, despite Kyra's actions.

With a start, Katherine realised she was shaking hands with Ratha. The older Councillor looked stern and haughty, even a little frosty. Something had changed in their relationship, although Katherine couldn't pinpoint what had precipitated it.

'Good luck,' said Ratha, in a detached, uninterested manner.

'Thank you, Joss,' replied Katherine, as warmly as she could.

For a brief moment it looked as if Ratha might move to make a speech, but fortunately, in Katherine's view at least, seemed to think better of it. For all her command and domination of meetings, Joss was a terrible public speaker burdened with the delusion she was inspirational. Her pronouncements invariably turned into protracted diatribes, interesting only to herself and a select group of sycophants.

Glad to move on, Katherine saw Roy Jacobs a few paces ahead. Like her, he was making an effort to pay the project team more attention than the dignitaries, which lightened her hearts. She couldn't help but smile, a gesture Jacobs happened to catch and reciprocate. He had reached Nara. Inexplicably captivated, Katherine watched as he shook her hand and lowered his head with unheralded familiarity and respect. As Katherine looked on, Nara did much the same. Some words she didn't catch were exchanged between them, and Nara fleetingly brought a hand up to cup Jacobs' cheek. Before she could blink, the moment had passed, and she wondered if she had seen it at all. She pushed it to the back of her mind, turning her attention to John Orchard, who stood before her, beaming.

'You're going to look after her, aren't you?' he asked, taking the role of the proud parent.

'Of course I am, John,' said Katherine, with a broad smile. 'Will she take care of me though? That's the question.'

'Katherine,' he said, in mock abashment. 'How could you ask such a thing?'

She took his humour gladly.

'Come home in one piece,' he said more seriously. She nodded and they exchanged smiles before moving on.

Nara shook Katherine's hand warmly. 'I'm proud to be on the Council with you, Katherine,' she said. 'I sincerely regret we haven't spent more time together. It seems absurd we've been sitting in the same building, attending the same meetings for so long but never got to know each other beyond that. Maybe when you return with Kyra we can make amends?'

Katherine, utterly floored, didn't know what to think. She tripped over her words but managed to say, 'I'd like that, Nara,' which seemed to be enough. Nara shrank back into the line, but with a look of admiration and something like happiness or satisfaction.

To Katherine's surprise, Vincent O'Brien and Tyler Olson stood next in line. She wasn't sure how they had got themselves here, but was grateful they had made the effort.

'Just checking you're not stealing the other one,' said O'Brien in a valiant attempt at humour.

'I sort of am,' said Katherine, pushing back a stray lock of hair. 'I'm not sure I was given any choice in the matter.'

'Well, good luck.'

'Thank you,' she said as he straightened a little and offered his hand, which she took before moving on to be greeted by

Olson. She wasn't sure what to say to him. He smiled and his eyes sparkled with that wonderful welcoming quality he had. For a fleeting moment she felt like they were the only two people in the hangar.

'You take care now,' he said, his soft voice carrying over the hubbub around them.

'I will.' She hesitated then began again, 'Look I'm so sorry...' but he cut her off.

'Please, we've talked through this. Maybe when you get back with your sister we could sit down and talk about it some more, if you feel you want to. But I'm fine with it.' Moving to change the subject he said, 'I'm retired as of the last shift,' and gave a mischievous grin.

'Congratulations,' she said, pleased for him. 'What will you do now?'

'Oh, I have an idea on that, but let's talk about it later.'

Katherine gave him a quizzical frown, and returned his smile. Turning to her right, she saw the end of the line. Standing expectant and unusually regal was her father, accompanied by a flustered-looking Megan. Kyle Devin greeted his daughter warmly, while Megan looked awkward and out of place.

'I'm grateful it's you doing this, Katherine,' he said and Katherine heard the truth of his words.

'I'll bring Kyra back, whatever it takes,' she replied, trying to sound convincing even to herself.

'I know you will.' He could see Katherine wanted to say something but was hesitating. 'Go on,' he said and Megan looked up as she recognised the seriousness of his tone.

'This whole thing,' said Katherine, not quite knowing where to start. 'Me going with ROOT, GVX, it seems very surreal. Did you get a say in it?'

'I did,' he confirmed.

'And how did you vote?'

'I voted for you to go,' he replied, holding her in a level gaze. Katherine looked away, feeling conflicted as she knew she would. On the one hand she was deeply gratified by her father's trust in her, on the other she wished for the simple protection a parent would naturally be expected to provide for a daughter. To her surprise, when he spoke next she found she had both.

'I voted for you to go, not just because you're the right person, Katherine. I voted for you to go because it will be safer for you to be away from Skala. I know that sounds contradictory, when you're going further into the ice than anyone has gone before.'

Katherine gawped at him. What he said next, directed at Megan and in a low tone so as not to be overheard, startled both sisters.

'I think you should leave too, Megan. I can't explain yet, it's too early, but things are changing in Skala and not for the good. You would both be better off somewhere away from here. Where that might be, I don't know. I can't make it look like I'm hiding you, it has to look normal. If either of you have any ideas, I'd be glad to hear them.'

Lost for words, Katherine looked to Megan, who seemed to be making up her mind on something.

'Dad,' she began hesitantly. The address made Katherine both profoundly jealous and happy at the same time. She wished she could call Kyle Devin 'Dad' again, but knew she never could. 'When I was with the Hadje, the Shaman, that's the tall guy with the cat eyes I told you about...' Kyle Devin nodded. 'The Shaman said I should go to Kul to find a man called Benjamin Kittala. That he might be able to show me the way to another city. He called it Tsarocca.'

'I've heard of it,' said Kyle in a hushed tone. 'But be careful who you mention that name to.' Then, to Megan's astonishment, he said, 'I think you should go, but Kul is a dangerous place. You can't go alone.'

Katherine grinned, much to the confusion of the other two. 'I have an idea about that,' she said and turned to head back up the line. She returned a moment later with Tyler Olson in tow.

She addressed her father formally but her tone was light. 'Councillor Devin, this is Tyler Olson. This is the man that followed Megan into the tunnel under the Vault.'

'We've met,' said Kyle with a frown. Olson, for his part, wore the satisfied look of a man whose expectations, however unlikely, had been fulfilled.

'Mr Olson is now retired from CID.' The link dropped.

'Have you ever travelled to Kul, Mr Olson?' asked Kyle.

'No, sir, but I'd sure like to,' said Olson with a smile.

'Then that's settled, provided you're happy with that, Megan?' Megan seemed to grow taller as her father spoke to her for the first time not as a child, but as an adult.

'Yes,' she said. 'I'd be very happy to travel with Mr Olson.'

'Then I'll speak to the quartermaster at Hellinar Research and organise transport for you as soon as we've finished here. He's requested a meeting for later this shift on another matter, so the timing couldn't be better. As far as anyone's concerned, you're on a field trip sanctioned by me.'

Without further comment, he turned his attention back to Katherine and they regarded each other for a moment. Then, taking a step forward, Kyle embraced his daughter for the first time in decades.

'Take care of yourself and your crew,' he said so that no one could overhear. 'And when you return…' his voice trailed off a moment before he composed himself and spoke directly across her ear. 'When you return, I suggest you approach Skala with care. Do you understand?'

'Yes, Father,' she said. He held her for a moment longer before they broke apart.

Although she didn't understand what he meant, the seriousness of his words was impossible to miss. She glanced at Olson, who looked concerned, then at Megan, who was looking at the floor.

'Good luck, Megan,' said Katherine and embraced her sister.

'You too,' said Megan and smiled.

The remainder of the crew had now filed past Katherine and she turned to follow them up the ladder to the platform. She took a last, long look at the assembled crowd and her family, from whom she seemed a little less exiled than she had thought. She took a mental photograph and turned, hitting the door release as she did so.

GVX's galley was a scene of frantic activity as the crew strapped themselves in and readied systems for departure. Amid all the activity, sitting one leg over the other in one of the sculpted leather passenger chairs was a lone female figure wearing a look of bemusement. In her mid-fifties, she was the oldest member of the crew and projected an aura of uncompromising experience. Wiry curls of black hair spilled down onto her immaculately fitting jumpsuit. Absently, she began removing a plethora of rings from her fingers and placing them in a small box on the seat beside her. As Katherine approached she reached up to her left brow with both hands to remove a small piercing that ran through her eyebrow. She placed this in the box, took a last look at the contents, then closed the lid with care.

'Councillor Kane,' she said, without looking up. 'I must say you've assembled a good crew here.'

'Thank you, Trish,' said Katherine with appreciation.

'That co-driver of yours though,' she let out a low whistle of appreciation. 'Shame on you for bringing a creature like that.'

She gave a little laugh and, raising her eyes to regard Katherine, propped her chin on the knuckles of her left hand.

'He's beautiful. A little rough around the edges maybe, but, wow.'

Katherine flushed and saw Myra, who was in earshot, staring at them with her eyebrows raised. Behind Trish Asher she saw Brendan Scott attempting to stifle a smirk. 'Are we going to have a problem, Trish? Now would be the time to say so.'

Asher dropped her arm and snapped instantly into a more professional tone of voice. 'No, don't worry. I'll keep myself to myself.'

'Good to have you aboard, Trish,' said Katherine in acknowledgement. Then she turned and headed for the cockpit.

'Quite the reception down there,' Jacobs observed, as Katherine climbed into the driver's seat.

'Well, Kyra and HEX apart, this is still quite a big deal.'

'Yes, it is,' he agreed, flicking switches and punching in commands on his control console to fire the V10s.

For the first time, there was no second-guessing; the crew knew exactly what they were doing and worked in harmony. JJ, Jayce and Scott all took their places while Myra diligently checked ROOT's telemetry for any anomalies, of which there were none. Jacobs activated the motors that retracted the slide-in compartments, and Katherine revved the engines a couple of times. She could hear a raucous cheer from the hangar below and for a brief, selfish moment, revelled in it.

'Control systems operating as expected, Katherine,' said ROOT silkily through a speaker behind them.

'I concur with that,' said Jayce. 'All systems nominal.'

'I suppose that means we're good to go,' said Jacobs,

covering his mic. He all but rolled his eyes at 'All systems nominal'. Katherine had to agree it was a daft catchphrase, but then it did serve a purpose.

'Something wrong?' asked Jayce when there was no response.

'No, Jayce,' said Katherine, who was trying not to smirk. 'Thanks, we're just locking in the torque converters.'

Jacobs flicked the switch to enable the drive line. 'Torque converters locked in,' he said, getting back to business.

'Okay,' said Katherine. 'Say goodbye to civilisation.' She throttled up and felt the drive engage as they began to roll. GVX broke into dazzling sunlight, magnified threefold by the water on the ground outside the hangar. The sectioned, spring-tread wheels threw arching gouts of spray into the air behind them as the V10s surged before being brought back to heel.

They skirted the outer edge of the Eastern District, heading south to meet the road that led to Aya. The new city lay further south than was ideal, and Kyra would almost certainly not have taken the same route. But being able to maintain maximum speed on a paved road for over 900 kilometres was an opportunity to make rapid progress. Katherine had pulled strings with the Aya Construction Department to have the road clear of traffic for a few rotations and, as they turned to join it, her wish appeared to have been fulfilled. Bureaucracy, for a change, had played in her favour.

She selected four-wheel drive, allowing the front four wheels to rotate freely, and throttled up to 80 per cent duty on the V10s. They accelerated up to nearly 120 kilometres a rotation and cruised comfortably eastwards. The concrete was smooth and new; the water sat like a film upon it, reflecting up at them.

They quickly passed what remained of Lake Eiraye, upon

whose receding shoreline Skala had originally been constructed. It looked unusually resplendent, a result of the last rainfall it was ever likely to see. Gradually, the green of the grasslands appeared on the horizon and the fields to either side began to look more fertile. Muscular livestock dotted the fields and the occasional tree gave way to small spinneys and outcroppings of woodland.

Ahead of them lay the darkness beyond the perpetual dawn. Katherine had never found time to visit the construction at Aya, despite it consuming her more recent working life. She felt a strange foreboding she couldn't explain and added another 2 per cent throttle. The journey had started and from now it was simply a race against time to find Kyra and HEX before any harm came to them. But first she would visit Aya and see the future she had helped to build.

033: Aya

Skala was only a little over eight rotations behind them when Katherine got her first sight of Aya. The transition from the heat and brightness of Skala into the sullen grasslands had been gradual. The sparkling of water on the roadway turned dull as light drizzle came and went at uneven intervals. Rear-facing cameras showed the sun falling ever lower in the sky, eventually necessitating the use of an anti-glare filter.

Aya itself lay around 100 kilometres southwest of a tall mountain range, colloquially known as the Teeth of Aumond because of its regular and serrated peaks. Who Aumond had been, Katherine couldn't recall, but she imagined her as one of the early tribal settlers of ancient history. Between Aya and the foot of the mountains lay what HEX had christened Har Lake, a thirty-five-kilometre-wide body of water fed by two slowly melting glaciers.

The approach to Aya took them due east, the city spread out a little to the south of their route. The road and its parallel railway turned slowly southeast until they faced the suburbs square on. The sun hung so low in the sky that it kissed only the tips of the huge skyscrapers littering the Central District. The bright concrete, white tile and blueish-green glass made

283

the taller buildings gleam between the shadows of the looming mountains beyond. The lower streets of the city extended out to surround the centre in a dark shroud.

A freight train trundled towards them, on its return to collect supplies from Skala. Despite GVX's speed, it took nearly a turn to clear, such was its length. The pallets and containers it carried were occasionally separated by huge lay-down gas tanks supported in metal cradles.

Nearing the city's boundary, the last licks of sun upon the road became darkness and the drizzle started once more. Katherine throttled down with a kilometre to go and GVX's progress slowed to a crawl by the time they passed between the first buildings. The roadway remained as wide as they entered the city and Katherine knew it continued as such, becoming a central thoroughfare as far as the Council Chambers, which were now under construction. Although some buildings, mostly residential, were complete, they were punctuated by partly developed plots around them, areas that had been purchased and would be developed by private companies who had yet to deliver on their commitments.

The crew of GVX remained silent as the huge vehicle rolled past shell after empty shell of buildings and under regular walkways in varying states of completion. Although pockets of floodlit construction equipment littered the sidewalks, it was eerily quiet. The residual warmth inside GVX, coupled with the streaking rain and deserted, spotless streets they flitted by, induced a soporific effect that was hard to fend off.

They slowed to a halt within sight of the construction area surrounding central Aya. From the cockpit, Katherine and Roy Jacobs could see the occasional site worker look at the hulking monster that had parked itself nearby, but none gave it more than a cursory glance before carrying on with their business.

Jacobs put the V10s into a fuel-conserving five-cylinder

idle-running mode, and initiated the command to expand the flanks before following Katherine out of the cockpit. Trying to fight back a yawn, he found the crew were standing in a semicircle facing the Councillor and made his way over to join her. The atmosphere was odd – he couldn't quite put his finger on it, but she seemed to have assumed a slightly sullen, resigned mood he didn't recognise. Maybe it was just the warmth and the tiring effect of eight rotations' travel.

'Before we go any further, I'd like Trish to brief you,' said Katherine. 'Now seems an appropriate time, while things are still safe and quiet.'

Trish, who seemed to be expecting this, pushed herself up and took her place in the centre of the galley, frowning her thanks to Katherine.

'Most of you know me already,' she said, in a soft but commanding tone. 'For those that don't, I'm Trish Asher. My role here is to keep you all safe. Trust me when I say Ayon is very unforgiving. My primary concern is risk management. Be under no illusions: should you fall down a crevasse out on the ice, you will not be rescued.'

She stared intently, first at Myra then at Roy Jacobs, to make sure the message sank in. The rest of the crew sat fidgeting or looking at the ceiling or floor.

'Should there be any sort of incident, our priority is to keep Councillor Kane and Roy Jacobs safe. I'm not suggesting the rest of you are expendable, but without drivers we're going nowhere. As I understand it, this bag of bolts is about the most sophisticated, complicated-to-operate vehicle ever to turn a wheel, so we need to keep both of them out of trouble.'

Trish saw nods around her. Katherine, who she knew would be feeling uncomfortable, was looking down at the floor.

'The next most important person here is Bren,' she said, looking at Brendan Scott. 'Bren and I go way back and I can assure you he's the best medic we could have with us. He's also a good cook. If you get hurt, he's the person that's going to put you back together again, so keep him safe.'

'Our biggest risk is Miss Cena here,' she said, pointing to Myra with the coupled fore and middle fingers of one hand. 'I mean no disrespect but you need to understand you're in at the deep end. JJ, Bren and Jayce have been out on the ice recently, so listen to them. Katherine, how long since you've been out?'

Katherine drew in a long breath, trying to remember exactly. She recalled the trip but not the date. 'A long time since I've been really deep into Ayon.'

'Then you need to re-acquaint yourself. I'll help you as much as I can. Now,' she said, looking around again, 'some housekeeping. JJ and Jayce, as soon as we stop in the tundra I want the mulchers filled, even if we don't turn them on. Keep them filled whenever you can. There is nothing less useful than all the bio-material that's sat behind you as the fuel gauge ticks down to zero.'

JJ and Jayce both nodded their understanding.

'Men,' said Asher, stirring them to attention. 'We're going to be out there for a lunar cycle at least, if not more. It's going to be hard enough for you to pee straight, so keep things hygienic.'

Asher turned to glare at Myra, who had put a hand over her mouth to cover a giggle.

'You might find it funny now, Miss Cena, but I guarantee when you're throwing up all over the place with a stomach bug, you won't be laughing.'

Myra looked a little ashamed of herself, but was still fighting hard not to giggle.

'Which brings me to my next point,' continued Asher, surveying the women around her. 'Our cycles will converge very quickly, you will be amazed how quickly. Bear it in mind, for your sake and the sake of the men. Menstruation is a reality, and it's not problem-free out on the ice. As with the men, keep things clean and tidy please. There is no shortage of sanitary supplies, so use them as you need. If you're feeling overwrought and snappy, most likely all four of us will be feeling the same. The last thing any of us needs is a catfight or a pack of us setting on the men. They need to do their jobs just as we do, so be aware of your body and cut them some slack. That works both ways, gentlemen. We all need to support each other.'

Everyone nodded their understanding.

'Good,' she said with finality. 'Now, when we get into the deep cold I don't want anyone going outside on their own. We operate a buddy system and everyone looks after everyone else. If GVX's toilets are blocked and you have to do your business outside, you go with someone. If you scrape the solar panels on the roof, you do it with a partner. Whatever it is, you keep line of sight all the time. Are we all clear on that?'

There was a collective murmur of affirmation.

'Very well,' said Asher. 'We've a long way to go before we have to put those rules into force, but the earlier we start observing them the better. When we do get out there, remember the basics. If you are outside you will use up a lot of energy, so keep that in mind. Bren will be helping you adjust your diet accordingly. JJ and Jayce, this applies to you more than anyone, as you're likely to be outside the most. I gather the panels on the roof will need periodic scraping?'

Jayce nodded.

'Watch how much you sweat if you're doing manual labour. If your sweat gets too cold you risk hypothermia. I know Jayce,' she said, as he made to protest. 'You know all about it but the others probably don't so I'm spelling it out.'

She grinned at Jayce a moment, and the others seemed to

sense he knew what was coming next. 'Keep your nether regions warm. It's not uncommon to contract urinary tract infections out here, particularly in men for obvious reasons. If you like pissing razor blades then fine, if not, keep wrapped up and warm down there.'

She looked at them each in turn to make sure they understood. 'Okay, that's it for now,' she finished and turned to sit back down.

'Okay,' said Katherine. 'We're going to be here for about three rotations for JJ and Jayce to have a look over GVX, before we head into the borderlands, then the tundra. Our next stop will be three shifts from now so check thoroughly.'

JJ nodded her agreement, Jayce kept his head down.

After a brief pause Katherine said 'I'm going to take a brief look around outside. Roy, would you come with me?'

'Sure,' said Jacobs, and made to gather his things.

'What do you think?' asked Katherine, speaking up over the distant sound of construction. It was cold outside and the floodlights above them made the sky look darker than it really was. The fresh, black tarmac under their feet glistened with an oily residue.

'It's very impressive,' replied Jacobs, after a pause that he hoped went unnoticed.

'No, really,' said Katherine, eyeing him critically. 'What do you really think?'

'It feels, well, I don't know.' He looked back at her intently and decided he might as well be truthful. 'It feels sterile.'

He wracked his mind for excuses as to why he felt this way and began to list them. 'Maybe it's because there's no one here. The buildings are just shells. Once they're fitted out and the streets are filled with people it will feel different. It just feels, I don't know,' he stumbled and saw that she was looking at him expectantly, almost willing him on. A thought had crystallised in his mind and he spoke it before he had time to properly consider his words.

'It's got Ratha's stamp all over it – you know, like a hundred variations on grey? I've heard people call her the 'Grey Lady', and it kind of fits.'

Katherine, who had heard people call Joss Ratha much worse, smiled but said nothing.

'Do you think she'll be the next Matriarch?' Jacobs asked seriously. 'That's the common view, that she'll be the first Matriarch of Aya.'

'I really don't know,' said Katherine. 'Possibly. What else do they say?'

Jacobs turned to her, a worried but defiant look in his eyes. 'That she's going to treat the position as more than just symbolic.' He let his voice trail off.

Katherine grimaced a little at the implications of his suggestion. Still, she couldn't deny the growing sense of unease she felt when thinking of her former mentor, but said nothing more. Jacobs looked back to the nearest building, looking for something positive to say but finding himself coming back to the same word – soulless. He scrutinised the curved glass frontage and realised he couldn't see the most fundamental of interruptions across its flank.

'Possibly I'm being dumb,' he said, suddenly more upbeat, 'but that building there? Where's the door?'

Katherine gave a snort loaded with irony. 'Yeah, where is the door?'

He waited for an explanation, which, after a deep resigned breath, she provided. 'It's Victor Urasa's new building. You see those glass pods?'

'Yes,' said Jacobs, confused. Three pods, evenly spaced at

about twenty metres apart, protruded from the ground a further thirty metres from the building.

'You step into one of those and an elevator takes you down into a tunnel. The tunnel runs across to the building, where you get into another elevator that takes you up to where you want to go.'

'Well,' said Jacobs thoughtfully, 'what happens if the elevator breaks?'

'There's a spiral staircase around each elevator. It kind of ruins the effect the architect was looking for, they were later additions for exactly the reason you've described.'

'Why not have just have a normal front door?' he asked. 'The sidewalk runs right up to the glass.'

Katherine crossed her arms and frowned in annoyance, he thought, but when she answered he realised from the sarcasm in her voice that her ire was directed elsewhere.

'Yeah, why indeed? I'll tell you one thing though, you can bet the font on every toilet sign is identical and every letter is within a few microns of the next.'

'I bet that took a few meetings to agree,' he said.

'You have no idea.' She rolled her eyes. 'The whole of central Aya was designed by committee and became control freakery gone mad. Those tunnels I just mentioned, they are linked to other tunnels, a whole network of them underground. They are supposed to be there to help prevent skin cancer, but if I were cynical, which I'm becoming, I'd say they were there because people like Victor Urasa don't want to have to mingle with the great unwashed of the general population.'

'That annoys you? It does me.'

'It frustrates me,' replied Katherine bitterly. 'The intention, when ROOT and I began to get involved more than a decade ago, was that Aya should accommodate all of society equally. I understand the need for culture and a little grandeur in the

Central District but, as time's gone by, it's degenerated into petty arguments over personal taste. Whose office floor area is bigger than whose, and more you just wouldn't believe.'

'You sure? I can imagine quite a lot of idiocy.' Jacobs regarded her closely and she took the hint. No doubt it wasn't just her world that could be so petty.

The rain had stopped, and activity going on in the distance had ceased, giving way to an eerie quiet. As he watched her, Jacobs realised Katherine was deeply troubled, and by more than arguments over font size. She kept biting her lower lip, and folding then refolding her arms. Eventually she took a step forward to put a token distance between them.

'What is it?' he asked, trying to catch her eye.

She stayed quiet and looked into the distance as if trying to make her mind up about something. As she stood, a breeze picked up and she drew herself in. Wisps of blonde, rain-strewn hair blew across her face. She absently brushed them away with cold fingers.

'The suburbs aren't big enough,' she said without further explanation.

'I'm not sure I understand?'

'The suburbs aren't big enough,' she repeated harshly and turned to look him straight in the eye. She looked more betrayed than angry. 'When we drove in, I thought the Central District looked too close so I started counting streets. There are way too few.'

'What does that mean?' asked Jacobs, recognising the faint traces of distress in her voice, but asking in a matter-of-fact tone.

'It means something's wrong. It means there isn't enough housing for the people of Skala and the slums.' She looked at him, but his reaction was unreadable. 'It means all the conspiracy theories I've heard, the pressure groups, all the craziness I've been arguing against, is right. It's a shock to have to accept, that's all.'

'But you knew it was the case,' he said evenly and hoping he read her right.

She turned her face away in shame and looked back out towards the partly completed Central Council building.

'Deep down, yes, I knew.' She bit her bottom lip again and drew in a reluctant breath. 'I've been living a lie. Another lie.' She gave a short, ironic laugh and turned back to him. 'Sometimes it feels like my whole life has centred around other people's lies.' She looked down and stubbed a toe into the rainbow mix of tarmac oil and water swirling slowly at her feet.

'It's not just you,' he said, with some assurance. Uncomfortable with the way the conversation was heading, he tried to change tack. 'I get it. You can deal with whatever it is that's going on once we get back with your sister. For now though, we need to stay focused. GVX has exceeded expectations so far, but it won't take much for it to bite us if we don't keep our eyes wide open.'

'You're right,' she said and seemed grateful for the reprieve. She turned back to look at GVX and JJ, who was meticulously inspecting the gaps between tread sections with a flashlight. 'We should get back. I want to check a couple of things with Myra and ROOT before we get moving again.'

She began to walk back and Jacobs fell in beside her. 'Sterile is the right word for this place,' she said, taking a last look around her.

'That's a first,' Jacobs laughed. 'Engineering grunts aren't known for their eloquence.'

'Eloquence,' she retorted, mirroring his humour. 'Another big word for an engineering grunt.'

When they got to the ladder, Jacobs ascended first. Katherine took another fleeting look around, despite herself, then forced her mind back to the present. As Roy had said, Aya would have to wait for the time being. She felt an irresistible need to get moving, to get away from Skala and Aya, out into the tundra and the ice beyond. Within a couple of rotations that was exactly where she was heading, and it calmed her soul, if only a little.

034: Kul

Megan and Tyler approached the city of Kul through a deep crevasse littered with the debris of old railroad. Twisted tracks and splintered sleepers lay strewn across the ground between near-vertical rock walls. Only the higher faces caught the sunlight, giving the place an eerie foreboding, magnified by the miasma of dust particles that hung motionless in the air. A solitary tree, growing out from low on the left-hand face, stood in defiant reminder that life had once thrived in this place.

Olson steered Pegasus 3 diagonally over the larger pieces of debris, turning occasionally to avoid the sharper, torn edges of the tracks. Megan, seated to his left, looked in wonder towards what, judging by the light flooding from it, must be an open space beyond. She had said little for the past 200 kilometres, in part to allow Olson to concentrate, but also because she felt restrained by an innate sense of trepidation.

Strange shadows played across the inside of the cab as they passed under the lone remnant of vegetation above. A single, dry leaf drifted down and lodged itself between the glass of the windshield and its surrounding support. Absently, Megan wondered what species it was that had survived out here with so little water. If it was still there by the time they reached

Kul, perhaps she would retrieve it and take it back to Skala to identify in the horticultural section of the Central Library.

As they made their way forward in fits and jolts, Megan began to see a faint impression of dark columns forming in the bright middle distance. Olson must have noticed them too for he leaned forward, squinting. As they neared the mouth of the canyon they began to make out a wall, topped with evenly spaced structures which filtered the sun in diffused rays.

'What do you think?' asked Megan, not taking her eyes off the shapes in front of them.

'I'm not sure,' said Olson, still squinting but being careful not to lose track of the debris they had yet to negotiate.

They exited the canyon, its steep sides quickly giving way to a flat plain of grit-laden earth. Now, free of the dust that hung in the air behind them, the wall and its towers became much clearer. It took a moment for Megan to get to grips with the overall picture before her. The wall, which stood around twenty metres high, was festooned with windows and slits. It had towers, each of which featured a prominent opening and a series of poles protruding both in line with and across its axis. But what took her time to grasp was the total lack of definition of the shape. It was as if the yellowish-grey stone had been melted like the wax of a candle.

Olson had noticed her stare from the corner of his eye. Approaching a gap in the foot of the wall where two distinct railroad tracks entered in parallel, he brought Pegasus 3 to a halt at the edge of the shadow cast down by the wall. He throttled back the turbine and, after a moment's pause to take in the sight, he turned to her with a smile.

'Sixty decades of abrasive erosion sure leaves a weathered look on a place, don't you think?'

'It certainly does,' said Megan in wonder. 'There can't be a defined edge anywhere. What do you think those towers are?'

'Wind traps is my guess,' he said without hesitation. He peered up at the once-rectangular structures. 'They catch the wind through those vertical slots and channel it down to circulate around the inside of the building. The air exits out of the back or sides of the tower, depending on the wind direction.'

He looked over and smiled at her. 'It's an older and more elegant form of air conditioning.'

Megan squinted but said nothing more. For a moment her mind flitted back to the Central Library and its undiscovered natural cooling system. She discarded the thought, as knowledge of such an extensively used principle couldn't have been lost in a mere thirty decades.

Olson, who was thinking along the same lines, but drawing a rather different conclusion, reached above him and flicked the switch that lowered the tailgate. He looked back to Megan.

'I think we should go on foot from here,' he said, levering himself out of the seat.

Grabbing a rucksack of provisions, Megan followed him back through the vehicle, down the ramp and onto the dirt. She was immediately struck by the silent desolation of the place. The sound of hot, moving air seemed remote and ghostly as it rushed into and exited the towers high above them. Straining, she heard the faint hiss of sand displaced by a young pit viper as it moved away from them, head tilted back in arrogant defiance. But there was little else; even the cawing of carrion birds was absent. This place, she thought, must truly be dead.

They walked up the remnants of the railroad towards a rounded, gaping hole that looked more like a pockmarked wound than the grand gateway it must once have been. Beyond it, they discovered a shadowy atrium illuminated by occasional rays of light that filtered through jagged tears in the roof structure.

As they crossed the threshold of the arch, one part of Megan suddenly broke out in revolt against the other. The nausea of fear clashed with a deep desire to be something more than she was, to emulate or better her older siblings. While Olson considered the Shaman's story of a monstrous creature within Kul as pure myth, she couldn't dismiss the look on Jean-Louis' face as the huge man had delivered his warning. Did she really need to take this sort of risk?

She fought to calm her mind: there was a choice to be made and she had to make it quickly. She called out after Olson. He paused, one foot atop a huge wooden beam that obstructed their path, and half turned to look at her. She saw that hardness in his eyes, just as she had during the descent into Buni Sound. She could tell he knew her mind and, as he turned back and stepped up and over the debris, she realised he also knew her inevitable decision. Shouldering the rucksack, she set off to follow him.

The atrium was a huge space, the twin parallel tracks dividing to six between raised platforms. Under the remains of crumbling wooden beams sat the hulking and morose shape of an ancient steam locomotive. Olson made his way over to it and ran a hand over one of the giant piston housings.

'You know, my great-grandfather was old enough to remember the last train to arrive in Skala. I'm sixty-eight and he must have been near enough a hundred before he died, so we're talking fifteen decades ago. They were rare back then, one in ten cycles or maybe less. I remember he said it belched steam out of it from all over and smelled like hot wet metal mixed with castor oil.'

He looked back and smiled at Megan, who stood motionless, admiring the immensity of the iron behemoth. 'I never thought I'd see one myself,' he said reverentially.

'What happened to the one he saw arrive in Skala?' she asked thoughtfully.

'That's a good question,' he agreed. 'Broken up for parts I guess. You remember that huge beam engine we saw buried in the floor of the Siphon?'

'Vaguely,' said Megan, recalling what she could in spite of the unreality of their first encounter with the Hadje.

'Same technology.' He smiled and patted the solid flank of the engine before turning to ascend onto the platform.

They climbed, moving to the rear of the space then through a high doorway that led back out into the sunlight. Kul, or what was left of it, lay below them. Unlike Skala, which was festooned with high-rise buildings, most of the rooftops were around the same height, two storeys at most. They were typically flat, punctuated by the occasional reed-covered, conical structure. The exception was a single dome that lay among worn, partially collapsed buildings at the city's centre.

'How could anyone still live here?' asked Megan. Olson grunted his agreement.

They stood slightly apart for a few moments longer, taking in the view. Only the faint whistle of the wind could be heard, giving the vast city an aura of desolation. Together they descended worn steps to a straight thoroughfare heading west. The going was slow, as they were forced to clamber over fallen stonework and the splintered remains of wooden beams.

Eventually they reached the dome, which bore a striking resemblance to the Council Chambers of Central Skala. One of the doors stood slightly ajar, cocked over on bent hinges, the gap just enough for them to squeeze through sideways, one at a time.

Followed by Olson, Megan stepped into the dim interior and took in the view before her. A few sections of the hemispherical ceiling had fallen in, leaving ragged tears of ethereal sunlight that caught a myriad particles of suspended dust. As her eyes adjusted, she began to recognise the eerily familiar layout. Ringed by a debris-strewn standing space was an exact, if slightly smaller, replica of the belvedere that was central to the chamber in Skala. The two semicircles and the divide between them were identical.

'I see it,' she said, 'but I don't believe it.'

'Believe it,' said Olson, equally awestruck.

They descended creaking, wooden steps leading down through the divide and into the belvedere. At the centre lay a pile of lumpy, charred material approximately three metres in diameter. Megan moved to its edge and gingerly nudged at it with her boot. It was lighter than she had expected and spread with ease, throwing up a small cloud of ash.

'It's the great table. The last one, I mean. After they burned it.'

Olson nodded his agreement but kept a respectful distance.

'I wouldn't have expected anything different, but I have to confess it's a real sight to see,' he said.

'Thirty decades ago a privy council sat here,' she said with a sweeping look. 'Do you think that's what they were called back then?'

'I expect so,' said Olson, looking up and around. 'Everything is so similar I can't imagine they would have called themselves anything different. Look up, you see the remains of the drapes?'

Megan looked and saw the drooping, somewhat ghostly shreds of loose fabric hanging from the ribs of the dome's framework.

'It's the same. It's all the same.' She shook her head in wonder.

For over a rotation they wandered the building, finding part-collapsed anterooms and annexes that evoked further echoes of the chambers in Skala. Undeniably there were differences, scale being the most obvious, but to both, it felt the same in grandeur and purpose. Each time they returned to the central chamber Megan got stronger impressions of the place being filled with people, debate and argument.

Trying not to break the spell, Olson quietly suggested they return to Pegasus 3 to sleep. Megan readily agreed, and they made their way back towards the heat of the sun-bleached streets.

Emerging sideways through the door, Megan thought she saw a flash in her peripheral vision from a rooftop to her right. She felt a sudden rush of adrenaline.

'Tyler,' she said urgently, under her breath.

'What is it?' he asked, turning back to face her.

She freed herself from the gap in the door and pointed in the direction of the movement. 'Something up there. I saw it from the corner of my eye.'

Olson squinted, but saw nothing.

'We're both tired and dehydrated. I'm seeing ghosts too.'

He offered her a bottle of water, and she took a long draw. Maybe it was her imagination but she still remained on guard as they picked their way back to the railroad. They climbed the steps up to the atrium entrance, but Megan held back a moment and scanned the city below her. She wanted to take in the sight again, but if she was honest she also felt a little paranoid, exhausted or not. Seeing nothing, she turned to follow Olson, who had already disappeared into the dim light of the atrium.

She called out, but heard no response. Then she saw him, stood stock-still on one of the platforms, silhouetted from the entrance on the other side of the space. He had one arm raised, the unmistakable gesture of his index finger held to his lips. She froze, listening. Again that burst of adrenaline surged through her and blood rushed in her ears. Blocking the sound out, she could just make out a soft creak from directly above her. Then she saw one of the beams of light darken momentarily as something flitted past. As she searched for the source, a huge figure dropped down from impossibly high in the roof to land in a crouch between herself and Olson.

Unable to move, Megan fixed her eyes on the form, which, with unnatural grace, raised itself up as if uncoiling. Its attention was focused upon her as, without realising, she let out an involuntary scream.

035: Benjamin Kittala

The Ruined City of Kul

Pure, unadulterated terror gave way to a concentrated panic that Megan could not begin to describe. Time seemed to stretch as the dark figure extended to its full height, well over two metres. Its first step toward her was languid but, with a second and third, it accelerated at a barely imaginable rate. With the fourth step it passed through a beam of sunlight and for a moment its features became distinct. Its skin appeared to be plated, a sort of armour or exoskeleton. The plates were flowing curves that moved across each other in soundless, rippling harmony.

The head was beautiful and terrible in equal measure. A malevolent, featureless mask of driven intent. Its proportions were humanoid, but formed in a serpentine curve that extended and reversed, flicking subtly upward from behind the crown. Strands of braided hair fanned out from a single point somewhere high above the neck. Each braid was adorned with multicoloured rings spaced at even intervals down its length, finishing in a series of extended white sleeves.

Megan saw the creature rotate its left forearm, as if offering up the vein of the wrist. As it did so, two long blades extended from the posterior flank behind the clenched fist, catching the light and reflecting it with the iridescent sheen of oil on water. The sight of the blades galvanised Megan and, with no conscious thought, she threw herself into the darkness to her left. As a diversion, she slung off her rucksack in a single, smooth motion and hurled it behind her.

Seeing a wide beam running down from an old cast-iron tank, she sprinted towards it and charged upwards. In front of her was a gantry, a crane of some sort for loading the locomotives. She scaled it, forcing her movements to be deliberate and slower than was natural. Reaching a platform, she ventured a look back. The creature was still at ground level, seemingly scanning around, apparently looking for Olson. She could see him crouched between the platform and the engine he had so admired earlier. The creature was now very close to him. It seemed to be sniffing the air, swaying as if trying to catch a scent and inexorably zeroing in. Olson, from his position below it, could not know how close it was.

Forcing her mind to calm, she tried to assess why the creature had not followed her. It was as if it were setting the scene, making sure it knew where both its targets were before deciding in what order to pick them off. With a sickening feeling, it dawned on her that the chances of them both surviving was essentially zero, but there was a possibility one of them might make it back to Pegasus 3 if the other could create an effective distraction. Instinct took control of Megan, pushing back the terror to bury the little girl that wanted to hide. She filled her lungs with stifling, dust-laden air and called out as loudly as she could.

'Up here! I'm up here!'

The creature's head snapped around and it bolted for the base of the structure, bounding across from one platform to the next with sickening agility. It began to climb the metal framework towards her as she saw Olson move and she hoped he guessed her intentions. She felt, rather than heard, a reverberation from below and guessed she had only a few moments to react. In the unreality of the situation she found a clarity. A phrase she had heard long ago came back to her, from where she had not the faintest idea. 'People always panic upward. If you want to survive, you need to do something different.'

She looked below her and saw a pile of debris, loose wood supports that might break her fall. It was a chance, if only a slim one. She made the decision just in time, throwing herself over the edge of the platform as the creature reached it. The sensation of falling ended in a crash of old, dry wood that gave way and splintered.

Expecting to be set upon a moment later, she looked up to see the figure standing high on the platform above, clearly distracted. From somewhere in the distance, Olson was shouting. Looking back around her for a means of escape, she saw a series of old mesh gratings set into the floor off to her right. One lay discarded to the side just a few metres from her, leaving an opening to the crawlspace below.

She plunged at the hole with an inelegant stumble. Finding the space below barely ample, she began to drag herself forward on knees and elbows. Fighting back pain from the fall, she heard the creature land somewhere off to her left.

Not a moment later, the screech of metal, as twin blades stabbed down through a grate behind her, brought a fresh panic to the fore. With a twisting motion the creature raised the section and tossed it aside. Possessed of a relentless speed, it systematically followed her, ripping up each grate in sequence.

She was sobbing, waves of nausea crashing over her as she willed herself forward. She knew it was over when the blades stabbed down within centimetres of her face. They paused for a moment, long enough for her to take a last appreciation of her dirty, sweat-covered hands. With the heel of her palm she pushed back a matted clump of her once-blonde hair, now reduced to a stinking, grit-infused mess.

With a deft flick, the creature flung away the last of her cover. It stood motionless for what seemed like an eternity, before squatting down to regard her curiously. Distantly she heard Olson again but couldn't make out the words. They didn't matter now. She felt sick emptiness mix with a resigned defiance and, against her every instinct, pushed herself up to face her end.

Before she was upright a powerful grip took the back of her neck as the creature lifted her out of the pit. The grip eased for just a moment before it threw her back against a wooden pillar. She crumpled to her knees as the twin blades drove with sickening force into the beam to either side of her neck, pinning her in place. The creature was squatting again, its smooth, blank face level with hers. It drew in, cocking its head to the side in a gesture dripping with intent and menace. Megan tried to turn away and felt a stinging heat as the blade's edge cut into the muscle at the base of her neck. She screwed her eyes shut and mustered every last remaining fibre of being she had for one last act.

'Tyler, get out of here. Forget Kittala. Just get out of here.'

Nothing happened. She ventured a terrified look at the creature, which was looking around, regarding its surroundings curiously. It brought its attention back to her and, to her utter astonishment, it spoke in a melancholy, slightly distorted rasp.

'You are looking for Benjamin Kittala?'

'Yes,' said Megan, in terrified confusion.

'Then I would say that you've found him. Mine is not a name many of your people would know.'

She felt the blades jerk from the wood and slide back past her neck before she collapsed in a heap. She saw the blades glint, then disappear; they didn't so much retract as disassemble themselves or dematerialise. It happened so fast Megan couldn't tell if she was making sense of what her eyes were telling her. She looked up at the towering figure above her. To her amazement it offered her a hand.

'What the hell?' she said, looking up in disbelief.

'You can come out, you're safe,' called the figure over its shoulder. Despite its metallic ring it reminded Megan of Jean-Louis' accented speech.

With trepidation, Megan took the hand that was still thrust out to her. It was undoubtedly synthetic, a plated armour of some sort. The feel of it was of a strong material that had just a little give to it.

'I'm sorry I frightened you. I thought you were looters,' the figure said.

Megan got to her feet. Her ears were ringing and she felt generally dizzy. From the far shadows she saw Olson cautiously approaching. He was as dirty as she was, and equally wide-eyed.

'Come, you're safe. I'm Benjamin Kittala. You were looking for me?'

'Yes,' said Olson, but sounded unsure.

'Fine. If you knew I was here, I am to assume you are friends?'

'Yes,' said Olson again.

'Your vehicle is outside?' He addressed this question to Megan.

'Yes,' she said shakily.

'Good. Mine also. We should leave this place if we are to talk. I have a camp three miles south of here. You follow me, and we talk there?'

'Okay,' said Megan, looking to Olson, who nodded his

agreement. 'How far is, what did you say, three miles? I don't know what that means.'

'Ahh,' said Kittala, as if enlightened. 'About five kilometres to you.'

'Okay,' said Megan absently.

'Then follow,' he said and turned towards the bright light of the entrance. Dazed, Megan found her rucksack, frowned in astonishment at Olson and followed.

Outside, the armoured figure of Benjamin Kittala made his way towards Pegasus 3, which sat as they had left it, about thirty metres away. Kittala bent his huge frame to peer underneath the chassis, then walked around to the rear, where the tailgate remained open. Following him around they found him performing a cursory inspection of the inside of the vehicle. Seemingly satisfied, he made his way back out, ducking his head through the opening as he did so.

'Can't be too careful,' he said in an offhand manner. Looking to his left he added, 'I'll meet you at the southernmost corner of the city.' And with that he turned and jogged off at a casual speed that would have put the fastest sprinters of Skala to shame.

Megan and Olson exchanged glances before moving to the cockpit. Olson began the ignition process and felt a pang of comfort as the familiar whine of the turbine reached his ears. Staring blankly ahead of her, Megan once again caught sight of the errant leaf stuck to the windshield. With a compulsion she didn't quite understand, she bolted back out of the rear of the vehicle and dislodged it carefully. Returning, and fumbling the lone piece of foliage between the pages of a field journal inside her rucksack, she heard the ramp clang shut behind.

Within a few moments they were moving, turning

southwards in the direction Kittala had been heading. They skirted the outer wall of Kul for a couple of turns before they saw him sitting astride a purposeful-looking hydrocycle. On seeing them, he spun the rear wheel and turned the bike on its axis to accelerate away as Olson throttled up to follow.

They drove in frantic pursuit as the plume of dust that followed Kittala turned to the right and disappeared. Throttling back, Olson saw the unmistakable form pulling up outside an outcropping of rock. The figure dismounted and indicated for them to stop outside the mouth of a cave eroded into the rock face. Olson did so and cut the turbine before lowering the tail ramp.

The cave was dark and surprisingly cool compared to the arid heat outside. Olson and Megan followed the hulking figure inside, both still unsure of their host, who bent down and, as if by sleight of hand, lit a small fire. Given the ambient temperature it was a baffling thing to do, but before either could express concern, Kittala placed a tubular structure around thirty centimetres tall atop the flames. Almost immediately the temperature around them began to drop to a tolerable level.

For a few moments, Megan and Olson stood in an uncomfortable silence. Megan reached up to her neck, which still stung from the cut. She ran a finger over it, finding that the damage was minimal. Satisfied with his fire and the refrigerant device atop it, Kittala turned back to regard his guests.

'We thought you were the monster,' said Megan, hesitantly.

'I'm not,' said Kittala, who raised his hands to his neck and began unhooking something below the flowing braids of hair. The faint hiss of slowly escaping gas passed within a few moments.

'Then why the suit?' asked Olson, with a jocularity he didn't quite feel.

'I hunt the monster. Don't want to get infected.'

Megan and Olson exchanged astonished glances. The possibility that a monster really existed in Kul took a moment to sink in. Looking back, they saw Kittala slide his hands across his faceplate and pull forward. It came away easily and he took a deep breath before turning to assess them with his own eyes.

Like the inhabitants of Buni Sound, he was dark-skinned but his features were fuller, as if better nourished, which he probably was. His face was purposeful but not unkind, though his stare was intense. He turned to stow his faceplate on a rack designed for the purpose, and as he did so Megan saw that he wore a sort of neck support that ran high up behind his head. The braided hair was not part of the suit. It was his own, channelled up through an orifice formed at the joint of the neck support and faceplate. Reaching for his neck he removed the support, which allowed his hair to fall down across his shoulders in a manner that made him suddenly far less intimidating.

'Sit,' he said simply, the synthesised quality of his voice replaced by a more natural tone. He gestured to a pair of plastic carry boxes and settled himself on a third.

'You came to Kul looking for me?' he asked Megan.

'We were sent by the Shaman of Buni Sound in Skala,' she said, not at all sure of herself.

Kittala gave a short laugh. 'That old wizard's still alive then.'

'Yes,' said Megan, who didn't recognise the word wizard but went along with it all the same. 'Are you Hadje too?'

Kittala seemed to consider this question for a moment. 'Not exactly,' he said. 'But for now let's say yes, I am Hadje of a sort.'

'The Shaman suggested you could help us,' said Olson, with that confidence Megan had heard in the Siphon.

'Did he? And what would I be helping you with?'

'We need to get to Tsarocca.'

Kittala frowned. 'Do you, indeed? And why is that?'

'Have you heard of the Intercessor Drive Cores in Skala?' asked Megan.

'Of course.'

'One of them has been stolen. We are trying to recover it, but...' Megan stumbled a little, wondering how to explain.

'There is a concern,' said Olson chipping in, 'that there is more at stake than we might understand. The Shaman suggested as much, but was cryptic to say the least.'

At this, Kittala regarded them with a hard stare, but said nothing.

'He suggested there's a bigger picture, a history that we know little about. By travelling to Tsarocca we might learn for ourselves. Why us, Megan and me that is, I don't know.'

Kittala considered this for a while before giving a curt nod. 'If the Shaman thinks it is required, then who am I to judge his wisdom? I will take you to Tsarocca, but I warn you now, it is a perilous journey.'

'We're getting used to perilous,' said Olson with a smile. It was the first time he'd looked that way for some time and Megan felt reassured by it. To her surprise, Kittala reciprocated.

'Then it is agreed,' said the huge man. 'We will eat now, and sleep. Then we begin.' He paused a moment before enquiring of Olson, 'Now I know Miss Megan, but you are..?'

'Tyler Olson,' said Olson, who thought he saw the faintest flicker of recognition in the man's eyes.

Megan and Olson retrieved food packs from Pegasus 3, while Kittala prepared a stew of a sort neither of them recognised. Its aroma filled the cave and for a few turns they ate in silence. Megan felt a calm come over her, a feeling that was growing familiar. She sat for a moment in silence, looking between the two men as the firelight flickered across their features. They seemed to see something in each other that she couldn't quite identify, a mutual respect between two people who recognised each other for what they were. Whatever it was, she felt at ease in their company. Feeling a little braver, she asked a question for herself.

'So, there is a monster in Kul?'

'Yes,' said Kittala. 'A hybrid. We are not sure what they are exactly.'

'They?'

'At one time there were at least five of them, but I believe there is only one remaining.'

'What are they like?'

'They're big, taller than I am, very strong and extremely vicious. They look a little like a human but have a thick, tough skin, as black as coal. We think they were created, not a natural occurrence. Many years ago my people found a laboratory high up in the mountains north of here. We think the first of their species was birthed from there.'

'But there is only one now?' asked Megan, who was still grappling with the alien way the Hadje measured time.

'For now, yes,' said Kittala. 'We take turns to hunt them, to stop them from breeding. I killed the last male about fourteen months ago, but there is still a female. I have been searching for her for many weeks, but she has gone into hiding somewhere deep in the sewers. That means either she's hurt or she's pregnant.'

'Pregnant?' said Megan, horrified.

'They have an unusually long gestation period, nearly three years. It is very plausible she is carrying offspring. If that offspring is male there is a possibility she can breed again.'

Megan pulled a face of disgust at this prospect and Kittala laughed.

'I think if your species were on the point of extinction you would find society's taboos a little less important.' He seemed to be about to elaborate on this, but apparently decided not to.

'And this female lives in the sewers?' asked Olson.

'I believe that is where she is hiding, deep in the darkness where she feels safe. I have travelled in that darkness, searching for the creature, but so far I have not located its nest.'

Again, Megan grimaced at the thought of a nest. 'You said something about infection earlier.'

'Yes, the creature harbours a potent biological disease, an elegant defence mechanism. More than one of my predecessors succumbed to infection, a fate I do not intend to emulate.'

'But we're safe here?' she asked, suddenly aware of the lack of protection within the cave.

'The creatures have never left the confines of Kul,' said Kittala firmly. 'That is not to say their pattern will never change, particularly now the last female is vulnerable. She might try anything. But I think it unlikely she would leave, or find us here. The danger is your kind entering Kul and providing her with the food source she so desperately needs.'

'Is that why you attacked us?' asked Megan

'Exactly. If she were to find you, months of effort starving her would have been undone.'

'You would have killed us instead?'

'No, no. But I think you would not have returned to Kul after you survived. Am I correct?'

'I think that's fair to say,' said Olson with a smile.

Seeing lingering discomfort on Megan's face, Kittala unclipped an ornate-looking rod from his left thigh and handed it to her.

'Here, take this if it would make you feel safer.'

Megan reached over and took the object, which resembled the blade-less haft of a sword. It was remarkably heavy and felt unwieldy as a weapon. She studied it intently, turning it over in her hand.

'It keys off nerve impulses,' said Kittala. 'Squeeze it with intent.'

Puzzled, Megan tried this, shaking it nervously and not knowing what to expect. After nothing happened she looked up, confused.

'Try again, but imagine the blade extending,'

She did so and, to her astonishment a long, straight blade appeared from the haft. Even to Megan's novice feel it was perfectly balanced, though much too large for her to use it in anything but the clumsiest manner. The length of the blade was engraved in a trellis design and ended in a curved tip which she traced gracefully through the air. Like the twin blades on Kittala's forearm, the metal shone with an odd, dark radiance in a manner unlike a normal polished surface.

'What is it made from? I've never seen anything like it,' she asked with appreciation.

'It's a binary-state metal, like these.' He offered up his forearm, which he flexed slightly before the blades materialised, then deconstructed again. 'The molecules can be programmed to take two distinct shapes, but they must be of the same volume. It's an ancient technology, very rare even in my society.'

'Ancient?' said Megan, astonished. 'It looks more advanced than anything we have.'

Kittala gave a soft laugh, but said nothing more.

'Thank you,' said Megan with sincerity. She squeezed the haft again, imagining the blade retracting which, after a couple of tries, it did.

'Just don't sleep with that thing in your hand,' said Olson, helping Megan up. Each thanked Kittala, who watched as they made their way back outside.

'Tyler, that stuff about the creature, the sewers, laboratories up in the mountains. Do you think that's true?' asked Megan as soon as they were alone.

Olson considered a moment before answering. 'We've no reason to doubt it. There are a lot of strange things hidden in the world. There are monsters in pure human form, trust me on that. I don't think this man or any of the Hadje have a reason to lie, do you?'

'I don't know,' said Megan, unsure. 'When he said about the mother breeding with the child he seemed to be about to say something more…'

'I noticed that, too. Maybe something in their culture…'

'I guess we'll find out soon enough,' she said as they entered the hold of Pegasus 3.

'Maybe,' said Olson. 'Sleep well, Megan.'

'You too,' she said. She didn't sleep, though. Her mind kept jumping from the frenzied pursuit in the atrium to nightmare visions of a creature, pregnant and starving in the dank blackness of the sewers below the dead, abandoned city. And the Council Chamber, its startling resemblance to that in Skala; that preyed on her mind most of all.

036: Tundra

Ayon Tundra, 1,506km East of Skala

After three shifts threading their monotonous way through the sparse forests that lined the foothills east of Aya, the crew of GVX finally saw the trees give way to a more open landscape. Dustings of snow became a more even covering across the olive-coloured spikes of wild grass that carpeted the borderlands of Ayon. Although it was darker here than it had been in the streets of Aya, the lack of any light pollution and the increasing presence of snow served to give the illusion of a brighter landscape.

The definition between land and sky gradually became indistinct: low cloud, snow, even the trees were colourless and visible only in shades of grey. Birch trees became a ghostly sea punctuated by occasional darker patches of drooping pine. Only the faint, brown tinge of grass provided any sort of hue.

'I imagined Ayon to be stark,' said Roy Jacobs. 'You can barely make out where the snow stops and the trees start. It's almost like there's a dark bleed between the two.'

'Photographs tend to make it look blue and white out here but it's really not like that,' agreed Katherine from beside him.

'Do you miss it out here?'

'Yes and no,' said Katherine after a pause. 'It's extremely

peaceful, beautiful in its own way, but once we get deeper into the cold it's also pretty dangerous. Having said that, there are six of us, which will make things easier.'

'I'm here as well, Katherine,' came ROOT's voice from behind them.

Katherine gave a soft laugh. Jacobs followed suit with a grin. 'And you, ROOT. I guess we're not in danger of getting locked out with you here.'

Jacobs regarded Katherine seriously. 'Level with me,' he said. 'Why do you think the Council let you leave with ROOT? It seems such a strange decision to me.'

'I can't disagree,' she said with a sideways glance. 'The rationale made sense at the time, but now we're out here and things are a little calmer, it does seem a big step at a critical time.'

'Back in Aya you said something wasn't right.' Jacobs said this cautiously, not wanting to press her.

She sighed and spoke in a reserved tone that carried with it a little confusion. 'There were some bits missing.'

'What do you mean, bits?'

Jacobs saw the muscles around her mouth tense. Taking her eyes off the undefined horizon for a moment, she looked at him as if deciding whether to elaborate or not. Eventually she turned her attention back ahead of her but began to talk hesitantly.

'The city centre seemed too close to the western border. When we laid it out we made a conscious effort to provide enough housing for the population that occupy the slums of Skala. I mean proper housing, not a shanty town. That's a lot of housing.' She looked over to him again to underline the point. 'But I'd say only half of it's there.'

'You don't think it's just not been built yet? The edge of

the city as it is now will move back towards Skala before the migration?'

'Maybe,' she said, but sounded doubtful. 'It didn't feel that way. I don't know, it just seemed smaller than I was expecting. The city centre looks grand even half erected but the suburbs just looked, well, limited.'

'You don't think it's simply that there's more around the rest of the city? To the north or south maybe?'

'Possibly,' she conceded. 'Maybe I'm imagining it.'

'I thought the same,' said ROOT. 'I compared the number of city blocks to the last plans HEX generated and I believe you to be correct. The city is fifteen blocks short.'

'I'm glad it's not just me,' said Katherine, who did not object to the interruption.

They continued in a thoughtful, subdued silence for a kilometre or more. Snow had started to fall in large, wet flakes that immediately turned to slush on the forward screen but began to settle on the ground.

'I'm starting to get pretty tired,' said Katherine.

'I'll take over for a bit,' offered Jacobs.

'No, we should stop.' She said this reluctantly but Jacobs could see sense prevail in her despite her fatigue. 'We need to check GVX externally anyway so we might as well power down for a few rotations. This race won't be won in a shift. You and I should get a couple of rotations' sleep and let JJ take a look outside.'

Jacobs keyed the microphone to talk to the rest of the crew stationed behind them. 'We're going to power down for a few rotations. JJ, you wanted to check around externally?'

'Yeah, that would be good,' JJ replied with a hint of relief.

Before they climbed gratefully into their bunks, Katherine and Roy had agreed to expand and level GVX to give the crew a little time to stretch their legs. Brendan Scott took the opportunity to prepare a fresh meal, a welcome change from the pre-packed food that had become the crew's staple diet while on the move. There might have been little advantage in sustenance, but fresh food provided a perceptible boost in morale.

As soon as GVX's flanks had locked into the open position, Joanna Joyce retrieved a coat, hat and gloves from her locker and headed into the damp cold outside. Jayce Baker went with her, undertaking his own survey of sensor pods and camera positions.

On the outside, JJ began a rigorous inspection of GVX's wheels, tread segments and hydraulic drives. To her pleasure, and later that of Roy Jacobs, everything remained fluid-tight. JJ was used to conditions in Ayon, having been out several times supporting more antiquated exploration vehicles. She knew the cold of the borderlands was often deceiving as a result of the damp. Minus seven centigrade out here felt significantly more uncomfortable than the minus twenty-seven centigrade she had experienced out on the ice. She was experienced enough to know that there was a distinction to be made between comfort and safety, and the nominally colder temperatures were to be ignored at her peril.

Continuing the inspection, she found the gill flaps that provided the intakes for the combustion air system were working perfectly and showed no sign of snow build-up. Jayce cleaned the transparent camera covers and sprayed them with a de-icing agent to ensure clear images would be projected to the cockpit. Climbing up a set of frigid rungs, the two of them inspected the solar panels that ran across the top of the chassis. Don Hoffer's crew back in SVA had no qualms about walking across these, but JJ preferred to stick to the central spine and ribs instead. In a moment of startling consideration, one of the designers had gone so far as to provide a sculpted recess in which was secured a convenient long-handled scraper for when the panels had to be cleared.

Climbing the ladder to the glowing warmth of GVX's interior, they found the rest of the crew eating together in good humour. JJ snapped the inner door shut before prising off her boots and hanging her damp coat on a hook, careful to bring as little snow inside as she could. Seeing her, Scott immediately set his bowl aside to dish her up a hearty-smelling stew of chicken thigh, carrot and… whatever else, she didn't care. He offered a second bowl to Jayce, who took it gratefully.

'Cold out there, JJ?' asked Scott.

'Not really, more wet than cold. It all looks good, though,' she said, to reassure Baker his readings correlated with the vehicle's actual condition. Baker gave her a nod of appreciation but, as was his usual way, he said nothing. She was grateful to be able to dig straight into the stew before getting some rest.

Less than a rotation later, GVX's flanks were retracted and Katherine, accompanied this time by Baker as co-pilot, settled herself back into her chair. The V10s gave their customary howl and GVX moved off to head into the remorseless grey of the tundra.

The scenery changed little for the following shifts. Katherine and Jacobs alternated as driver, supported by Baker or Joyce as co-driver. Myra Cena kept a watchful eye on ROOT, who remained uncharacteristically quiet. When she could stand it no more, she collared an exhausted-looking Katherine to plead for something useful to do. Katherine, heading to her bunk for the minimal amount of sleep she now took, was caught off guard and could think of nothing, but promised to give it some thought. Overhearing their conversation, Brendan Scott took pity on Myra and took her into the medical compartment.

'If you're at a loose end, there would be no harm in you familiarising yourself with the medical supplies. I take it you've done the first-aid course?'

'Of course,' said Myra, a little surprised. 'They wouldn't let me near GVX without doing it.'

'Glad to hear some common sense still prevails at SVA,' said Scott, who was pulling an extremely old-fashioned-looking wooden box from a shelf. 'You wouldn't know it from the layout of this thing,' he said, referring to GVX. 'These boxes should be right by the door, not way back here.' The box was one of several of similar design. All were painted white with a red cross and all were held closed by plain-leather, wrap-around straps.

Catching her eye, Scott began to explain. 'The first lesson of Ayon, as Trish over there will no doubt drill into you over the coming shifts, is "keep it simple". We use wooden boxes because they can be easily repaired and they don't freeze up like metal, or get brittle like plastic.'

'That makes sense,' said Myra, taking his point.

He removed the strap and flipped the lid open. 'Call me Bren by the way. I've no use for formality.' From his pocket he retrieved a small box of matches and clamped one between his teeth.

'I'm Myra,' said Myra, and offered a hand, which he shook. His skin was rough, dry and pleasantly warm. She took in his face, as if for the first time. He was not handsome but he looked hardened and strong. His chin already showed scratchy stubble, brown with flecks of grey.

'Okay Myra, listen up. You need to strap something down outside, you use rope. Metal clasps, clips, carabiners can freeze up. Rope or leather is ideal. Get Trish to teach you how to tie knots and practise until they're second nature. By that time your fingers will be bleeding and you'll need to come see me again.' He gave a short laugh.

'I'll practise,' Myra assured him seriously.

'In here is a rudimentary first-aid kit. You'll recognise most of it if you've done the course. If for any reason we need to camp outside the vehicle, this box goes at the front of your tent. That's not a suggestion, it's essential. If someone gets hurt they need to know exactly where the box is and get at it easily.'

'Is it likely we'll have to camp outside?' asked Myra, a little horrified at the thought.

'No, but you can't ever tell what's going to happen out here. Added to that, this machine's new and untested. A Freon leak or unexpected build-up of carbon monoxide might force us outside.'

Myra took this in, appreciating for the first time that she had taken for granted things would go to plan. She began to feel trepidation, but also a sense of excitement, as GVX listed over rough ground before jerking level again.

'I'll take you through the first-aid kit, piece by piece,' said Bren.

When they were done they repacked it carefully, Myra noting exactly where each bandage, saline bag and anything else was located. Bren was a good teacher and she took to him easily, his occasional humour belying the seriousness of what lay ahead.

Over the following few shifts the going got slower as they wound their way around the foothills of mountains, unseen above the low blanket of cloud. Snow squalls became frequent, before finally giving way to an unrelenting blizzard that obscured all conventional vision. Katherine held out as long as she could before switching to a radar-based terrain projection. She had been forced to use this system before and disliked it, despite its capabilities. Even with GVX's advanced systems it was no more elaborate than a series of projected, meshed contour lines that gave a crude idea of the terrain ahead. The mesh itself, unable to differentiate between natural elevation and dense clumps of trees, also needed a little human interpretation. But it was good enough to work with if the landscape was obscured which, by now, it truly was.

For the first time in more than two shifts, Katherine and Jacobs found themselves driving together and, for a change, had swapped places. Katherine, who usually liked the cockpit brightly lit, had reduced the light level to a dim, bluish hue, knowing it was how he drove when she wasn't present.

This was not lost on Jacobs, who'd in turn noticed Katherine grow introspective. He appreciated the gesture, while at the same time wondering whether she was trying to hide herself a little. 'We're getting close to the Nastra research station,' he said, hoping to rouse her from her thoughts.

'Yes, I know,' she said in a resigned tone.

'It'll be a relief to top-up on supplies and fuel, to finally get going.'

When she didn't respond, he gave an involuntary sigh which she seemed to pick up on.

'I'm sorry Roy, I don't mean to be obtuse.'

'You're worried.'

She picked up on the statement with apparent relief. She swept her hair back and to one side in an uncharacteristically female gesture that he tried his best not to find attractive. She looked over to him and smiled.

'I'm worried. But we're doing fine so far, despite this.' She gave an overt sideways glance at the snow rushing over the cockpit's screens.

'I think we'll do fine, too.' From the corner of his eye he noticed her brighten a little for a moment, before her thoughts seemed to sink back to the never-ending blizzard that engulfed them.

037: The Balance of Power

The Meatpacking District, Skala City

'I kept this place as a reminder,' said Ratha, pushing open a heavy, metal door to lead her small delegation into a frigid space beyond. She offered no further explanation and the clinical functionality of the room only served to heighten the group's collective confusion. The floor was painted a dull red and had been made deliberately rough. It sloped in a little from dirty, tiled walls that must once have been white. From the ceiling, just below the harsh glare of strip lights, a series of metal rails were suspended on bulky, forged brackets. At odd intervals, large, curved hooks hung from the rails with menacing intent.

'Councillor Ratha,' said a woman, with an air of exasperation. 'You've brought us to an abattoir. Are we supposed to feel threatened, or has your morbid sense of humour finally got the better of you?'

Ratha looked back with disdain at the tidy form of the senior corporate accountant, Delta Reva. Then her features softened and she gave the group a rueful smile.

'No threat, I simply want to impress upon you how close to disaster it is possible to find yourself if you choose not to keep your house in order. Do you know what this room is? What it represents?'

'I've no idea,' said Reva, who found herself standing a pace ahead of the rest of the group. Her brazen tone left no one in any doubt she was humouring Ratha and had little patience for such talk. Some of those behind her fidgeted in discomfort.

'Well you had better learn fast,' spat Ratha, jabbing a pointed finger. 'You think you're clever, hiding up there in your comfortable glass tower, but trust me, if you are going to survive in this world you had better learn how far you can lean over the edge before you get pushed.'

Ratha eyed the group, a pitiful mix in her estimation. Most were women, but there were a couple of men who she regarded with grudging admiration. She glared at them a moment longer, then began again in a more measured tone.

'A decade ago there was an agreement, an alliance between myself and some of your predecessors in the private sector. We achieved some great things together for this city. But the arrangement became compromised by a single bad apple – an accountant, much like you, Miss Reva. He was brought here, but due to the utter incompetence of his captors he escaped.'

Ratha pointed directly down to a drain beside her. They all stared at it for a moment, then looked impassively back up at her. She looked frustrated, as if recognising that the message was not getting across.

Emboldened by the Councillor's apparent failure to get through to the group, Reva took another step towards her. 'We've all been working with this syndicate of yours. What exactly is it you want?'

Ratha fixed Reva with a venomous stare, her eyes narrowing to slits. Then, as if she had got the measure of the woman, she looked back to the group and said simply, 'Discipline. I want discipline. Make sure your house is in order.' She looked down to the grate beside her. 'Fortunately, the little bastard that slithered into this drain is no more than a corpse rotting in the sewers, but I don't ever want a repeat of that episode. Is that clear?'

'You've made your point,' said Reva, glibly. 'Now what about our concessions?'

Ratha smoothed the material of her grey robe, propped her hands on her hips and pushed her chin forward. 'Nothing changes,' she said flatly. 'The mining subsidies will keep flowing for as long as is practical, the same goes for the refineries. There is nothing more I can do about the fulgurite situation, that's down to the weather and even I can't control that.'

'What about the water supply?' asked a tall man from the rear of the group.

'Ah, Mitchell Crowder,' said Ratha, affecting mock recognition. 'I had forgotten you were here. Maybe you can explain to your colleagues the significance of this room in more detail? After all, it was your company that caused us all so much grief.'

When Crowder didn't respond, Ratha continued. 'The arrangements for the water supply and filtration remain unchanged. The necessity is still assumed.'

'With regard to Aya, there was a concern,' began Crowder, but Ratha cut him off. 'There was. It's no longer a concern. Councillor Kane is not a factor. Whatever she might have discovered, which I suspect is very little, doesn't matter if she's not here.'

'And the Intercessors?' asked Reva with a raised eyebrow. 'They are both out of the picture too. Was that your doing?'

'Partly,' said Ratha, who could not take credit for whatever madness had taken Kyra Devin. 'Isn't it amazing how a little push in the right direction can get you what you want, if you can take advantage of the prevailing circumstances?'

'Whatever,' said Reva dismissively. 'I'll ask you again, what is it you want from us? Discipline is all well and good, but it's hard to imagine that's the limit of your needs.'

Ratha bridled, but kept control of her temper. 'I want your support, when the time comes.'

'You want to be Matriarch,' said Reva, with ill-concealed exasperation.

'That is already assured,' said Ratha. The statement clearly startled Reva and had a discernible effect on the rest of the group. In the pause that followed, the Councillor took on a significantly more formidable persona. 'What I want is for you to deliver me, via your employers, the means to change how our people are governed. You want change as much as I do – we've done enough skulking around trying to keep Skala going while pandering to the bleeding hearts. It's time we cut off the dead weight and severed the red tape. We're not going to repeat the mistakes of the past. There will be no slums in Aya, no divide in the chamber. It will be one city, where the righteous rule for the benefit of all. That's what I will give to you if you choose to take it. If you don't, then you'd better get the hell out of my way.'

Reva looked momentarily surprised at this unexpectedly eloquent speech. She blinked a couple of times then, as if speaking for the rest of the group, shrugged and said, 'Well that sounds desirable.'

Ratha was clearly not impressed by Reva's offhand manner and narrowed her eyes once again. 'I assume you know what some people call me, Miss Reva?'

Reva gave a little snort. 'The Grey Lady.'

'No,' said Ratha, her tone dangerously low. 'They call me the Hellion Bitch. Do you know what a Hellion is?'

'I don't,' said Reva cautiously. She had in fact heard the name, but was nonetheless astonished Ratha had any awareness of it.

'A Hellion is a daemon of the old world the bards speak of. I don't expect history is a subject you have time for, between orchestrating your covert tapping of the Skala water supply from inside your plush office and your disgusting sexual liaisons outside of it.'

An incandescent anger welled up in Reva as she felt the withering look of Crowder upon her from behind. That Ratha could be aware of either of these things was utterly unthinkable. What else did she know?

'Do you see what I mean about the discipline now, Miss Reva?'

'I do,' said Reva, through gritted teeth.

'Good. I expect Mr Crowder here will want a little chat after I've done with you. I trust we are clear on where we stand?' This was apparently addressed to the group as a whole. 'Don't think Miss Reva is the only person I can dish the dirt on. I expect you all to stay in line and vote favourably when required. Do we have an understanding?'

There was a collective murmur of assent while the Hellion Bitch assessed them with contempt.

'Be under no illusions. Katherine Kane may be out of the picture for now but Kyle Devin is very much in the picture. If there is a threat to the Syndicate, it will almost certainly come from him.'

'What about Nara Falla?' asked Crowder, his anger at Reva held in check.

'Nara's hardly a problem. Her position is effectively redundant and she seems occupied starring at lumps of ice, so I see no reason to dissuade her from that noble pursuit.'

'And Urasa's onside now?' asked Reva, recovering some of her former confidence.

'Victor has his own agenda. He's reduced the Privy Council to a state of disarray, which strengthens our position. Selwyn Abbot has effectively removed himself as a chamberlain, but I don't think he knows that yet.'

'I heard he won a no-confidence vote,' said Reva, but Ratha cut in to correct her.

'Quite the opposite. The vote was a confidence vote, not a no-confidence vote. No one voted in Abbot's favour, he just didn't notice. Petty I agree, but those are the rules.'

Joss Ratha gestured to the open metal door and waited patiently for her guests to file out. It was lost on none of them that a single rack of meat hooks had been arranged next to the exit, each clearly engraved with a name. Not a single member of the group was left in any doubt who was in charge and, as Reva and the rest were soon to discover, this was just the first play of a much longer hand.

038: Reunion

Nastra Research Station, 5,100km East of Skala

GVX's progress steadily improved over the course of two shifts as the blizzard eased. Thoroughly exhausted, Katherine had been relieved to switch back to normal visual mode, exchanging mesh projections for a grey landscape lit by the diffused glow of a pink moon. ROOT was apparently keeping his own counsel and had not uttered a word for several rotations. Jacobs had nodded off beside her and she'd let him sleep – the mountainous terrain made the driving punishing, and neither could last long before needing a break.

After some time searching, Katherine finally found the narrow, orange beam of a guidance light that reached up to the heavens from a distant vale. She steered towards it and a few kilometres later, a settlement came into view. Through flecks of falling snow, she could just make out the slim trellis structure of a communications relay pylon amid sparse, prefabricated buildings. Pushing forward on her splints, she throttled down and GVX came to a gentle, controlled halt just inside the tangled remains of a perimeter fence. The change in engine note made Jacobs stir.

'We're there?' He sounded groggy and looked shattered.

'Yes, we're there,' she said, resigned and a little sad. 'I think it would be prudent to wake the others and expand the flanks. We could be here a few rotations or more.'

'No problem,' said Jacobs. 'I bet expanding will wake them up anyway, so…' Reaching over to the console, he activated the controls to spread the hull. Motors whirred as the compartments moved out of the central chassis and locked into place.

Katherine peered out of a side window projection at a nearby cylindrical tank. 'I guess that's the fuel pickup.'

Jacobs, now fully awake, quickly verified all was well before putting the V10s into five-cylinder idle mode. Katherine stared expressionless out to a hut that stood dark and resolute amid the falling snow. For a moment, light spilled from an open door before a single figure blocked it. Trepidation gripped her stomach as she watched. The backlit figure pulled a fur-lined hood over its head and started out towards GVX.

'Man, at least there is someone still alive out here,' said Jacobs, noting the figure as he worked his control pad.

Katherine climbed out of her seat with a speed that took him by surprise, her movements almost aggressive. Confused, he levered himself up to follow, finding her already stripped of her jumpsuit and pulling on a thin, woollen base layer.

'You seem in an awful hurry to get out of here,' he said, more sharply than he intended.

'Let's just say I want to head off any problems early,' she replied, putting a leg into waterproof trousers. 'You stay here and get Jayce and JJ to organise the refuelling.'

'I'm coming with you,' he said firmly, retrieving his own gear. 'Whoever that is has probably been here a long time, and it's not exactly unknown for these Deep Ayon Research people to go a little bit nuts. No disrespect.'

'He's been here four cycles and he's not going to be nuts, trust me,' she sighed. Flicking her hair through a neck sleeve, she was at the exit before he could ask more. Frigid air streamed into the galley as the outer door opened. Jacobs pulled on his thermals, relaying the instructions for Jayce and JJ as he did so.

By the time he was down the ladder, Katherine was at least twenty paces ahead of him. The air was the coldest he'd experienced and was strangely tasteless. Loose power hissed across the surface of deep, dry snow that juddered underfoot as he walked. Intermittently, the sound was loud enough to drown the gusting winds that howled though trees high up in the surrounding hills.

Katherine approached the lone figure and, although Jacobs couldn't make out their first exchange, he sensed an intimacy between them that stopped him short. He stood for a moment, hearing only the patter of fine particles against his coat and face before hesitantly approaching to within earshot.

'I'm not insane, Iain,' Katherine said, clearly exasperated. 'I've got a job to do. We're passing – collecting fuel, supplies and that's all. I thought you might actually help us out.'

The hooded figure looked up and in the dim light Jacobs caught straggles of hair strewn across a male face. 'Help you? You're mad. How in this world can I possibly help you? I'm here alone with scant resources, not to put it too mildly. Take the fuel, that's nothing to do with me. But I can't help much with this almighty thing.' He gestured toward GVX which, in contrast to the dilapidated shack behind him, was a technological palace.

Resignation washed over him and he sighed. 'For the love of God, come inside. Bring your friend if you must.'

Not looking at Jacobs, Katherine followed the man a pace or two behind. The crunch of the snow turned to a squeak as it became compacted around the boundary of the station. They headed past the wire of an inner fence towards a door, which screeched open on overstretched springs. The warm glow of sodium light spilled out onto the snow as they entered the building, the door banging shut behind them.

The man pulled down his hood to reveal shoulder-length black hair and a strong, good-looking complexion hidden behind grey-streaked stubble. He rolled his eyes at Katherine, then reached past her to shake Jacobs by the hand. Jacobs greeted the loner with a restrained uncertainty.

'Pleased to meet you, I'm Iain. What the hell has she roped you into?' There was ill-concealed disrespect in his voice. Jacobs, deciding discretion was the better part of valour, looked to Katherine for an answer, but none came.

'Good God woman, get your things off and go through there. There's a rec room of sorts. Be with you shortly.' He turned abruptly and pushed at another door. It banged shut behind him on a failed damper.

Katherine reluctantly fought her way out of her coat, which was sodden with snow despite the short time they had been outside.

'You know him?' Jacobs asked.

'Yes,' was all she offered.

'Worked together?'

'No, we never worked together.'

'Then what?' Jacobs couldn't help feeling annoyed, at her recent dark mood and now this evasiveness.

She reluctantly came to a decision, and spoke in a sharp, disapproving tone he had not heard from her before. 'He's my husband.'

'Your what?'

'My husband, Iain Kane. We've been married seventy cycles but...' her voice trailed off.

'But you're not together now?' he asked.

'It's complicated,' she said. 'I knew this was coming. I'm

sorry, I should have told you.' Her eyes were filled with apology and self-pity.

Jacobs shook his head, trying to make sense of it. 'I should keep out of this,' he said, genuinely wanting no part of any sort of retribution.

'Just stay here,' she said, in a pleading tone. 'He's been out here for cycles and, like I said, it's complicated between us. He's not dangerous or anything,' she said, suddenly defensive. Seeing his wide-eyed expression, she assured him, 'It's just a mess. He wanted to get away and now here we are. It's not exactly fair on him either.'

Jacobs wasn't willing to take that assertion at face value, but nevertheless agreed to stay out of the way.

'I'll be a while,' she said. 'Don't be too alarmed if there is some shouting to be done.'

Jacobs drew in a deep breath. 'Whatever you say, ma'am.'

The rec room was sparse, with only a couple of partially disintegrated armchairs offering comfort to the inhabitants of this most far-flung outpost of humanity. Picking the nearest, Katherine perched on the edge of the worn seat cushion. It wasn't long before a second door creaked open and Iain Kane entered, settling himself into the other chair. He was holding a short length of corroded steel tube, apparently a fence support. He didn't look at her, preferring to concentrate on winding a length of leather twine around it. His hair, much longer than it had been when she had last seen him, drooped forward, partially obscuring his face. Before he spoke, he reached behind him to a low shelf and dragged a bottle from it, taking a swig before he finally looked up.

'What the hell are you doing here Katherine?'

She thought a moment, picking her words carefully. 'I'm not here for you, Iain, but it is nice to see you.'

'Bullshit,' he said, in a disbelieving tone.

'I said I'm not here for you,' she flung back at him.

'Yes, I realise that, but I can't imagine it is nice to see me.'

She shifted uncomfortably, unsure of what to say. 'You came out here of your own choice.' She had hated these exchanges back in Skala but here, in the meagre dilapidation of his exile, the feeling was a hundred times worse.

'Choice – that's rich, coming from you,' he said, placing the bottle carefully at his feet. 'You left me long before I came out here.'

'How?' she said, simply but with conviction.

He looked down at the tube. This was an argument she guessed he must have had a hundred times over in his mind, just as she had.

'You left me the moment we were married. You preferred to spend more time with work and your colleagues than you ever did with me.'

'That's not true,' she insisted incredulously. 'I gave up some of my work for you. It was my whole life and then there was you.'

Again he didn't look up. 'You gave up some of your work, that's great. I gave up everything for you. I waited in that apartment every shift, not knowing when or even if you were coming back. Every shift, Katherine. Every single bloody shift.'

She didn't respond right away. When she did it was in a measured tone. 'What I was doing, what I am doing now is important.' She paused again, the silence briefly hanging over both of them. She went on, conviction strong in her voice. 'I was planning the migration of our people. A necessary move to Aya. That is more important than anything any generation has had to face in nearly thirty decades.'

He fed the leather twine around the pole, making a knot with his strong fingers. Katherine noticed the muscles in his exposed forearms. They were every bit as strong as they ever were back in Skala, where he trained every shift without fail.

Presently he spoke again. 'Ratha – that woman is poison and you know it.' He fixed his eyes on her as he reached down to the bottle to take a swig.

'She's misunderstood, and not just by you,' she said in a supplicatory tone. Seeing derision writ clear on his face she started again. 'She's abrasive, I'm not disputing that, but she's got good hearts. She has helped me my whole life.'

Kane shook his head at her slowly. 'That woman took you. She monopolised your time, shift after shift, and for what? Every time you came back with the same story, the same conversations over and over again. Okay, she advanced your career, but for her gain, not yours. Can't you see that?'

Deep down Katherine felt some truth in this, but natural defensiveness got the better of her, as it usually did. 'She did help my career enormously, and I owe her for that.'

'You don't owe her shit. She used you – your father never did that. He stood you on your own two feet and trusted in you, he didn't interfere. But Ratha did, and you let it happen to the detriment of you and me.'

'My father has nothing to do with this,' she said vehemently.

'Exactly,' replied Kane with a deliberate calmness that clearly intimated he had already predicted this answer. 'He knew better.'

Silence descended upon the two of them for a turn or more, each in their own way trying to calculate their next move. It was Iain who broke the stalemate.

'So, what the hell are you doing here?'

'You wouldn't believe me if I told you.'

'Try me anyway,' he said, pausing in his work.

Not knowing how to frame the craziness of the situation, Katherine blurted it out as best she could. 'Kyra has stolen HEX – took her from the Vault a little over twenty shifts ago and headed out into Ayon. ROOT says he knows where she's going, but he's being evasive.'

Iain reached down for the bottle and drank deeply, taking in her words with the fiery liquid. Katherine, who had despaired of his descent into alcoholism towards the end of their cohabitation in Skala, forced herself not to react. He lowered the bottle and eyed her intently from behind long straggles of wild hair.

'You're mad,' he said simply, not taking his eyes off her. She looked off to the side in resignation. 'Kyra's a bit wild, there's no denying that, but she'll have taken HEX for a reason. She's a straight thinker.'

Katherine bridled. 'Unlike me, is that what you're saying?'

'Yes, unlike you,' he snarled. 'You think in complicated patterns. Always. The simple answer will never do for you. It's always engineering, complicated by politics and how to avoid a fight. Kyra, for all her faults, decides on a path and follows it. She normally has it set out right at the beginning.'

'You've always had a thing for Kyra,' she flung back at him, phlegm unintentionally spitting from her lips.

'I have not,' he spat back at her. 'I respect her, but I've never had a thing for her. I know you thought that back in Skala, but it's a product of your own insecurity. I've never slept with her and I've never had the desire to. That's what you seem to miss in me. I loved you, but you loved your work, your colleagues and Ratha more. A person can only take that for so long.' He swept the bottle to his lips and took a long, violent gulp before spitting some of the black liquid onto the floor in front of him. 'You cared about you, that's all.'

He began again, more level, meeting her eyes this time. He

could see she was holding back tears and, despite his rhetoric, he didn't wish to hurt her. 'So how are you going to find Kyra?' he asked.

'I don't know exactly, follow her. We've got a survey drone...' she said, hopelessly, looking down at the floor. 'ROOT is convinced he can take us to where she's going, but I can't get him to explain where or why.'

'You have ROOT with you?' Iain asked in amazement.

'Yes,' said Katherine, still finding the circumstances hard to believe herself. 'He's kind of stuck in there, in GVX I mean.'

'That thing out there is John Orchard's project? I saw plans some time ago. I didn't realise it was finished.'

'It's about finished. Enough to get us here, anyway,' she explained. 'Whatever it is that's going on – and I can't pretend I have any understanding of Kyra's motive myself – my father seems to buy into it. He helped get us here.'

Iain's face hardened and she saw a degree of acceptance in it. When he spoke, his voice was quieter and more measured. 'If Kyle believes in it, then I guess I should treat it seriously.'

She looked at him and nodded. 'I think it's real, too. The whole thing might seem crazy but there is a ring of truth to it I can't explain.'

'What do you need from me?' he asked.

She looked at the floor, not sure how to answer. 'We don't need anything really, this was just a last stop-off. We're heading out onto the ice as soon as we can get to it. If there is anything you can tell us, then I guess that would be appreciated.'

He looked at her for a long time and they locked stares; hers tearful but resolute, his dark and questioning. He smiled, not in mirth but with the genuine smile she had long ago fallen in love with.

'There are a lot of big, furry creatures that are really pissed off,' he said, with a fleeting grin. She hesitated, then put a hand out, reaching for the bottle, which he passed to her. She took a swig and choked, the liquid spilling from the corners of her mouth.

'Sorry, it's fairly strong.'

'Strong?' she laughed. 'This stuff is like battery acid.'

'Best we can do out here.' He held out a hand and took the bottle back as she stifled a retch. 'I can probably find you a glass, though,' he said wryly.

039: The Southern Reaches

Even stripped of his armour, Benjamin Kittala was huge. The armour itself looked like a second person hung in the rear hold of Pegasus 3 and Megan had found herself startled more than once on catching sight of it. She was getting tired and a little jumpy. After giving Olson loose instruction on the route he should take, Kittala had slept almost constantly. He had stretched himself out next to the elegant hydrocycle, strapped down to the chequer-plate floor. How he could sleep with all the jostling and lurching of the vehicle Megan wasn't sure, but she was beginning to feel she would probably do the same if she had the opportunity.

Fortunately, with no immediate rush, they had been able to stop at regular intervals as they threaded through the canyons east of Kul. Olson had done the bulk of the driving, but where the terrain turned flat he allowed her to swap places and get a feel for the machine. It was exhilarating but, as he took back the controls at the sight of the smallest obstacle, the feeling was short-lived. He had promised her more seat time on the return journey to Skala and she hoped he would allow her a little more latitude when the time came.

To Megan's surprise, what Kittala called the 'canyon

country' was more populated than she had imagined. She had visited a few of the outlying settlements to the north and south of Skala, but had not expected to find people living so far into the inhospitable drylands of Hellinar. These were not temporary settlements either. As the rock walls smoothed into plains, she could see outposts the size of small towns. Megan assumed these must be relics of the time Kul had been the capital. Those of more recent construction she guessed were the product of the 'seedings' that were occasionally dispatched from Skala to establish a wider civilisation. Whereas a few had permanent stone shield-walls, eroded like those of the dead capital, others featured a patchwork of corrugated steel to protect them from the sandstorms that occasionally swept in from the desert. Sporadically they passed scattered herds of ravaged gaur, thin and gaunt by comparison with the magnificent satin-coated bovine stock farmed in grasslands east of Skala.

At Kittala's insistence, they kept their distance from the settlements, but Megan found herself intrigued. She made a mental note to return and explore further if the opportunity arose. The answers to even the most basic questions of survival out here eluded her, and she felt there could be more to learn than might be immediately obvious. Such had been the case with the Hadje beneath Skala, a lesson she vowed not to forget in a hurry.

Progressively, the signs of scattered habitation became ever more sparse as they turned south again to pass along the outer edge of the looming mountain range that formed the boundary of the Southern Desert. Even out here, six or eight hundred kilometres beyond the cusp of Hellinar, the mountains were capped with snow.

After two shifts' travel, the barren, rocky landscape gave way to the red dust of arid drylands. Strange, sometimes precarious-looking outcroppings of rock punctuated the even horizon and beneath them the solid ground became a carpet of fragmented, loose platelets.

She kept coming back to thoughts of Kyra and the impossible enormity of her situation. In the whirlwind of the events leading up to Katherine's shock departure with the GVX crew, she'd felt sure Kyra must have been justified in whatever had motivated her to steal HEX. Now, out here in the searing flat rubble of Hellinar, she had started to doubt her assertions. Lost in these thoughts, she propped an elbow on a raised knee and watched through the side window as the jagged shards of rubble passed by. She could almost see the heat emanating from them, and began to consider that the emptiness of this place was enough to alter a person's way of thinking.

'You want to swap?' asked Olson, gently bringing her back to the present. 'Not much you can hit out here. I could really use a little sleep.' He nodded and began to slow Pegasus 3.

'Sure,' said Megan in a flat, over-decisive voice that she immediately regretted. 'I mean, of course. I'd be happy to,' and gave him what she hoped was a warm smile.

Olson made his way back into the hold to a now-awake Kittala, who wordlessly moved forward to the passenger seat as Megan took the controls. He barely fitted but she was grateful for the company. She moved off, a little clumsily at first, but soon smoothed their acceleration into a stable fifty kilometres per rotation cruise. The loose stone beneath them produced an almost constant clatter as it was thrown up to bounce off lined wheel arches. Occasionally, an errant rock would fly up and strike the metal hull with a high-pitched clang. It was little better than travelling in a tin can.

'How in the world do you ride a hydrocycle across this?' she asked Kittala.

'It's about technique,' he said, not taking his eyes off the horizon. 'It's stable enough once you're at speed. Turning is another matter, you have to dig the front wheel in and turn the bike from the rear using the throttle. It's a little intimidating at first but, once you have the measure of it, it's quite easy.'

'I find it hard to imagine you intimidated by anything. You don't worry about running out of fuel?' she asked, knowing the bike was far too small to carry a mulching system, not that there was anything to mulch out here anyway.

He laughed, a gentle, prolonged sound that Megan found calming. He turned and looked at her quite seriously, his massive frame almost completely obscuring the side view. 'I worry about it all the time. That's why it's in the back.'

She looked at him and smiled. 'It's a very distinctive-looking bike'.

'If such a thing can be, yes it is,' he agreed. 'It was a gift,' he said with a finality Megan didn't want to challenge.

'Can you tell me about Tsarocca?' she asked, to change the subject.

'It's better you see it,' he said, staring out into the distance. 'It's not a place that's easy to describe in words.'

'Is it like Skala?' she persisted.

'No,' he said with a burst of humour that filled the cockpit. 'It is nothing like Skala. Wait and see. It's not much further, a shift at most.'

After the endless flat of the rock field, the terrain finally became more undulating. The ground returned to a smoother, dustier surface, giving them a respite from the constant din of the hull strikes. From time to time Megan thought she saw small tufts of grass, although it seemed impossible any flora could survive out here. These sightings became more regular and, despite her tiredness, she became convinced she was not seeing things. Nevertheless, she was pleased to trade places with Olson for a few rotations' sleep.

When she woke it took her a moment to get her bearings. Pegasus 3 was no longer moving and she could see Kittala's suit was gone. Blearily, she realised the tailgate had been lowered, a hot breeze streaming into the hold and with it a host of unfamiliar sounds. The air was different. Not the dry heat of the desert she had experienced over the past few shifts, but damp and humid.

She pulled herself up and slid her feet into her boots, tucking the laces into the tongue rather than stopping to tie them. She moved towards the loading ramp, blinking against the bright malevolence of the sunlight that silhouetted two figures of disparate height. Stumbling a little down the ramp towards them, she found, to her disbelief, that she was staring at a vast landscape of plant life.

'What?' she gasped, shocked by the sight. They were pulled up on a high ridge looking across a valley covered with exotic trees, the like of which she had never seen before. 'How long was I asleep? Did we turn around?' She felt confused and disorientated.

'You slept about a half-shift,' said Olson, who seemed similarly wonderstruck. 'It's quite magnificent isn't it?'

'Where are we?'

'Close to Tsarocca,' said Kittala, pointing. 'It's just beyond that valley. We will have to go on foot from here.'

'It's hard to believe all this life,' said Megan.

'The area has its own micro-climate,' explained Kittala, fastening the arm straps of his suit as he did so. 'On the other side of this valley is a lake. That's where we're heading.'

Within fifteen turns they were on their way, following in the wake of the towering Hadje. He brushed the plants aside with a grace that belied his size. The wet heat intensified as they progressed deeper into the foliage. The occasional croak of bullfrogs and other animal sounds Megan didn't recognise became a constant haze of noise. As her senses grew more attuned, she could pick out individual animals, the gentle hiss of a nearby snake tasting the air, or the high-pitched buzz of a dragonfly flitting between trees.

Where hanging branches and vine became impossible to penetrate, Kittala deftly cut a path with his sword. It looked much better-proportioned in his hand than it had in Megan's but, for reasons she was reluctant to admit to, she found a longing to hold it again. An object that responded to thought, or at least the electrical impulses generated by thought, had forged a connection she never even suspected could exist. If Tsarocca was full of such objects, who knew what was possible. Still, she remembered him saying it was a rare technology even among his people. And ancient, which didn't make sense.

Upon finding the occasional clearing, Kittala would pause their relentless march, allowing a moment for Olson to recuperate. Perspiration dripped from him, saturating the collar of his jumpsuit, which he had zipped open as far as was decent. The infrequent stops were short-lived but enough to keep exhaustion at bay, and he continued to keep up with an energy that should have belonged to a younger man.

'Can I ask you something?' he said as they paused to rest once more.

'Of course,' said Megan, who herself was glad of the chance to recover.

'That note I gave you when we first met in the library. The one Katherine wrote. What did it say?'

'Oh, that,' said Megan, clearly amused. 'It was some rambling nonsense, typical Katherine. I can't remember exactly, something about you being a better version of her. Something daft like that.'

Olson smiled inwardly. 'That was a kind thing for her to say.'

Megan merely shrugged, not understanding, but the sentiment gave him a degree of renewed strength. He pushed himself up again and Kittala, who had observed their exchange without comment, took this as a signal to start moving again.

Further into the jungle the ground began to rise a little, causing Olson to pant at the exertion. Megan was worried about him. After ten turns of steep incline they halted in another clearing. Megan thought she could hear lapping water and wondered if they had finally reached the lake they were looking for.

Kittala stood strident before them, sniffing the air with obvious pleasure. 'Don't worry,' he said, donning his faceplate with a single hand, fingers splayed wide across the smooth face. 'We're very close now.'

Deftly, he reattached an electrical connector and what Megan had recognised as a gas drybrake at his neck. After the shifts of travelling it was strange to see him covered once more. The form she had initially assumed to be a monster now looked elegant but simultaneously powerful and lithe. He stepped forward, brushing a huge fern aside for them to pass. A few metres further on the ground became mossy and firm, before giving way to smooth, grey stone. Breaking out of the foliage and back into the blinding light of the sun, they saw the lake stretched out before them. From their vantage point high on a ledge, the water glistened below them, seeming to swirl a little as it did so.

'It's stunning,' said Olson, who was unashamedly awed by the sight. 'When I was a kid I saw lakes and rivers up in the north, but nothing like this.'

'It's amazing,' Megan agreed.

They took a moment to take it all in and Kittala, holding back a supple branch to allow them a clear view, was encouraging them.

Presently, Megan came back from her reverie to look up at him. 'So where's Tsarocca, Benjamin?'

He looked down at her, his obscured features unreadable. When he spoke it was in that slightly muted, electronically manipulated voice she recalled from their first encounter in the atrium of Kul.

'It's below you,' he said.

'Below us? I don't understand.'

'You've seen a great deal in recent times, have you not, Megan Devin?'

'An unbelievable amount,' she agreed honestly.

'Then you must trust me. You have to jump.'

'Jump?' she asked, horrified. It was at least a twenty-metre drop to the water.

'Jump,' he said, releasing the branch behind her.

He took a step forward and, to her utter astonishment, leapt off the ledge. The time it took before she heard the splash of contact with the water was sickening. Peering over, she realised she couldn't see him. She stared at Olson, who looked concerned, but not alarmed. He leaned forward, peering to examine the water below.

'Well,' he said thoughtfully, eyes wide with excitement. 'The man's right, we've come a long way, you and I. I guess we've got to trust him.'

And with that, Olson too stepped forward, pausing a moment to compose himself before stepping off the ledge and falling into the swirling surface. Megan waited but, like Kittala, Olson did not emerge from the water.

Hesitantly, she took a step forward. Despite racing hearts,

she managed to calm her mind. Fear, she realised, was now a thing she was getting used to. It was not her friend, but it was no longer the enemy. She looked up at the sky, at the sun, higher here than she'd ever seen it. She looked at the greenery around her and the shimmering lake below her.

She screwed up her eyes and thought of her parents. Her father and what political fallout he was dealing with now Kyra's treachery was openly known. What grand, drunken, repetitive parties her mother might be flitting between back in the Central District. It all seemed a far distant place from here. This was real though. This was now.

She drew in a last lungful of the hot, damp air, savouring any aroma, any sensation she could discern from it. She caught the smells of plants and animals, felt the freshness of clear air flowing across her face and cooling her sweat-soaked skin.

She took it all in and opened her eyes to look upon it all, a last level stare.

Then she jumped.

040: Beyond Nastra

Nastra Research Station, 5,100km East of Skala

To Roy Jacobs' astonishment, Katherine and Iain Kane emerged from the rec room in good spirits. Moreover, they were giggling like a pair of adolescents. If he didn't know Katherine better he would have said she was slightly drunk. Any hostility between the pair had evaporated, for which he felt very relieved.

He had sat alone outside the rec room for as long as he could bear. The bitterness passing between them was audible through the tin walls, even if the words themselves were not distinct. Feeling uncomfortable, he had wandered back outside to check on JJ and Jayce, who were doing what they could to de-ice the couplings on the remote fuel tank left for them some shifts before. Whoever had delivered it must have done so in a hurry and not covered the connector, which was now frozen solid. For a while, he watched Bren launch the survey drone, flying it up to a height at which it was barely visible. It descended a few turns later, its battery drained prematurely by the biting cold.

Reluctantly, he returned to the prefab to find the acidity between husband and wife had died down.

'I'm sorry,' said Katherine on reaching him. 'I should have made proper introductions. Roy Jacobs, this is Iain Kane. Iain's a meteorological scientist and part-time geologist. He did a lot of the early work modelling environmental conditions in Aya. More recently,' she continued hesitantly, 'he's been stationed out here at Nastra.'

Jacobs stood and again shook hands, more warmly this time, as Katherine made the reciprocal introduction.

'Roy Jacobs was the Chief Engineer on the GVX project and offered, inadvisably, to come along.'

Iain Kane looked impressed. 'I remember Katherine mentioning you in the past. You've worked together before.'

'Never on anything quite as intense at this,' Jacobs said modestly. 'But yeah, we've worked together.'

'It's hard going out here, you have to look after yourself.'

Jacobs nodded his agreement. 'You're out here on your own?'

'Most of the time. It's been okay actually,' said Iain, pleasantly surprised. 'The living space is a little cramped but the work's interesting. If you're going out on the ice there's a whole lot of fascinating stuff, believe me.'

'Like what?' asked Jacobs, who had imagined the ice to simply be a single open space for as far as the eye could see. He could easily have posed the question in an incredulous tone but that wasn't his way. Out here, where his understanding of the environment was limited, he preferred not to make naive assumptions and to trust the experience of others. It was a quality Katherine had observed, as had the rest of the crew, most obviously Trish Asher, and they respected him for it.

'Well, for one thing,' began Iain, warming to his subject, 'there are small communities out there.'

'You're joking?' asked Jacobs, astounded.

'I'm not. Ask Katherine.' Jacobs looked to her and saw the truth of it in her eyes. 'They call themselves Inuk, we've known about them for a decade now. Not that we've learned much, mind you, but they're out there. The population is denser, if you can call it that... let's say, less sparse, up to the northeast, where the ground still provides some shelter.'

He paused a moment and looked a little awkward. 'What is it?' asked Katherine, sensing his hesitation.

'I actually saw their figurehead,' he said, unsure of himself. 'You remember some time ago there was talk of a wandering hermit they regard as a sort of spiritual leader?'

He looked Katherine straight in the eye and she returned the stare with a questioning curiosity. 'You met her?'

'Him actually. No, not met exactly, I did see him though. Trust me, once you've set eyes on someone like that you're unlikely to forget the experience.'

'Why?' asked Katherine, fascinated.

'He's tall. Very tall. You'll think I'm nuts, but his skin is dark, like it's been dyed or something. He was wearing thick robes and a hood, but I could just make out the face underneath. I've never seen anything like it.' He hesitated again, and both Katherine and Jacobs waited for him to continue. 'The strangest thing was his eyes. The pupils were split or atrophied or something. They looked more like the eyes of a cat than a person.'

Katherine looked at Jacobs, then back to Iain. 'I don't think you're nuts, Iain. This is a long story, and I don't know all the details myself, but Megan, with a man called Tyler Olson, encountered someone who fits a similar description.'

'Megan?' asked Iain with a mixture of affection and amazement. 'Where?'

'Skala. Somewhere in the coolant tunnels deep under the city. There's too much to tell now, but maybe you should ask her about it when you get back.' She stopped herself short of saying 'home'. 'So this figurehead, you said he was a hermit?'

'That's what the Inuk say, and I've no reason to doubt them.

I got the impression he only appears occasionally, and always from the east. Out to the east there is only ice, although that in itself is very interesting.'

'The ice is interesting?' Katherine narrowed her eyes, hearing the inflection change in his voice as he found surer ground.

'I've been spending a lot of time on the ice this past cycle, while the moon's been high for a few shifts. I've been drilling and assessing the core samples. Something's come up that I wasn't expecting.'

He faltered a moment, as if deciding whether to continue or not. When he did so it was in a hesitant, almost disbelieving tone. 'There's water under it, Katherine. I mean a lot of water, and it's moving.'

'Moving?' she asked, astonished. 'Like a river you mean?'

'Something like that, yes.' He paused again while Katherine processed the information. It meant little to Jacobs, who had no training in any sort of geology, but it was clearly significant to her. 'There's something else, it's really strange though.'

'Go on,' she urged, intrigued. 'Nothing could be stranger than the goings-on in Skala in the last cycle, believe me.'

'I don't know, it's pretty weird. Here's the thing. The water below the ice, the water that's flowing… It's loaded with sodium chloride. And I mean loaded.'

Katherine's brow furrowed. 'Salt? There's salt in the water?'

'And bromine, lots of bromine. I told you it was weird.'

'That could tell us a lot,' she said, trying to grapple with things Jacobs could only begin to imagine.

Iain took a deep breath before he spoke again. 'Anyway, I don't know what ROOT is proposing, but on recent experience I'd suggest turning northeast and keeping to the edge of the ice. The further north you go the thicker the ice becomes, according to the trend in the measurements I've taken. That's going to be important, with a vehicle that size.' He looked out of the window across to the hulking form of GVX, the fuel line now attached to its underbelly.

'It's fitted with a sonar probe,' said Jacobs thoughtfully. 'It can measure ice thickness, to try to prevent cave-ins over crevasses and the like. It's not that accurate measuring ice over loose snow, but we might get better results with ice over water. The difference between solid and liquid should be more defined.'

'That will definitely be useful,' Iain agreed. 'What about data? You're sending it back, right? Are you going to relay it through here?'

'I think that's the only realistic option,' Katherine agreed. Looking uncomfortable, she added, 'Could you relay it over this frequency only?' She pulled out a prepared note, written shifts before, and offered it to him. On it was a sequence of five numbers with a decimal point before the last.

'Sure,' said Iain, regarding the scrap of paper with perplexity.

'It's Nara Falla's private frequency. I don't want to explain too much, but the data should go to her and her only, if that's okay?'

'I know exactly what it is,' said Iain, to Katherine's visible surprise. 'I broadcast on that frequency pretty much every shift.'

'Why?' asked Katherine.

When he answered, he spoke with an air of reluctance or resignation that immediately put her on edge. 'Like I said, there are a lot of weird things going on up here. There's the water, the indigenous tribes and a whole bunch of other stuff. The Inuk talk about lights in the sky way up to the north. I thought it was nonsense, but I've seen it for myself. Nara and I felt we should wait until we understood more about the environment out here before we spring it all on the Council.'

'You mean on me?' said Katherine indignantly.

'I knew you'd take it badly,' he said with a shake of his head. 'You have so much going on with Aya and all that shit. You barely had time for me, so if I had come to you with all this stuff back in Skala what would have happened?'

Katherine looked at the floor. Jacobs saw shame traced across the soft lines of her face. 'I would have sent you away, said I was too busy.'

'Yes you would,' Iain agreed. 'And there is another reason,' he added. 'We wanted to keep Ratha out of it for now. And Erin, if I'm honest. There is something going on between Erin and Ratha that I don't understand. Sometimes it's like the two of them are operating in concert with each other.'

Katherine frowned. 'How do you mean?'

'It's hard to explain exactly. When one zigs, the other zags, I don't know. One will overtly support say, a field expedition she doesn't want, while the other will undermine it.'

'That's pretty normal,' Katherine interjected. 'We're all squabbling for funding.'

'On the face of it, yes, I agree with you. But it's the regularity with which it happens that I started to notice. Nara had picked up on the same thing, and we started making a record between us. This is going back cycles before I left to come here. In fact I could date it almost exactly back to when HEX came online. Maybe that's coincidental, who knows?'

'It sounds to me,' said Jacobs after a pregnant pause, 'like whatever the situation is, or is not, we should send as much data as we can back to Nara directly. I think that's what you agreed anyway, isn't it, Katherine?'

'It is,' said Katherine, who was amazed and a little confused that Jacobs would have any knowledge of this confidential agreement. In that moment, she felt inexplicably separate from the two men, who watched her closely. They didn't know each

354

other – Jacobs had no idea she was even married until a rotation or two before – but they seemed to share a common and very strong bond, a loyalty to Nara Falla.

The three of them fell silent for a few moments, before Katherine drew in a breath and suggested they see how the refuelling was going. The two men agreed and all three began fighting on boots and coats to head back into the dim, pinkish glow of the moonlight.

A few rotations later, Jayce Baker and Joanna Joyce had the refuelling complete and fresh food stores on-board. To JJ, who did the bulk of the heavy lifting, replacement of only a quarter-cycle's worth of sachets didn't seem worth the effort, but it was always better to be prepared than not. Katherine had slept fitfully in her bunk, fighting with the conflict of exactly how estranged she was from her own husband. In the end, her bunk seemed a safer option than the prefab and she knew Iain wouldn't protest.

He had hung around, though, talking briefly with each member of the crew and looking over GVX. He resisted the urge to take a look inside, partly to give Katherine some space and partly because he felt that the two of them should not be together with ROOT present. At one time, the IDC had taken an interest in their private lives, causing the first of many fallings-out. For her part, Katherine was in no doubt ROOT knew Iain was at Nastra. After all, he could access GVX's external cameras. But, if he had any view on the situation, he was keeping it to himself for now.

At a loose end and unable to sleep, Jacobs spent the next few rotations with Nastra's sole inhabitant. The engineer found the scientist to be engaging, knowledgeable and, despite his early misgivings, likeable. Among other things, the two discussed the communications relay system in detail before Katherine finally re-emerged onto the snow.

'So this is goodbye again,' said Iain, as Jacobs returned to ascend the ladder to the galley. 'I'm pleased to at least do it face to face this time.'

'I'm sorry about that,' she said, and meant it. 'I'm sorry about everything. Will you be here when we get back?'

'I don't know. How long will it take?'

Katherine sighed. 'I have no idea.'

'Then 'maybe' is the best I can tell you.'

'Well, I hope you're here. Even if it is all over.'

'I think it probably is, don't you?' he asked as gently as he could. There was no malice in his voice, just a little sympathy for both of them.

Katherine looked into the distance and nodded. 'I guess it probably is,' she said.

Turning back to him, to the surprise of them both, she embraced him. Not as a wife to a husband but as a friend to a friend, as it had been when they had first met.

'Goodbye, Iain.'

'Take care, Katherine. Best of luck. Go find Kyra.'

She nodded and turned back towards GVX. She felt like her body was three times its normal weight as she climbed the ladder, but she forced herself not to look back, not to turn and run to him. Reaching the platform, it took all her mental strength to push the button to close the outer door behind her, but somehow she managed, and felt a little better.

For the first time in several exhausting shifts there was a sense of anticipation in the galley. It seemed the crew had realised that, although they had left Skala thousands of kilometres behind them, it was only now that they were truly about to get going, leaving humanity as they knew it and venturing into the unknown.

Katherine pulled on her jumpsuit and adjusted the fit carefully, feeling a rising sense of occasion. Asher buckled herself in, her black hair pulled tight against her scalp into a ponytail, as Myra scrolled through ROOT's data with more vigour than uninteresting straight lines deserved. Bren was redistributing food sachets into organised boxes, while JJ and Jayce jointly discussed some minor technical point. At the very rear, the faint glow of ROOT's chassis seemed brighter than usual from his bulkhead interface.

Her feelings of loss and remorse gave way to excitement and trepidation, as she turned and made her way into the cockpit. Roy Jacobs was already flicking through checklists and making preparations for their departure. She deftly swung herself into her seat, a motion now second nature in contrast to her clumsy first attempts back in the arid hangar of SVA. She settled her arms reverently into the splints and began to run through her own, now familiar checks.

'Five-cylinder running disabled,' said Jacobs from beside her, and the V10s surged as each picked up onto ten cylinders. 'Retracting chassis and locking in torque converts.'

'All systems nominal, Jayce?' asked Katherine wryly.

'Yes ma'am,' came Jayce's even voice over the com system.

'Are we ready?' she asked Jacobs.

'Ready as we'll ever be,' he replied, and grinned.

'Here we go then,' she said, pulling her splints back to throttle up.

The V10s roared, filling their exhausts with that shrill howl that sounded even more dramatic out here in the cold than it had back in Skala. A moment later they started to roll. Instinctively, Katherine looked across Jacobs and out towards the settlement. For a fleeting moment she saw Iain walking away from them, one arm raised and waving. Then he was gone.

Katherine accelerated away vigorously, in an intoxicating world of her own. As the speed built, it felt as if she were shedding her skin, peeling back dead layers and discarding the withered husks to reveal the purer soul at her core. Every cloaked lie and half-truth was cast off, no longer a part of her. Her failed marriage; the pressure of politics; a career awarded her on the strength of good timing and a stupid accident as a bereaved teenager; the estranged and confusing relationship with her father and half-sisters; and Ratha, who, out here where the world seemed simpler and clearer, she suddenly didn't trust. She was free of Ratha as well.

Settling GVX into a steady eighty kilometres per rotation cruise, she disabled the drive to the front four wheels, hearing the V10s' revolutions per rotation drop in compensation for the reduced load.

'From here on it's an economy run,' she said to Jacobs. 'I've set a target 'plate angle' of eight degrees for the rearward hydraulic drives and zero for the front. I guess we're about to find out how far we can eke out a full load of fuel.'

'It'll do better than you think,' said Jacobs with pride. 'I'll start the mulchers in a rotation.'

Acclimatising to the pace, she allowed her mind to turn to her purpose, finding Kyra. How far ahead her sister was she had no way of telling. Her co-driver sat beside her in silence, alert but introspective. For a while he made occasional adjustments to their fuel economy settings, before eventually giving in to the laws of diminishing returns. She was glad he was with her; his easy dependability kept her grounded. In that respect he reminded her of Nara, which triggered a memory from their last moments in SVA.

'Roy,' she asked impulsively. 'Can I ask you something personal? Is Nara your mother?'

Jacobs laughed, making her feel instantly foolish. 'No,' said Jacobs. 'She's my aunt.'

'Your aunt?' said Katherine, wide-eyed and grateful for at least a degree of vindication. 'I didn't know Nara had a sibling. But that's how you knew that she'd asked me to send that data back to her alone?'

'Yeah,' said Jacobs. 'Nara told me about that. She's a strong-willed lady, just like my mother, who, believe it or not, moved to the slums of her own free will when I was old enough. My father brought me up after she left and I ended up taking his name, Jacobs. Really I'm a Falla. I see her from time to time, she does a lot of good there but it's no easy life.'

'Does she know you're out here?'

'Oh yes,' he said, very seriously. 'She practically signed me up. Don't get the wrong impression,' he gave her a look of reassurance. 'I don't do everything she says, of course.'

'I'm sure you don't.' Katherine now knew him well enough to recognise he was strong-willed in his own right.

'Some of her people, as she thinks of them, her flock if you like, left with your sister. She's worried to death about them. Besides,' he added, 'I was going to volunteer anyway. GVX MK2 is some way off and I needed a little excitement before getting into that.'

Katherine said nothing more, her gaze levelled fixedly ahead. The sky was completely clear and littered with a million burning stars. Across the snowy landscape, the greyness was bathed in the diffused, pink glow of moonlight, which kissed the tips of far-away trees as if giving a spark of life to their inert, grey bodies.

'Time to start thinking about turning north, Katherine,' said ROOT in a soft, thoughtful tone. He was right; they were within sight of the edge of the ice.

'Agreed,' said Katherine, readying herself. She pulled gently back on her left splint and the view yawed gently in that direction. The V10s picked up, as if momentarily roused, before returning to a lazy slumber as GVX straightened and headed out towards the far northeast.

041: Epilogue

The woman's eyes flew open as a shot of adrenaline took hold. She felt the cold line of a blade against her throat give way to a stinging heat, as it made a shallow incision, stopping just short of the cartilage of her windpipe. For a moment, she gripped the rails of her camp bed, using the compression force of her palms as a means to focus. She drew a slow, measured breath of cold, dry air, not daring to put any more pressure against the razor edge of the metal. She felt dribbles of warm blood meandering along different paths down her nape, before reaching the confluence of a blooming, damp stain on the rolled-up shirt she used as a pillow.

She moved her eyes down, a stage at a time, until the gaunt, snarling features of Jody Vaughn came into focus through the dim, blueish light that illuminated the cave. She couldn't see the blade he held but she was sure it was the stubby skinning knife he carried and had put to good use practically every shift over the course of the last half of a frantic cycle. He was saying something, but she couldn't read his lips, the angle was too acute. She moved her eyes to the right, trying to indicate she needed her hearing aids to understand him, but he seemed not to recognise the gesture and became more aggravated.

361

She tried again, but Vaughn was caught up in his own rhetoric. He moved forward until his face was above hers, and she felt an increase in the pressure exerted on her neck. She would have to do something fast if she was going to avoid serious injury. She didn't dare speak and was not at all confident the words would come out clearly if she tried. Tensing the muscles in her left arm, she flicked her eyes to the right. This time he followed her gaze and, after a moment's hesitation, registered her meaning. It was all the time she needed.

Before he could react she brought her right arm up fast, making contact with the pommel of the knife. Pushing it away she exerted all the strength she possessed to turn her body and swung it hard into the man beside her. She uncoiled her legs in a fluid motion that took Vaughn's feet from under him. In the blink of an eye, he was on his back on the floor with her straddling him, the knife, still in his hand, pointing down at his left eye. She pinned his other arm, with her shin pushing down into his bicep. Shifting her weight a little, she dug it in harder, just to make a point.

She leaned into him, using all her upper-body strength to bear against the knife, forcing it closer to his eye. He strained to keep it immobile as her blood dripped onto his face, making him wince.

'Whatever it is you want, Vaughn, I can't hear you without those.' She nodded over to the two aids, which had been carefully placed next to HEX on a small ground mat less than a metre away. He appeared to understand, so she supposed the words must have come out as intended. 'We're going to relax, we're going to put the knife down and move away so we can talk through whatever your problem is. Is that acceptable to you?'

She could see by his expression that it was, just. He was an ugly but straightforward man, which made him easy to read. She thought of him as a dog, but bereft of loyalty. Reducing the pressure on his hand, she felt him reciprocate. He released his grip on the knife and she took it, then flung it to the side. Climbing off him, she backed towards the camp bed and sat down, reaching behind her for the two sculpted earpieces which she inserted with the instinctive familiarity of a lifetime's practice. The moment they were in place, HEX's voice hissed through them as if present in her mind.

'He's got a shiv tucked into his belt, it's around the back on his right side. There's a second knife in his left boot, concealed on the inside under the trouser leg. Clearly right-handed this one...'

Without a moment's hesitation she launched herself off the camp bed and into Vaughn, taking him by surprise. As he fell back with an agonised grunt she reached around him and found the shiv. She pulled it out and threw it back into the cave in the same direction as the skinning knife. It clattered against the hard rock surface of the cave's uneven floor. She dug a knee into his stomach to wind him. With deliberation she reached down to his trouser leg and found the second knife. Withdrawing it slowly, to emphasise to him that she had known it was there, she brought it into his eyeline. Vaughn looked in pain and was clearly startled: he must have believed he had kept this last weapon to himself.

She admired the long blade as it glinted in the cold, artificial light cast by the globe she had placed next to the camp bed rotations before. The metallic surface was ground perfectly flat, and polished enough that she could see her dim reflection upon it. She examined the cut to her throat. It looked superficial, but there was a significant amount of blood soaked into the grey shoulder straps of her vest. She fingered the edge of the blade and was impressed by how keen it felt. It looked very new and unblemished by the scratches inflicted by manual sharpening.

'It's very nice, this one,' she said, hearing her voice clear and strong this time. 'I might keep it. Now what the hell did you want, Vaughn?'

He drew a deep breath and she realised she had hurt him more than she'd intended. Worth remembering, if the situation were to occur again.

'Like everyone else,' he said, and winced as he tried to rise, 'I want to know what the hell I'm doing out here, Kyra.'

She drew in a deep breath, polluted by the foul stench of the man's body odour.

'Tell him nothing,' said HEX in an emphatic whisper. It was a suggestion that didn't need repeating.

'You're being paid, that's what you're doing here,' she said, pointedly. 'You're Rika, aren't you? You're supposed to be used to this sort of thing.'

'Yeah,' said Vaughn, with a trace of sarcasm. 'But not in this environment. Harsh doesn't cover it, it's bloody murder out there.'

'Just deal with it,' she replied with disinterest, and moved as if to tuck the knife into the belt of her trousers. Realising she had no holder, she thought better of it and offered it back to Vaughn.

'Take it,' she said to the man now sitting propped up on one arm. He was holding his gut but managed to reach out for the blade. 'Just don't pull a stunt like that again.'

'Sure,' he said, in a tone that implied the word meant nothing.

She sat back on the camp bed and pulled on her boots, wondering where the other crew were. Preparing to undock Unit Hydra, she hoped. Tying her laces she gave Vaughn a last scathing look. He met her eyes with a level, slightly amused glare that unsettled her. She had to remind herself that, despite his complaining and now this apparently mutinous outburst, overall he was an asset.

'I'm going outside,' she said. 'Are you coming or are you going to stay in here and sulk?'

'I'll come,' said Vaughn and levered himself upright. He was tall and a thug, but a reliable enough man when he wasn't holding a knife to her throat. Reaching the mouth of the cave, the heat and the dazzling light of Hellinar hit Kyra full force. She was used to it, of course, but it never failed to arrest her attention after a few rotations under cover. The sun seared through the invisible layer of barrier cream she wore and into the skin of her face, shoulders and arms.

The cave's entrance was cut into the exposed strata of a bare rock face, overlooking a depression that extended out to a bank of compressed shale. In the centre of the depression, docked together to form a three-legged star, were the vehicles that made up Unit Hydra. They faced nose-in to each other with lowered tail ramps pointing out, three faded tarpaulins strung between the hulls supported midway along their edges by poles driven deep into the fissile mudrock.

'Do you really think we're safe, staying out here this long?' asked Vaughn as they approached the ad-hoc shelter.

'Why wouldn't we be?' asked Kyra, an amused inflection in her voice.

'Because the Council's going to throw everything they can at following us, maybe?'

'They'll be looking in the wrong place, if they're looking beyond Skala at all,' she said confidently.

'Because of the snow chains and the other crap we had to ditch?' said Vaughn, grunting sarcastically. 'That'll be a tenuous misdirection at best.'

'Big words for you,' she said in a patronising tone. 'But yes, you're right. On their own the tracks are tenuous, if they were found at all before the dust eradicated them. There's a lot more to it you don't know about.'

'Like what?' he said, doubtfully. After all the effort she had put into getting this far, his insinuation riled her, and it was clear in her voice when she explained.

'Like the man Connor had convert Hydra for Ayon – we made sure he kept the drawings. Like the photos I had him take in the slums, the ones that show Hydra kitted for Ayon. Connor even used his own name to infiltrate T24, so he can mislead anyone asking questions into thinking we're out on the ice. That was a huge risk for him. The whole operation's been thought out in ways you'd have no appreciation for, and that's before we even start to talk about actually getting HEX out without anyone knowing.'

'Yeah, about that...' said Vaughn, intrigued despite his simmering anger. 'How the hell did you do that without being caught?'

Kyra considered her answer. She thought back to the endless rotations she'd spent in the dark corridor of the abandoned part of the Vault. Huddled with her back to the original door to HEX's chamber, she had listened to the Intercessor impart her incredible story, her version of history, through hearing aids she could inexplicably link to. When she had finally convinced Kyra she had to act, they had conspired to get the door to work again. Through a single, sleepless shift she had fillered, rubbed and matched the joint to make the opening invisible. They'd had some close calls as the Vault's monitoring staff came and went but HEX, through the CCTV, had always given Kyra a precious few moments to get out, seal the door and disconnect the emulator that masked her presence from the chamber's environment sensors. Throughout the whole ordeal she was sure someone would notice the cracked plaster and the progressive repairs she was making. However, HEX, revelling in antagonising the staff, kept any visits brief and attentions diverted. As far as she could tell, no one had noticed a thing.

She went back further, to the terrifying exploration of the 7075 service tunnel and her encounters with the mysterious dark-skinned people that called themselves the Hadje. She felt a pang of guilt – they had after all taken her deep into their own territory, welcoming her and appreciating her interest in the history of her people, the 'Cauldron Born' as they referred to her kind. That in the terror of their first encounter she had misspoken her own name amid the ringing of her hearing aids, ironically added yet another layer of confusion for any would-be pursuers. The inhabitants of Buni Sound, Hadje and up-worlder alike, knew her only as Myra.

She drew a breath and looked back to an expectant Vaughn. 'That's a story for another time.'

'So what next, boss?' he asked, clearly disappointed.

'I'll show you.' She turned to walk past Hydra towards the bank.

Together they climbed, scrabbling up the loose rock, which further disintegrated underfoot. Cresting the escarpment, Kyra drew herself upright. Vaughn, a few paces behind her, noted the determination in her posture. She stood with her feet slightly apart, arms folded across her chest as her long bound hair swayed with serpentine grace in the hot breeze. A moment later he joined her and drew himself up, similarly resolute in the face of the view set out below them.

The ground was gently sloping and even for around half a kilometre before them. Beyond that was a sheer drop of indeterminate height. From its base extended an unending expanse of rocky canyons and craters, mountains and deep, deep valleys.

'You see the cliff?' she asked.

'No,' said Vaughn. 'But I see the drop. It's mighty big.'

'It is,' she agreed. 'It's literally called the 'drop-off'. We've had geologists this far out before, but they can't figure out how it was formed. The most popular theory is that it's glacial, from when this part of the planet was Ayon. But for that to be true, you would expect there to be a wall the other side, and there isn't one.'

'And we've got to get down it? How?'

'Those winches you fitted, they'll get us down,' said Kyra. 'There's a pass, like a pathway down that we can take some of the way. After that it's remote-release ground anchors and lots of wires.'

'Then what?' asked Vaughn, as if the descent wasn't enough.

'Then,' said Kyra, looking out into the wilderness. 'Then we cross Hellinar.'

'I didn't sign up for that,' he said with a trace of malice.

'No,' she agreed, not looking at him. 'But that's what we're doing.'

The big man grunted and pushed out his lower jaw. He stood with her a moment longer, then turned and descended the slope, skidding over the loose rocks underfoot. She considered again HEX's reasoning for the journey and how her account of history had been reinforced by the stories of the Hadje. She had seen the ancient city of Mayak for herself, the tombs in which ROOT and HEX had been imprisoned countless ages before. She had seen and heard enough to find HEX convincing, but explaining it to the others was a risk she was not willing to take. For the time being at least, it was safer if they didn't know.

She wondered whether her father had discovered the truth yet, that it was she who had removed HEX. A part of her hoped that he had. She was sure he would be as shocked as anyone, but equally she knew he would be impressed by the audacity of her actions. Katherine would no doubt be preaching some moralistic diatribe, vilifying her. Megan would be left as confused as their mother.

She thought again about Katherine. If there was a danger it would likely come from her. She might be overcomplicated and frustrating to be around, but she wasn't stupid and had an infuriating knack of putting things together where others could not. If anyone were effectively marshalling resources to retrieve HEX, it would be Katherine at the helm. If she had even the slightest suspicion Kyra was involved, which by now she most likely did, her zeal would at least be doubled.

Kyra stood a while longer, considering the immensity of the task before her. The cloudless sky was hazy in the distance, the horizon lost to an indistinct blur. Heat radiated up from the rock below, as the unrelenting sun beat down on her from above. Presently, she heard the unmistakable ringing of aluminium poles being piled and loaded. She took a last look across Hellinar then turned to descend the slope after Vaughn.

Glossary

Aya

A new-build city set 1,009km east of Skala.

Ayon Borderlands

Mountainous region lying from approximately 1,000km to 2,500km east of Skala.

Ayon Research

Large Council-owned building in the Eastern District of Skala City. The building itself has been extended multiple times. Occupants include Privy Councillors Katherine Kane and Nara Falla.

Ayon Tundra

Vast area of frozen wasteland located to the east of Skala City. Experiences perpetual darkness.

Buni Sound

Water storage and accompanying network below Skala.

Fulgurite Fields

Large areas of desert located to the south of Skala lined with lightning conductors to produce fulgurite glass from sand when a strike occurs.

Gygath Slum

One of three slums bordering the western edge of Skala.

Hellinar Plains

Vast area of desert located to the west of Skala City. Experiences perpetual sunlight.

Hellinar Research

Council-owned building in the Western District of Skala City. Due to the perceived lack of need for research in Hellinar the building has suffered a lack of investment. Occupants include Privy Councillors Joss Ratha, Kyle Devin and quartermaster JT Gilbert.

Kul

Previous centre of civilisation prior to the migration to Skala circa 300 years ago.

Mal-Kas

Large-scale ore mine operated by MineVision located in the mountains north of Skala.

Nastra Research Station

Farthest established outpost in Ayon. Used to conduct meteorological research.

Siphon

Water storage pumping facility below Skala.

Skala

Current major civilised city of the temperate band.

Skala Grasslands
Verdant area located directly east of Skala.
T7 – Hellinar Research
Hellinar Research storage and vehicle maintenance facility located southwest of the Central District of Skala.
T24 – Hellinar Research
Hellinar Research storage and vehicle maintenance facility located near the northeastern edge of the Eastern District of Skala.
Temperate Band
A north–south band of fertile land around 1,200km in width between Hellinar and Ayon that creeps eastwards at the rate of approximately three kilometres per year.
Tsarocca
Hadje settlement.
Vault
Facility located beneath Ayon Research to house the Intercessor Drive Cores ROOT and HEX.

TECHNICAL

Gas Turbine Engine (GTE)

An internal combustion engine of axial compressor/ combustion chamber/turbine design. Used as the primary drive in medium-sized long-haul 'Unit' vehicles and commonly as an ancillary power source.

GVX

Advanced mobile science research station designed specifically for operation in extremely low temperatures and over rough terrain.

Mulcher

A device used for converting bio-material into a viable fuel for burning in internal combustion engines.

Platform Control

An active suspension system that works to keep the body of a vehicle level by hydraulically controlling wheel movement.

Pneumatic Valve Spring

A gas spring used in place of a steel coil spring to return an inlet or exhaust valve to the closed position when not depressed by a camshaft.

Power Pack

Interchangeable power unit designed specifically for GVX to assess pros and cons of various power sources on a large-scale vehicle.

374

Splint

Frame in which a driver can place her (or his) arms to enable intuitive control of GVX's complex drive functions.

Thomason Plate

A plate forming the base of a pneumatic valve spring that itself is sprung by a light steel coil spring. Under normal operation, i.e. when the pneumatic valve spring is pressurised, the Thomason Plate remains stationary. However, in the event of a loss of pneumatic pressure, the plate rises on its coil spring and acts against the valve retainer to close the valve when not depressed by a camshaft.

Torque Converter

A hydraulic pump and motor coupling that converts the mechanical power of an engine to a controlled flow of hydraulic oil able to power wheels, steering, platform control and other functions.

Unit Vehicle

Part of a three-vehicle group that commonly travel together. Can be docked together nose-first in a star pattern, to form a single structure joined by three awnings. Units such as Hydra and Pegasus are driven by gas turbine engines positioned alongside a double-berth cockpit.

V10 Engine

An internal combustion engine of reciprocating piston design featuring ten cylinders arranged in two banks of five to form a V shape as viewed from the front.

Acknowledgements

Patrick and David would like to thank the following for their contributions to *Trinity*.

Kris Nash and Oliver Johnstone for their superb insight into mining and living in a desert city, respectively. Jon Gowdy for sharing his experiences in the British Antarctic Survey team. Paula Rissanen for organising the trip to northern Finland and for her company. To Jade Gurss for his invaluable advice. Emma-Jane Lewis for photographing the two worst subjects in her illustrious career. Also to Fraser Sinclair and Lucy Sinclair, Mark Robinson and Julie Monk. Alan Thomason, for his loan of the 'Thomason Plate' Patent (https://patents.google.com/patent/US9399933), and Ian Watson for his help with the illustrations.

Above all we would like to thank our families, without whose support this would never have been possible. To Cathy for looking after us and to Celia for her tireless sub-editing; we are both so very grateful.

Unbound is the world's first crowdfunding publisher, established in 2011.

We believe that wonderful things can happen when you clear a path for people who share a passion. That's why we've built a platform that brings together readers and authors to crowdfund books they believe in – and give fresh ideas that don't fit the traditional mould the chance they deserve.

This book is in your hands because readers made it possible. Everyone who pledged their support is listed at the front of the book and below. Join them by visiting unbound.com and supporting a book today.

Bret Gordon
Jane Graham
Rob Hallifax
Mark Hearn
Keith Hicks
Ruth Hill
Peter Hogan
Philippa Hurwood
David Iddles
Simon Ingram
Tom Johnston
Oliver Johnstone
Dan Kieran
Charles Kimbell
Mit Lahiri
Emma-Jane Lewis
Andrew Lockey
Elaine MacKenzie
Dan McBryde
John Mitchinson
Andrea Morgan
Celia Morgan
Florence Morgan
David Murdoch
Rhel ná DecVandé

Stu Nathan
Carlo Navato
Reema Pal
Justin Pollard
Jon Powell
Graham Pretty
Matthew Price
Mark Robinson
Gemma Robson
Danny Saunders
Bernadette Shail
Neil Shorter
Ellie Sinclair
Taff Smith
David Steare
Philippa Stenning
John Stiner
Phil Stoner-Graham
Luke Trethewy
Gill Turner
Sonja van Amelsfort
Ulrich VanAyrd
Louise Whitbread
Andrea Williams
Grant Wilson